To Richard,
Pish! Posh!
 Enjoy reading!

Charles Gordon

NEVER RULED BY MAN

BY

PHYLLIS BARONE AMEDURI

WingSpan Press

Published in the United States and the United Kingdom by WingSpan Press, Livermore, CA

The WingSpan name, logo and colophon are the trademarks of WingSpan Publishing.

ISBN 978-1-59594-626-3 (pbk.)
ISBN 978-1-59594-662-1 (hardcover)
ISBN 978-1-59594-939-4 (ebk.)

First edition 2018

Printed in the United States of America

www.wingspanpress.com

Library of Congress Control Number: 2018958102

1 2 3 4 5 6 7 8 9 10

DEDICATION

There are quite a few people who could be named here: those who encouraged, who questioned, who gave constructive feedback, plus the one or two who were blunt in their criticism and fueled a massive rewrite that clearly improved the final version.

Please accept my sincerest gratitude, but understand that there is truly only one person to whom this book should be dedicated.

To Mary Ann McDonough McLoughlan Richards Bascombe. This one's for you.

Contents

CHAPTER ONE: THE FEMALE LAWYER

It was Ladies' Day in court.

The plain wood door entrance to Police Court flew open, and in shuffled a small crowd of unlikely criminal characters. At the center of the procession walked two strikingly pretty and well-dressed young women from the infamous neighborhood of Rocky Hollow, Stapleton. Each had been summoned to the stuffy, cramped courtroom of the Justice of the Peace, Charles K. Taylor. The ladies made sure not to look or speak in the other's direction, each having entered the building under the escort of a separate nattily attired Richmond County police officer.

It was a bitter February morning, and the supporters and nosy neighbors who followed them inside were greatly relieved at last to have the opportunity to come in out of the cold. Court was held inside the Richmond County Police Headquarters, a nondescript three-story brick structure that was located on Beach Street, one of the busier thoroughfares within the town of Stapleton. It was situated in the heart of the commercial district, and those who frequented the courtroom were somewhat used to the steady intrusion of outside noise - sounds of the bay, the hustle and bustle of cargo being loaded or carted down to the waterfront, and nearby traffic on the streets. Boat horns, laborers yelling back and forth, horses, wagons, carriages, and folks chattering away as they passed by the windows provided a periodic and oft times welcome distraction to the perfunctory courtroom proceedings. On this particular day, however, those present resolved to block out the sounds of the outside world. All bets were on that today's inside commotion would far exceed any spectacle beyond the walls. Their expectations hinged upon on the court appearance of a third woman.

She was a middle-aged lady who likewise lived in Rocky Hollow. The lady followed behind the court officers and took her place standing next to one of the young women. She was tall, of medium build with gray strands of hair and a handsome but serious face. There was nothing remarkable about her at all. Yet, within a minute or so of entering the room she made sure to stand out to all who did not know her. This nondescript matron was not here to comfort, testify, or pay silent witness.

Pish! Posh! Time is money, she thought to herself.

Without invitation, the woman suddenly made straight for the desk of Justice Taylor. Her steps were bold and heavy, and she did not stop until she planted herself directly in front of the man. As she started to speak she looked straight at the Justice, but in mid-sentence turned with great pomp to face the room. She raised her index finger and pointed it stiffly at one of the pretty young ladies. Then she spoke, in full possession of an air of complete and utter self-confidence. The words flowed from her mouth, much like the crisp, clear waters of nearby Gore's Brook.

"If it please Your Honor, I am present here on behalf of the defendant, Mrs. Kennedy, whom this girl Mattie Dell accuses of assault and battery."

In a corner of the tiny crowded room, one man's interest was immediately piqued. The gentleman, who had been slouching in his seat and idly doodling caricatures of those around him to pass the time, lifted his eyes upward to take a close look at the woman. It took but a moment for him to realize what was going on.

Well dang it, if that's not the lady lawyer these locals go on and on about! he thought.

There had been talk circulating among the New York City reporters about a woman who lived in Rocky Hollow and defended the down and out in court but he had yet to see her at work. The reporter fixed his eyes upon her for a minute or two to take in the full magnitude of the woman's presence. Next, he closely scrutinized the face of the Justice, and then dropped his face down to start rapidly scribbling on the paper in front of him.

The reporter wasn't the only one who snapped to attention

after hearing her words. The Rocky Hollow citizens who had stood outside in the frigid cold to get a seat in the courtroom now elbowed and shushed each other. They craned their necks to see past the heads of their neighbors. Each considered themselves quite the lucky ones to have gained entrance into court to watch the day's drama unfold.

Shuro, they whispered, *but t'isn't this goin ta be the talk of the neighborhood for weeks on end!*

The crowd expected the Justice to react to the woman's words but to their surprise, he did not flinch. Some thought he didn't hear her, but he did and was even a tad annoyed. Taylor ached to bang his gavel and say *Aye but hold your horses Mrs. Bascombe and wait yer turn,* but as a professional he was not given to angry outbursts. Taylor answered the woman's declaration only with the calm request that she kindly take her seat.

Taylor did not show his feelings because he knew that even if the well-known Mary Ann Bascombe was quite the talent at putting on a public display, it was still he who controlled the comings and goings of his court. It was February 1882, and Taylor had sat on the Richmond County police court bench as a Justice of the Peace for many years. He was close to eighty years old, and the combination of age and experience gave him the confidence to deal with any and all outlandish situations.

Over the years, Taylor had witnessed a profusion of odd characters marched in and out of his small courtroom by the Richmond County men in blue. They were not only audacious like this gray haired lady, but also quite often drunk, disorderly, and disruptive. Assault, battery, robbery, theft, public menace, animal cruelty – these were just some of the more familiar charges he had seen.

Taylor knew that sooner or later anyone could show up in his court. Men, women, and children - rich and poor - sailors from near and faraway places - public officials - Germans, English, Irish, Italians, and people of African descent. All shapes, sizes, and varieties of mankind and, yes, even the occasional animal was led in to stand before his desk. And, in almost every case, they were in a hurry to speak. Just like this presumptuous woman standing before him now. Folks were always itching for the chance to tell their side of a sordid tale first.

Justice Taylor served the Middletown region of Richmond County, which encompassed all of Staten Island in the southern-most part of New York State. The island's name came from the explorer Henry Hudson who first called it Staaten Eyelandt. The island was located at the entrance to New York harbor, separated from the rest of the state by the Narrows on the east, and from New Jersey by Newark Bay and the Kill Van Kull on the north, by Arthur Kill on the west, and by Raritan Bay on the south. Self-governance was of great importance to Staten Islanders, as wit-nessed by the numerous independent local town and county gov-ernments. Rocky Hollow, where these three women hailed from, was a part of Stapleton, which in turn was a part of the incorpo-rated Village of Edgewater within the region of Middletown.

Taylor and his magistrate colleagues were charged with car-rying out an important civic duty, and, in return, the good folk in town made certain they earned their wages by keeping the offi-cials busy at their work. As a Justice of the Peace, Taylor was not a lawyer but an elected official who served a term that was stag-gered in conjunction with three other local justices. In his role, Taylor had the power to set bail, send someone to county jail, or commit them for mental examination to rule out insanity. If the charge was more serious than a criminal misdemeanor, Taylor was required to refer the alleged criminal to the higher county court in Richmond.

By 1882, Taylor was in the twilight of his career and would soon be shocked to learn of its abrupt end. There were signs, but Taylor had been overlooking them. Like when Justice Kassner retired and the new justice on the block was assigned Kassner's courtroom. It was directly across the hall from Police Headquarters and one hundred feet closer than Justice Taylor's space. Since law dictated that prisoners would be taken to the nearest court, by technicality this novice was being assigned more cases than Taylor. It was a slight and a warning but it was not heeded. Life would go on as usual for Justice Taylor until a year from now when his career received the actual death blow.

A lawyer challenged one of his rulings, declaring that he was too old to serve as a justice. As a result, New York State law was brought forth and examined. Taylor had served ten years beyond the mandatory statewide legal retirement age. He was forced to step down from the bench.

Well, this did not matter today for Taylor's impending retirement was not on the agenda. Taylor pulled the eye glasses sitting on top of his head down on the bridge of his nose and studied the complaint papers set before him on the table. From what he could gather, his role was to sort the fallout from a local love triangle. Did he personally care one way or another about the situation? No one in his courtroom was able to tell. Because he was skilled at meting out justice without emotion or prejudice, the spectators in his courtroom often debated whether the particulars of a case amused or disturbed him. Today, Taylor's initial calm suggested he would remain stoic throughout. However, a few men in the crowd vowed to watch his face closely. A pint of ale was on the line as a bet that before the hearing was over Taylor would lose his composure with the lady lawyer.

Mary Ann's initial approach to the bench was brazen and made it clear she intended to test his patience. He could have taken issue with her, but since there were no pressing court matters that day, Taylor decided he would not openly challenge her. As long as she was reminded when needed that he remained in charge of the proceedings, why not go along and break up the monotony with a little local entertainment?

Justice Taylor settled back into his seat to get comfortable for the exhibition about to begin. Living on an island separated from the mainland of New York State bred citizens who were bold and self-reliant by nature, and that fiery independent spirit permeated the local courts. Taylor was sure to hear two greatly animated and radically different versions of the circumstances. His task, as in all his court proceedings, was to listen intently to both sides and labor to strip away the various layers upon layers of irrelevant information. Taylor's work could be likened to the way one stripped the inedible outer leaves of an artichoke in order finally to arrive at the fleshy inner core. The Justice got to the heart of the matter and then rendered an official ruling. That was his job. The two major tenets of his work were that his final say made good legal sense and it was made quickly. All decisions had to be swift, as the police courts were usually backed up.

Taylor thumped his gavel and began the proceedings by asking Miss Mattie Dell to step up to his desk and tell him what happened. Miss Dell, the complainant in the matter, stood up, smoothed her long skirt and sashayed up the main aisle to face the Justice.

Mattie set her pretty eyes directly on Taylor, ignoring all others in the packed courtroom. She started out by admitting that all in all, life had been going well for her until just recently. Over the past year she had been cheerfully keeping company with Mr. Kennedy, a young village carpenter. They spent many happy days together, and while courting he gave her a tintype image of himself which she treasured.

Mattie was well composed and fluid in her speech, but as she continued those paying close attention in the room noted the gradual change of inflection in her voice. She was becoming increasingly annoyed. Yes, that Mr. Kennedy was indeed a sweet talker who had much finesse and was quite pleasing to the eye but woe it turned out in the end because apparently, he had never learned how to be a true gentleman. Mattie had no knowledge of it at the time, but while the carpenter was spooning with her, Kennedy had also been hedging his bets by keeping company with another pretty Rocky Hollow neighbor by the name of Miss Baxter. One day the Kennedy-Dell romance took a bad turn, and her young beau bailed out of the courtship. The carpenter then exercised his other available option and took Miss Baxter as his wife.

Mattie Dell turned to the crowd. Her eyes were now watery as she explained how awful she felt after learning about the marriage from her neighbors. At first, she was shocked but then a severe melancholy overtook her. She brooded for Mr. Kennedy day and night, and did she not have that right? After all, she was wronged by the man! Mattie knew that the courtship was over, but she did not discard the tintype. She kept the image because it would have torn her inside out to let it go. Mattie continued to show the tintype to others, but it was not out of spite. She was using it to tell her story and help manage her broken heart.

Mattie claimed she had no idea that the new Mrs. Kennedy wanted the tintype. Two months after the wedding, his wife paid a social call to Mattie. She did not ask about the image. She gave no indication of her intentions but when Mattie left the room, Mrs. Kennedy took action.

Mattie stopped talking for a moment. She reached deep into her right skirt pocket, pulled out a fancy hanky, and then slowly dabbed at each eye. The crowd, captivated by her testimony, waited anxiously for her to resume. In whispers, they gossiped about what she had said so far.

Shuro, but that Mattie's got a fine gift of gab, hasn't she?
Oh, the poor girl! T'is a pity what she's been through!
Such a horror!
What yer think she'll say next?

Mattie heaved a loud, drawn out sigh. She folded the hanky neatly under the right wrist sleeve of her blouse and proceeded with the story.

When she reentered the room, Mrs. Kennedy looked nervous. Mattie knew that something was wrong. She looked around and saw that the tintype was missing. Mattie asked and then demanded that Mrs. Kennedy return it. She told her she had no right to take the image. That was a gift to her!

They argued and then a loud and vicious struggle ensued. Mattie said she could not remember who grabbed at whom first. Mattie wrenched the photo out of the young wife's hand. Mrs. Kennedy got so mad that she slapped Mattie in the face. Mattie claimed that the sound it made was so loud it could be heard by all her Rocky Hollow neighbors. Mrs. Kennedy then grabbed the tintype and ran off. As soon as she recovered from the shock, Mattie made her way down to the Stapleton police station and had a warrant issued for Mrs. Kennedy's arrest.

Mattie's face and neck were now deeply flushed. She took out her hanky and blotted the corners of her eyes once again. Justice Taylor asked her if this was all she had to say. Then he thanked the young woman and instructed her to step back. Mattie spun around and sashayed back to the bench next to her police officer. She intentionally avoided eye contact with Mrs. Kennedy and Mrs. Bascombe by turning her head to the side as she passed.

Throughout Mattie's testimony, Mrs. Kennedy had been shifting around nervously in her seat. By the time she was finished speaking, the young wife had slid so far forward that she was at serious risk of falling off the cold wooden bench onto the floor. Her stomach churned as she hoped that somehow the angst did not show all over her face.

Ever since she had been taken into custody, Mrs. Kennedy had been consumed with fret. There was no way she could afford to pay any fines. And she most certainly did not want to go to jail! Mrs. Kennedy realized she needed a good legal defense and was thankful that her husband's family were neighbors of the well-known lady lawyer. Mary Ann Bascombe agreed to defend her and was now readying to speak.

Justice Taylor gave a nod over to Mrs. Bascombe. Mary Ann, who then stood up in plain view of everyone in the room, was a hard woman to characterize. There was rarely a consensus among gossipers. Those who were fans called her tall and graceful while those who were less enamored labeled her masculine with harsh features. There was only two points they agreed on: she was a middle-aged woman and her own brand of unconventional.

Mary Ann had been somewhat impressed by her young adversary. She rose from the bench thinking, *Admirable job there Miss Mattie but Pish! Posh! It's now time, my dear, to watch and learn from your elder.* Mary Ann smoothed her skirt slowly and deliberately, bringing a rush of anticipation to all those who had braved the February winds and the cramped conditions inside the Police Court. They knew Mattie had been the opening act but now it was time for the main attraction to begin. Mary Ann ceremoniously stepped up to the front of the room and looked Justice Taylor straight in the eye.

A lifelong resident of Rocky Hollow, Mary Ann had a big heart but was also a no-nonsense Stapleton businesswoman. She held substantial real estate in town which provided her with steady income. She also owned a small store and local saloon. Mary Ann had been married three times, but her financial success had not been attained through the help of a husband. She was independently wealthy. Armed with a keen mind and fast tongue, Mary Ann had what it took to outlast her opponent and win almost any argument on the street, at a government public hearing, in the Village tax office, or in court.

Her words were good enough to seal the deal but for added insurance the lady of Rocky Hollow often carried with her a most unusual travelling accessory - a stout club. Though she insisted it was just a prop, her third husband and neighbors knew full well she would not hesitate to make use of it if she felt the need. Because she was so skilled at swinging the club, few dared to anger the woman. Justice Taylor had been quite relieved to see that the lady lawyer possessed the good common sense to keep the onerous object out of his courtroom on this day.

Legally she was now Mrs. Bascombe, but the locals who knew her way back when enjoyed calling her by one of her many nicknames. She was *Mary Ann Mack* to those who had first known her as the only daughter of the late Thomas McDonough or through her first husband, John McLoughlan. Before becoming Mrs. Bascombe she had been married a second time, so a few others in town remembered her as *Mary Ann Richards*.

Some locals called her *Counselor Howe* or *Lawyer Howe*. Her voluble speech and larger than life delivery earned Mary Ann this comparison to the well-known city lawyer, William F. Howe. The real Counselor Howe was a famously flamboyant Manhattan criminal defense attorney who was always being written up in the New York newspapers. A few lucky Staten Island residents had seen Counselor Howe in the flesh a few years earlier when he tried a Stapleton murder case. A young woman who was one of Mary Ann's neighbors had been butchered and her husband put on trial for the heinous crime. Although Howe lost the case, her neighbors had not missed the similarity in styles between the renowned esquire and the champion of the poor who now stood most self- assuredly in front of the Justice's desk.

In 1880, there were over 60,000 males but less than a hundred fully fledged female attorneys in all of America, most of whom were forbidden to practice because of state restrictions barring women from a career perceived as not fitting for a lady. It would be a few more years before New York State authorized the first female to practice law in New York and years after that before women broke the gender barrier to gain admission to the Richmond County Bar.

Although she had no formal education or legal training, Mary Ann Bascombe made an excellent lady lay lawyer. She was well versed in the rights of individuals in the courts. She kept abreast of all the ordinances and as a property owner frequently argued in court and at public meetings for tax reductions, better roads, storm sewers, and the like. The lady lawyer was so authoritative, loquacious, and tenacious in her debates that the municipal officials frequently gave in to what she wanted just to make her go away. Because Mary Ann was so successful in her own endeavors her neighbors, who were mostly poor and could not afford a real lawyer, began to seek her out when they got into trouble with the law. *Lawyer Howe* obliged their requests for help, and she became a regular face around the Stapleton courts. *Lawyer Howe* was a kind of local folk hero in Rocky Hollow. She had saved many poor unfortunates from having to pay fines or go to jail.

Justice Taylor eyed Mary Ann and in a tone of voice that was solemn, yet held a slight hint of mocking, he asked the matron to state her name for the record. It was a legal formality, as all present were well-aware he most certainly knew the answer. Mary Ann, who up to this point had been projecting the demeanor of a solemn and highly dignified professional, could not help but be herself in the response she gave. Since Mattie's theatrics had taken away some seriousness from the proceedings, with a unique and fine spirited sense of humor she replied, *Mrs. Bandbox.*

Mary Ann was conveying to Taylor that she thought she looked and felt spectacular - as if just out of a bandbox. Her answer hit the right note, as many in the crowd stifled a good chuckle. If he had been in a bad frame of mind, Taylor could have chastised the dame right then and there, but he had already given into the notion that there was no way he was going to stop Mary Ann from performing. Thus, Taylor played along with the woman's tease. He acknowledged the name and asked *Mrs. Bandbox* to proceed with a statement of the facts of the case.

Aha! That the Justice of the Peace did not challenge her joke greatly encouraged her, so Mary Ann began a most articulate and passionate appeal on behalf of Mrs. Kennedy. The reporter wrote fast and furious as the words gushed from her lips:

"Your Honor will perceive, if you have any gumption at all, and I credit you with as large an amount of it as most persons- that is most men – you will perceive that at different times and at the same time my client and the complainant were cocking their caps at Mr. Kennedy. Now you will also perceive that Mr. Kennedy could accept only one of them, and in that case I would say 'Go in and let the best girl win.' Well my client probably gave the most taffy to her fellow – and that's the only way you can win one, because they are all fools – and she won. Why did not Mattie Dell take her defeat like a sensible girl, and as the poets say, tear him from her memory and ogle some other fellow? Does she not know that them are as good fish in the sea as ever were caught? What delight could she take when she lost the substance and reality, in keeping a miserable old piece of tin containing a wretched likeness of a good looking fellow who didn't care for her? A last memento of blighted love, indeed!"

Her audience nodded their heads to agree with the sense she was making. The lady lawyer paused momentarily, recognizing this as a good time to start showing Mattie up in terms of dramatics. She turned and shot a fiery glare over at Miss Dell. Then, with a tone of earnest disgust she declared,

"Bosh! Spooney! These girls make me mad!"

Mary Ann next dropped her voice down low to demonstrate a bit melancholier. She began to plead most vehemently to the Justice that it was Mrs. Kennedy who was the aggrieved party in this case. Her look was most sincere as she explained that marriage changed everything. As his wife, Mrs. Kennedy now had control over her husband's destiny. She was his counsel, guide, and protector and required to act in his best interests. Mr. Kennedy's possessions were now hers too, and any likeness of him was Mrs. Kennedy's sole and unquestionable property. So as such, the tintype should remain with her.

Mary Ann switched to a somewhat bolder voice to make her next points. She took issue with the notion that the slap caused an injury. She rolled up her sleeve and held her own arm up for all in the courtroom to see. It was incredibly muscular and of very powerful proportions for a woman. The visual aided her argument but it was no big shock to most present. Mary Ann was widely known to be a strong woman capable of wielding tools the equal of any man. She was commonly seen driving a horse cart throughout town laden with various construction materials and did the work of a carpenter and brick layer when necessary to accommodate her business interests.

Mary Ann explained that Mattie would have good reason to complain if she had been hit by someone bearing the full weight of an arm such as hers, but since all could see that her client's hands were quite delicate, this was not the case. Why clearly, a slap from Mrs. Kennedy couldn't hurt even the smallest cock robin!

She emphasized that this was merely a war of words between two ladies which led to the circumstances for which they were in court together today. Mattie's feelings had been hurt and she had lashed out like a sore loser. She asked everyone to think for a moment about the characters of Charles Dickens. Mary Ann likened the relationship between Miss Dell and Mrs. Kennedy to that of Fanny Squeers and Tilda Browdie in *Nicholas Nickelby*. Mattie Dell became ill tempered because Mrs. Kennedy called her names. Mattie, like Fanny, was vain and way too proud.

After this last jab at poor Mattie, Mary Ann suddenly shifted the tone of her speech. She was no longer the harsh lady lawyer but instead a soft and tender mother. With the utmost compassion in her face, Mary Ann turned to look Mattie straight in the eye, then spoke to her gently, like she was the only person in the room.

Ah, but she knew full well that young Kennedy was a dandy

lad – he had grown up just a few doors away from her home. Still, she advised Mattie to forfeit the likeness and set her cap for another man. Mary Ann wished her the best of luck in the future and said that it was her highest hope that Mattie's next beau would be a *"handsome six-footer who will be able to buy you all the sleighs and light wagons your heart can desire."*

Mother Bascombe paused for effect, then after having given it her very best effort, stepped aside to let *Lawyer Howe* return for the final monologue. The lady lawyer hammered home a powerful final plea on her client's behalf. *Lawyer Howe* concluded her defense with a warm smile, reiterating that she had only good wishes to impart.

"Now then," she urged, *"in God's name drop this row, shake hands and take a friendly cup of tea together. Kiss each other, and Mattie, you have my best prayers for a good husband in no distant date."*

Mary Ann's words were followed by the swish of her skirt as she crisscrossed the room and lowered herself back down in her seat on the bench. The room was in awe. In her ten minute oration, this middle aged mother of eight had succeeded in capturing the hearts and minds of nearly everyone in the room with the exception of Justice Taylor and poor Mattie.

Few had been paying attention to Justice Taylor while Mary Ann spoke, but now that she finished all eyes turned in his direction. It was time for him to step back into the limelight and bring this drama to an end. Taylor asked Mary Ann if she would be willing to pay the court fees. She replied of course but that it was still up to him as Justice to decide the matter. He could send the case to a higher court if he liked. Justice Taylor answered no, that he would rule on the matter and dismiss the charges so long as the defendant paid all costs.

Before letting them go, Taylor tried his own hand at trying to be a peacemaker. He asked the two young ladies to come up and shake hands in front of him.

"No– never, never!" shouted Mattie, tossing her head back defiantly.

She hastily gathered up her coat and belongings. Mattie then

13

snubbed Mary Ann's willingness to pay the court costs. She opened her purse, took out fifty cents and flung it at the clerk before stomping out of the room.

From his seat in the far corner, the reporter leaned back in his wooden chair and let out a smirk. *Dang,* but he had surely hit pay dirt on this assignment! His editor was always riding his staff to go out and find local stories that would titillate the readers. Using Mary Ann's words alone, the reporter knew he had the makings of a great news item. He could not wait to deliver the finished product to his boss. The gentleman jotted down one more key observation to include in the article as he began packing up.

"She talks with the unerring fluency of a phonograph, and is capable of saying or doing the most extraordinary things."

Rather than summarize the hearing in a line or two for the Staten Island section of the newspaper, he sat down and wrote a full article. And, his hunch about the article turned out to be correct. His finished product was such an attention-grabber that his editor not only published the piece, but subsequently sent the story off to affiliate newspapers in other cities. Readers far and wide would read about Mrs. Bascombe, Mrs. Kennedy, Mattie Dell, and Justice Taylor.

The newly christened *Mrs. Bandbox,* also known as *Lawyer Howe, Counselor Howe, Mrs. Richards, Miss or Mrs. Mack,* and legally as Mrs. Mary Ann Bascombe, was quite satisfied with the result of her efforts on behalf of the young Mrs. Kennedy. She lingered in the courtroom for a few minutes after the conclusion of the hearing to relish the thanks and compliments she received from those present. It was a grand feeling but did not last long. Justice Taylor soon broke up the festivities by informing the occupants that his court needed to be cleared for other legal business.

Mary Ann prepared to leave. She set on layers and layers of sweaters and scarves to bundle up for the raw February winds outside. Mary Ann donned her heavy wool coat and hat and bid her good days to Justice Taylor, Mrs. Kennedy, the police officers, and her other Rocky Hollow neighbors. Leaving her identity as

Mrs. Bandbox behind in the courtroom, Mary Ann stepped out of the police station into the chilly air of downtown Stapleton and into her other life which was full of vastly different interests and responsibilities.

She did not forget to offer her thanks.

Dear Lord, thank you for helping me fix things for that dear young woman!

Mary Ann's spirits were flying high. She was grateful to be of service, for she knew there were not many places in 19th century America where a woman would be allowed to do as she wanted.

Stapleton was a special place, and my, how Mary Ann loved her hometown! It was such a grand mix of peoples. There were the worker class folk like Mattie Dell and Mrs. Kennedy who resided in the modest neighborhood of Rocky Hollow, the more prosperous merchants and businessmen who lived on the quaint streets close to the waterfront, and the wealthiest residents who owned large estates in the surrounding picturesque hills. There were also a lot of outsiders - day vacationers that came by ferry and sailors who frequented the town while their boats were in dock. They shopped in the same markets, attended the same community functions, and worshiped side by side in the churches. Stapleton was full of all kinds of people leading different kinds of lives, but with an unspoken measure of respect for each other. Yes, and even if you were a woman. Mary Ann smiled at the thought. In her mind, there was no better place to live and raise her family.

On foot from where she stood on Beach Street it was a brisk fifteen or so minute hike uphill to her home at the corner of Broad and Gordon Streets. Normally she walked the distance but since the weather was so cold, Mary Ann traveled today by horse and wagon. Not one to waste time or money, she preplanned the trip to combine the free legal defense work with her downtown errands. Mary Ann left her horse tied up while she conducted some nearby business on foot.

Mary Ann moved quickly to stay warm, weaving in and out around the numerous wagons and carriages on the street, stepping carefully to avoid plunging her boot heels into any icy snow patches, un-shoveled horse droppings, or slushy mud ruts in the road. Mary Ann visited The Staten Island Savings Bank on Bay Street, then the local government offices. As she walked, Mary Ann passed Washington Park. She was a lifelong resident of Stapleton, and had memories of when the park opened after the Civil War. The park was a fine addition to downtown Stapleton. It was a patch of welcome green in the spring and summer and a glistening blanket of white at this time of the year. Washington Park was one of the more popular places in town because of the summer concerts and many public meetings and debates held there. She nodded at that thought and kept going. When done with her business downtown, Mary Ann returned to the wagon. She unhooked her horse's bridle from the hitching post, hiked up her long skirt and stepped up into the buckboard. Mary Ann settled herself onto the bench seat and then drew up on the reins to direct her horse to begin its trot.

It was a simple route home. From Beach Street, she turned right onto Canal Street at Washington Park and then right again at Broad Street. Other than the park, the most remarkable sight along the route was the large brewery building which towered over the small one and two story frame structures at the top of Broad Street. Stapleton was like any other similar sized communities of its time, except for the breweries and the unusual number of saloons and beer gardens. The streets she travelled were main thoroughfares, so along the way she passed a variety of merchants. In Stapleton, it was easy to procure goods and services as there were millinery and clothier shops, druggists, cigar shops, blacksmiths, grocers, bakers, and butchers in town. Mary Ann enjoyed the practicality of her route home. She decided to stop and grab some fresh produce and bread for the night's supper.

At the market, she ran into some Rocky Hollow neighbors. They made casual chit chat about the day's court hearing and also asked Mary Ann to opine on a few local matters.

Do yer think the Trustees will git around to macadamizing our street before next winter, Mary Ann?

Did ye hear of the mischief the School Board is up to now?

Shuro, but who will yer be supporting in the next Democratic campaign?

It was not an unusual occurrence. Mary Ann was often sought after for information and advice and truth be told - she did not mind one bit. Gee Gosh! The woman relished being the center of attention.

Mary Ann made a few more stops on the way home. She passed one of her investment properties and got out of her wagon to examine the quality of her hired contractors' work. Then she checked in on a tenant because she heard her child was ailing.

Eventually, Mary Ann came to the section of Broad Street where a simple wooden mission chapel was under construction. It was being built by her beloved Rev. Father John L. Lewis, pastor of St. Mary's Roman Catholic Church in nearby Clifton. Mary Ann had at last reached the heart of her beloved Rocky Hollow neighborhood and was about two blocks away from home. She slowed her horse down a bit, shifted both reins into her left hand, and raised her right to make the sign of the cross over her forehead and chest. Then she whispered a few words of prayer for the continued good health and prosperity of her family as the wagon drifted past the storefront which served as the temporary home of St. Mary's Chapel of Ease.

Minutes later, she unhitched her horse from the wagon and returned him to the barn. James Bascombe heard his wife clapping her boots against the side of their unpretentious wood frame home. He opened the door and gave her a light peck on her cheek. Mary Ann called out to greet her clan, received a few shouts back from various corners of the house, then removed her wet boots and carefully hung up her hat, scarves, and coat to dry. She went into the kitchen and stood near the stove to warm up a bit, then used the wash basin to clean her hands. After that, she rolled up her sleeves and called for assistance as she got to work starting supper. It was a big family, and everyone was expected to help.

The Bascombe family rarely knew when to expect the arrival of their infamous mother, but James and her eight children were almost always eager to see her when she did show. She was full of rich and colorful tales. Over supper, there was some minor bickering which took place between the children. James broke it up by asking the offenders to pass over their bowls so he could ladle out the stew. They ate and discussed the events of the day. Mary Ann asked about the things her younger children learned in school and what happened to James and the older children at work. While James spoke, Mary Ann paid close attention to the accounting of his hours and scrutinized him for signs that he may have imbibed one too many beers.

The children listened closely to Mary Ann's fascinating story of her day in court. She was most pleased to help one of the Kennedy clan. They lived just a few doors down from the Bascombe family and were good neighbors. Still, Mary Ann felt sad for how things turned out for poor Mattie Dell. She really should stop pining for that silly Kennedy boy!

The Bascombe residence was rarely peaceful, buzzing with the activity of eight children of varying ages who traipsed about the small house and grounds at all hours of the day and night. Mary Ann felt very blessed that all her children were hardy. It was so rare in the day not to have suffered the loss of at least one child to disease.

Mary Jane, the eldest, was a prepossessed twenty-two year old beauty. Baby Joseph, at just a year old, was the youngest of the family. In between Mary Jane and Joseph were sisters Mary Ellen and Mary Emma, and brothers William, Thomas, James, and John. Mary Jane and William had the last name of Richards, having been born during Mary Ann's second marriage. The rest of the brood were fathered by her current husband, James. All children still lived at home. Mary Jane was technically married, but it was a complicated matter no one openly discussed. William was a carpenter while Mary Jane and Thomas worked in a local paper factory. Mary Ellen, James, and John were students at the Broad Street district school. Mary Emma, and of course, baby Joseph were not yet of school age.

Once the meal was over and the children finished cleaning up, Mary Ann sat down to take care of any pressing maternal demands, which could vary depending on the night. There could be loose buttons to sew on Thomas' shirt, the ironing of Mary

Ellen's frock for school tomorrow, or listening to James' recitation of the time tables. Baby Joseph was too cute to be ignored so she made sure to give him ample attention. She held the baby in her lap and rocked him until he became drowsy enough to gently lower into his cradle for the night.

One of Mary Ann's greatest pleasures of the day was the time she spent with Mary Emma. She was a small child, but clearly musically gifted. Mary Ann delighted in listening to her sing. They said prayers together and after lots of hugs, Mary Ann tenderly tucked her daughter under the covers for the night.

There were times when the Bascombe children wished their mother didn't work or have to be so involved with others in the neighborhood. Even though the real estate business allowed Mary Ann more flexible time to be with them than a mother who slaved away as a factory worker or servant, they felt cheated. True, she had figured out a highly successful way of making a living and earned more than enough money to provide them all with the necessities of life, but they resented always having to compete for her attention.

If only mother would make enough money to quit her business and be a home keeper who was always there to tend to our needs!

They moaned and groaned among themselves but none of the children dared to voice the complaints to their mother. They feared that if said, she might take her stout stick to their behinds for uttering hogwash.

Late into the evening, when chores were complete and the youngest children fast asleep in their beds, Mary Ann finally sat down to tend to her financial affairs.

Pish! Posh! Always one thing or another to do...

First, she pulled out her bank ledger book to write out a few payments to local contractors. Next, Mary Ann took out papers to pour over the plans for a new home she wanted to build.

Fortunately, other than the parents of young Mr. Kennedy (who came over with a cake to thank Mary Ann for the time spent defending their new daughter-in-law) there had been no callers after supper. And, there were also no outstanding volunteer promises to fulfill for the church or the fire company for the next day. Tonight, she relished the notion of a full night's sleep so long as Joseph or one of the other children did not wake her.

Mary Ann bundled up and grabbed a lantern to make a quick frigid run to the privy, then returned back to the house to wash up before retiring to bed. James was already asleep, so Mary Ann turned down the kerosene lamps in the living area before retiring to the bedroom. She was a lady who was rarely depleted of energy, but it was getting late. Time had come to rest up for whatever tomorrow would bring.

Mary Ann let her hair down and brushed it out. Then she changed into a plain flannel gown. The lady lawyer crawled into bed, moving cautiously so as not to wake James. She pressed up against him ever so slightly to steal a bit of his body heat, and then arranged her head upon the feather pillow.

At the end of a long and productive day, it was time to give thanks.

She lifted her right hand to her forehead and started the Sign of the Cross.

In the name of the Father, the Son, and Holy Spirit: Dear Lord, I humbly beseech you to bless my dear father and mother and brothers up in heaven. May you also continue to bestow your blessings on the living. Keep husband James, children Mary Jane, William, Thomas, Mary Ellen, James, and John, and my dear babies, Mary Emma and Joseph, free from sickness or debt. Bless my brothers and their families. Help me to be an admirable wife and mother, to make wise decisions, and to provide well for my family. I ask you this, oh ever living God, for through you all things are possible.

Amen.

Though many gifts had been bestowed upon her, Mary Ann considered being born and raised in Rocky Hollow, Stapleton as one of her finest blessings. She firmly believed that her parents, Thomas and Mary McDonough, had been guided by God's good graces to make their homestead at the corner of Broad and

Gordon Streets. With the help of God, she had overcome many losses here, and in Stapleton Mary Ann felt nearly invincible. She was in her early forties now, and well on her way to obtain the things she desired most in life.

Mary Ann settled in, pulling her quilt up snugly around her neck, secure in the knowledge that today she had held sway over her little corner of the world.

And, with this comfortable thought, she fell into a deep sleep.

Chapter Two: A Delightful Yet Unsavory Neighborhood

Thomas McDonough and Mary Smith were the parents of Mary Ann Bascombe. They came to America filled with hope and dreams as part of the initial wave of Irish immigrants who fled the rising government oppression, religious discrimination, unemployment, and untenable housing conditions imposing an intolerably low standard of living in their homeland. Like other Irish passing through the port of New York, Thomas and Mary first settled in the city. Thomas went out to find work as a laborer. Mary set up house in their tiny quarters. Initially, the couple found that living alongside Irish brethren had advantages. They did not feel so alien in the unfamiliar surroundings and enjoyed the camaraderie they shared with fellow nationals. Thomas was able to secure steady work and Mary was close to the markets. These were pluses, yet they soon discovered the uglier aspects of urban living. Violence, crime, and disease were common in the immigrant community. So, it was not long before the couple agreed. The city would not be their permanent home.

Mary gave birth to a handsome boy they named John. Soon after his birth, the couple began to talk more seriously about making a move. Thomas kept his eyes and ears open for good possibilities, and then one day his diligence was rewarded. He heard about a new community just formed on Staten Island. It was called Stapleton and not far by ferry from Manhattan and Brooklyn. Stapleton was a small town along the New York shoreline surrounded by delightful hills and countryside. According to his sources, the town was growing fast and in need of day laborers.

Thomas could hardly contain his enthusiasm. Bolting up the stairs of their tenement two steps at a time, he was nearly out of breath by the time he reached the top floor. Thomas threw the door wide open and spied his wife sweeping the floor with a broom. Her back was to him, so Thomas ran up to Mary and grabbed her from behind. He spun her around.

Mary gave him a startled look, then pushed him back gently. Thomas asked for her attention as he had great news to share. Mary stopped sweeping, smiled, and then leaned on her broom to pay full attention to her husband's words. Excitedly, Thomas told her what he had learned, concluding by saying:

Maire! If t'is true what they say about Stapleton, we shud be packin' our bags this evenin'!

Thomas had a gift for persuasion which rarely failed to win Mary over, so long as it made some sense. She listened carefully to his argument, and then told him she was amenable to relocating but only after a bit more investigation. They agreed that Thomas should go see Staten Island and report back, so he quickly made the arrangements for a day excursion.

Thomas impatiently counted the days until the trip. He was a responsible husband and father, but Thomas also had a passion for living which had not been stamped out by the hardships of immigrant life. He was a thoroughly practical man who had not yet lost the capacity to dream. A few years earlier, Thomas' dreams had taken him clear across the Atlantic Ocean. Now, his dreams would propel him once again, this time across the New York waterways.

Thomas left in the early morning hours to have sufficient daylight to explore. He arrived at the docks and got in line alongside a small group of men, women, and children likewise seeking passage to the Stapleton ferry. There was sufficient room inside the cabin of the sailing vessel, but Thomas chose to remain on deck after boarding. It would be a much better view of the harbor, so long as he could bear the elements. Thomas braced his coat lapel up around his neck to defend against the anticipated wicked harbor wind. When the boat began to move it was certain to whip him viciously about the face. Thomas circled the boat until he found a preferred spot against the railing and then leaned back to watch the deck hands ready the sails.

Thomas reminisced that the last time he traveled this water route the boat was pointed in the opposite direction, sailing up through the Narrows at the end of a long and perilous journey from Ireland to New York. Back then, Thomas overlooked close scrutiny of the harbor due to the combination of cold and fatigue. This time he made sure it did not happen again. Thomas took note of the features of the land on all sides of the boat, then turned his focus exclusively towards the distance. There was morning fog, and the ferry would need to get closer to its destination before he could clearly see land.

Yea, but t'will be a glorious view, Thomas predicted.

It was a relatively short ride. As the ferry coasted closer to its dock, Thomas noted the gentle green rises which bordered the northern and western edges of the town of Stapleton, sloping down in graceful fashion until the land met the sandy shoreline. He was intrigued before his first step off the dock.

Thomas was one of the first passengers to disembark the ferry. He first meandered along the Stapleton waterfront. Thomas hailed a few men at work near the dock and inquired about the demand for local laborers. He verified that there was more than enough steady work. The reports he heard were accurate.

He toured the streets closest to the docks first, and then began to fan out to explore other parts of town. Thomas found a local pub, where he sat down to take in a whiskey or two and make small talk with the patrons. After chatting it up for a while, Thomas was thoroughly convinced that this new town of Stapleton was where he wanted to be. It seemed that from the Stapleton docks one could venture out almost anywhere. Stapleton offered a valuable water transportation link to other parts of New York, with commercial docks and a regular ferry service already in place running back and forth to Manhattan. Stapleton was also an important transportation hub on land. Gore Lane, a country road which had been named after a local farmer, was the main artery in town. It began at the waterfront and ran straight through the middle of the village up to a point where it intersected a major inland toll parkway called Richmond Road. The toll road ran north to the town of Tompkinsville and south to the landlocked county government seat in Richmond.

He thought to himself.

Shuro, but t'isn't this also a place of grand convenience!

Thomas dallied a bit longer than Mary would have approved of at the saloon. He thoroughly enjoyed the companionship of the men and could have lingered there all day, but in the back of his mind he did not forget he was on an important mission. After his third or fourth whiskey, Thomas reached deep into his pocket and placed a coin on the counter. He thanked the men for their time and company and went on his way.

Thomas wandered and eventually found his way over to a long straight wagon path which disappeared up in the direction of the hills. The hills! Thomas, practical dreamer that he was, was energized by the notion of what he could see from atop those heavenly green slopes! He began hiking faster and faster up the road, which he found out later was the Gore Lane he had been told about. The path was a steady incline, and soon he reached the bottom of a steep hill.

Without hesitation, Thomas began to scale the hills he had ogled from the ferry deck. Locals told him the elevation had been called Signal Hill during the War of the American Revolution but in present day it bore the name of a wealthy family called Grymes. The rabbits hopping about at his feet did not seem to mind, but Thomas moved cautiously as the primitive trail he uncovered was steep and thick with prickly briars. It took time, but eventually he cleared the top of the rise. Thomas turned around and then tripped and nearly fell. He was overcome by the grandeur of what his eyes spied.

Praise be t' God! I give thanks fer allowin' Thomas Mack, yer humble servint, to behold such a glorious sight!

Thomas plopped down on a rock at the top of Grymes Hill to catch his breath and savor the view. The morning fog had lifted, replaced by a piercingly bright blue sunny day, and the panorama before him appeared to stretch clear to the ends of time and place. To the far north, Thomas spotted the fringes of

25

the Palisades on the New Jersey side of the Hudson. By panning right, he had views of Upper New York Bay and the Isle of Manhattan. Looking to the east, Thomas noted the Narrows and near and far stretches of Kings County. And, as he turned southward, Thomas' gaze met the Lower New York Bay, with a hint of Sandy Hook and the Highlands in the far distance. The view below him was also amazing. Here he saw the billowing sails of vessels big and small as they slowly made their way up and down the glistening waters of the Narrows.

The Irishman leaned back, utterly mesmerized. He had never been this high up, seeing the New York waterways in such a grand fashion. When finally tiring of the view, Thomas shifted his eyes to look even more downward and scrutinize the tiny town of Stapleton. Other than the small cluster of civilization at the water's edge, there were few signs of human life beyond a sprinkling of cattle or a modest roof top here and there. The scene was serene and pastoral and most appealing to his senses.

Shuro, but t'is no noisy, grimy, hostile city here!

Stapleton was a prosperous community with sufficient work to occupy the hands of a skilled laborer, and yet with so much open space and natural beauty to be enjoyed. Thomas had verified everything he heard back in the city. He was sold on the move. Full of excitement, he started the descent back into town.

That night over supper, Thomas discussed the day's adventure with his wife. He could not stop repeating himself.

T'is where we belong, Maire!

Mary, always the more sensible of the pair, was not yet convinced. She told Thomas to take hold of his britches. As a religious woman, she felt strongly that they must take time out for thoughtful reflection to arrive at the proper conclusion.

Meybe so husbind, but ferst we must pray and ask fer God's blessins on the move. Shuro, as t'was He the one who ferst guided us in aur choice to leave the homeland and He who shud direct us now.

Thomas valued his wife's opinion above all others, so he reluctantly acquiesced to her point of view. Over the next few days, they talked and prayed about the matter. They agreed that

Thomas would not be at a loss for work if they moved. This was good, but it could not be the deciding factor as there was also ample work in the city.

Both liked the notion of being close to New York yet living in a place where there was plenty of fresh air and countryside. In Stapleton, they could grow crops and have a cow, horse, and some pigs, just like back home in Ireland. But living on Staten Island could never measure up to home completely because in Stapleton they would be a distinct minority. Like the city, the old guard was of Dutch or English descent and not accustomed to outsiders. A small contingent of Irish lived on Staten Island, but they were clustered mostly around the factories where they worked on the north shore. Stapleton was located on the east shore. It was quite possible that would feel like loners in this new place.

Thomas and Mary were sensible enough to realize that a move to Staten Island was an escape from the city but not from all of life's problems. They prayed and concluded that with the help of God's good graces, they were making a sound decision. The McDonoughs would make the move to Staten Island.

Thomas and Mary packed their belongings and left the city. Thomas found work right away. The prejudice against their nationality turned out to be minimal. They found rooms to let, moving into cramped living quarters which they shared with others. The tight space was barely tolerable, but Mary was without complaint as Thomas, still dreaming, told her of the grander plan fermenting in his head.

Shuro, Maire, but don't ye agree that ownin' land is the one true measure of Amerikin success?

Thomas was convinced that they could not go wrong with the purchase of land. Stapleton was being marketed in New York as a delightful place to live, and tens of thousands of dollars were being invested in real estate speculation. In 1836 alone, over 130 parcels of land had been sold, clustered primarily on Gore, Gordon, and Targee Streets and along Richmond Road. The subdivisions were affordable to a variety of budgets, starting at $40 a plot. Thomas promised Mary they would soon be in a position to buy one of the available properties.

The Irishman drew upon all the mental and physical faculties bestowed upon him by the Almighty Creator to labor steadfastly toward the goal. He toiled long hard hours, and although he still managed to down a drink or two now and then with the other men at the local tavern, Thomas put aside from his wages, a little at a time, to fuel the dream. Thomas gave all the credit to Mary, as he knew he may never have achieved this purpose without the partnership of his beloved. Mary cherished Thomas for his gregarious enthusiasm and unstoppable energy and he adored her for the level headed encouragement and support she provided. Mary helped Thomas by understanding the need for them to be frugal. She did not fritter away money on unnecessary household purchases. Plus, she kept an eye on Thomas' drinking, knowing how easy it was for a man to lose his head over whiskey. Her smart and savvy household practices helped Thomas maintain his focus. He worked, saved, and waited for the right land deal to come along.

In the later part of 1840, Thomas had accumulated sufficient money to feel confident in making a credible real estate offer. Mary was expecting another child, and husband and wife agreed it was the proper time to invest in larger living quarters. Thomas put out inquiries and learned of a property for sale which sounded quite appealing. It was located in the part of Stapleton they called Rocky Hollow, at the base of the beautiful hills that overlooked Stapleton.

No one was certain how the area came to be called Rocky Hollow, but Thomas heard that it was named after the caves near the top of Gore Street. Legend had it that the Hessians carved them out of the hills when they camped there during the War of the Revolution. Thomas took off after work to examine the property he wanted to buy firsthand. It was situated at the corner of Gore Street (the former Gore Lane) and Targee Streets, close to the intersection of Richmond Road. The land ran adjacent to Gore's Brook, which well pleased him. Thomas could use the nearby water source to support livestock and crops. The land also had close proximity to main roadways. This would be useful in getting back and forth to places of work, and, as the property was far enough away from the hustle and bustle of the business district of Stapleton, it would likewise be a peaceful place to dwell. Thomas, who was handy with tools, envisioned building a house at just the right angle on the property where a window might capture a wee bit of that magnificent view of the Narrows.

Thomas grinned. *Shuro, 'nd t'isn't that a grand idea!*

He went home to Mary. The couple talked. They prayed, and then Thomas struck the deal. In November 1840, Thomas dressed up in his Sunday garb and borrowed a horse to travel down to the office of the Richmond County clerk. With graceful strokes of his quill pen, Joseph Egbert recorded the real estate transaction, noting that a sum of one hundred dollars lawful money of the United States was paid to George Coyne by Thomas McDonough for the sale of the land.

Alleluia! Praise be t' God!

Thomas McDonough shouted out loud when he left the building. He was now officially a New York State land owner! He made haste to return home, eager to show the paperwork to his wife and down a few celebratory shots of whiskey.

Thomas and Mary liked Rocky Hollow from the start. It was a small and tight knit community whose inhabitants were an agreeable mix of people from English, Irish, and African backgrounds. Merchants, lawyers, carpenters, masons, butchers, coachmen, gardeners, and a teacher all lived within walking distance of their new home. Everyone got along and the McDonoughs felt well accepted. Mary found the women to be pleasant and helpful. Thomas fit in well with his male neighbors who congregated at the local tavern to enjoy a wee bit of whiskey now and then after work to discuss politics and the news of the day.

Shortly after settling in, they themselves became the news of the neighborhood.

Aye, neighbor, have ye heard? A healthy girl baby has been born to Thomas and Mary!

Mary Anna McDonough (the girl who would grow up to be Mary Ann Bascombe) came into the world on December 14, 1840. Her birth, just a few days before Christmas, made the celebration of the McDonough's first holiday in Rocky Hollow even more joyful. She was a new life in a new home within a newly founded community, and her parents took this as a good omen. God would bestow special blessings upon their baby daughter to carry her throughout life.

They were devout Catholics, so word was sent to their priest as soon as possible after Mary Anna's birth. Bishop John Hughes of the Archdiocese of New York had opened the first Roman Catholic parish on the island just a year before, and Thomas and Mary felt quite fortunate that the baby would be baptized on Staten Island.

Reverend Ildefonso Medrano, an exiled Spaniard priest, was the first pastor of St. Peter's Church. Three days after Mary Anna's birth, Father Medrano arrived in Rocky Hollow on horseback to baptize the baby in the presence of her parents and sponsors, John Garrett and Elena Smith. Father Medrano used the flask of holy water he brought with him to anoint Mary Anna's forehead and welcome her into God's family. Mary, still weak from childbirth, leaned on Elena and her new neighbors to help with a modest repast after the sacrament was administered.

Mary Anna slept through much of the ceremony but towards the end of the meal she began to wail loudly in her cradle. Mary got up to attend to her, and Father Medrano followed. He watched intently as Mary tenderly soothed the infant. The priest remarked that God had blessed Mary Anna with robust lungs. He predicted she would grow up to be a strong and courageous woman of faith. Mary looked back at him and smiled.

In 1840, Father Medrano's flock consisted of about one hundred faithful Staten Island and New Jersey parishioners. Among them there was not sufficient money to build a church, so mass was held inside St. Peter's temporary place of worship, a former north shore gun factory. A church on Staten Island was good for parishioners as they were no longer forced to travel to Manhattan or Brooklyn for services, yet it was still not easy to get to Sunday mass. The faithful journeyed on foot, by horse, wagon, and row boat, but travel was restricted to daylight and fair weather. Staten Island roads were of very poor condition, consisting of either packed down dirt or plank board construction, and were notoriously treacherous to travel on in rain or snow storms. Flooding and/or excessive muddy conditions often forced parishioners to forego the trip.

On dry and sunny Sundays, however, Thomas and Mary enjoyed the ride to and from St. Peter's. Thomas hitched horses to the wagon while Mary swaddled Mary Anna in wool blankets to guard against seasonal chills. Mary was helped into the back of the wagon and the baby placed into her loving arms. Then, Mary Anna's toddler brother John was hoisted up by Thomas and took his place next to his mother. When all were settled, Thomas climbed into the front buckboard bench seat and took off.

Sometimes, Thomas took the wagon down Gore Street to the docks, and then made a left and followed the shoreline. Other times, he started up Targee Street and travelled along Richmond Street from Stapleton into Tompkinsville. This hilly route had fabulous views but it was difficult to negotiate after a rain, so eventually it earned the nickname Mud Lane. A third route to get to church on special occasions was to travel to the end of Gore Street and turn onto a toll road which had been known in former days as the Old Kings Highway.

Dry weather meant safer travel, but Thomas drove with caution no matter the elements. He needed to skillfully avoid major ruts in the road which made the ride uncomfortable or worse yet, could damage their mode of transportation. A slower wagon pace also benefited the new baby. The steady clip clop of the horse served as a natural pacifier for Thomas' precious cargo.

There was one precarious part of the weekly trip. In order to get to the gun factory, Thomas had to travel in the vicinity of the lazaretto quarantine. The quarantine had been established during Colonial days by the New York State legislature. A prime 30 acre waterfront property in Tompkinsville owned by St. Andrew's Episcopal congregation was taken by eminent domain and a hospital was built to treat victims of smallpox, yellow fever, and other deadly diseases.

The Quarantine was a most significant public health threat to Staten Islanders, and each Sunday Mary was on edge until they were well past its walled borders. Thomas made sure never to give his horse occasion to rest or offer rides to strangers near the lazaretto. It was a foul and dangerous place.

On the way to and from church, Thomas and Mary had the opportunity to chit chat about matters for which they had no time during the rest of the week. Most often the conversation circled around the children or neighbors. Sometimes it was about Ireland and the past. Other times they discussed the local news and small-town politics. Their conversations made the ride all the more enjoyable.

Thomas was proud of his new hometown and enjoyed sharing his growing knowledge of Stapleton's history with his wife. The Lenape Indians had been the first to live along the shores of Lower New York Bay, followed in time by hard working Dutch farmers with last names such as Vanderbilt, Coursen, and Van Duzer. Area development in large part was tied to the prescience of a New York State Governor who later became Vice President of the United States. Daniel D. Tompkins was a visionary who recognized that the Staten Island shoreline held extraordinary real estate appeal. Tompkins borrowed heavily in 1815 and bought 700 acres at the most northeastern point of the island. The Governor mapped out a series of streets which he named after his immediate family members. He called the new community Tompkinsville.

In 1833, Tompkin's son Minthorne and New York City business partner William J. Staples expanded upon Daniel's foresight by purchasing and sub dividing Vanderbilt farm land just south of Tompkinsville. They created an attractive network of wide streets and buildable lots. The region had gone by a variety of names such as Second Landing, Cole's Ferry and Darby Doyle's, but they decided to rechristen the place. Since the Tompkins name had already been used, they agreed to name the new development in Staples' honor. Tompkins and Staples organized a day of festivities to publicize the renaming of the community. They invited local citizens and guests to a grand party held at the elegant Bay Hotel by the water's edge in July 1836. The old timers told Thomas that the townspeople celebrated in splendid fashion that evening. Spectators were treated to a glorious nighttime display as fiery rockets and gun salutes were discharged into the dark summer skies.

HooRAH! HooRAH! Cheers for the new town of Stapleton!

Oh, how Thomas wished he had been there that night! At its beginning, Stapleton consisted of just a few dozen houses, the Bay Hotel, a small hospital for sailors, and a cemetery, but soon a mix of small and distinctive clusters of neighborhoods began to emerge.

When Thomas made a detour through the small streets nicknamed The Nook, it allowed him to pass in front of the Stapleton sailor hospital. The Seaman's Retreat had been established in 1831 as the first hospital in New York State dedicated to the care of aged and infirmed sailors. It was situated on a grand spot with a magnificent unobstructed view of the shoreline, just south of the business district at the border of Stapleton and Clifton near the Vanderbilt ferry. The property was a sprawling 40 acres, which stretched from the sandy eastern shoreline over to the western woodlands bordering Rocky Hollow.

At first, medical services were provided inside a small farmhouse. However, by the time of the McDonoughs' move to Rocky Hollow, a permanent structure had been erected. The new hospital was a stately building admired by everyone for its fine construction. It was three stories high and built of grey granite ashlar in Greek revival architectural style, complete with porticos and Doric columns. Situated on a high bluff overlooking the waterfront, the hospital provided recuperating sailors with a most therapeutic milieu.

As they approached the hospital, Thomas, the perpetual dreamer, expressed his sincere wish to work at the Retreat someday. Then, he could boast that he labored for good purpose at the grandest property in town. Plus, he would also get a chance to see some of the area's finest views of the Narrows from the third floor of the hospital building!

The small frame house that Thomas built was not far from the heavily wooded area at the western border of the Retreat. As they approached the corner where Thomas planted the seeds of his American dream, he began to tug at the reins to bring the wagon to a slow halt. Thomas helped his wife get John and Mary Anna out of the wagon. Mary brought the children into the house, then walked down to the brook to draw a bucket of water and cool them down after the dusty ride. Thomas unlatched his horses from the wagon and walked the animals over to the trough to unwind. He smiled as it popped into his head just how much he enjoyed this town of Stapleton. How blessed he felt to live here, in a place with so much to offer the everyday man.

Stapleton realized slow but steady growth, yet continued to offer Thomas and Mary a relatively peaceful existence. The town was publicized as a worthy destination for day trippers, thanks to the city newspapers. One agreeable autumn day, a reporter ventured out to Rocky Hollow to write a piece for the brand-new publication *Harper's Weekly*. He hiked high up into the hills above the McDonough home, sat down in the grass, and took in the expansive views. The reporter took paper and writing implements out of his bag and started writing. He noted the purple line of hills that dipped toward the Hackensack, the misty heights of Morristown, the far off Highlands of New Jersey, the shoreline of Long Island, the long, curving Communipaw coast, and the sparkling Newark Bay. He remarked how the views of the Narrows were unchanged from the days of the Lenape Indians and Henry Hudson.

The reporter wrote of the beauty of nature but also the reality of civilization:

"The lowing of cattle, the cackle of fowls in neighboring barnyards, the sound of children's voices ringing in the perfectly quiet air, the barking of dogs, the occasional distant cry of boys driving the cows homeward, an evening bell from the village below...Down in Rocky Hollow and all over the island, there are indeed poverty and suffering; but they are the exception, not the law."[1]

Like the writer, Thomas was well acquainted with the idyllic aspects of his home along with the full understanding that God provided no true paradise on Earth. Rocky Hollow was a pleasant place to live but like anywhere else had its share of problems.

The forces of nature were a huge challenge that Thomas and

his neighbors faced. The flooding of Gore's Brook was a routine part of living in Rocky Hollow. The brook would bring fame and prosperity to the area someday, but in Thomas' time it was often more of a nuisance than a blessing. Named for the same farmer who once owned much of the land through which the waters flowed, Gore's Brook was by far the biggest tributary in the area. It commenced in the hilly section of the nearby town of Clifton and flowed directly through Rocky Hollow. Under normal conditions, it provided a readily accessible water supply. When the brook overflowed, however, it posed serious threats to the health and livelihood of citizens.

Living in an era before storm sewers meant in bad weather the residents of Rocky Hollow could do little else but pray when it rained heavily. Crops were submerged and ruined while the streets turned into big muddy, rutted messes. Wagons and carriages were hampered in their ability to navigate the streets. Sometimes the roads washed away completely.

When storms grew intense, the rising waters extended beyond the fields into homes and businesses, inundating basements and the first floors of buildings. Thomas' home was situated on higher ground than other parts of Rocky Hollow so his family escaped most occasions of harm, but their neighbors were not as lucky. At times, the fierce rains resulted in so much flooding that citizens were forced to flee to the second floor or even their roof tops to stay dry. When disaster struck, Thomas pitched in with all the other able-bodied men. They used rowboats to rescue stranded inhabitants and help salvage house contents. Mary did her part too, sheltering and cooking for neighbors until the waters ebbed.

Flooding was bad enough, but even worse were the outbreaks of invisible and quite deadly disease. Stapleton, as part of the New York waterways, was a cosmopolitan place. Sailing vessels converged here from all parts of the world, bringing cargo and travelers but also all forms of uninvited sickness. Thomas and Mary were always on guard for reports of yellow fever, smallpox, typhus, typhoid, scarlet fever, and influenza. They took precautions as best they could when epidemics flared.

The Irish Potato Famine began in 1845, resulting in a great influx of new immigrants to America. They endured perilous journeys across the Atlantic Ocean. Many died on ship or arrived very ill. Those who harbored the symptoms of contagious diseases were brought to the quarantine on Staten Island, swelling the numbers of patients being treated at the facility. As the numbers of afflicted individuals rose, Thomas and Mary joined a growing number of citizens in the community who were united in their opposition of the facility. They argued that until the quarantine closed, dangerous living conditions would persist for all men, women and children living in Richmond County.

The cries of protest were not limited to the poor or working class. Local physicians, health officers, and clergymen openly supported the removal of the hospital. Elected officials tried repeatedly to convince the New York State legislature to close the facility. Time and again their pleas were overlooked, so the notion of taking matters into their own hands to rid Staten Island of the hospital once and for all became a frequent open topic of discussion in homes, churches, and local taverns.

New York health officials labeled 1848 a *Yellow Fever Year* because of major outbreaks throughout the region. Yellow Fever was a torturous ailment, causing fever, headaches, nausea and vomiting in its milder form, and jaundice, mental confusion, and stomach bleeding in its more progressive fatal stages. Nicknamed the *Yellow Jack*, the disease was all too familiar to those who lived in Rocky Hollow. Learned men of the day postulated that *Yellow Jack* was spread solely through the bite of infected mosquitoes, which made perfect sense in Rocky Hollow because of the presence of Gore's Brook. The brook routinely overflowed in the summer months, leading to an accumulation of pools of stagnant water. If infected mosquitoes laid their eggs in the water, it would bring on the disease. Not all local citizens believed this theory, but they did agree there was something in the environment causing the disease. They dreaded the possibility of yet one more epidemic.

In the summer of 1848, the *Yellow Jack* made land in both Tompkinsville and Stapleton around the same time. In Tompkinsville, a carpet weaver who had purchased bed sacking found floating in the waters off Upper New York Bay was the first to succumb to the fever. His friend who cared for the man during his illness was next in line to die. A local fisherman and a shoemaker were sickened soon afterwards.

In Stapleton, the first fatality was a store owner who had recently purchased old lumber and rubbish which washed ashore. The trash, which beached next to the Stapleton Malleable Iron Works, was blamed as a source of disease since soon after many men employed at the factory fell ill. A fisherman, a hotel worker, and a part time undertaker likewise succumbed to the contagion.

Living less than a mile from the Stapleton waterfront, Thomas and Mary scrambled after hearing the news to take what precautions they could to protect themselves. Mary instructed the children to stay indoors whenever possible and avoid contact with others in the neighborhood. John and Mary Anna, eight and seven years old respectively at the time, protested but it was in vain. They obeyed their mother, although it was unbearably hot and stifling in the house. All prayed for an end to the epidemic as soon as possible.

The McDonough's concerns about this particular outbreak were not to be minimized. By mid-September, over fifty people had been officially diagnosed and twelve had died. The extent of the *Yellow Jack* epidemic stretched as far south as the town of Clifton at Stapleton's southern border after reports that the sister of the chaplain at the Seamen's Retreat had also become a victim.

Yellow Jack was a scary disease because it did not behave like other contagions. There seemed to be no guaranteed immunity. Older Stapleton residents recalled that back at the beginning of the century a well-respected physician named Dr. Richard Bayley died of the *Yellow Jack*. Bayley, who was the chief medical officer at the Quarantine, had been exposed repeatedly to the disease without serious consequence, and then one day became violently ill and never recovered.

Mary Anna and John continued to object to their isolation but the decision would not be reversed. Allen B. Whiting, health officer at the Quarantine Hospital, noted that new cases of

Yellow Jack were being reported on a daily basis. He suspected that three vessels from New Orleans docked at the Quarantine carried the disease. Whiting ordered the ships as far away as possible from the shore to obviate any further danger to the citizens.

Whiting was not a physician and relatively new to this kind of work, so he called upon on a team of local experts for guidance in managing the crisis. To thwart the Angel of Death, the health officials of Tompkinsville, Stapleton, and Clifton decided to close the docks. No steam ferries or any other boats would be allowed to touch land or take on passengers until the ban from the Board of Health was lifted.

The bustling Tompkinsville and Stapleton waterfronts fell silent and devoid of human life. Men who depended upon the bay for their livelihood pulled up stakes and moved to the north shore of Staten Island or south of Stapleton to do business. The wealthy residents who were fortunate enough to get out of town before the shutdown escaped harm, but they had to do without their belongings. Trunks, bandboxes, and carpet bags lay abandoned in piles all over the docks. They contained some valuable items, but none dared touch them, fearing they might be tainted with disease.

The local hotels and boarding houses emptied out. The private schools in town were closed, and the boys who boarded and could not be sent home were cloistered with their instructors somewhere inland. All stores were ordered to close between 4 and 5 o'clock in the afternoon so that citizens could get indoors before the onset of what officials believed was a perilous night air.

When seasonal chills arrived, the Yellow Fever epidemic of 1848 began to ebb, and slowly but surely life returned to normal for the citizens of Stapleton. They had survived the *Yellow Jack,* yes, but this gave them but limited comfort. All knew it was only a matter of time before another round of infectious disease would emerge to terrorize the community.

Cholera, an acute intestinal disease contracted by ingesting food or water contaminated by feces, was another commonly recurring illness and even more dangerous than Yellow Fever because it was not limited to the warm weather months. In Thomas' time, it was not known that cases of cholera could be prevented if citizens better understood how crowded and unsanitary conditions contributed to susceptibility. On ships that crossed the Atlantic, the breeding grounds for the disease were the tight, dark, germ-infested living quarters of those traveling in steerage. In communities like Rocky Hollow, it was dirty streets and the absence of a municipal garbage collection system which accounted for the problem. Heavy rains mixed with human waste and animal droppings spread contamination throughout the neighborhood.

During an acute outbreak, health inspectors were sent out to investigate and found unclean privies and grubby hog pens. Animals wandered the neighborhood at will, left to graze anywhere and everywhere. On at least one health inspection, just a few doors down from the McDonoughs on Gordon Street, pigs and cows were found living in the basements of neighbors.

The county health officers imposed severe fines, even imprisonment for violators. They ordered the sacrifice of suspect animals and mandated strict street cleaning and outhouse disinfections with chemicals such as chloride of lime, coal tar powders and sulfate of iron. These were sound practices but took place only after an epidemic was already in progress. A regular schedule of health inspections and street cleaning would have helped greatly to prevent Cholera epidemics, but it was not yet a practice of local governments.

As the population of Rocky Hollow grew so did the number of cholera victims. New York newspapers began shifting their reports of fanciful Rocky Hollow day trips to the grittier news of the day. They dropped the references to Rocky Hollow as a delightful place to live. Instead, they relabeled the neighborhood as an unsavory place of poverty and filth where citizens brought on their own disease by engaging in disgusting living habits.

Thomas and Mary took umbrage when they learned of such comments. Their humble way of life was being attacked by outsiders who disrespectfully lumped everyone together in the same boat. Thomas labored long, exhausting hours at his trade, providing the necessities for his family. Mary toiled day and night at home as the keeper of the home and children. They kept a tidy house and property. There was nothing disgusting about their habits or the dignity of the way they lived their lives. The reporters were wrong to generalize!

Time went on. The combination of Thomas' hard work and Mary's frugality helped them continue to save money. They were so successful that Thomas was able to add to his property by purchasing a neighboring lot. The acquisition gave him all the land he needed to construct a fine new barn for the livestock.

Mary became pregnant three more times. Baby Eugene did not live long, but Michael and Thomas were hardy babies and a welcome addition to the clan. Father Medrano's prediction for the little girl in the family turned out to be accurate. Mary Anna was growing up as a strong and fearless child. She was friendly. She was talkative. She was enthusiastic in declaring her love for God, her family, and her Rocky Hollow home.

As the only girl in the family, Mary Anna was recruited at an early age to help with the house chores. She did not relish these tasks, but Mary Anna did not complain. Instead, she chose to treasure the one on one time spent in the company of her mother. She was a lot like her mother, so she enjoyed hearing the strong and fearless woman share her personal beliefs about God, hard work, home keeping, and other subjects during their side by side labor. Mary told Thomas how proud she was of Mary Anna for shouldering her daily share of work without grumbling. She praised John too, for he likewise fulfilled his many chores cheerfully. John and Mary Anna each took turns supervising their baby brothers, which was Mary Anna's favorite chore of all. Gregarious and full of fun, she thrilled at the opportunity to run about the property with the boys. Mary Anna was not a sissy girl. She hiked her skirts to scale trees and climb hills. She splashed around at the brook. Mary Anna caught frogs and made her fair share of mud pies with the little ones.

When Thomas trudged up Gore Street at the end of a long, grueling day at work and spotted his children outside at play, he could not help but feel at peace with the world. Why, he was living the grandest of dreams! He had his land, the children, and best of all, he had Mary at his side to comfort, support, and offer wise counsel. Thomas smiled. He was convinced he owned everything one could ever want for in life.

Thomas was happy, but unfortunately this contented time of his life did not last. Misery arrived at the McDonough doorstep amid the blazing heat of the summer of 1849. Labeled a *Cholera Year* by New York health officials, Rocky Hollow became part of the year's wide sweeping epidemic which led to over twenty-two thousand New York deaths.

When the outbreak hit Stapleton, Thomas and Mary took the usual precautions to avoid exposure. The children were confined indoors except to carry water from the brook, help in the garden or in the barn. Mary prayed that all would be spared from the disease, but suddenly one morning, nine years old John began to complain of stomach pain. He vomited, had a few bouts of loose stools, got woozy, and collapsed into his mother's arms. And shortly thereafter, his thirty-eight years old mother started experiencing the same symptoms. Their vomiting and diarrhea continued until both were too weak to stand. Mary and John took to bed together.

Thomas came home from work that evening and went to work at once caring for his wife and child. He was panicked inside but tried not to let the children see. Thomas sent his two youngest sons to the neighbors down the road and asked his neighbor to call for a doctor. Then, he went back to his house and wracked his brains. Was there anything else he could do other than change the bed sheets, empty the chamber pot, offer sips of water, and place wet rags on hot foreheads? To steady his nerves, Thomas turned to the cupboard near the fireplace and took a few swigs of whiskey. Then a few more.

Thomas instructed his daughter to tend to the animals in the barn, so he was startled when he returned to his wife's side and caught little Mary Anna curled up in the corner of the room. Thomas barked at her to leave, but she flatly refused. The small girl, eyes red and lined with tears, prayed silently.

Mother and son lay close to each other, enduring unrelenting waves of vomiting, diarrhea, and cramps. In spite of her agony, Mary Anna saw that her mother tried to ease John's pain. She ran her fingers through his hair and whispered in his ear ever so softly.

Mama! Mama! Can't I help?

Little Mary Anna called out to gain her mother's attention. Mary lifted her head up slightly from the pillow. With a vacant look she answered in a weak but stern voice.

Leave this room. NOW, Mary Anna!

Mary Anna's feelings were severely injured but she dutifully obeyed. She left the house and walked down to the brook. Michael and Thomas were there splashing around, so she sat on a nearby rock and pondered the circumstances. Mary Anna had only wanted to make things better, yet her mother had been so uncharacteristically harsh. Why?

Back at home, Thomas tried to offer water to the pair, but with little success. He was fighting a losing battle and could only comfort, pray, and beg his wife and son to hang on.

Maire! Johnny boy! Dun't give up! Sweet Jesus, h've mercy! Grant me luved ones strength ta overcum!

The symptoms continued, and neighbors coaxed Thomas to allow them to summon the priest. The pastor administered the Catholic sacraments of the dying, and shortly afterwards Mary lapsed into an unconscious state. Mary succumbed to the cholera first. John kept up the fight but died three days later.

The McDonough household was thrown into a tizzy by their deaths. Thomas' neighbors came to help, knowing he could not handle the situation alone. They carried out Mary's body wrapped in clean linen sheets. After John's death, they removed him, then burned the straw mattress and cleansed the surroundings as best as they knew. While they worked, Thomas wandered in and out of the house in a mental fog, the whiskey bottle never far from his sight. Mary Anna, likewise in a daze, alternated between crying and trying her best to take care of Michael and baby Thomas. Because she was the eldest child and a girl to boot, Mary Anna was immediately thrust in charge of household affairs. Friends of her mother came to help and Mary Anna was glad for their kindness, but it did little to ease the confusion in her head or emptiness in her heart. She listened to them and did as she was told.

The next few weeks were horrid. Thomas tried to master his grief, but he remained inconsolable. Alcohol became his refuge from the world. He was not going to work. He ignored the children. Thomas gave instructions to Mary Anna to care for her brothers and then left them alone for hours on end. She obeyed her father but became increasingly fearful about his state of mind. The drinking binges were becoming more and more frequent. Thomas hid behind the whiskey bottle until his cronies cornered him. They took him aside and scolded him severely. He needed to face up to his responsibilities like a man.

Thomas told them he was drinking out of sorrow and also because he was fully aware that the family situation was too difficult to manage on his own. Mary Anna was only eight years old. She could help in some ways but was not yet physically mature enough to tend to all that needed to be done around the house. Her brothers Thomas and Michael were very young and could not go about unsupervised. Thomas did not want to let go of his devotion to Mary, but he needed help. The only sensible solution they told him was to remarry.

One day soon after this discussion, Thomas introduced a new Mrs. McDonough to his children. Like his first wife, Julia McDonough was a native of Ireland but twenty-five years younger, making her closer in age to Mary Anna than her new spouse. Michael and baby Thomas were young enough to adjust quickly to having a strange woman in the house. Mary Anna, old enough to fully comprehend that her mother was being replaced by this stranger, remained aloof. All the change was too sudden for her to grasp.

Recognizing that Mary Anna would be a distinct challenge to win over, Julia asked the girl to give it time and pray for acceptance. There was clearly a need for another woman in the house, and Mary Anna saw that Julia possessed a sense of practical wisdom which was similar to her dear departed mother. This was comforting, although in her heart she held firm that her Mama could never be replaced.

Time passed. The distraction of daily routines and responsibilities slowly helped Mary Anna work through her emotions of sadness and anger. Together, Julia and Mary Anna shouldered the weight of running the home. Each took turns at chores like kneading dough, churning butter, peeling potatoes, and keeping the fire stoked as they prepared the daily meals. They suffered the charge of doing weekly laundry. Mary Anna used the scrubbing board to rub chunks of homemade soap over their dirty clothes. Julia manned the huge kettles of boiling water used to pour over the garments to rinse them. Both hung the clothing out to dry.

In addition to helping her stepmother with the cooking and cleaning, Mary Anna continued to supervise the boys. She made sure her brothers were done every day with their chores before allowing them to run off and make merry among the woods, rocks, and waterways of the Hollow.

Mary Anna's innate personality which was friendly and out-going, slowly returned. She was giggly and chit chatty like other girls her age, but as she continued to grow other traits emerged that set Thomas McDonough's daughter apart from the others. Mary Anna, like her father, possessed a mind which was rarely at rest. She was always trying to better understand the world around her and never hesitated to fire off a series of well thought out questions when intensely curious about a subject. A few frowned at such behavior in a girl, but her father delighted in this conduct. He egged her on, instructing her to never pay any mind to what others thought about her.

Whenever possible, Mary Anna volunteered to deliver her father's meal pail to his place of labor. Here she stole a few precious minutes away from her chores to watch Thomas laying bricks or wielding a hammer. She was naturally inquisitive about the details of construction work. At home, she asked Thomas to let her handle a few tools under his watchful eye. Naturally, he agreed.

Mary Anna thoroughly enjoyed listening in on the conversations of her male neighbors. Their topics of discussion were so much more interesting than women talk! She hid in the shadows to eavesdrop whenever her father and the neighborhood cronies gathered to discuss the events of the day. Mary Anna was most eager to hear their opinions.

Who do ye think will win the election for town supervisor?

Do yer think Gore Brook will overflow in the next big storm?

Did ye hear what happened down at the docks last night?

Thomas' friends were kind and gregarious. If they spotted her in hiding, they never shooed Mary Anna away. In fact, on occasion, they even threw her a question or two, so she could likewise weigh in!

Mary Anna was truly her father's daughter whenever she set her mind on a goal and in such cases there was no stopping her. Near Richmond Road there was a tiny district school house, only a short walk from her home. She ached to go to school there and learn to read and write. Mary Anna asked her father if she could attend, but sadly he told her this was not possible. The school charged fees which he could not afford. It was a difficult conversation for Thomas, as he could see the intense yearning of his bright young daughter. Her father urged her to find a way to learn on her own.

Mary Anna took on the challenge. There was no reason to pout so long as she did not accept defeat. She thought about it and asked a few of the literate adults in the neighborhood. They recommended using the Bible and old newspapers as textbooks. With a little help, Mary Anna learned her letters and numbers. She studied daily and over time, became quite proficient at both reading and arithmetic.

On the Sabbath after church and supper cleanup, Thomas liked to take Mary Anna and little Michael on hikes up into the hills. Amid that most glorious view of the Narrows they sat and passed the time watching the tall ships sail by. Thomas taught his children about the history of their community. He wanted them to understand that they were living in a special place. Thomas, who was never at a loss for words, also took these opportunities to lecture them on his way of thinking.

Mary Anna 'nd Michael, remembr, ye must work hard t' reap the rewards of life. Be kind t'a family 'nd neighbors. Be

45

op'n to changin yer mind. But most of all littl' ones, dunt forgit ta chase yer dreems. Aur home was my dreem and see! T'is real teday! Ne'er let yer dreems git away.

Around 1850, Mary Anna and her family took note of a new group of enterprising young immigrants coming to town. Just like Tompkins and Staples who founded the town in the 1830's and Thomas McDonough who bought his property in the 1840's, these were men of vision. They were Germans, who discovered that Stapleton had just the right combination of natural resources needed to manufacture a great tasting beer. Combining old world knowledge with new world acquired business skills, these men would go on to create an industry destined to change Mary Anna's quiet neighborhood forever.

To be fair, the first to brew beer commercially on Staten Island had been two Italians, Giuseppe Garibaldi the famous general and his inventor friend Antonio Meucci. They opened a brewery in nearby Clifton, but the business did not prosper. A few years afterwards, a German immigrant by the name of John Bechtel came to Stapleton. It was he who changed everything.

Bechtel was the owner of New York City's first lager beer saloon. He had been getting his beer from a Philadelphia supplier, but after learning about the cool clear artesian springs of Rocky Hollow, decided that the time had come to brew his own label. Stapleton water was the perfect ingredient Bechtel needed to produce an excellent tasting beer. Plus, the caves in the hills above Rocky Hollow were cool and damp and made excellent storage facilities, just like back in the old country.

Bechtel purchased a large tract of land on Richmond Road at the top of Gore Street and began building a brewery. All the children in Rocky Hollow were fascinated by its construction. Each day after the chores were done, Mary Anna and her brothers ran up the road to watch the workers from across the street. Michael couldn't help but remark:

Gee gosh, that's gonna be one geegantic building just two blocks away from our house!

The brewery brought new sights, sounds, and smells to the neighborhood. It was a thriving business from the start and encouraged even more Germans to come to town and open rival businesses.

Mary Anna and her brothers grew, nurtured by the love of their father and stepmother in the peace and tranquility of their hometown. Like her father, Mary Anna loved Rocky Hollow with a passion and was forever grateful to him, the Irish dream chaser, for coming to America and choosing to settle here. In Rocky Hollow, she saw firsthand that hard work paid off. Here, she was accepted and encouraged to pursue her own interests. Here, she acquired a solid belief in herself. If you had God's blessings, anyone with the right combination of guts and grit could be successful.

Yea, even if one was only a girl.

Chapter Three: This Factory Girl's A Money Maker

Thomas McDonough, the man who made it safely out of Ireland and led his family from city ghetto to a land of peace and prosperity, departed the earthly life in December 1852. A few days before his demise, the family joyously celebrated Mary Anna's twelfth birthday, but these good memories were obliterated by the tragedy of the days that followed. His death was just shy of Christmas, a dreadful time of the year to be in mourning.

Sitting at his desk downtown, the local health officer let out a sigh. He withdrew his pen from the ink bottle, blotted it carefully, and then wrote the words *Delirium Tremens* as Thomas' cause of death in the vital records ledger. Stapleton was a small town, so he knew Thomas McDonough personally. The Irishman had been a likeable, hardworking soul who never failed to provide adequately for his family. Aye, but Thomas McDonough had one serious downfall which led to his ultimate undoing.

He drank too much.

Delirium tremens was a torturous disorder with symptoms of severe and sudden agitation, confusion, hallucinations, vomiting, and seizures. When Thomas was dragged home by his cronies on the day after his last drinking binge, Julia was initially more angered than panicked. It was not the first time she had seen him in such a state. Julia knew there was no prescribed treatment other than wait for Thomas to dry out and purge the alcohol out of his system. She rolled her eyes but said nothing.

Thomas' cronies placed him in bed. Then, Julia took over. First, she took steps to shield the youngest children from the scene. Over their litany of protests, Julia packed clothes for the boys and dispatched them to a neighbor's house down the lane. She turned to Mary Anna and barked out orders to fetch wood and keep the fire going. When the children were out of earshot, Julia let out a frustrated sigh. Then, she steadied her nerves, rolled up her sleeves, and put the kettle on to boil water.

Over the next few days, Julia attended to Thomas, watching over him closely to meet her husband's needs. Julia offered sips of soothing tea when Thomas was at rest, prayed for him while his body shook, toweled him dry as he sweat, and changed the sheets after he vomited. When the stink got bad, Julia threw covers over him to keep him from shivering as she opened the windows to let the cold drafts air out the room. When it got too cold, Julia closed the windows and covered up the glass, thinking if Thomas fell asleep in the darkened room that it would help let the liquor dissipate out of his system. She was exhausted but had no choice.

Mary Anna worked bravely side by side with Julia. Mary Anna had questions but knew not to ask. She listened closely to her stepmother and did as she was told. She wanted to help in any way possible so her father would recover.

Both sensed that Thomas' condition was more desperate than in the past. He was so very agitated and mean, filled with wild mood swings and behaviors. He grabbed at Julia twice and threw the water goblet Mary Anna offered him against the wall, shattering the glass. In between outbursts, he curled up in bed looking pitifully helpless. By the time Thomas lapsed into a final state of unconsciousness, he was no longer the man they loved. Here lay a crumpled heap of human flesh, not the joyous human being who was their husband and father.

Fighting back the tears, Julia and Mary Anna bore witness as Thomas' spirit drained away with his last breath. When the ordeal was over, they collapsed into each other's arms. Each held the other tightly for a long time. Julia raised her hand and stroked her stepdaughter's head gently. Softly, she told Mary Anna they had done all they could. Then she instructed her to lie down and rest while she went down the road to ask the neighbors for assistance.

Mary Anna could not obey her stepmother. After Julia left, Mary Anna did not leave the death scene. She sat on the floor in a corner of the room. Mary Anna stared blankly at her father's lifelessness, and then let go of everything she had been holding back over the past few days. She cried softly at first and then got louder and louder in a wretched crescendo. The uncontrollable sobs took hold of her physically and she began to heave as the breath was sucked out of her chest. She wailed until there were no more tears, and then blew her nose a few times with the edge of her skirt. She was sad, so sad, but then suddenly a different emotion began to take over. Mary Anna, still alone, started cussing under her breath.

How could you do this to me Dada? Do this to all of us! We loved you so! Blasted whiskey! Why, Dada, why? Why be so needy for fool's drink!

Over the next few days, Thomas' wife, daughter, and young sons struggled to endure the exhausting ritual of a wake and funeral. Although Thomas was in his early 50's at the time of his demise, Julia was still only in her twenties. During their marriage she had given birth to two more sons, so Julia was now left with the heavy burden of responsibility for three step children, a son, and a newborn.

After the burial, Julia put her mourning on hold as soon as it was socially respectable. She grieved, but knew she had to harden her heart and deal with the reality of her circumstances.

Julia needed control of the family finances. Cipriano Miranda, her kind South American neighbor, offered to assist. One early January morning, Cipriano hitched up his wagon. He helped the young widow get settled in her seat, then climbed into the buckboard next to her and gave a pull on the reins to start the horse up Gore Street. When they reached the top of the road, he bore left onto Richmond Road and headed in a southwesterly direction. Their destination was the county courthouse.

Thomas McDonough did not have a will, so Julia needed to obtain the permission of a judge in Richmond County Surrogate Court to take legal possession of her late husband's assets. Unable to read or write, she made an "X" as instructed on all the documents set before her and was appointed the administratrix of Thomas' estate by Henry B. Metcalfe. By the end of the morning, all legalities were put in order. She was awarded property and assets valued at three hundred dollars.

It was slightly more than a five mile roundtrip between Rocky Hollow and the courthouse, allowing plenty of time for conversation. Julia confided in Cipriano. She talked openly about her marriage to Thomas, his good and bad traits, and the challenges of having so many young children to care for. Though she was well aware of the seriousness of the situation, Julia was not distraught. As a woman of faith, she was certain that God was on her side. Julia had comfort and security knowing she owned the home on Gore and Gordon Streets. It was free and clear of any lien, so no one could force her to move from the property that her husband loved so dearly. Between the crops they grew and the chickens and cow they owned the family would not go hungry. What she had to do one way or another was figure out a way to manage the taxes.

Cipriano listened to Julia attentively, a bit taken back by the logical approach of his young neighbor. He was not used to women sounding so strong and courageous. Cipriano had been certain that Julia would be consumed with grief and unable to think clearly after Thomas' death. Why, it was the main reason he had offered his assistance, feeling sorry for her plight. What Julia was saying was in direct contrast to Cipriano's personal beliefs about women. He felt that God created woman with an incapacity to make the important decisions in life without a man. Yet, here was Julia sitting beside him, alone and illiterate, ready to meet the world head on.

Cipriano's thinking was not outrageous. In fact, his beliefs were well in line with what many men of his day thought. A local Staten Island newspaper, the Richmond Republican, summed up the prevailing mindset:

"When a woman aspires to ambitious situations, she steps out of the sphere allotted to her by nature, and assumes a character which is an outrage upon her delicacy and feminine

loveliness. No female does so unless she be an infidel; none but atheists and libertines sanction the aberration."[1]

The author's message was clear. Women should exist as objects of desire rather than desire for themselves. Thus, Cipriano let Julia speak and made no comments. *Such a naïve female*, he thought to himself. Soon, she would find out. Julia needed a man to survive.

Just a few years earlier in 1848, the first women's rights convention was held in Seneca Falls, New York. The movement was still in its infancy, but sentiment was growing in support of major changes in the status of women in America. Julia had no knowledge of the movement, but the young widow's attitude was demonstrative of some of their core beliefs.

Julia was confident that she could make ends meet, but not as sure of herself in dealing with Mary Anna's state of mind. Thomas and Mary Anna enjoyed a special closeness, bonding years before in the grief over Mary and John's deaths. They were father and daughter, but their connection ran deeper. Thomas and Mary Anna were kindred spirits. He could read her mind and she finish his sentences. Her presence always brought a smile to Thomas' face while in turn, he had an uncanny way of making Mary Anna laugh. Thomas inspired Mary Anna to dream big, just like him. He was like no other to her and his untimely death was clearly affecting her personality. Normally cheery and outgoing, she was now sullen and detached. Julia winced as she listened to her sob uncontrollably in bed at night.

Julia tried her best to console Mary Anna, promising her that in time things would get better.

H've hope, Mary Anna! Yer faith in the Lord t'will heal ye.

Every night, Mary Anna got down on her knees, as her dear departed mother had long ago instructed. She made the sign of the cross. Then, she asked for some form of divine intervention to lift her from the gloom.

Dear God, please deliver me from this grief!

Mary Anna appreciated Julia's concern and did her best to follow Julia's advice out of respect for her stepmother. Mary Anna was appreciative that her father married well on both occasions. Mary and Julia were both born and raised in Ireland, a place where women were traditionally less dependent on men. They were smart and strong ladies. Mary's wisdom was like a compass that steered Thomas' enthusiasm in the right direction. She did a stellar job keeping him on task to limit his drinking and save the money needed to buy the land he wanted so badly. After her death, Julia bravely stepped into the deep void Mary left in the family. She assumed the difficult role of second wife and stepmother and earned the love and admiration of Thomas and Mary's children. Julia used all her available energies to manage Thomas' growing dependence on alcohol. Even though she was only twelve years old, Mary Anna could now see that Julia had shielded the children until the end.

Mary Anna had no choice but to muddle through the troubled days and weeks that followed Thomas' death. In time, she turned away from the lingering sadness and began to refocus her thoughts on happier events. The pain did not leave her, but it got easier to live with. Julia's concern for her stepdaughter led the pair to become closer than ever.

Julia was unable to read or write but understood she must track family expenses. Thus, she asked Mary Anna to set up and keep a log. One day, while they were discussing the log, Julia knew the time had come. She instructed Mary Anna to find Michael and bring him to her. Julia needed to have a serious talk with the two eldest children.

She began the conversation gently. They had all been through a trying time. The family was still officially in mourning, but this period must come to an end. Julia had worked out in her head how the McDonough family would make ends meet and frankly, they did not have the luxury of unlimited time to grieve. Fortunately, Thomas was a hard worker and left them money when he died. The good news was that his savings would tide them over in the immediate future. The bad news was the inheritance would not last indefinitely. Without additional means of income, there would be future money problems.

Julia went on to explain that the children's lives had been a healthy mix of work and play, but their carefree days spent roaming the woods, rocks, and tributaries of Rocky Hollow were indulgences the family no longer could afford. Every able McDonough had to pitch in now to make their way. Julia would take in the wash of wealthy folk in town but only part time as she was still required to tend to the needs of the boys too young to be left on their own. She needed both Mary Anna and Michael to step up to take on more chores as well as contribute financially to the grieving household.

Michael, who was eleven years old at the time, was surprised. He put up a mild protest. Michael thought it was unfair that he and Mary Anna needed to find jobs in addition to their chores at home while seven-year old brother Thomas wasn't being given any extra duties.

Michael looked over to his older sister for support. She was frowning so severely at him that he stopped midsentence. Mary Anna then responded for them both. She said she and Michael understood and would comply.

Ever since she could remember Mary Anna had been helping in the home as well as overseeing the chores of her younger brothers. A job would just be a natural extension of her current family responsibilities. Her stepmother's request wasn't a shock like it was for Michael. She had been logging the family expenses for a few months and knew of the dwindling cash.

Mary Anna was also clearly in support of Julia's request because it came at a time of major transition in her life. Thomas' death occurred when Mary Anna was on the cusp of young womanhood. She had been starting to daydream about stepping out on her own. An outside job was good for the family finances and perhaps just the right kind of distraction she needed to manage her grief and feel good about herself.

Mary Anna set out door to door to ask her neighbors for work. She started doing odds and ends household tasks for the elderly and infirm but quickly realized she could not make a reliable income this way. She needed a full-time occupation. Mary Anna and Julia sat down at the supper table one evening to consider the options. Just what were the best job prospects for a young girl from Rocky Hollow?

There were but two obvious choices. Mary Anna could work as a house servant or a factory worker. Julia believed she was capable of either job but cautioned Mary Anna that wherever the girl worked she'd have to learn to hold her free spirited tongue in check. Mary Anna had the potential to talk too much. She asked too many questions and held far too many personal opinions. These traits could get her into trouble if an employer lacked sufficient patience or humor.

Mary Anna got up the next morning, helped Julia prepare breakfast for the boys, then got dressed and walked down Gore Street to the center of town. Her outgoing nature was to her advantage as she visited the local shopkeepers to ask whether they knew of any available jobs. In short order, she secured a position as a housemaid for one of the well-to-do families in town. Mary Anna raced home to proudly announce the news.

Julia! Julia! Look here! I am a full time working girl now!

Mary Anna started her new job with great enthusiasm. She relished sharing the details of the day's events with her family over the evening meal. She was thrilled to contribute financially to the household, even though her wages were a pittance. For all her daily hard work washing and ironing clothes, dusting, polishing, serving meals, washing and drying dishes, Mary Anna was paid $1.25 per month.

Mary Anna's excitement over landing the job did not last long. Quickly, she found out she did not enjoy the work. It was tedious and at times discouraging. There were times she felt disrespected and wanted desperately to complain but knowing her family needed the money, Mary Anna kept her mouth shut tight. She toiled as hard as possible while keeping her eyes and ears open for a better opportunity.

When afforded the luxury of time, Mary Anna often daydreamed about the past and the freewheeling days spent with her brothers. Together they had explored the great outdoors of Rocky Hollow - its woods, brooks, caves, and spectacular views from the hills - and enjoyed watching all kinds of interesting travelers make their way back and forth on Gore Street. At the supper table each night she sighed longingly while her brothers reported some of the impish things they had done that day, such as their mischievous exploration in and around the new brewery. She envied the adventures they were having without her.

The McDonoughs, like all who lived in Rocky Hollow, were affected by the rapid expansion of John Bechtel's business. New distinctive smells from the brewery filled the air. Mighty work horse teams became a daily sight. The rattle of the wagons hauling heavy kegs of beer up and down Gore Street assumed a familiar clatter. People who spoke only the German language began moving into town to live within walking distance of their jobs. They were strangers at first, but Rocky Hollow was a small community. Soon they became familiar faces and neighbors.

Life was hard but there were still days of fun for Mary Anna and her family. Lively celebrations were a happier part of life. After John Bechtel opened a beer garden next to the brewery, bubbly German tunes began to spill out into the local streets. Mary Anna liked the music. The tunes themselves were unfamiliar but the musicians played with such gusto! Soon, more beer gardens and dance halls were built, bringing additional music as well as an influx of visitors from all parts of New York. It gave the whole neighborhood a merry and lighthearted feeling on weekends and holidays.

Mary Anna and her brothers looked forward to the town celebrations. Stapleton parades were common and since Gore Street was a main road, it was customary for many processions to pass by their house. Oh, how Mary Anna loved that her family always had front and center seats on the grass of their front lawn! No matter if the parades were political or celebratory in nature, for they all included marching bands, decorative flag waving, fireworks, and gun salutes. On parade days, Julia's frugality gave way to a bit of indulgence. Money was tight, but she always tried to put a little extra aside for celebrations. Each child was given a coin to buy firecrackers, candy, or delicious ice cream.

Mary Anna worked as a domestic for more than a year before deciding she had enough of being at the beck and call of rich women. She began to search for a factory job. Mary Anna knew she would make more money doing this and was confident she would have no trouble finding work. Manufacturing flourished on Staten Island since the early part of the nineteenth century. Indeed, there were so many factories in one section of the island that it called itself Factoryville. The demand was high for this kind of labor, and young girls had a strong advantage in being hired. Factory bosses knew that most of the time young women only worked long enough to find a man, get married, and leave. Girls worked hard and were very productive. They had fewer complaints and were rarely considered troublemakers. Plus, they could be paid less than male workers who did the same job.

As a sign of maturity, Mary Anna assumed the more adult name of Mary Ann. Tall for her age and armed with a natural gift of gab, Mary Ann gave the impression she was older than her thirteen years. Quickly, she landed a job at a local factory. Mary Ann was ecstatic. It was a huge leap in salary. She would now be paid $2 per week!

The hat factory foreman shortened her last name and began to call her *Miss Mack*. Mary Ann didn't mind, and soon others called her that too. Mary Ann put forth her best efforts in this new line of work but found out almost immediately that factory work was almost as bad as being a house maid. It was so repetitive and boring! From time to time she could not keep her mind from drifting. She pondered the magnitude of financial uncertainties the family experienced because of her father's unexpected passing. When this happened, Mary Ann fought back feelings of resentment. Though she was unhappy with her life situation, she knew that Thomas did not deliberately create their troubles. It was not his fault.

Still daydreaming, Mary Ann recalled a time when she was a little girl sitting at the table listening to her parents' conversations. Mama spoke, and her father agreed. She said it was important to practice frugality, for it was only through a combination of hard work and economical practices that one could guard against the hard times in life.

Mary Ann smiled. Her mother had been so wise. So, while she

was no great fan of the work, the young factory girl heeded the words of the woman whose memory she held so dear in her heart. She poured heart and soul into her labor. Paid by the piece, Mary Ann vowed to work as fast as her hands could manage. Money meant safety and security, and she yearned to feel the comfort of such sanctuary.

Mary Ann made a conscious decision to look forward to the day of her financial independence. Someday, she would not be forced to work at such an unbearable job. The resolve became her salvation from the day to day monotony.

The factory girl's days were extra-long and tiring because she continued to maintain major responsibilities at home. Mary Ann rose well before dawn every day of the week except the Sabbath. Her first job of the day was to wake her brothers, so they could begin their chores. Then, she headed to the kitchen.

Mary Ann tended the fire in the wood stove while her step-mother prepared the morning meal. Julia set the table and then all sat down to a hearty breakfast which at different times included eggs, oatmeal, biscuit, potato, or a rare piece of pork sausage or ham. After the meal, Mary Ann carefully wrapped the leftovers in a napkin, packed it into her lunch pail. She cleared the table, helped Julia clean the stove, and washed pots and dishes. When all was done, she was free to get ready to head out to the factory.

Mary Ann strove to look her best every day but traipsing up and down dirt roads and wood plank sidewalks regularly defied her good intentions.

Blasted dust and mud!

It was not very ladylike, but at times she could not help but mutter a cuss word under her breath as she looked down at herself upon her arrival at the factory. Her polished boots and long skirts were like magnets, attracting the streets' fine powder in dry spells and mucky goo on wet days. Mary Ann had a multitude of obstacles to dodge while walking: the droppings of horses, dogs, and livestock, flies circulating around fetid garbage found on the streets, as well as the errant misses of inconsiderate males attempting to hit outdoor spittoons with their tobacco juice. Even if she kept her clothing relatively clean by the time she reached the factory, Mary Ann often felt she was wearing the stench of her route. Her nostrils retained the smells of open garbage, animal wastes, and stale brewery aromas which filled the streets.

Miss Mack was often required to travel to and from work in the dark. There were no gas streetlamps, so the moon served as her only illumination. No matter how well she knew her way around or how delightful the neighborhood could be, Mary Ann was repeatedly cautioned by her step mother that it was not totally safe. A young girl walking alone in the dark was at risk for injury or robbery or matters far worse.

Although Mary Ann felt at ease in the neighborhood, she understood what her stepmother was saying and heeded Julia's advice. Mary Ann refrained from walking in places that were desolate or where one could not hear a cry for help. She kept her eyes and ears open to avoid contact with strangers. One day, Mary Ann came across a stout branch on the side of the road. When she tried it out Mary Ann discovered it was useful as a walking stick, providing handy assistance in hiking over steep hills. She also realized it served as a means of self-protection. Once or twice in her life she had come across an animal that she had to shoo away. A stick like this could keep an unfriendly animal at a safe distance. And, it could also make any offensive male think twice before approaching. Mary Ann was physically strong, not as much by nature but from hard work and necessity. The factory girl used the strength in her upper arm muscles and learned to wield the stick with the requisite sense of authority. Soon, it became as natural for her to wield a stout stick as it was to carry a purse.

Around the same time that Mary Ann was beginning her new job, the town of Stapleton was likewise at the threshold of great change. Two major events would take place in the next few years – the expansion of the local beer industry and start of the Civil War – and each of these happenings would greatly alter the peace and tranquility of the community. But for the moment, the key elements of what had first drawn Thomas McDonough to the neighborhood of Rocky Hollow remained to be enjoyed by his widow and children.

Mary Ann experienced a series of emotional highs and lows in the years following her father's demise. She was pleased with herself for all she was accomplishing, but even more proud because she had met and overcame challenges she never could have imagined. She conquered having her way of life turned upside down. She managed to overcome a broken heart. These experiences helped Mary Ann to establish a fundamental belief which she would carry into adulthood.

Sometimes you just had to make do and move on to survive.

She was unaware of it at the time, but Mary Ann was just starting out on a journey to achieve what no one could have predicted. She was on her way to becoming a most remarkable woman.

CHAPTER FOUR: A REMARKABLE WOMAN

"*M*rs. Bascomb in her youngest womanhood proved herself exceptionally clever in business. She was eager to acquire real estate, and whenever she saw a chance to 'put money into the ground,' she did so."[1]

Mary Ann clung steadfast to her dream of achieving financial security. She worked harder and faster than all the other factory girls combined. At sixteen, Mary Ann was pleased beyond measure at how far she had come. Mary Ann was now earning close to $11 a week, a sum well beyond the minimum take home pay!

The factory girl worked tirelessly to fulfill her duties at work and home as the oldest child in the McDonough family. Over four difficult years, she had helped her stepmother make ends meet. Mary Ann pulled her stepmother aside one morning and spoke to her candidly. Weren't her brothers old enough now where they could bear the major responsibility for contributing to the household expenses? Her stepmother agreed and told Mary Ann she would handle it. At the supper table that night, she announced it was time for the boys to take over as the family's chief wage earners.

Gee gosh! What a relief for Mary Ann! Julia understood and was giving her the chance to move on. Mary Ann had been continuing to fulfill the role of dutiful child, but lately a resentment had been building. Handing over her wages to Julia every week had been fine in the past, but times were changing.

The biggest change was that Mary Ann was now keeping company with a man by the name of John McLoughlan. It was only a short time after her conversation with Julia that Johnny fell on both knees and expressed his undying love for Mary Anna. The young woman's eyes filled with happy tears as he proposed marriage. At a temporary and uncharacteristic loss for words, Mary Anna wiped her face and took a long pause. Then she gushed.

My Gosh, Johnny Mack! Well, yes! Of course, I will marry you!

Hand in hand, they went to break the news to Julia. She acted surprised, although Julia expected this would happen. Mary Ann's stepmother held conflicted feelings about the couple. Mary Ann was a bright girl and a fairly good judge of character, but John was her first serious romance and she was acting far too giddy to make Julia feel at ease. She kept the uncertainties to herself, however, because she knew her headstrong stepdaughter all too well. Mary Ann was flying way too high emotionally to be swayed by any practical advice. Expressing her reservations would have just caused friction between them. So, instead she hugged Mary Ann, wished them happiness, and somehow managed to hold her tongue.

The wedding date was set for August 22, 1857. The night before Julia helped her stepdaughter get ready by ironing her best Sunday frock and curling her hair in rags. That morning, Julia brushed Mary Ann's long brown hair and pulled it up off the back of her neck. Then, she helped her into her fanciest petticoat.

Mary Ann was acting like a small child at holiday time. Once dressed, she kept pacing and peeking out the window. She shrieked with delight when she saw John arrive with his wagon. He rapped at the front door and entered the house with a telling grin. John held out a large bouquet of bright yellow daisies for his future wife. Mary Ann took the flowers, cradled them in her arms, and gazed back at him with a broad smile.

No. This is not a dream, she thought. *It is really happening!*

Mary Ann and her family went outside. John hoisted the women up into the wagon. Then her brothers piled in the back and they started off on the bumpy ride to church.

St. Peter's had long abandoned the use of the old gun factory. Services were now held in a small brick church on a steep hill overlooking the busy waterways of New York harbor. It was a typically hot summer day, and despite efforts to fend off the sun's effects with parasols and fans, by the time they arrived all in the wagon were dripping in sweat. No one seemed to care, however, because the joyous nature of the occasion far outweighed any personal discomfort. John secured the horses and helped the ladies out of the wagon. Julia held the bouquet as Mary Ann dabbed a hanky at her wet hairline and smoothed down her hair and skirt. Then she took the flowers in one hand, grabbed John's arm with the other, and together they climbed the precipitous steps leading up to the front door of the church.

Father Murphy greeted the assemblage and gave them instructions on where to stand and sit. Then, he began the Roman Catholic marriage ceremony. The group recited prayers, genuflected, and received Holy Communion as dictated by the scripted formalities of the Latin mass. Though there was a wee bit of a breeze wafting in from the open windows, the air was still miserably hot and uncomfortable inside. Midway through the mass, Mary Ann became acutely aware of a steady pattern of sweat dribbling from her hairline down her back. It tormented her for the remainder of the ceremony.

Before dismissing the assemblage, Father Murphy spoke briefly in English, bestowing a final blessing upon the couple. When mass was over, John took the hand of his bride and led her down the main aisle and out the front door of the structure. The blinding rays of the hot August sun were in deep contrast to the dark interior of the church and temporarily blinded the crowd.

Mary Ann put her right hand up to shield her eyes. She paused briefly on the front steps to take in the beauty of the harbor and her surroundings. She wanted to savor this precious moment in her life. It was all so glorious! Marrying Johnny was the beginning of a whole new life for her, the girl who had been forced to grow up too quickly.

Before descending the stairs, Mary Ann offered up a silent prayer.

Thank you, Lord, for bringing Johnny into my life. Thank you for the gifts you will bestow upon our marriage. Bless us always with good health, long life, and an abundance of family and friends.

Mary Ann firmly believed that God had recognized her past suffering and all the hard work and devotion she gave to her family. A happy future would be the reward for her faithfulness. She was totally unprepared for what happened next.

Mary and John were not destined for a long and fruitful marriage. The McDonough- McLoughlan union ended up being measured in days, not years. Mary Ann had barely set up house-keeping when Johnny suddenly died. Like a summer storm, as quickly and dramatically as Johnny had come into her life, he was gone. John McLoughlan left this world with little to mark his passing other than his heartbroken teenage bride, too tall and skinny to properly fit into her stepmother's hand me down mourning clothes.

Julia and the neighbors tried their best to comfort her, but Mary Ann found it difficult to stomach their condolences. The emotional pain was excruciating. God had taken away the second most important man in her life, but in the end whose fault was it? In her angst, she blamed herself.

Was I too smug, Lord? Was I conceited to parade Johnny around as a grand prize in front of my family and friends? Did you think I was not deserving of true happiness because of this? Oh, my poor Johnny. First Father, now you. Why, oh why, do this to them and to me, God?

To make matters worse, Mary Ann's financial situation was as dismal as the rest of her life. She did not have sufficient money to go it alone, so Mary Ann gave up her rented rooms and moved back in with her stepmother. Not much had changed over the course of a few months, but she took little consolation in the familiar routines. Mary Ann brooded day and night. She found herself edgy in the company of her brothers, snapping at them for no reason. Then, afterwards she felt deep guilt and shame.

Mary Ann sequestered herself inside the house for weeks. Julia, greatly concerned for the well-being of her stepdaughter, counseled Mary Ann that what she was doing was not helpful to the mind or spirit. Mary Ann needed fresh air and a new start.

The argument did not work, so she thought it over and came up with a different, somewhat harsher approach.

Julia appealed to Mary Ann's practical side. If Mary Ann was going to stay with Julia and the boys, she must get a job and help with the household finances. No babies had been made during her brief marriage, so nothing was holding her back from returning to work. They were not a wealthy family, so she should stop acting like she was entitled.

This approach did get through to Mary Ann. Her stepmother was right. Supporting the family took precedence over time to grieve. Weary of the factory, Mary Ann made a few inquiries and secured employment as a domestic for a wealthy family just outside of Stapleton. Their large home sat on a bluff that overlooked the U.S. military fort built at the entrance to New York harbor. The work soon became just as monotonous as her previous jobs, but she made no complaints. Mary Ann liked the trip out of town every day. It was a welcome change of scenery from the familiar streets of her hometown which taunted her with bad memories.

Long hard days of labor proved to be a solid distraction for her grieving heart. Mary Ann helped her stepmother pay the household expenses, while also saving a little money for herself on the side. She tried not to lose hope for the future. Each night when she went to bed, Mary Ann got on her knees and prayed for better times to come.

Soon after the official period of mourning for John McLoughlan ended, the better days arrived. Mary Ann was introduced to another young man by the name of William Richards. He hailed from Connecticut, a fact which fascinated Mary Ann. Connecticut sounded so exotic to a girl who had never travelled any farther in her life than the northern side of Staten Island to attend Sunday mass! They started to keep company and within a short time, once again, Mary Ann felt the pangs of love.

William knew she had gone through a lot when John passed, so he did not rush Mary Ann's feelings. He was kind and gentle. When at last William asked her to marry him, he promised a new beginning. He was from farm country and wanted to bring Mary Ann back home to live.

Start over with me. I will make you happy, Mary Ann.

William's words were soft and healing and just what Mary Ann wanted to hear. She desperately wanted to move away and leave all the bad times of her life behind. She prayed, and this time talked it over with her stepmother.

Julia approved of the match. Although she was not sure how she felt about Mary Ann moving away, she genuinely liked William. His caring had helped so much to draw Mary Ann out of her melancholia.

Though the emotional pain was still fresh in her mind, Mary Ann resolved to be unafraid. She would let love back into her life and let it renew, refresh, and lighten her heavy heart. Mary Ann agreed to move to Connecticut and marry William.

She had few possessions, so the packing was far less difficult than saying goodbye to friends and neighbors she had known all her life. On the morning of her departure, Mary Ann lugged the satchel which contained her belongings aboard the ferry which would take her from Stapleton on the first step of the journey to a new home. When she looked back from the boat railing to see her stepmother and brothers standing on the dock, she could not help but feel conflicted. Feeling a bit uneasy, she repeated over and over to herself that this was the right decision. She saw the sadness in the faces of her family members. She was sad herself. Mary Ann winced at the thought that she did not know if or when she would ever see them again.

William realized that Mary Ann would miss her family and did all he could to make her happy. The marriage of Mary Ann and William turned out to be a pleasant and fruitful union. Soon after the wedding Mary Ann was delighted to find out she was with child, and in 1860 she gave birth to a healthy baby they named Mary Jane.

Mary Ann relished being a new mother. There was great joy in watching her infant girl learn to talk and walk, but as the baby grew so did the intensity of homesickness within her. Although William's family was nearby, Mary Ann sorely missed Julia, Michael, and her other brothers. Her pregnancy and delivery had been without complications, yet the during the entire time

Mary Ann longed for her stepmother. Now, she craved Julia's motherly advice on how to best raise the baby.

That was bad enough, but Mary Ann also realized she seriously disliked farm life. In rural Connecticut, the pace was dull and repetitive. Mary Ann was talkative, inquisitive, and outgoing by nature yet here there was such limited opportunity to interact with others. She felt socially isolated.

Mary Ann concluded that her natural temperament was much better suited to the daily hustle and bustle of Stapleton and so she needed to return. She resolved to badger her husband until he agreed. In heart to heart pillow talks at night, she made her case.

Oh Billy, why not please your dearest Mary Ann and move us back to Rocky Hollow? After all, it makes such fine sense. Julia can help with the baby and there will always be plenty of trade work there for you.

William initially shrugged her off, but Mary Ann was persistent. She continued to come at him, using every argument that came to mind. One night, she even threw in the eradication of the dreaded Tompkinsville Quarantine hospital.

You must admit Billy, that the island has changed so much for the better since we left. Why, you know even that swarming refuge of filthy contagion on the northeast shore is gone forever!

Secret meetings which had been held to plot the Quarantine's demise dragged on until finally one dark night a group of locals took action. They gathered bundles of straw, boxes of matches and bottles of camphene, and used battering rams to knock down a section of the brick wall surrounding the hospital. At great personal risk they entered the building, carried the sick outside onto the lawn, and burnt the wretched structure down to the ground. The perpetrators were taken to court and received weak sentences, and ultimately the hospital was officially closed.

William's counter arguments proved no match for the hard stance of his wife. She was unrelentingly convincing. They said their goodbyes to William's family and loaded their belongings into trunks and barrels. Then, the family of three made the return trip via wagon, stagecoach, train, and ferry back to Mary Ann's beloved Rocky Hollow.

Good gosh! Home at last!

An audible sigh of relief escaped from Mary Ann's lips as she stepped off the Stapleton ferry on the last leg of their tedious journey. It was comforting to have family and friends close at hand once again, especially in light of the escalating pandemonium on the national political scene.

Mary Ann watched over her tiny daughter with one eye while keeping the other fixed upon the changing environment. Stapleton was home, but it was no longer the peaceful village she knew as a child. A bloody war between the states had erupted and Stapleton, as part of the New York Harbor, played a critical role in meeting the needs of the Union Army. The waterfront was now in a state of perpetual activity. Supply boats and ferries transporting military men and supplies arrived daily at the docks. Shipbuilders labored from dawn to dusk to meet the military's demand for new vessels. Soldier encampments sprung up close by in Tompkinsville. And, the McCullough Shot and Lead Works on Bay Street became a major supplier of lead balls for Union Army artillery.

The presence of the U.S. Army brought some clear economic benefits to Stapleton. Laborers were in demand because of the need for new construction. Vendors who sold apples, candies, oranges, nuts and other items to soldiers well profited. The breweries, beer gardens, and saloons flourished because of the many thirsty soldiers.

William and his brothers-in-law relished the chance to make more money, but like other locals saw downsides to the rapid change. The resources of the U.S. Army were far too tempting to the more mischievous citizens in town, causing the crime rate to soar. It became way too common to hear of local hooligans sneaking into the camps at night to take off with government issued saddles, sacks of oats, and horses.

Drinking among the enlisted men was also a big problem. Though the rows upon rows of white tents and full dress blue parades on Sundays made the encampments seem somewhat enchanting, the reality of housing many young men so close to a town with an overabundant supply of lager ale caused major headaches for everybody. When soldiers ventured out of camp their destination was quite often a Stapleton saloon. They got very drunk. They offended the local ladies with foul language and bad behavior. They got into fights with each other and with the townsmen. The military police often had to be called in which led to jurisdiction disputes with local law enforcement.

To try to keep the peace, General Sickles issued orders for his officers to live with their regiments and enforce regular military drills. He warned that there would be severe punishment for trespassing or interfering with local property or persons. The general gave orders to prohibit the sale of intoxicating liquors in or around camp and for an indefinite period placed a guard at the door of every popular saloon. Local patrons were not enthused by the military presence at the entrances to their favorite drinking holes. They did, however, appreciate the assistance if and when an inebriated soldier carrying an Army issued weapon decided to pick a fight.

Blasted alcohol! Mary Ann complained to William.

Mary Ann was perpetually confounded by men's overreliance on alcohol. Though she still could remember some pleasant times when her father hoisted a few pints with his cronies, his violent death had become her predominant childhood memory. Thomas McDonough was a good man, but he had flaws and those flaws destroyed him and devastated his family. Mary Ann often asked herself what might have been if her father had not been a patron of the poison. The notion made her acutely vigilant in monitoring the consumption of her husband, brothers, and all others she cared about. She applauded the general's orders.

Mary Ann once again started carrying a stout walking stick. When she walked past groups of drunken soldiers on her way downtown to errands, who knew what was on their minds? She needed to protect herself. Wielding the stout stick would hopefully make any inebriated male think twice before venturing too close to her or her daughter.

It was a difficult time for the nation, yet Mary Ann was

personally full of joy. She was with child once again. William Richards was born amid the blazing heat of mid-August 1862 and baptized a few days later at St. Mary's Church in the nearby town of Clifton. St. Mary's was a relatively new parish on Staten Island, founded in 1852 by the New York Archdiocese to meet the needs of a growing Roman Catholic population. Mary Ann liked her new parish. It was a shorter wagon ride to mass than the weekly trek to St. Peter's. Plus, St. Mary had a most extraordinary pastor, the Reverend Father John L Lewis. He was a humble man who was tireless in his work on behalf of the people. Lewis had a gift for speech and used this talent well to inspire his flock to accomplish great things. Why, in just a few years, he raised the money to build a handsome brick church with distinctive mansard roof on New York Avenue to replace St. Mary's modest wooden predecessor.

Mary Ann held Fr. Lewis in the highest regard, so it gave her great personal satisfaction for him to administer the sacrament to William. Mary Ann and her family watched in reverence as the pastor anointed the baby with holy water at the baptismal font. The newborn apparently did not appreciate the wet welcome into the Roman Catholic faith, letting out a loud wail that echoed throughout the church. Mary Ann tried to hush him, but at the same time could not help but think,

Little William has healthy lungs. Oh, what a gift, dear Lord!

The Civil War raged on, but the battle between the states meant little to Mary Ann. Her husband and children were her world. She kept busy during the day keeping house and tending to the needs of her small children, and before she knew it, a year had passed.

The summer of 1863 started with no clues that it would be any different than its predecessors. There was predictable heat and an increase in the mosquito population. Mary Ann could never imagined the trouble that followed.

If she had been paying more attention to the outside world, Mary Ann would have realized that the actions of the Federal government were churning up ugly emotions within the local citizenry. Earlier in the year, President Lincoln issued the

Enrollment Act of Conscription because the Union army was in dire need of more troops. A draft lottery was established. Black men were exempted from the draft because they were not considered citizens. White men who could afford to hire a substitute or pay three hundred dollars to the government could buy their way out of service. These caveats made the draft overtly unfair to poor white men.

The Enrollment Act came just a few months after Lincoln issued the Emancipation Proclamation freeing slaves in the southern states. Though the Emancipation Proclamation was applauded by most, not all Northerners were in favor. Some feared that freeing slaves would result in a migration northward and intensify existing labor competition between blacks and poor whites.

Draft quotas were set up in all the northern states. In New York City, the Irish, who generally were more impoverished than other immigrant groups, were incensed at the move. Tensions percolated, and in mid-July finally boiled over into physical violence. Protests that began during the drawing of draft numbers turned ugly and rioting ensued. Over the next few days hundreds of fires were set in Manhattan. Innocent blacks were killed. Thousands were savagely beaten and terrorized. It was a week of holy hell, which spawned a series of smaller riots elsewhere.

Rocky Hollow, unfortunately, was one of the places where violence spread. One hot summer night, this neighborhood where people of different races, religions, and nationalities had lived together in peace and harmony for many years, suddenly snapped. The small community of blacks who lived in the modest shacks and cabins near the woods at the western border of the Seaman's Retreat were viciously attacked.

Mary Ann and William had drawn the shades and gone to bed early that night. Suddenly, they were startled out of their sleep. There were the sounds of gun shots, cussing, dogs barking, people screaming, and babies' cries.

Dear Lord! Billy! What's that blasted racket!

The young mother flew to the window. She craned her neck outside to see what in blazes was going on. Mary Ann smelt smoke and saw a few men running in the direction of McKeon Street which was just a few blocks from her home.

Since Mary Ann and William could not ascertain what was going on, they were not sure of what to do. Should they stay put or pick up their sleeping children and run? They quickly talked it over. The couple decided to close the windows, draw the shades, and remain in their rented rooms until first daylight when they could better see what was happening. Mary Ann grabbed her stout stick from its resting spot against the wall in the kitchen. *Just in case,* she said to herself. Then she got down on the floor next to her sleeping babies. Mary Ann prayed the outside noise would not rouse the children. If they awoke and began to cry, she feared that she would not be able to quiet them.

The next morning, William ventured out and learned the details of events from the night before. Young men of Irish backgrounds had gotten drunk and stolen muskets from a local meeting hall. They descended upon the poor blacks of McKeon Street, breaking windows and tearing down the front doors of their homes. The men threw peoples' furniture and belongings out on the street. They looted a grocery store, then gutted and torched a few houses. The hoodlums tried to burn down the Union African Methodist Episcopal Church, but luckily the fire was put out before any major damage occurred. The black residents of Rocky Hollow were rightfully terrified. Some fled for their lives into the nearby woods. Others brave enough to stand up to the rioters were dragged out of their homes and severely beaten.

Mary Ann was visibly shaken when she heard the news. Such an ugly event unfolding on the streets of her beloved neighborhood! Rocky Hollow was such a pleasant community. She knew many of the perpetrators and victims her entire life. This was very wrong!

The rioting continued over the next few nights. Mary Ann and William did not evacuate as they were far enough away and in no immediate danger. They watched as a police and military presence took over the streets. MaryAnn stayed indoors most of the time with Mary Jane and baby William. As the rioting dragged on, Mary Ann became angry as hell. She wished she could do something tangible to put an end to the affair. Oh, if only she didn't have the babies to look after for if not, she would have gladly taken her stout stick to the hides of those heathen boys!

Mary Ann heard from a neighbor that there were a few good men like George Bechtel helping the victims. They were doing God's work at a time when she could not, and she was grateful. Mary Ann vowed to seek George out and thank him after the crisis was over.

Mary Ann held a great deal of respect for George Bechtel, the young and enterprising son of John Bechtel, the brewer. Everyone in town knew him. George was a successful businessman, but also a man of the people. Although George had attended Columbia College, he understood that the best way to learn the brewery business was from the bottom up. Hence, he had spent long hours toiling side by side with his father's employees in knee high boots and blue jean jumpers.

Having spent much of his youth in Rocky Hollow, George empathized with the plight of its most unfortunate citizens. He knew he could not halt the rioting but wanted to do something to help. He instructed his workers to deliver food into the woods for all who were in hiding until it was safe enough for them to return.

Meanwhile, local authorities scrambled to end the violence. A few miles away in Clifton, a public meeting was organized. Fr. Lewis was enlisted to speak to the crowd of anxious men, women, and children. In his speech, Lewis did not chastise the rioters. Instead, he said he understood the anger of the situation. Lewis emphasized that the young men had every right to protest but no right to disrespect the law. He called for peace. Handbills signed by government officials were distributed at the gathering, announcing that the draft had been halted. These measures calmed the crowd and got the message through to the rioters.

After the rioting stopped, citizens took stock of the damage. There had been numerous assaults and a great deal of property damage, but fortunately no serious injuries or deaths. A cleanup started but talk about the riot lingered on for weeks and months afterwards. In the end, McKeon Street acquired a new and notorious nickname among the locals. They now called it Battle Row.

Mary Ann had lived far enough away from the violence to feel safe, yet close enough to witness a great many unpleasant sights. The riot was a life changing experience for Mary Ann. She had never witnessed a situation where undue hatred was so overt. Mary Ann vowed to herself that she would never turn on a person solely because of something as arbitrary as the color of their skin. She would do what was right no matter the consequences. God demanded this of her.

Bosh! Spooney! All hardworking, Godfearing people deserve to live in peace!

July ended, and a sense of day to day normalcy returned to the people of Rocky Hollow. Folks returned to their usual complaints about the heat, humidity, and bugs. Mary Ann continued in her maternal role at home and then suddenly, the second upending disaster of the summer of 1863 struck. Just days after his son's first birthday celebration, her second husband suddenly died.

Mary Ann plunged into an emotional freefall after William's death. This was so much more painful than losing Johnny Mack! Her first marriage had been barely more than a blip in time. She was a child bride and acted giddy and immature. Her second marriage was so vastly different. Her affection for William was deep and rich. He had recognized Mary Ann's pain and tenderly rescued her from grief. He offered her a new beginning and delivered on that promise. She entered into a comfortable life with William. She was happy. She was a mother. Mary Ann felt safe and secure. The loss she felt was indescribable.

As Mary Ann buried William, her mind swirled with negativity. She felt cheated and was very, very angry. She openly chided God.

Oh Lord, how could you let this happen to me again? Did I not serve as a devoted wife to William? Now, there will be no more happy days to share. What will I look forward to without William at my side? How will I take care of my babies? How will I make ends meet? God in heaven, I ask you! Show me the wisdom in taking yet one more man away from me!

The young woman with enough self-assurance to contemplate chasing down drunken rioters with her stout walking stick just a few weeks earlier now doubted everything around her. She was young and able but consumed by the notion that there was no future without William.

The practical arguments pitched by Julia were overlooked. Offers of help from others were kind but did little to ease her pain. Days passed, and then one day in a brief unstable moment Mary Ann pondered ending her existence. It was a notion that came and went in a flash but left her terrified. She cussed under her breath, acknowledging she must immediately banish such thoughts from her mind.

Blasted Mary Ann! What are you thinking? You have young babies to care for!

Mary Ann had finally reached her low point, as far as her unsinkable spirit would allow. She began to turn away from the despair. It was time to spring back, take control of her life, and solidly crush any remnants of doubts left within her. Life was unfair, yes, but she was not undone. God had NOT abandoned her. He had given her two beautiful children to love. Plus, He made sure the ever-wise Julia was there to help.

Her father suddenly popped into her head and Mary Ann realized that the spirit of Thomas McDonough was there for her too. She smiled at the notion. It was her first real smile in weeks. Years ago, Thomas gifted his daughter with a strong sense of believing in herself. Now, it was up to Mary Ann to use that gift to manufacture hope and somehow navigate through this very grim time of her life.

Have faith. Be a good mother. All will work out.

Mary Ann called upon all the reserve she could muster to cast out the down and defeated feelings. It was a good thing too, for truthfully, there was precious little time to wallow in self-pity. Mary Ann was her children's sole source of support and there was only a modest cash reserve. Mary Ann had not worked since the birth of Mary Jane. Now, she needed to find a job to pay the bills. Mary Ann asked around and found employment as a washerwoman for a wealthy family living atop Grymes Hill. They were charitable people, allowing Mary Ann to bring the children with her to work. She was grateful, since Julia was not able to look after them every day.

Mary Ann assumed a daily routine which was exhausting. She woke the babies up every morning at daybreak. She fed and dressed them and packed lunches. Then she scooped William up in her arms and took Mary Jane by the hand. Together they walked over to Richmond Road and climbed the steep winding trail near the entrance to the brewery up the hill to her employer's home. The children played nearby as she drew water from the well, scrubbed clothes at the washboard, rinsed and then hung clothing out on the line to dry. On rainy days, the children played in the kitchen while she ironed inside. After her long tiring work was done, Mary Ann and the babies made the return trip down the hill back to their home. Mary Ann ended each day changing clothes, washing little hands and faces, overseeing supper, supervising the privy, and making sure evening prayers were said before collapsing into bed next to her children.

The former factory girl was a real gem when it came to scrimping and saving, but from the start realized it would be next to impossible to support her family indefinitely without a plan. She searched for inspiration and found it in the example set by her stepmother. Julia McDonough was such a strong woman. She had proven to everyone that one could well survive the loss of a husband. Reminding herself of what Julia had endured helped Mary Ann get by. Instead of circling back to the despair she felt over the loss of her husband, Mary Ann made a conscious decision to keep her mind focused on a better future. She would take good care of the children and make her husband proud.

Don't look back! It's gone forever Mary Ann. Keep moving forward woman!

Mary Ann worked harder than ever, saving every penny she could. She thought about what she would do with the money being saved. Mary Ann prayed for guidance and direction. Rather quickly she received an answer to her prayers, in sharp contrast to the War Between the States which lingered on and on.

One night, in a quiet moment of reflection, Mary Ann found her true-life compass.

Mary Ann could not sleep. She tossed and turned carefully so not to wake little Mary Jane who was dozing next to her. As she laid there in the dark, her father, Thomas the Dreamer McDonough, came to mind. Remembering his happy go lucky grin, Mary Ann relaxed and let her thoughts run free. She started a silent conversation with him.

Daddy, I miss you. You were always so full of life and laughter! True, you had your faults, but most certainly you served as an excellent provider for the family. I remember you always said that the purchase of the Rocky Hollow property was the best move of your life and you were right. Not for a moment after your demise did any of us fear being thrown into the streets or forced into the county almshouse for the poor and destitute down in Richmond. We did not suffer after you were gone because of your wisdom. God bless you always for that.

Mary Ann then began to shift her thoughts to her own situation. Thomas demonstrated that owning a home free and clear was key to providing well for the family. So, if she managed to accumulate enough money to buy a small house in Rocky Hollow, could she likewise ensure domestic stability for her children?

Pish! Posh! Why, of course!

Well, that was it! Mary Ann needed a house! She would keep working, keep saving, and eventually buy a house! Then, if or when she needed help with the bills she'd just take in a boarder.

It was impossible to fall sleep after such a revelation. Mary Ann got out of bed energized, eager for it to be morning so she could further investigate the idea. She went down to Town Hall and made some inquiries. Happily, Mary Ann confirmed that she needed no man to make such a dream come true. In New York State, a woman could independently buy and own property with all accompanying rights and privileges. It was a grand thing for Mary Ann to learn, since life kept proving to her over and over again not to count too heavily upon the men in her life.

It was almost an impossible dream, yes, but Mary Ann did not care. She was convinced she would be successful. Days spent scrubbing clothes and running after her two small tots continued to be long and exhausting but after her revelation, Mary Ann's daily grind took on a greater sense of importance. She got little to no sleep most nights, but she saved and remained focused on making her dream come true.

Julia did not challenge her but other family and friends advised Mary Ann to come down from the clouds. She was bound to get deathly ill working so hard. Mary Ann did not listen. Worries or criticism would not distract or discourage Mary Ann. She felt strong and on top of the world. She was proud to be challenging the status quo of the times, just like some of the highfalutin women she read about in the dailies. Famous women, like Miss Fanny Wright.

Fanny Wright was perhaps the most audacious woman alive in the years before the Civil War. She was an English heiress who immigrated to America in the early 1800's. Fanny was an abolitionist, a suffragist, and an enemy of organized religion. She attempted to start a utopian community to demonstrate how slaves could be freed and then educated. She was the first woman in America to address a mixed male and female audience at a public gathering. Miss Wright was grossly maligned by her detractors. They called her masculine, loud, and distasteful in attire. Critics chastised her for traveling around unescorted and for having free and open relationships with men.

Though they lived in two very different worlds, Fanny and the young Rocky Hollow widow shared some similar personality traits. Both ladies believed they had a right to live life as they saw fit. Mary Ann was beginning to acquire a few less than flattering labels from neighborhood gossipers, but like Fanny, she let the criticism slide off her back. What others thought did not matter. Mary Ann held unshakable confidence in herself and her master plan.

The War Between the States wore on, seeming as if it would never end. Her brother Michael, who up to now had stayed out the conflict, enlisted in the Navy in 1864. The whole time he was away Mary Ann feared that he would never return, and she would lose yet one more man she loved. She wrote Michael as often as she could to tell him how much she missed him.

Mary Ann was twenty-three years old in the spring of 1864. Mary Jane was four years old and William almost two years. Life was hard. She was working day and night, pinching pennies in every possible way she could. There was no time for a man. Family and friends believed she had sworn men off altogether.

Indeed, Mary Ann *was* strictly adhering to a policy of male avoidance up until the day James Bascombe sauntered into her life. It was never well explained so no one was quite certain how Mary Ann and James met or what attraction she felt for him in the first place. Perhaps she was amused by his wry sense of humor or the little crinkle at the corner of his eyes when he told a tall tale? Maybe it was his blimey English accent? This was just pure speculation, but one thing was certain. Mary Ann most certainly did not marry James Bascombe for his money. James had practically none to his name on June 15, 1864, the day he and Mary Ann climbed the steep steps of St. Mary's Church to exchange wedding vows in front of the beloved Fr. Lewis.

It had been yet one more whirlwind courtship, each with its own unique set of circumstances. The first time she fell for a man, Mary Ann was still a child. She lacked maturity and went into marriage like a lovestruck teenager. The second time around Mary Ann fell deeply in love with William in part because of her need for nurturing support and affection after John's death. This third time, the marriage seemed more or less a strategic maneuver. After William's death, Mary Ann beliefs about marriage had changed. In her mind, the foundation of a successful third marriage was to put emotions to the side and enter into the union with a clear sense of practicality. She no longer felt that marriage was all about love. No more starry-eyed relationships for her. Mary Ann had suffered way too much.

James met most, if not all, of her key conditions of marriage. He was a laborer by trade who didn't mind sharing home keeper duties. He said it was ok for Mary Ann to be in charge of family finances. And, most importantly, he did not care if she owned real estate independent of him.

Just to confirm he was no threat to her overall plan, Mary Ann checked again at Town Hall. Yes, her personal assets were protected even if she married. The Married Women's Property Act which had been passed by the New York State legislature just a few years prior ensured that married women could own property separate from their husbands and collect rents and profits as if a single person. Though she hadn't known James very long, Mary Ann was quite attracted to how he did not put up a fuss given her stipulations. From her vantage point, she imagined this could be a fairly heavenly match.

Mary Ann and James were about the same age but came from very different backgrounds. Born in England, James was abandoned as a young child and grew up in a home for paupers. Small in stature, he got by with his combination of an affable demeanor and natural talent for easy going gab to get him out of sticky situations. When he became a teenager, James wanted out of the home. He became enamored with America and somehow finagled his way onto a boat headed for New York.

James had a huge secret which he hid from Mary Ann. Four years after arriving in the states, James got into some serious trouble with the law. While working as a bell boy at the popular Pacific Hotel on Greenwich Street in lower Manhattan, James decided to plan a robbery. He swiped the duplicate key to the hotel's big iron safe and then plotted for the right time to make a move.

One day young James took off with $1200 in gold coins, gold dust, and other valuables belonging to the distinguished hotel guests. At first, he was not considered a suspect, but then Mr. Patten, who was the owner of the hotel, learned that James was aboard a river boat bound for Troy, New York. He called the police and a telegraphic dispatch was sent to the Canadian authorities asking for help. They intercepted James as he attempted to enter Hamilton, Canada.

It was an open-shut case for the prosecution as most of the stolen goods were still in his possession at the time of arrest. James was convicted of grand larceny and sentenced to imprisonment at Blackwell's Island, one of the two large penitentiaries in New York State. Blackwell's was a cigar shaped island located in the middle of the East River. It housed a prison, lunatic asylum, workhouse, almshouse, and hospital. At the penitentiary, James kept company with a thousand other criminals who were serving out their various misdemeanor sentences. Upon his release from prison, James sought redemption. He served a short stint in the U.S. Army and was honorably mustered out in 1864, just before his marriage.

Mary Ann and her new husband got along amicably from the start. James more or less kept to his own interests, and she hers. Spring gave way to summer and brought with it the usual round of scorching heat, intense humidity, and nasty mosquitoes. Everyone was grumbling about the conditions except Mary Ann. For her no matter the bugs or weather, it was going to be a grand and glorious summer.

Mary Ann was happy as a lark but not necessarily because of her new husband. A wonderfully unexpected surprise arrived one day in the mail from brother Michael. While serving in the U.S. Navy, Mary Ann had faithfully corresponded with Michael to keep her brother up to date with all the happenings in town. In one of her letters, Mary Ann shared the dream of owning her own home someday. Michael was touched and wanted to help his sister. He sent her a bank draft attached to a letter.

You have worked hard to manage your lot of troubles Mary Anna. Take these funds and invest in a home for you and the babies. I believe in you and your dream, dearest sister.

Mary Ann was thrilled by her brother's generosity. Adding his contribution to what she had put aside from washing and ironing rich people's frocks day and night over the past few years, Mary Ann knew she had finally accumulated enough money to go house hunting!

She began a careful examination of the local real estate market. Mary Ann discussed the various options with her new husband, but was careful not to ask for his advice or financial help. James accepted the role she assigned him, apparently seeing no downside in obtaining a new home without having to pay for it. Mary Ann found a lot for sale that was close to her father's property. She knew the land well, liked it very much, and could well afford the purchase. Mary Ann made an offer which was accepted.

On August 8, 1864, Mary Ann's great dream came to fruition. That morning she nervously polished her boots, ironed and re-ironed her best Sunday frock, and fretted over which bonnet to wear. Mary Ann wanted to look her finest on this very special occasion. She laced up her boots and took a last look in the mirror before kissing her kids and new husband and walking out the door. Mary Ann hitched up the wagon and drove to the county clerk office.

After signing the required legal documents, Mary Ann removed three hundred twenty-five dollars from her purse for cash payment of the lot near the intersection of Gore and Gordon Streets. When the transaction was complete, Mary Ann stuck her right hand out towards James and Harriet Coyne, the sellers. Though it was an impulsive gesture, the move came natural to Mary Ann. She felt like she already knew them, for it had been another Coyne who sold her father the land at Gore at Gordon back in 1840. James was a bit taken back by the brash unladylike move, but his wife obviously thought, why not? She stepped forward, placed Mary Ann's hands in her own, and gave her a ladylike pat. She wished the young woman the very best of fortunes.

The county official packed up and made ready to leave. Mary Ann, however, gave a minor excuse to lag behind. She needed a moment by herself to bask in the significance of the occasion.

Whoopeeee! Thank you Thomas Mack for sharing your dream with Mary Anna!

The twenty-three years old woman was tickled silly. Now she, James, and the children would have a place to call their own. Even better, Mary Jane and William were now guaranteed to grow up in the same Rocky Hollow neighborhood as Mary Ann and her brothers had!

Before she left the building, Mary Ann made sure to also thank He who made all things possible. She clasped her hands together, bowed her head, and whispered under her breath.

Thank you oh gracious Lord, for bringing your humble servant Mary Ann to this time and place. It is a glorious day. I ask you to grant me continued guidance in all future decisions I make for the benefit of my family.

Mary Ann's hands went up to adjust the bonnet on top of her head. She smoothed her skirt, picked up the purse lying on the bench next to her, and draped the bag over her elbow. Mary Ann smiled to herself. Then, she walked out the door into the blazing hot sun and a new chapter of her life.

CHAPTER FIVE: THE VETERAN HODCARRIER

Mary Ann was, by nature, an early riser. As a young girl, there had been no choice. She had many chores to do around the home before dressing and going to work. Now, as a grown woman she continued to get up early because she knew it put her at an advantage over others. There was so much one could accomplish in a day, especially if a body got moving at the crack of dawn.

One summer day, however, she was awakened in a most non-routine manner. The common early morning sounds – the crow of a cock, a wagon passing, her children giggling in their beds – were drowned out by the loud shouts of men and a cacophony of various animal sounds.

Pish! Posh! What in blazes is going on outside?

Mary Ann and her neighbors had not been notified of a recent decision made by the trustees of the Village of Edgewater. They were not going to put up with untethered livestock running amok on the streets any longer. It was both a public embarrassment and a boldfaced insult to their authority. So, in the wee morning hours of June 22, 1878, they dispatched the entire Richmond County Police Department to the streets of Stapleton. Their mission was to enforce an existing ordinance prohibiting goats, sheep, cows, hogs, and geese to run loose.

Mary Ann threw on a light cloak and stepped out her front door. A few of her children who had also been awakened by the commotion spilled out behind her. One by one the neighbors opened their front doors to see what was happening. Soon, almost all the citizens of Rocky Hollow were standing out on the street. They stared in amazement and amusement at the sight.

The work had barely begun and already some of the police seemed flustered and over taxed in their efforts. Two officers were sweating like hogs themselves as they dragged an uncooperative billy goat down the road. Another officer stood at the side of the road visibly shaken. He had been carefully shepherding a lot of goats down to Canal Street and the front gates of the pound when suddenly a long and loud whistle pierced the air. It was one of Mary Ann's neighbors calling his property home. When the obedient animal bolted, he took all his neighborhood companions with him. The poor officer was caught in the middle of the resulting stampede. Mary Ann and her neighbors, who had ample time to side step way out of the path of the oncoming herd, called out to each other how lucky the officer was not to have been crushed.

The round up went on all morning. As she dressed to go out and run her errands, Mary Ann could not help but feel sorry for the poor officers who were out there doing their duty. The majority were incurring an awful tongue lashing from the neighbors. No doubt, neighbor Rodger McGinley was among those being chastised.

Rodger was a well-known and respected young officer from Rocky Hollow. That day, he was stuck between doing his duty and currying the favor of his neighbors. Rodger kept his eyes low to the ground and focused on walking slowly and cautiously behind a flock of geese to gently shoo them towards the pound. While doing so, a local woman walked out her front door to watch. She kept silent at first, her eyes firmly fixed upon the young officer. When she had seen enough, however, she raised her arm, held out her right index finger and shook it angrily in the air as she yelled over to him.

"Shuro, McGinley, and haven't yees anything betther to do than that? Yees, who was born and raised in Rocky Hollow, ought to be ashamed of yeeself to thry and injure the poor folks! Yees ought to go home now and pray for yure sowl."[1]

Rodger tried his best to ignore his neighbor. He agreed that the trustees shouldn't go about bullying the hardworking folk of Rocky Hollow if they weren't hurting anyone outright.

And yet, Rodger also understood the need to eradicate the conditions that drove the officials to take action. The streets were a filthy mess with animal droppings, and his beloved Annie and little boy Thomas Rodger risked physical assaults by geese and goats every time they walked to market! Rodger turned away and continued his assignment. He made peace in his head by concluding that what they accomplished today would not matter. The round up was not a permanent solution for the problem.

By the end of the day, the pound was overflowing, and the streets clear for citizens to walk about unmolested. Village officials proclaimed the raid as a victory for humankind, but Rodger was correct in his assumption. It did not last. Animals and humans would continue to cohabitate on the streets of Stapleton for years to come.

A newfound desire to corral animals which were accustomed to running free on the streets was a good example of the changes that Stapleton was going through in the late 1800's. The War Between the States was over but it had left its mark. The surge in population after the war dictated a need for major civic improvements. The once sleepy little waterfront village was moving in high gear.

Gore Street officially retired its status as a quaint little farmer's lane when the road was macadamized. The adults of Stapleton were glad to be rid of the dirt, dust, and deep ruts of the old roadway. The children of Stapleton loved watching the process of widening the thoroughfare, as workers replaced the dirt with a smooth hard surface made of compressed stone. When the work was complete, Village officials changed the name of the road to Broad Street.

The paving of Broad Street led to increased wagon and carriage traffic, which led to more stores and homes being built along the avenue. Mary Ann was delighted to have access to a host of new vendors just a stone's throw from her home. She would have less need to drive her wagon down to Canal Street for daily necessities.

Mary Ann was likewise pleased to see that new technologies

and modern conveniences were making their way into town. Having grown up with only candles to light the way, she had been thrilled when gas lamps came into being during the Civil War. Now, she would get the chance to see if Edison's invention was all it claimed to be. George Bechtel was making plans to convert from gas to electric illumination of his brewery.

Workers sent from The New York and New Jersey Telephone Company began erecting wooden poles and mounting overhead wires on the streets. The horse drawn trolleys that ran along Richmond Road and up and down Broad Street were being replaced with electric vehicles.

The Crystal Water Supply Company established a reservoir atop Grymes Hill and started to pump water into Stapleton. It would still take years for the installation of sanitary sewer lines, but the reservoir eliminated the need for water pumps, wells, and cisterns. Indoor plumbing became all the rage as wealthy Stapleton residents began to acquire systems with sinks and bathtubs.

At the Bascombe residence, eight eager children chomped at the bit with all the new spangled innovations springing up around them. Well, why not have electric lights and water pipes in our house too? They got together and took a vote. Mary Jane, as the eldest, would plead the case to Mary Ann on behalf of all the siblings.

Mary Jane knew this would be a difficult task. Her mother was hard to convince, so she needed to plan out her argument. She took her time, seeking the best opportunity to speak to Mary Ann. One rainy day, she found the perfect setting. Her mother had volunteered to run the refreshment table at the upcoming fireman's fair and there was much baking to do. Mary Ann was in the kitchen up to her elbows in yeast, flour, sugar, and eggs. She wasn't going anywhere. Knowing it was now or never, Mary Jane began her pitch.

Dearest Mother, I speak for all of us. Please give some fair consideration to your children's request to convert to electric lamps. You are always telling us to read more and this is such a good way! Every family that can afford it will be doing so. And Mother! How wonderful it would also be if you could lay pipes inside the house. We'd have all the water we'd need at our disposal. The girls could take long steamy baths while the boys do other useful chores instead of constantly lugging heavy buckets back and forth from the pump!

She went on as her mother picked up her rolling pin, leaned over the table, and put her muscles to work flattening out the dough. Mary Ann waited until her daughter finished and asked for a reply. Then, instead of a yes or no, she shooed her away.

Pish! Posh! Not now, Mary Jane! Can't you see I'm busy?

Mary Jane did not speak another word. She turned and walked out of the room.

Good try, Mary Ann mumbled under her breath, *but no child of mine will tell me what to do.*

Yes, she understood that Mary Jane's request was made because it was obvious that things were going well in Mary Ann's business. But what Mary Jane did not realize was that she would never have been this successful if she had spent all the money she made on frivolous luxuries. It was expensive to install indoor plumbing and likewise to make the switch from gas to electric. Someday, it would make sense to do as Mary Jane wished. Then and only then, she would bargain with the providers, talk them into discounting the installation costs for all her homes, and make a handsome deal for the utility services.

Mary Ann was alone in the kitchen now, so she focused on her tasks. She whipped eggs, sifted flour, and kneaded dough. It was humdrum work. She could not help but find her mind drifting to relive some events of the past.

My, but when she looked back it seemed that what she had accomplished so far in life was truly amazing! How gutsy a girl she had been in her mid-twenties when she bought the first Rocky Hollow property! There were a few who tried to talk her out of what she was doing at the time, but they failed. There she was, the young mother of two small children with barely enough savings to go through with the deal, yet she made her dream come true without the help or permission of her new husband. She used her own money and in this way made sure James had no rights to the property.

Soon after she acquired the land, Mary Ann bought a barn which she moved onto her property and converted into a house. She remembered how confident she felt as she wrapped her family belongings in preparation for the move. The house on Gordon Street was just a stone's throw from her father's property at the corner. She could check in with her stepmother and brothers daily. The children would have an easy hike down the road to school. Plus, just a few feet away there was the convenience of the variety of stores popping up along Broad Street.

It was a time of great excitement, but Mary Ann never let it go to her head. She kept following the internal compass acquired during the difficult period after her father died. Money was security in bad times so it was important for her to earn back the money used to purchase her home. Mary Ann continued to work at the local hat factory while James, Julia, and other family members pitched in to help care for her children.

The Bascombe family lived in the dusty old barn for ten years. Thomas, Mary Ellen, and James were born there, and in time their tiny home became tight living quarters. Eventually, Mary Ann accumulated sufficient savings so that they did not need to live there indefinitely. It was time to contemplate a move.

She knew the property she wanted to buy but wondered, was it the right time to ask? Well, she would never know unless she gave it a try.

One evening, she sat down with Julia and Michael over a cup of tea and discussed the plan she envisioned in her head. Would the family consider parting with their shares of the McDonough property on the corner of Broad and Gordon Streets? Her arguments were convincing and the buyout fair and equitable. Julia and her siblings could not resist the offer. They agreed to sell out to Mary Ann.

Good Gosh! Wasn't she ecstatic!

On the day of the sale, Mary Ann got up extra early to drive her wagon down to Richmond with husband James. She watched with giddy glee as the county clerk slowly and carefully dabbed his pen in the inkwell. With fine penmanship, he recorded the $600 sale in the county deed book.

This transaction held such great personal significance to Mary Ann. She could sense the same degree of thrill which Thomas must have felt when he purchased this land many years before. Here she was, keeping her father's dream alive! Mary Ann was so excited she did not watch what the clerk was writing in the ledger. He left off her first name, identifying the buyer only as the *wife of James Bascom*. It was an obvious and deliberate slight.

Lucky for the clerk that she never saw it.

Every fiber within Mary Ann's being wanted to shout to the rafters, but somehow, she composed herself until she got outside the building. Mary Ann grabbed James' elbow and gave him a playful tug on the arm. Then, mimicking her father's rich Irish brogue she looked upward and said:

Well Daddy! Shuro, but uren't ye prowd teday in heven of yer littl' gurl awl grewn up?

That night, the Bascombe family celebrated with cake and special homemade desserts. Mary Ann remained euphoric for a few days, until it was time to settle down and make another important decision. She owned two properties now. Should she sell or keep the barn home?

Mary Ann wasn't sure. Maybe she needed some fresh air to help make up her mind? Mary Ann grabbed her bonnet off the hat stand and took off down the street. She wanted to take a walk on her newly acquired property.

Good gosh, she thought. *How I do love my father's land!*

Mary Ann meandered awhile near the brook, and then circled the house and barn a few times. How pleased she was at her ability to put together the funds to make this happen. Mary Ann stopped for a while under a shade tree. When at last she decided to move, she felt a slight tug. Mary Ann looked down and saw she had absentmindedly sunk her boot heel into the dirt. She twisted her foot a bit to loosen up the soil.

Not surprisingly, she felt a connection with her father much stronger here in this moment than any time in the recent past. She looked up, stretched her arms wide open and threw her dilemma out to the heavens.

Well Thomas Mack, you tell me now. What's your darlin' Mary Anna's next move?

No sooner than she uttered the words did she receive an answer. It was crisp and clear, just like the crystalline waters of Gore's Brook.

Collect rent money. Buy another property.

It is God's plan for you.

A simple but brilliant plan suddenly flooded Mary Ann's brain. Mary Ann needed to rent out her small house, take that money, and buy another home. Then, rent the second home, take that money and purchase another property. Keep repeating the process. Use cash. Don't borrow. Each home would pay for the next.

It was incredible, but Mary Ann truly believed that her father had spoken directly to her. She rushed home and began an intense study of the subject, devoting every possible waking hour to the plan. She sent her son William to the store each day to pick up the newspapers so she could scour the real estate section. She began friendly chit chats with her butcher and grocer down on Canal Street. They were gossipers and often knew more about a piece of property than could be gleaned from the papers alone. She informed her husband that he would have to watch the children more frequently now. James did not protest, because he knew Mary Ann too well. There was no stopping his lady when she set her mind to a task. Julia and James cared for the children as she continued to work long hard hours in the factory to accumulate more seed money.

Mary Ann opened a savings account at the Staten Island Savings Bank downtown. Then, she began to carry out her plan. Her sound yet simple business strategy was immediately fruitful because Stapleton was in a period of rapid expansion with a shortage of affordable housing for workers and their families. Mary Ann learned that the best buys in housing were often tied to a death or foreclosure, so she decided to make this an important part of her plan. The strategy was brilliant. Mary Ann started attending the public auctions held downtown. At one lucky estate auction, she paid only $1 for land which had been owned by a deceased grocer.

She quit the factory job after she saw that her weekly wages no longer matched what she could earn in real estate. This move gave her more valuable time to devote to her business and the needs of her growing family. As long as James continued to pitch in here and there with the raising of the children, everyone benefitted from the new work arrangements.

Thank God for James!

Though James' easygoing demeanor made it easy for Mary Ann to do as she pleased, others shook their heads at the union. It seemed that Mary Ann, so ambitious and driven to achieve, had not married her equal the third time around. James never worked harder than he had to on any given day. He showed little interest in the things that Mary Ann cared most deeply about. James was not embarrassed to live in a house owned by his wife. He took no issue with her holding a separate bank account. So long as he could top off his day with a beer or two, James was content with Mary Ann carrying the weight of main breadwinner for the family. Her family, seeing all this, were not huge fans of James, but since Mary Ann seemed happy, they kept mum.

Indeed, a main reason the couple got along so well was that they rarely had disputes over money. Mary Ann controlled the house finances, and this helped her overlook her husband's lackadaisical nature and occasional beer binges. She concentrated her earnings on building a solid nest egg for the family, and gave James an allowance to pay for the recreational beers he enjoyed. They both contributed to purchase food, pay household bills, and provide for the needs of the children.

Her assets began to grow and as she continued, Mary Ann realized there was even greater profit potential if she purchased undeveloped lots. Land was cheap, and it allowed her the flexibility to build as she wished. No one in the family was eager to support the idea of Mary Ann as a general contractor, but she paid them no heed. Mary Ann was certain she was up to the task. She had been a keen study of her father's trades as a child and knew the basics of carpentry and masonry. If there was something about construction that she didn't know, why she would ask and learn!

Mary Ann resolved to limit her earliest purchases of land to within walking distance of her home. That way, she could keep a closer eye on her investments. When building a house, she employed her own family members whenever she could. Mary Ann made daily inspections of the work being done on her properties and regularly conferred with the hired carpenters, painters, and laborers. If the men were running low on supplies, Mary Ann helped out. It became a common site for neighbors to spot Mary Ann making her way up Broad Street in a wagon loaded with bricks, lumber, and other building materials.

Mary Ann was a tireless worker and expected no less effort from the men she employed. She was not one to tolerate laziness or shoddy work. One day, a hot and heavy dispute erupted at one of her construction sites. The men had stopped working and were standing around arguing. One of her neighbors saw what was going on and ran over to tell Mary Ann. She was livid.

Bosh! Spooney! What kind of folly is this?

Mary Ann grabbed her stout stick and took off down the road. She shouted to the men to cease their fighting but they did not, so Mary Ann went over to the pile of building materials. She gathered bricks in her skirt and walked over to a ladder leaning against the side of the home. With one hand she held her skirt tight and the other held on to the rungs. Mary Ann climbed up the side of the building, dumped the bricks, went down the ladder, and picked up a hod filled with mortar. She shouldered the hod and reclimbed up the ladder. Then, when she got up on the roof, Mary Ann began to brick the chimney.

The men stopped arguing, stunned by what they were seeing. *Dang it!* one workman cussed. *That woman's plum crazy!*

They called out to her to get down, but Mary Ann did not stop. She bricked until the strikers were sufficiently embarrassed and agreed to go back to work.

As her real estate enterprise grew, Mary Ann began to generate a few ideas for side businesses to bring in extra income. The kitchen table was her business office and rarely a quiet working space. There were eight children spanning a twenty-plus year age difference running around competing for the boss lady's attention. In between financial matters, Mary Ann always had some type of child rearing issue to contend with. There was sibling rivalry and the periodic fights to break up. And there was her daughter Mary Jane, who was growing up high spirited and requiring close supervision. When her offspring were acting up or she was bogged down with work, Mary Ann turned to James for help. With a smile he was accommodating and dealt with the concern without grumble or complaint. She appreciated this although she sometimes fretted that his easy going ways were fueled by his growing penchant for beer.

The couple did not argue over money, but they did spar over his alcohol consumption. And, they were not alone. The steady growth of the Stapleton brewery business brought with it a proliferation of saloons, beer gardens, and liquor stores around town, causing problems for many. Some husbands found it far too difficult to resist drinking binges with their pals on pay day. Wages were spent even before they got home because of a compulsion to buy their cronies round after round of drinks. Bad enough, but after squandering their pay, these same men often went on to torment their wives at home with their drunken behavior.

Mary Ann abhorred drinking, yet she set up a small saloon inside a small store she established on Broad Street. Its main purpose was to make a little extra money but perhaps equally important was that by doing so she could keep James home and out of the local saloons. There had been a recent incident she did not want repeated.

Mary Ann was proud of her actions that day and not a bit embarrassed when a few days afterwards a New York City newspaper reporter came rapping at her front door. On the prowl for sensational news items, he heard a rumor downtown and asked around until he found her. Cautiously so as not to offend, he asked Mary Ann whether she could confirm a story that had been circulating in the community. Mary Ann smiled back at him amusedly. She told him to come into her parlor and sit down for she'd be happy to give him firsthand details.

In her version of the story, the day in question started out quite peacefully. Mary Ann was in her store. She was playing with one of her babies, savoring the little one's laughter as she bounced the child up and down on her lap. Suddenly, a neighbor appeared at the door. She was out of breath and looking somewhat shocked and appalled.

Mary Ann! Mary Ann! Come quick! James just went into Mrs. Baker's house!

Mrs. Baker was a widow who resided a little ways down the road. She shared her home with another widow by the name of Mrs. Nietze. They were famous in Rocky Hollow. Their home was a place where married men such as James Bascombe should have had the good sense not to enter in broad daylight.

Mary Ann did not flinch at the words of her neighbor. She put the baby down calmly and told one of her older children to watch over him. Then, she walked to the corner of the room and grabbed her stout walking stick which was leaning against the wall. With club firmly in hand, Mary Ann marched out of her store and down Broad Street. She went up to the front door of the house in question and used the door knocker to rap loudly and repeatedly.

Mrs. Baker appeared at the door and Mary Ann used her wondrous gift of gab to somehow talk her way past the woman. She entered the house, and made a quick move to grab the key left in the door. Mary Ann turned the lock and placed the key inside her skirt pocket. Then, she called for James to come out of hiding. It took a few moments, but James finally complied after realizing that Mary Ann was not about to leave. Sheepishly, he appeared from a dark recess of the house.

The reporter, who was looking down at his paper, could not help but smirk at the images her words were conjuring up in his mind. Mary Ann saw that her story was being well received. It encouraged her to continue. He wrote swiftly, trying not to miss a single word.

James began to blubber. In the attempt to explain himself he kept tripping over his words, in part due to a large quantity of ale he had consumed. Mary Ann dispassionately ignored him. She ordered her husband to take off his coat. James hesitated. Then, after scrutinizing the look on his irate wife's face, he obeyed. He was drunk but not stupid.

Next, Mary Ann commanded James to lean down over the side of the sofa. He obeyed, and she took her stout walking stick and whacked him over the buttocks. Then Mary Ann told him get down on his knees and offer up an apology to her.

Mrs. Baker cowered in great horror, wondering what came next. After James expressed sufficient regret and vowed to go straight to the confessional when released to rightfully atone for his sins, Mary Ann turned to face Mrs. Baker. Mary Ann said she blamed her much more than her husband. Baker had taken advantage of a man clearly not in control of his senses.

James pleaded mercy for the woman but knew better than to put his hands on Mary Ann to try to stop her. Mary Ann gave the woman a taste of her stick and then dragged her man back home.

The reporter asked if Mary Ann had any regrets for what she had done. She laughed loud and heartily.

Why, Bosh! Spooney! NO! she replied.

James was cured. The next time Mrs. Baker tried to tempt, he would turn away. Mary Ann, however, was concerned about the fate of other wives in Rocky Hollow. Mrs. Baker and her lady friend would surely continue to prey on the weaknesses of other husbands. She told the reporter:

"I have my eye on other married men who go around there and I intend to form a vigilance committee of married women to chase them home. I fear neither man nor devil."[2]

The reporter's smirk turned into a broad smile at the last remark.

Ah yes, but you are all that they say about you, Mrs. Bascombe, he thought.

The man packed up his writing accessories, thanked Mary Ann for her kindness, and scurried down Broad Street towards his office in downtown Stapleton. If he wrote fast enough, he might beat the deadline for the next edition of the newspaper. Why, this story was surely frontpage material!

The words Mary Ann had for James after she got him back home she did not share with the reporter. That night at supper, James sat on a pillow holding his throbbing hungover head in both hands while Mary Ann scolded him like a child.

Why do you drink so much James? Just what kind of han-ky-panky were you into over there? How many times have you been there before? And why did you think you could get away with embarrassing me with such atrocious behavior?

James made no attempt to defend himself. He remained silent and let her rant until her she just about lost her voice. When Mary Ann lay down in bed that evening she looked over at him snoring away next to her and cringed with disdain. That was the night she decided to set up her own saloon. Mary Ann would make James's life more comfortable. If he could enjoy a few leisurely drinks a day without worry of paying the tab, maybe he would stay clear of further trouble. Mary Ann fell into a restless sleep, wondering if it had really been worth her while to marry him.

Lucky for Mary Ann that her real estate enterprise continued to grow by leaps and bounds for it provided a welcome distraction from James and his errant personality. Mary Ann's favorite time of the month became the day her rents came due. She would get dressed, eat a quick breakfast, grab her stout stick, and then visit each of her properties to collect the monies owed. Sometimes a tenant invited her in for tea. Mary Ann accepted, appreciating the hospitality and tasty homemade jellies and tea breads. The chit chat with her tenants was pleasant but the greater satisfaction by far was the thrill she felt sitting at their table, chatting away while running her fingers over the smooth coins in the deep pockets of her skirts.

The feel of currency never failed to excite her.

She began expanding her real estate interests outside of Stapleton, yet for the most part Mary Ann continued to concentrate most of her real estate transactions within a few blocks of home on Broad, McKeon, Patton, Meadow, and Gordon Streets. Several properties she bought were located at the edge of the woods bordering the Seaman's Retreat. This had been the poorest section of Rocky Hollow since her childhood, a place where folks lived in rundown shacks and cabins. When Mary Ann purchased land there she set a goal of remaining profitable while at the same time improving the living conditions of these people.

Clearly Mary Ann was out to make a profit, but money was not all she cared about. She had a genuine concern for the welfare of all her tenants. She became known as a smart and independent business woman who was also a fair and honorable landlord. The Richmond County Clerk may have slighted her in the past, but Mary Ann's neighbors were a loyal breed. They gave her proper respect for her accomplishments. In stark contrast to the conventionality of the times, she was rarely if ever referred to *Mrs. James Bascombe* inside Rocky Hollow. To them, she was always *Mrs. Mary Ann,* and uniquely one of their own.

In bed at night, Mary Ann often thought about the people who rented rooms from her and over time acquired a philosophy which was key to her success. She believed there was a reciprocal relationship between renters and owners. While tenants must be responsible to have jobs and pay the rent on time, she was required to keep their apartments in good working order and make all necessary repairs. The living conditions of renters were not a high priority for other landlords, but Mary Ann felt this was not only the right thing to do, but a good business strategy. While other landlords had trouble finding tenants, Mary Ann rarely if ever had any vacancies. She had no need to advertise for her empty apartments were filled quickly by word of mouth.

Mary Ann's kindness as a landlord travelled outside the neighborhood until one day another newspaper reporter came to her door. He asked to speak to her for a few minutes about her business. Mary Ann gave him this quote:

"When a tenant comes to me and says 'Mary Ann, I haven't the rent this month,' I do not tell him to look for lodgings elsewhere but I ask him if he has plenty to eat in the house or is in need of any money. When that man leaves me he no longer looks upon me as his landlord, but as his friend, and he will slave his fingers to the bone when he does get work in order to pay me my due. You see, I am a believer in the honesty of the poor."[3]

While other landlords didn't hesitate to throw their tenants out on the street for failure to pay the rent, Mary Ann was quite the opposite. She tried to work it out with them whether it took a month or an extended period to catch up on payments. One day, a female tenant rapped on the front door of Mary Ann's home. She asked to speak in private with her landlord. Mary Ann welcomed her in, noting the strained look on her face. The woman began weeping uncontrollably as soon as she sat down. Her husband had been out of work for many months, and she was with child approaching her time of confinement. She could no longer work and it would be impossible for them to pay the rent next month.

As Mary Ann listened, she was immediately taken back to her own dark days after William died. Mary Ann knew quite well how it felt to be desperately down on your luck. She held out a hanky and told the woman to blow her nose and not to fear. Mary Ann would not throw the family out on the streets. She sent the woman home with a hug and a basket of fresh baked bread. Mary Ann was not a charity, but she told her she would find a sensible way to help.

Of course, being a benevolent landlord was a risky business practice. It could get her into a severe financial fix if she was not careful, but in prayer one night she came up with a novel idea that helped. If a tenant's life was insured, Mary Ann could ask to hold onto the insurance policy as rental security. And if not, she could insure them herself. Mary Ann paid the insurance premiums and in the event of a tenant's death, she'd collect the payout as their beneficiary. Mary Ann could then provide the deceased a decent burial, deduct what was due her for back owed rent, and turn over the rest of the money to surviving family members. She tried it out and the system worked well. It fit well with Mary Ann's own philosophy of hard work and charity. It became yet another big reason why Mary Ann never lacked tenants.

Her success proved she did not need a man, yet as Mary Ann's business grew she found herself spending more and more of her time in their company. The men she associated with came from all walks of life. She dealt with merchants who supplied her with lumber and construction materials. She supervised the painters, carpenters, and masons who worked on her building projects. And, she got familiar with most of the local bankers, lawyers, policemen, and judges.

As her real estate holdings grew, Mary Ann saw the value of nurturing a positive relationship with local politicians and officials. It was not just for herself, but for the benefit of the entire community. There were long standing public health concerns in Rocky Hollow, and she now had the power to speak up and be heard. It had been so painful to watch her dear mother and brother succumb to cholera as a child. What if their deaths could have been prevented? Back then there was not enough understanding of infectious diseases, but what was the excuse for poor health department practices now? It was commonly known that regular inspections of latrines, outhouses, and livestock pens, along with scheduled street cleaning were needed to control contagion. Yet, Rocky Hollow had no street sewers, and livestock still roamed loose on the streets.

Gore's Brook was another major public health concern. Despite its value to the brewers, the brook had been flooding Rocky Hollow and serving as a breeding ground for nasty summer mosquitoes for as long as Mary Ann could remember. Because the brook ran contiguous to her property at Broad and Gordon Streets, Mary Ann knew that health inspectors were only dispatched to the scene when there was flooding. There was no serious attempt being made to fix the problem. God gave Mary Ann a strong voice and the gift of gab. It was up to her now to use her gifts and make sufficient noise so that things would change!

One day after breakfast, Mary Ann told James that he would have to mind the children because she was needed elsewhere. She helped clear the table, then grabbed her coat off the hallway rack, and went out to the barn. She hitched the horse and drove her wagon down to Village Hall.

Mary Ann tied the horse to a post, then walked up to the front steps of Village Hall. She saw a group of men standing at the door and asked where the Trustees were holding their meeting. When she walked into the courtroom, Mary Ann saw that she was the only woman present, but paid this no mind. She walked past all the men in the room and sat down in the first row of seats front and center before the Trustee's table.

The meeting began with the pledge of allegiance and a roll

call. Mary Ann paid close attention to the proceedings. During the meeting, officials and experts were called upon by the Trustees to give testimony on a variety of issues. After listening for a while, Mary Ann realized she knew almost as much as the Trustees about these same concerns!

Mary Ann sat on her hands, eager for the time when the public was allowed to ask questions. When that time came, she raised her hand high and when called upon, spoke smoothly and with great confidence.

I am here as a citizen of Stapleton, born and raised in Rocky Hollow, to serve witness upon you that those who you supposedly represent are suffering greatly from inadequate street cleaning, a lack of storm sewers, and safe roads!

Mary Ann went on to deliver a most elegant oration. She spoke of the history of Rocky Hollow and her firsthand experiences dealing with these concerns. She outlined the financial as well as the health benefits of storm sewers. It was a well thought out presentation. She ended by chiding the Village officials to take action, reminding them that they were responsible for continued harm to the community as a result of their delays.

Stapleton was still a small town, and word of her presence at the meeting spread quickly. Her Rocky Hollow neighbors applauded her efforts and urged her to continue. In short time, Mary Ann was regularly attending Trustee meetings serving as their unofficial community spokesperson.

More frequent health inspections were remedied rather quickly. Obtaining funding for the installation of storm sewers was a mightier task. It took years of intense public lobbying by Mary Ann and others for the government to finally get around to authorizing the construction of a 3000 feet long storm sewer alongside Gore's brook. The project cost was around $30,000 and although everyone agreed it was a fine thing to do, some taxpayers were displeased with the resulting tax burden. They argued that Gore's Brook originated outside Stapleton so neighboring communities should shoulder part of the financial burden.

People had a right to their feelings, but Mary Ann knew these sewers were necessary! She campaigned personally around Rocky Hollow to set her neighbors straight. The flooding was going on in their community not elsewhere, and that made the tax fair and just. Besides, as the biggest property owner in the neighborhood, didn't they realize if she thought the tax was unreasonable that she would be first in line to complain?

Amid the battle for storm sewers, Mary Ann realized how much she enjoyed her growing involvement in Stapleton politics. Her business connections flourished as she started hobnobbing with local democrats who dominated the political scene. Some men were a tad uneasy at first including Mary Ann in their salty discussions, but quickly she won them over. Mary Ann was armed with logic and a knowledge of the facts to craft arguments that were difficult to dispute.

Although she was unable to cast a vote in any election, Mary Ann became an important member of the Democratic machine. Her male tenants and neighbors respected her and she could influence them to swing an election. Plus, she had a bulging purse to help fund the campaigns of her favorite politicians.

Mary Ann's neighbors clearly saw the benefits of her civic activism. She was fast becoming an authority on local ordinances, keeping up with any changes to ensure her own personal rights as a land owner were not compromised. She honed her public speaking skills at the Village Trustees meetings, so much that family and friends began to ask her to accompany them when they were required to appear in court. Mary Ann rarely if ever said no, for she relished the opportunity to stand before the justices and deliver legal arguments.

As Stapleton grew, the courts became so jammed that they opened a small police court annex just down the road from her house. The tiny one room courthouse was close to the intersection of Broad and Canal Streets, sandwiched between two large beer saloons. This made her legal defense work even more convenient. Why now she could defend a citizen early in the morning and still be home in time to help with supper!

Her *Counselor Howe* nickname stuck, and she was swamped with requests for help although what was needed was not always a legal concern. If Mary Ann was invited to afternoon tea, it was often associated with a favor. Fathers asked about construction jobs for their sons. Mothers inquired about suitable beaus for their daughters. Those in the market to buy their own home asked for advice on where to start. Even brother Michael wanted her counsel, asking his sister how to best invest his savings.

Mary Ann's success made her grow increasingly bold. The woman who was known to speak vociferously and carry a stout stick openly questioned Staten Island's most powerful men - county officials, village politicians, local justices, school trustees, and clergy – and did not back down. Staten Island newspapers, more conservative and less sensationally inclined, tended to overlook her existence by omitting or downplaying the stories about her but once discovered, the New York City reporters could not get enough of her. They knew that Mary Ann Bascombe was, indeed, a remarkable woman.

Proud of her accomplishments, Mary Ann clipped out newspaper articles written about her and kept them in an album on the credenza. She tried not to let the newspaper stories go to her head. Instead, she praised God for giving her the talents she used to help her family and others.

Mary Ann was fearless except for how she felt about two things: contagious disease and fire. She was always concerned about the health of her loved ones because of the losses she suffered in her youth. And she was terrified of fire because of its potential to kill, maim, and destroy. Mary Ann cringed every time she read a story in the paper about a child who was scorched playing too close to a fire or a woman whose skirts caught flame while cooking. The damage a fire could do to her own pocketbook was also scary. Most of the homes she owned in Rocky Hollow would burn to the ground in minutes. They were small wood frame structures heated by coal furnaces and lit with candles, kerosene, and gas lamps.

Mary Ann could not stamp out fires, but she vowed to assist those brave men who did in any way possible. As the population of Stapleton grew, so did the number of volunteer fire companies. The oldest fire house, the Enterprise Hook and Ladder Company

No. 1, was located on Bay Street. There was the Excelsior Bucket Company on Thompson Street and Protection Engine Department No. 7 which was the closest to her home on Broad Street. The Edgewater Fire Department formed around the same time as the Trustees' decision to build a big new fire tower. It was located at the edge of Washington Park near Canal and Water Streets and soared forty feet high. The bell in the tower weighed more than 2600 pounds, and when it was rung, it could be heard throughout Stapleton.

When smoke or flames were spotted, citizens took off in all directions to track down a police officer. It was the job of the Richmond County Police to go to the tower and ring the bell. It sounded sensible, but in practice this was not very efficient. Stapleton was patrolled on foot, and precious firefighting time was lost as the officer ran to the park. When Mary Ann was a child, firefighting equipment was pulled by hand to the scene of the fire and water hand pumped from a nearby creek or cistern. Now, in the late 19th century horse drawn engines were used and the water came from the Crystal Water Supply Company. The installation of pipes and fire hydrants in town helped to provide easier ability to extinguish flames.

There were glitches other than the fire itself which were at times responsible for buildings burning to the ground. At times there was a delay in the fire fighters getting to the scene. Sometimes, the firefighting equipment failed to work properly. And, other times, rivalries between the various fire companies got in the way. There was no central coordination, so when multiple fire companies showed up at the same time, buildings burned until agreement was reached on who would do what.

Mary Ann showed her thanks for the efforts of the brave firemen by serving as a lady volunteer. She secured the help of her youngest daughters, Mary Ellen and Mary Emma, and together they ran the Refreshments Table at fireman fundraisers. It was a job well suited to Mary Ann. Anyone within earshot could not escape her sales pitch to purchase home baked goods and lemonade. Her girls served the food while she collected the donations.

As Stapleton continued to grow, so did the needs of the population. There was a commitment among the wealthier families in town to support newly created benevolent organizations. In the later 19th century, it became respectable for society ladies to work for worthwhile charitable causes so Stapleton women put forth great time and energy to run fundraisers which were successful because of their husbands' generous philanthropy. The Diet Kitchen had a laudable goal of feeding the sick and needy through donations of food and monies. The S.R. Smith Infirmary was a community hospital which did not charge fees, relying on the donations of well-to-do Staten Islanders to fund its good works.

Mary Ann was pleased to see that the wealthy women in town were sympathetic to the down and out, but she personally took no interest in joining their ranks. Truthfully, Mary Ann spent very little time in the company of females other than Julia and her daughters. Day to day, she lived in a world dominated by men – at Village Hall, in the courts, at the bank, and at construction sites – and she liked it that way. When introduced to a new couple in town, she usually found she had more in common with the husband than the wife. With a man she could launch into a deep and fascinating discourse on politics, finances, and other big news of the day. With women, she was a fish out of water because of her limited interest in gossip, fashion, or cooking.

She was atypical and didn't mind it one bit.

Time went on, and Mary Ann's name was showing up in the newspapers on a more frequent basis. Mary Ann chuckled loudly at the kitchen table the day she read that the *New York World* nicknamed her the Hetty Green of Richmond County.

Pish! Posh! she thought. *Is this a compliment or a dig?*

Henrietta Howland Robinson Green was born into a rich family. Hetty learned about business and finance from her father and grandfather. After her father's death, relatives tried to place Hetty's inheritance in a trust fund to be managed by a male relative. Instead, Hetty took charge. She analyzed her positions, and invested cautiously. Over time, she increased her portfolio to more than one hundred million dollars. She owned railroads, theaters, cemeteries, hotels, office buildings, and real estate in 48 states.

When Hetty married Edward H. Green by mutual consent the couple kept their finances separate. She was dubbed *The Witch of Wall Street* because of her crafty business practices, tight-fisted spending, and typical attire of long black dresses. Because she was born at a time when women were widely believed to be incapable of handling money, men kept trying to take advantage of her. Some thought it was a farce and she really did not understand finance, while others believed that God may have given her a man's brain. No matter, for she survived and thrived despite the hostile male environment. Hetty broke through male dominated societal barriers, blazing the way for women to follow in her steps.

Mary Ann did have some traits in common with this wealthy woman. Like Hetty, Mary Ann was an astute businesswoman who held her own despite the prejudice against her in a man's world. Mary Ann was frugal like Hetty. She kept her personal finances separate from her husband. And, she was a bit odd, not because of the clothes she wore but because of things she did, like hauling around her stout club and climbing on roofs to lay brick. Why, who knew what little Mary Anna the orphan girl could have achieved if she had been endowed with even a fraction of the inheritance of young Hetty!

One day, Mary Ann was contacted by the *New York Journal*. She had been asked for interviews before, but this time it was special. The reporter asked to hear her life story and the article he wrote was fantastic. It celebrated Mary Ann as a remarkable woman who had found financial independence through a combination of hard work and shrewd business acumen. Male or female, she was a great example of self-made American success!

Mary Ann learned that reprints and offshoots of the article found their way into newspapers across the country. Readers in cities like Washington D.C., St. Louis, Kansas City, and Los Angeles now knew her name. Mary Ann cut the item out of the paper and placed it carefully inside her album. Years from now, when she looked back at all the articles written about her, this piece would make her the proudest.

Mary Ann did get a bit perplexed at times, however, by the bias of the different newspapers. The only local paper which wrote fair and accurate stories about her was a Stapleton weekly called *The Staten Islander*. The other Staten Island newspapers virtually ignored her while the New York dailies like the *New York Evening Telegram* and *New York Herald* wrote less than flattering commentary. They used adjectives such as *peculiar, eccentric* and *a character* to describe her. The paradox was baffling, yes, but in the end the lady of Broad and Gordon Streets shrugged it off. Mary Ann rationalized that it was she who had the last laugh with all that she achieved, was she not? The lack of coverage and the less than kind words that were written must mean they just didn't know what to make of her.

Pish! Posh! Yes, and may God curb their jealous hearts, she added.

Given her real estate success, some found it surprising that Mary Ann never moved her family to another part of town. As time went on, the once homogenous neighborhood was fast becoming a cultural stew. Italians and Eastern Europeans were newcomers to Rocky Hollow and were not well accepted by many of the English, Irish, and Germans living in the neighborhood. That, plus the continued expansion of the beer industry seemed to be creating more and more local crime and mischief.

By the late 1800's, her large family was busting at the seams of their small wood frame home and Mary Ann had an important decision to make. She knew the answer in her heart but felt God was asking her to factor the sentiments of her brood into her deliberations. At suppertime, she queried the group.

James, children. What are your thoughts? Should I build a new home for us here in Rocky Hollow, look for land in The Nook or in Stapleton Heights, or go elsewhere?

Mary Jane looked up from her dish and frowned.

Since when did our Mother give us choices about anything? she thought.

She stayed mum while James and the other children

responded. A few mentioned they thought Rocky Hollow was a good location because they could get to and from almost anywhere on Staten Island from their home. Some said they loved the convenience of having a shoe shop, meat store, barber, grocer, hat shop, drug store, cigar shop, tobacconist, gun shop and church within one walking block of home. Everyone had a close friend living in Rocky Hollow they did not want to leave behind. They came to agreement at the table. Rocky Hollow was still more of a *delightful* than *unsavory* place to live. They wanted to stay.

Mary Ann was relieved to hear their answers. It set the stage for her big announcement. When she pondered the move, Mary Ann realized there was more than enough land on their current property to build a new home. She already had the plans drawn up in her head. She wanted to build a three-story multifamily brick structure. A storefront on the first floor would provide more room to expand her general store/ saloon business. They would live in the first floor apartment. The other floors would be available if any of the children got married and wanted to live there. If not, she would rent out the rooms.

James and the children thought it was a brilliant idea. This delighted Mary Ann because truthfully, she did not want to leave the corner where she had been born some 50 odd years ago. She felt a deep spiritual connection with her father here and feared it might not be the same elsewhere. Thus, with her family's blessing, Mary Ann began to take the necessary steps.

GOODNESS! HOW MY MIND CAN WANDER!!

Mary Ann had enjoyed reliving some of the high points of her past, but it was time to return to the here and now. She had a lot of baking left to do for the fireman's fair. She placed the bread dough she had been kneading into a pan and put it in the oven.

Hmm, now where was that Mary Jane? she wondered.

After being dismissed from the kitchen by her mother, Mary Jane had sat on her bed listening to the rain fall. Then, when the rain stopped she walked outside and sulked for the longest time near the water hydrant. The ground was a bit muddy but what did she care? She was so angry. Her mother was so impossible at times!

Mary Jane suddenly reappeared in the kitchen. Without saying a word, she helped herself to a handful of fresh baked oatmeal cookies cooling on the table and walked away.

Mary Ann was concerned. Her oldest daughter had always been a bit of a handful but recently it seemed to be getting worse. Mary Jane should not have taken the cookies without first asking permission, but Mary Ann let it go.

She made a mental note to herself.

I need to do a better job of getting through to that girl.

Chapter Six: Othello in a Police Court

Stapleton was abuzz with excitement in the dark winter months of 1881. The annual charity ball to benefit the S.R. Smith Infirmary was to be held the weekend before Washington's Birthday, and all fancy ladies and gents were busy preparing to attend.

The local papers fed into the genteel society's eager anticipation of the event by publishing advance details. They predicted the ball to be the premier social event of the season. Ticket sales were brisk, and the list of those invited constituted a *Who's Who* of the most highly esteemed professionals, businessmen, and socialites within the county. George William Curtis, arguably Staten Island's most famous citizen, was lending time to the event. A nationally recognized author and lecturer who was the chief editor of *Harper's Weekly* and served as Chair of Ulysses S. Grant's Commission for Civil Servant Reform, Curtis graciously carved time out from his busy schedule to chair the Reception Committee.

Over four hundred women from prominent Staten Island families were patronesses of the event. A grand march was planned, followed by a scrumptious supper held at Stapleton's German Club Rooms at the corner of Richmond and Prospect Streets. The main ballroom would be decorated like a forest with Grafulla's Seventh Regiment Band on hand to entertain guests throughout the afternoon upon a stage lined with lavish palms, ferns and camellias in bloom.

It was a lot of hoopla, but all for a worthy cause. The S. R. Smith Infirmary was Staten Island's first real hospital. It was opened during the Civil War and named after a well-respected local physician, the late Dr. Samuel Russell Smith. Risking his own health many times over, Smith courageously served the people of Tompkinsville and Stapleton during the dark days of the Quarantine's operation. Following in the example of Dr. Smith, medical care at the Infirmary was provided to all, regardless of the ability to pay.

It was all the talk downtown, but certainly not big in the minds of those living and working in Rocky Hollow. They were just plain folk trying to get by and way too busy to take notice. Mary Ann was one of the few citizens of Rocky Hollow who could afford the price of a ticket, but she too took no interest in the event. Though she handled many fine gowns in her time as a washerwoman for the rich people on the hill, it had never inspired her to wear one herself. Mary Ann was not one for fancy hats, fine gowns, or jewelry.

Pish! Posh! she thought. *Let the well-to-do have their hoity-toity occasions. I'm content to roll up the sleeves and deliver my own brand of sensible charity.*

When Washington's Birthday weekend finally arrived, curious locals gathered midday at the side of the road to watch the procession of horse drawn carriages winding their way over the rutted bumpy roads to Prospect Street. And, as a strange coincidence, at the same time of day Mary Ann was also in route, but to a distinctly different Stapleton destination.

While Staten Island's elite made merry at their festive event, Mary Ann had serious business to attend to just a few blocks away.

BANG!

She threw open the door of the Richmond County Police Headquarters on Beach Street and stomped up to the front desk. Mary Ann raised her voice deliberately so that every officer within earshot could hear. She asked for the paperwork to file a complaint. Mary Ann inked her pen and scratched out information on the required form. Then she shoved it back to the officer at the desk and sniped at him.

Pish! Posh! Get to it! And, she stormed out the door.

Back home, the Bascombe household was in an uproar. A

most terrible thing had happened. Mary Jane Richards, Mary Ann's beautiful dark eyed eldest daughter, had been abducted at gunpoint!

Mary Ann fumed but was not panicked. Mary Jane's kidnapping had not been at the hands of a stranger. Mary Ann knew the culprit all too well. It was the fast talking, charming but good for who knows what Denis O'Leary! That hooligan just would not leave her young and impressionable daughter alone!

Mary Ann went to the police station as a last resort. After the abduction, she had first taken to the streets with her trademark stout walking stick in hand, seeking to track down the whereabouts of Mary Jane. Eventually, she caught up to O'Leary, but her daughter was not with him. When Mary Ann demanded Mary Jane's safe return, O'Leary laughed and adamantly refused. That was when she turned matters over to the police.

With the complaint on file, Richmond County patrolmen hit the streets in search of the young man. Denis was easy to catch. He was the younger brother of the well liked, fellow police officer Cady O'Leary. The officers tracked him down, arrested him, and took Denis down to the police station. There he would sit in the backroom jail cell until the charges against him were heard in court the following Tuesday, George Washington's Birthday.

Mary Ann grumbled when she learned that David B. McCullough was assigned to the case. McCullough was a relatively new man on the Stapleton bench. He had been a Justice of the Peace for only a year while all the other Middletown justices had decades of experience. Though functional at his work, Mary Ann felt he was still a bit wet between the ears. She weighed the pros and cons of a rookie justice hearing her complaint. Then, she tried her best to put matters out of her head until Tuesday.

For McCullough, being a man of the court was a distinct change of occupation. His family had once owned the McCullough Shot and Lead Works located in New York City and Stapleton. During the Civil War, the company was a major supplier of lead buckshot and round balls to the Union Army. Everyone in Stapleton knew the lead works because of the tall company tower which loomed over the waterfront. Atop the tower was a huge cauldron where lead was heated until it reached its molten temperature and then released through a sieve. As the metal fell, it solidified into small lead balls which landed inside a large water basin to cool. After the Civil War, the company suffered as the demand for ammunition radically declined. Eventually, the business was shuttered and McCullough had to go looking for other work.

McCullough was voted into office in part because of the name recognition. After he took his seat on the bench, many citizens came up to tell him how much they missed his family's business. It had been replaced by a factory which manufactured cream of tartar. Now, instead of dropping lead, the tower spewed noxious odors into the air. The smell was bad – so putrid - that a group of angry Stapleton residents threatened to burn the tower down in the middle of the night, just as the Quarantine had been torched earlier in the century.

The justice held a respected government post, yet he had few perks of office. McCullough's work quarters were far from commodious. As he had the least seniority, McCullough was assigned the overflow court cases held in the newly designated police court annex building on Broad Street. It was a block or two down the road from the Bascombe residence. Court was held in a small but functional twelve square foot space. The room's walls were bare other than some deal board pigeon holes, an old order of sale, and an auctioneer's flag. The only permanent furniture in the room was the desk and chair he used and a wooden bench for jury seating. A railing separated his desk from the rest of the room. Lawyers, when called upon to be present, borrowed chairs from one of the two beer saloons which bordered the building on either side.

Washington's Birthday came and the justice arrived early at the annex to get the fire going in the wood stove behind his desk. As the room began to warm up, McCullough sat down to look over the schedule of complaints.

Oh, sweet tarnation! That presumptuous Mary Ann Bascombe was coming to court today with a complaint against her daughter's sweetheart!

McCullough leaned back into his chair. It was going to a real hum dinger of a day. He promised right there and then to reward himself with a tall frothy mug from the saloon next door before travelling home for supper.

Over the past year, McCullough had gained a great deal of experience rendering decisions in strange and unusual court proceedings. Now, whenever a case before him seemed trivial or mundane, McCullough found his mind drifting back to some of the more outrageous spectacles of the past. Once he heard a complaint against a vagrant who was camping out on the ferry. The man resisted arrest, adamantly defending his right to do whatever he wished because of the claim that he was German royalty. McCullough found that case quite amusing. He ruled to grant His Highness an extended stay at the Richmond County Almshouse.

Some people were thoughtless or even vicious, especially when it came to animals. In a year, he had presided over a series of complaints involving animal cruelty. Some were cut and dry judgments, such as the case where a man proudly mutilated a live fox at the end of a hunt by cutting off its tail for a souvenir. Others were more complicated affairs, such as the case of Mr. Brock's dog.

Herman Brock was a man of German background who owned a canine which was a big and powerful cross between a St. Bernard and Newfoundland. Brock was training the animal as a rescue dog. One day while training on the Middletown ferry, he pushed the dog overboard. The dog was lucky. He narrowly escaped serious injury after falling into the direct path of another vessel. Brock was less lucky, though, because the dog lovers aboard the ferry disembarked and went straight to the police station to have him arrested.

Those who passed near the court annex certainly got an eyeful and earful on Brock's day in court. The Society for Prevention of Cruelty to Animals summoned an angry throng of men and dogs to stand outside the building and show their disapproval of Brock's actions. The crowd was large and noisy and would not leave the premises. When the doors of the courtroom opened, both men and dogs pushed their way in. Those who could not get a spot to stand remained outside on the street with their yipping, yapping animals.

Brock had a lawyer who demanded a jury. McCullough complied with the uncommon request after collecting an additional $1.50 administrative fee. He directed the police in attendance to go out and round up six true and good men. After a brief time, they returned with the prescribed number of adult males. McCullough did not say anything, but it seemed to him that the volunteers would have preferred hearing the case in the saloon next door rather than his courtroom. The men made themselves comfortable on the jury bench by opening up a few pouches of tobacco. They listened to the testimony, all the while chomping, dribbling saliva, and taking turns aiming for the spittoon in the corner of the room.

Brock's trial was long and tedious and tested McCullough's patience. After the last witness testified, the entire courtroom including the justice adjourned to the saloon next door to wet their whistle while waiting for the jury to deliberate on their verdict. Everyone, including McCullough, downed a few ales. Some time passed, and then there was the signal from the court officers to return. The jury vote was 5 -1 to convict, but it had to be unanimous. McCullough sent them back to try again for a verdict. More mugs of ale were consumed. Hours later, the jury returned with the same result.

McCullough cursed under his breath. He started to explain to those present that there would have to be a new trial but a loud chatter filled the room. McCullough banged his gavel repeatedly on the desk. Someone in the court shouted out he thought the justice should take Brock's dog home overnight to keep him safe. McCullough, fatigued and a bit taken over by the ale he had consumed, got annoyed. He forgot he was a politician who might want to run for re-election someday. With a repugnant look on his face, McCullough fired back. If the dog was left with him, he'd find someone to shoot him. His comments filled the room with a mix of angry cries and belly laughter.

McCullough wanted this trial over soon with and got his wish. Someone shouted that he'd take the animal home because he was far less harmful than the prosecuting attorney. The lawyer, just as fed up as McCullough, turned and looked daggers at the crowd. Then, without a word, he packed his bags and left the room. Case dismissed!

Mary Ann may have thought he was inexperienced, but in fact McCullough was quite good at his job. He had learned through mistakes how to quickly sort through the frivolous and bizarre charges and move along legal proceedings. Managing behaviors was a major part of his work. Hostility was commonplace in his courtroom and often linked to excess lager consumption. With three large breweries and a multitude of beer gardens and saloons in town, wrong doers were often dragged in off the street and into the court annex by the police before the alcohol sufficiently passed out of their systems. McCullough found out by trial and error that the best solution in such cases was to send the alleged offenders off to jail and let them sleep off their intoxication. It was safer and more productive than attempting to settle a dispute with folks in a highly agitated state.

Beer, quite thankfully, did not seem to play a part in the complaints set before him today. McCullough shuffled his papers, and then looked up to see that the court officers had arrived. They were stationed at the entrance, waiting for a sign from him to open the doors to the public.

He waved to the men and they swung open the doors. It was a bitterly cold morning, and the crowd that had been shivering outside rushed in to fill the room. Mary Ann Bascombe elbowed her way up to the front of the room and positioned herself as close as she could possibly get to McCullough without leaping over the railing. He was careful not to look directly at her, but from the corner of his eye he could spy the scarlet rising up from her neck. She seemed about ready to catapult through the roof.

Court was called into session. McCullough instructed the police officers to bring in the prisoner. Officer Rooney went outside and returned with Denis O'Leary. He was a handsome, young, six-foot tall Hibernian who was quite a popular fellow around town. Appearing quite unabashed, O'Leary grinned as he passed those in the room who gawped at him. Mary Ann looked scornfully as he walked past her, but O'Leary seemed not to notice. He stopped at the railing. Officer Rooney moved in quickly from behind to stand squarely between the plaintiff and defendant.

That the alleged kidnapper was related to a police officer was of no surprise to McCullough. Another thing he had learned in his first year as a justice was that anyone, including politicians and local government officials, was capable of breaking the law. He recalled the former Richmond County Treasurer who had been arraigned before him for attempting to load his boat with beach sand belonging to a South Beach woman. And, the prominent politician and member of the Richmond County Democratic Committee who was so clearly in violation of the alcohol tax ordinances as a liquor store owner that McCullough was forced to send the case to a higher county court.

McCullough had seen a variety of complaints filed against employees of the Richmond County Sheriff's Office and Richmond County Police. The chief clerk of the police department had recently come before him. He had been accused of felonious assault upon an Italian organ grinder and his wife. The unlucky *paisanos* missed the last ferry back to New York and made the unfortunate mistake of camping out on the front stoop of the clerk's home overnight. The clerk attacked the couple because he could not get them to stop cranking out their blasted tinny music. Thankfully, McCullough mused, the monkey had been spared from harm and no animal advocates showed up for the hearing.

Focus on the matters at hand, David! Focus!

McCullough derailed his train of thought and got back to the events of the day. He asked O'Leary to give his side of the story. The young man took the request as permission to take a few steps closer to the justice. He looked McCullough straight in the eye and began to speak. His speech was fluid and without hesitation.

According to O'Leary, the night in question had been a thoroughly pleasant winter evening in Rocky Hollow. He went out for a walk along Broad Street in the vicinity of the Bascombe residence. His intention was to pay a social call to his sweetheart,

Mary Jane Richards. As O'Leary approached her front door, he heard a fierce commotion coming from inside the house.

Yes, it was true. He busted in unannounced, but it was only because of the dreadful screams coming from the residence!

O'Leary said he was shocked by the sight when he entered the kitchen. There was Mrs. Bascombe, holding tight onto her daughter's leg. She was forcing a shoe which was way too tight onto Mary Jane's foot, causing her terrible distress. Mary Jane was in tears pleading for mercy as her cruel mother continued to inflict pain. O'Leary was crazed. He did not stop to think. He grabbed Mary Jane by the arm, pulled the girl to her feet, and led her out of the house. Then he helped find her a safe place to hide.

The young man asked Justice McCullough for leniency. He had done nothing wrong. He had merely taken steps to rescue his sweetheart from the torments brought upon by her own mother! He turned to his audience in the courtroom and reminded everyone that Mary Jane was of consenting age and left home of her own accord. Also, that it was at Mary Jane's own request that her whereabouts were a secret.

Denis O'Leary's colorful details enlightened and entertained all the family, friends, and curious onlookers who were crowded into the court annex. It was a powerful defense. O'Leary concluded his testimony by emphasizing his undying affection for Mary Jane. He vowed he would marry the girl despite any hazards.

What passion and conviction! What love he shows for his girl!

Voices in the crowd egged him on to continue, but Justice McCullough had heard enough. He instructed those in the room to be silent. Then, he directed O'Leary to step off to the side and asked his accuser to please rise and come front and center.

A highly agitated Mary Ann stepped forward. She grabbed onto the railing in front of McCullough's desk to steady herself. Throughout O'Leary's testimony she looked ready to pounce upon him. All knew she itched to serve him justice at the end of her stout stick rather than inside this courtroom.

At last, she thought. *MY chance to tell the TRUTH!*

Mary Ann took in one large, deep calming breath. Then, she

started in on a most vociferous condemnation of the affair. Mary Ann had never much approved of the courtship between O'Leary and her daughter. Mary Ann was proud to be a self-made woman and hoped to inspire a similar degree of accomplishment in her daughters. But, if this was not to be, then it was her duty and responsibility as their mother to help her daughters find men who would provide well for them. Mary Jane worked at the paper mill and her wages were meager at best. O'Leary was a nice enough lad, but there was no way he could provide sufficiently for Mary Jane. Over the past few months, she tried her best to stop Mary Jane from seeing O'Leary, even to the point of making persuasive arguments out of soapsuds, boot jacks, and broom handles. But *Pish! Posh!* Nothing seemed to be working.

After laying the groundwork for her story, Mary Ann launched into a detailed account of the night in question. Mary Ann and stepfather James had been talking to the girl about the perils of marrying without parental consent. She reacted by pouting and insisting that she and O'Leary would be married no matter what her mother thought. During their talk, Mary Jane asked her mother to assist with her footwear. Mary Ann picked up the girl's shoe and started to place it on her foot, but it must have been more or less uncomfortable because Mary Jane gave out a little cry.

While making the adjustments for her daughter, the door suddenly flew open, and the O'Leary boy burst into the house. *HER home!* O'Leary ran to Mary Jane's side and seized the wrist of her daughter with one hand. Then he pulled a pistol out of his jacket pocket. O'Leary pointed the gun straight at her husband's head and swore that all would see the inside of James's scrambled brains if anyone dared to stop him. Mary Ann and her husband kept silent. They were no fools. They allowed the pair to take off into the night.

Mary Ann spoke slowly and deliberately, using inflections and hand gestures to dramatize her testimony. She was an expert at winning the sympathy of a crowd, but the one she really needed to impress sat on the other side of the railing with a gavel in his hand.

Breaking into my home, threatening my husband with a gun, and abducting my eldest daughter! Why, this is criminal behavior of the highest degree! Justice McCullough, you must deal with this O'Leary boy severely!

Mary Ann demanded that O'Leary be punished but not before forcing the young man to return Mary Jane back to the custody of her mother.

McCullough, who had been working hard to remain deadpan while listening to both of the melodramatic presentations, now turned back to face the defendant. He asked O'Leary to respond to Mary Ann's request. Would he produce her daughter?

Yes, he told the justice. He'd tell him where to find Mary Jane if a single condition was met. Mary Jane needed to be allowed to speak and act according to her free will. McCullough mulled it over. Since the girl was of legal age he answered that this was a fair proposition.

Mary Ann winced at the notion of O'Leary being treated so evenhanded. She put up a protest. It was not easy, but McCullough got the irate woman to calm down and accept the terms so that the hearing could proceed.

O'Leary leaned over and whispered into the ear of one of the court officers. The officer went off, and soon after, Mary Jane sashayed into the courtroom on his arm. Mary Ann's daughter was, by far, one of the prettiest girls in Rocky Hollow. She had dark eyes, rosy cheeks, and a bright smile that turned heads wherever she went. Most of the men in the room couldn't take their eyes off her, but McCullough was not much impressed. These shenanigans had taken up way too much time of his valuable time.

The justice cut to the chase. He turned to O'Leary and asked if he loved this woman to which the lad replied that he surely did. McCullough next turned to Mary Jane and asked if she loved O'Leary. Her response was measured but the impish look gave it all away.

"Well, I don't dislike him," she answered.[1]

McCullough then proposed that he marry them right then and there.

NO! NO! NO! Mary Ann yelped. *What in blazes are you thinking McCullough?*

Mary Ann may have been struck down with apoplexy in the very spot where she stood if not for what happened next. The lad who so adamantly declared his love for Mary Jane did not answer right away. He hesitated, and when he did reply it surprised everyone.

Denis O'Leary thought it proper that they should wait to be wed in a Catholic church.

Good gosh! Somehow, for the first time since the start of this fiasco, Mary Ann and the young Hibernian were in agreement! Mary Ann was relieved but her daughter felt quite the opposite. She glared at her beau. Why say this? Had he contracted a sudden case of cold feet?

O'Leary's response started up a whole new round of arguments back and forth between Mary Ann, Mary Jane, and O'Leary. McCullough sat back and let it go on for a while, hoping the three of them would come up with some sort of resolution on their own. It was not to be, however, so he took back control of the proceedings. The justice gave O'Leary an ultimatum.

Denis. Get married or go to jail. Choose.

O'Leary was boxed into a corner. Over the very loud protests of his soon to be mother-in-law, the brawny Hibernian opted for wedding bands over jail bonds. They were married by Justice McCullough, who ended the proceedings by boasting that he had given the couple a most memorable Washington's Birthday present.

McCullough dismissed Mary Ann, Mary Jane, and her new husband from his courtroom, well aware that their argument would continue out into the street. This was of no concern to McCullough. He was behind schedule and had others waiting in the wings to air their complaints. Another thing he had learned in the past year was that pleasing both parties in a Stapleton court decision was more of an exception than a rule.

The story of the Washington's Birthday marriage was fodder for the New York dailies, but the reporters lost track of what happened next. After they walked out of the courtroom, Mary Ann put her foot down. Under no circumstances would she allow her daughter to go off with O'Leary. She insisted that Mary Jane remain home until the marriage could be ratified by a priest.

Putting her foot down proved to be a wise move. O'Leary was forbidden to visit Mary Jane at the Bascombe home and time and distance did not make hearts grow fonder. He never followed through with a priest. The church wedding never occurred. Over time, the entire Richards-O'Leary union became shrouded in mystery. No one was sure whether Mary Jane and her young Hibernian even consummated the marriage. An estrangement ensued and they parted ways.

McCullough was somewhat disappointed to learn that his spur of the moment marital union did not take. He considered the act one of his finer moments in this often unrewarding line of work. When it came time, he thought long and hard whether to seek a second term on the police court bench. There were some good moments, but also dark episodes, such as his encounters with Mickey the Duck.

Dang that thug!

David McCullough would be haunted by the memory of that man so long as he lived. What a disrespectful delinquent! Mickey's disregard for McCullough's authority was so egregious it was actually written up in the *National Police Gazette*.

Mickey threw open the door to McCullough's courtroom one day while court was in session. In a highly inebriated state, he stomped up to the railing, stared the justice straight in the eye, and yelled at him to get off his *binch* so he could give him a *damn strapping*. Then he threw off his coat and started whooping it up all over the front of the room doing a sort of war dance.

McCullough ordered the two brawny police officers present to remove Mickey from the room. Mickey resisted, and a free for all ensued. McCullough watched in horror as an entangled mass of human arms, legs, and torsos flailed about the room. They knocked a lawyer flat to the ground. Then, they knocked down the railing in front of McCullough. While trying to wrestle Mickey to the exit all three stumbled and fell through the doorway out onto the street. The officers scrambled and got back up first. They barricaded the door so Mickey could not reenter but he continued to disrupt the proceedings. The building had low windows, so the Duck had access to the eyes and ears of everyone in the court annex. He darted from window to window, continuing to curse and threaten. McCullough was disgusted. He ordered the officers to go back outside, arrest the Duck, and throw him in jail without bail.

Later in the day, a contingent of Mickey's friends came to court, begging the justice to let Mickey apologize after the alcohol dissipated from his system. He agreed, and the next day Mickey returned after his release from jail.

Mickey stepped up to the damaged railing and sheepishly asked if this was where he should stand to apologize. McCullough replied yes, and then Mickey began to rant once again. Just to make things clear, Mickey said, he apologized to no one except God. And, sometimes, not even to HIM!

Dear God! Mickey's taunts were worse when he was sober!

The gavel came down. The Duck was fined $10 and ordered to leave. Mickey started to go but as he stepped into the doorway, he turned back. Mickey just couldn't resist firing off one last shot at the Justice. He called McCullough a sucker and no good and yelled out that he'd never be reelected.

McCullough's decision to step down from the bench was influenced in part by the encounters he'd had with cretins like Mickey the Duck. The family business was gone, but surely he could find a better way to make a living.

Meanwhile, back at the Bascombe residence, Mary Jane was quite melancholic over the way things turned out with Denis. She resumed work in the paper factory and settled back into the daily routines at the overcrowded house on the corner of Broad and Gordon Streets. The police court annex was just a few minutes down the road and Mary Jane was forced to pass it every time she went downtown. She grew to deeply resent the wooden structure as it was a constant reminder of her uncertain status in life. Mary Jane complained but drew limited sympathy from her mother, who repeatedly instructed her to forget the past and make the best of what she had.

The fact that Mary Ann downplayed her daughter's predicament came as no surprise to Mary Jane. For her entire life it seemed that she had been needing but not receiving her mother's full attention. Mary Ann had so very little time for her when she was a small child. They were very poor and her mother was forced to work long hard hours to pay the bills. Now she was remarried and they had money but her mother's growing obsession with things outside the home like real estate and politics took up almost all of Mary Ann's free time. Mary Jane was always being told by her mother to look after her younger siblings. Well that was fine and dandy, but didn't Mother see that sometimes she also needed a small dose of care and concern!

Mary Ann's eldest daughter yearned to find someone who would pay full attention to her. Someone she could confide in and trust to share her most inner feelings. Eventually, she did find that person, but by that time the relationship with her mother was so strained that Mary Jane felt no obligation to inform her.

A few Washington Birthdays passed. One day, Mary Ann was out supervising her laborers at a handsome new brick home she was building. The lady was in high spirits that afternoon. Things had certainly been going her way of late. Four of her children had been cured of the measles. Town officials had agreed to lower taxes on her properties. And, the construction of this house was progressing way ahead of schedule.

It was rent collection day and the pockets of Mary Ann's long skirt jingled with the sounds of the coins as she walked the property with her foreman. Mary Ann was all smiles and laughter until a messenger arrived and walked up to whisper in her ear. All who were present witnessed a ghastly change come over Mary Ann's face. She went chalky white at first, but then as the messenger continued to speak, her cheeks and neck flushed deep scarlet. She excused herself from the men and hurried home.

Mary Jane Richards (or was it O'Leary?) had run away from home again but this time it was surreptitiously. Whether her daughter had been trying to show a degree of sympathy to her mother or was just trying to make it easier on herself was not clear. There had been no hint of what she planned to do at the breakfast table that morning. Mary Jane engaged in the usual family chitchat while everyone ate. Then she volunteered to wash and put away the dishes. Mary Ann bid her daughter a good day as Mary Jane calmly waved back. She waited until her mother was gone. Then she made her escape.

Mary Ann interrogated the neighbors one by one and found out who assisted Mary Jane's departure by moving a substantial amount of clothing out of the Bascombe home. She knew her daughter's accomplice fairly well. He was a young bricklayer and plasterer named Harry Marshall who lived on Gordon Street. Mary Ann set out on foot with her stout stick in hand to track him down.

Bosh! Spooney! Wait until I catch up with you Harry Marshall. I'll be most happy to back up any words with my stick!

Harry was at work high up on a ladder just a few blocks away. When she found him she called out, demanding that he tell her what was going on. She was loud and livid but Harry refused to raise his voice to match hers. He told her very plainly that he had been expecting her and would be happy to answer all her questions. Harry climbed down from the ladder so that they could stand eye to eye. His soft and respectful demeanor worked. Mary Ann stopped ranting and calmed down. She let him explain the situation.

Yes, he admitted. Harry helped Mary Jane move out because she asked for his assistance. Her daughter was taking action because she needed to move on and nullify her marriage to be free of the past. Harry reassured Mary Ann that he loved her daughter very much. He pledged to ask for Mary Jane's hand in marriage in proper fashion as soon as she was legally able. Harry vowed to be a hard worker who would provide well for his wife and family.

Mary Ann scrutinized Harry's face as he spoke and felt a bit guilty. Mary Ann had been overlooking her daughter's needs for way too long. Harry Marshall appeared to be a mature and responsible young man who truly cared for Mary Jane. These circumstances were not a repeat of what had been experienced four years earlier.

When the city reporters got wind of what happened, they set out to track down Mary Jane. They found her living in rented rooms in New York City and asked her for an interview. The reporters gleaned from her responses that the rift between the girl and her mother had not healed well over the past few years. Mary Jane informed them she ran away because she could not trust her mother to approve of her actions.

She needed to find out if she *"was a wife or maid"*, adding *"and as my mother won't help me, I'll find out myself."*[2]

Mary Ann stayed in hiding until her first marriage was annulled. Then she married Harry in a church ceremony in front of her entire family. After the wedding, the relationship between Mary Jane and her mother softened. Mary Ann offered and the couple agreed to move into one of her homes two blocks away from the Bascombe residence. Mary Jane and Harry settled down to a quiet life in Rocky Hollow. Harry lived up to his word as a good provider. Mary Jane would end up having eight children, just like her mother.

On Saturdays, Mary Ann made it a practice to go to confession. After saying penance, Mary Ann then prayed for everyone she cared about, both living and dead. When it came time to pray for Mary Jane, she was always grateful that her daughter had been given a fresh start in life and thankful for God's help in repairing the wounds they suffered as mother and daughter. Mary Ann asked God to grant Mary Jane the motherly wisdom she had lacked. It was her sincerest wish that Mary Jane would do a better job handling the trials of her own daughters someday.

CHAPTER SEVEN: SHANTYTOWN SENSATION

"*One of the most useful women of the period lives on Staten Island, and her name is Mrs. Bascombe. It is recorded of her that by the sheer force of her perseverance, exerted by means of her tongue, she has forced the corporate authority to improve the drainage in the vicinity of her property, forced the assessors to reduce her taxes and compelled the courts to protect her rights. It is a little late now, but what a woman Mrs. Bascombe would have been to argue with the Board of Health on the subject of street cleaning."[1]*

It was a favorite time of day in the Bascombe home. The children ran about performing their assigned duties. Chairs were dragged from all over the house to set around the crowded table. The older boys went out in the barn to milk the cow and fill pitchers. The older girls grabbed towels to remove hot biscuits from the warmer on top of the oven, then got cups and dishes out of the cupboard for the main meal. The youngest children set the table.

Supper was ready. They were all famished, so it was a quick thank you to God for the blessings they were about to receive followed by a mad rush to pass around the platters of meat and potatoes.

As busy as she was all day, Mary Ann made it a point to get home in time for supper. She looked forward to the nightly jibber jabber of conversation. Typically, there was talk of the weather or the children's day at school or who had been spotted downtown. On this chilly winter night, however, the topic of supper conversation was unique and of interest to each family member.

There was a hot new scandal in Rocky Hollow and not of the typical kind, for this one did not involve women, beer, or politics. Tonight, the topic of discussion was murder! A neighbor was going on trial tomorrow, accused of butchering one of the Rocky Hollow's most popular inhabitants.

Bridget Fitzgerald, the alleged murderess, lived only a few blocks away on Patten Street. Billy McKow, her victim, resided in Rocky Hollow but spent most of his time high up in the hills overlooking Stapleton. Mary Ann started the conversation off by saying she felt sorry for poor Bridget. She was a naturally high-strung woman who in this case let frustration get the best of her. The children chimed in that they heard her yell at Billy many times in the past and were unanimous in condemning her cruelty. James said it was plain to see the ole gal had gone bonkers and should be sent to a rest home. All agreed that Bridget would have fared much better if only she had gone to the police and filed a complaint.

Mary Emma innocently asked if anyone was going downtown in the morning to witness the proceedings, but before any of them could open their mouths to respond Mary Ann adamantly *Pish! Poshed!* the notion. She cautioned her eldest children not to dilly dally about and risk their bosses docking them a day's pay. Then, she warned her youngest children that she better not hear from any of their teachers that they skipped school to hang out at Town Hall. Her words brought about some protests, but in the end, they reluctantly agreed. Mary Ann could outlast them all in any verbal contest, so it was just easier to give in.

The next morning James was walking down Canal Street on his way to work when he saw a gathering crowd ahead.

Blimey, James thought as he kept moving closer. *That's quite a crowd out to crucify poor Bridget!*

When he reached the corner of Canal and Wright Street, James did not stop. He grinned and waved to a few of his tavern pals and then turned a sharp left to continue on his way.

Joseph Bascombe, Mary Ann's youngest son, took a slight detour from his regular morning route. He hid himself behind a nearby tree to gawk at the crowd of neighbors before heading over to the Broad Street School. It was a pretty exciting event, and the lad seriously toyed with the notion of disobeying his mother by playing hooky to watch the proceedings. Then, Joseph imagined the look on his mother's face and how she might pick up her stout stick and use it on him after finding out what he had done. It convinced him to get moving.

John Bascombe ended up being the only family member willing to risk the wrath of his mother. A laborer by trade, he was between jobs with free time on his hands. John told no one his plans. He left the house last in the morning so that no one could see in which direction he was headed. Then he made haste down to Village Hall.

It was a nippy December morning. John joined up with a few cronies who were milling about in the cold. They were all anticipating a mad rush which would take place as soon as the doors to the municipal building were opened. A few folks were there out of curiosity like John but many more were present to demonstrate their disgust. John and his friends huddled together and made a bit of chit chat to pass the time.

Well, why was it that none of us knew we've been livin' down the road from a disturbed woman all these years? Good gosh Almighty!

After what seemed a very long time, the doors of Village Hall swung open. Two Richmond County police officers emerged and positioned themselves at the entrance to prevent a stampede. Men and women lined up and elbowed each other trying to squeeze through the central hallway to get into the main court room. John and a few lucky others were able to grab seats. The rest of the crowd stood, taking up every available space around the perimeter of the room. No one complained. The room was cool, but the body heat generated by the large crowd would soon warm the air temperature to satisfactory comfort.

BANG! BANG! BANG!

Justice Michael McGuire picked up his gavel and leveled it loudly and repeatedly against the top of his wooden desk. McGuire was the unlucky justice assigned to the hearing and wanted to get the circus side show over with as soon as possible.

McGuire asked Constable Goggin to bring in the accused. Goggin left and reentered with Bridget Fitzgerald. The poor soul looked quite disheveled. She sat down and looked around the room with a confounded look on her face.

John leaned back in his seat and shook his head. It seemed that Bridget still had not figured out what the fuss was about. She had seriously misjudged the community's deep affection for Billy. To Bridget, Billy McKow was merely a goat, but to the rest of the neighborhood he was their unofficial mascot. He occupied a special place in the hearts of just about everyone who lived in Rocky Hollow.

Billy was John McKow's pride and joy. He was a strikingly attractive creature who had been born in Harlem and brought to Stapleton as a small kid. From an early age, Billy sported a fine beard which as he grew matured into a set of long blonde whiskers. His frame was large with a colossal set of horns which along with his whiskers provided him a most authoritative presence.

Billy was a part of the everyday landscape of Rocky Hollow. He could often be seen poised majestically atop the hills overlooking the neighborhood. As he stood there motionless, Billy may have been mistaken for a statue if not for the occasional gusts of wind which blew at him and gently feathered his whiskers. Billy's countenance was so impressive that he had been sketched by a number of local artists. Why, his likeness had even been under consideration as the logo for one of the local beer labels.

Despite his imposing features, Billy was a kind and friendly goat. He showed no unprovoked malice towards other living things. Billy enjoyed a carefree existence in Rocky Hollow, grazing contentedly upon the tin cans and available refuse he found in his travels. He knew every rock, hill, nook, and cranny of the neighborhood. Billy was given carte blanche access by his human neighbors to wander at will through the streets and yards. He frequented the interior of his neighbors' homes if they ever happened to leave their front or rear doors open. At times, Billy descended from Rocky Hollow into downtown Stapleton to fill his stomach with the trash left over from a carnival or street rally.

Billy commonly disappeared for days a time and returned fat and dyspeptic so that he would have to prostrate himself until feeling better.

Sadly, it was the combination of Billy's freedom to roam and appetite for things other than tomato cans which led to his ultimate demise. One day, looking down from his perch high up in the hills, Billy spotted Bridget's linens on her clothes line and meandered down to take a look. Ah, but her clothes blew oh so tastily in the breeze! Billy began to regularly stalk the Fitzgerald laundry and before long, he was addicted. He could not resist the temptation. Whenever Bridget hung her garments out on her clothes line, Billy jumped the back fence of the property to enjoy a meal.

Bridget grew to despise the white-haired animal. Her days were spent sitting guard with a broom to chase him whenever her wash was on the line. Her nights were spent dreaming of ways to shoo him away. One day after yet another afternoon raid, Bridget snapped. Her hatred for the animal drove the otherwise demure housewife to pure madness. She announced publicly to all within earshot that she was looking for an opportunity to put an end to the goat.

Justice McGuire called John McKow to the witness table. He took an oath and then launched into his testimony. After the Christmas holiday, McKow realized he had not seen Billy in many days. He went outside and called for him. The goat did not come home. McKow searched the streets and enlisted a few small boys in the neighborhood to help him look. After the search failed to locate Billy he contacted the Richmond County Police. Bridget immediately emerged as their prime suspect, since she had so openly voiced her hatred for the creature.

McKow received a tip that Billy was being held at the Fitzgerald home, so he walked over to Patton Street and pried opened Bridget's barn door. McKow was sickened by the gruesome find. His beloved goat had been skinned and was hanging by his hind legs from one of the rafters! McKow scoured the neighborhood until he tracked Bridget down. He pumped her for answers, using every ounce of self-control he could muster so as not to physically lunge at her. Bridget tried to play dumb about Billy's death, but McKow did not believe her. He flagged down a police officer and had her arrested.

There were a few key testimonies at the trial. Two black men from Rocky Hollow were sworn in first. They told the justice that they were walking past the Fitzgerald home when Bridget stopped them and asked for help. Bridget said she had bought Billy and was trying to lead him into her barn. Billy was putting up a fierce resistance to being tied up, rearing up on his hind legs and plunging at her with his horns. They agreed to assist and with some effort managed to drag the goat into the barn.

An Italian was sworn in next. He said that Bridget approached him about killing Billy and they struck a deal. He would slay the goat and she would pay him 50 cents along with part of the carcass for dinner. The man performed the dirty deed with his stiletto but said that Bridget reneged on payment. In broken English, the man said that since she did not live up to her end of the bargain, he had no problem testifying against her.

John looked around him at all the angry faces in the room. Although he did not condone the butchering of someone else's animal, he was not about to join in the uproar over Billy's death. John agreed with the views of his mother, who felt that the neighbors were missing the point in their hysteria. Animals who ran loose caused problems and not only because they consumed the neighbors' wash. The cows, pigs, dogs and goats who roamed the streets of Rocky Hollow were just as dangerous. They should not be allowed to block the path of vehicles or spread infectious contagions from their animal droppings throughout the community. Why, there was a new century approaching, she often said, and Rocky Hollow must change with the times!

Justice McGuire, born and raised in the neighborhood, tried to maintain a non-committal look on his face. He next called Bridget to rise and stand before him and give her version of what took place.

Bridget did her best to glean some sympathy from the justice and hostile crowd. Bridget told them she tried everything she could think of to keep the offender away. She changed her laundering habits by hanging the clothes out at odd hours of the day. She put out trash for Billy to feast on instead of her garments. The poor troubled woman even went to see Billy's owner, John McKow, and repeatedly asked to have him tied up. She kept a list of her damages and as an example shared with Mr. McKow that on one day alone Billy consumed a bonne bouche of three shirts, a nightgown, half a dozen neckties, some cuffs and collars, a nightcap and napkins off her line! McKow dismissed her time and time again, ignoring her complaints and refusing to compensate Bridget for Billy's meals.

Bridget adamantly insisted she did not harm the goat. The two black men that testified stole the goat. The Italian lied when he said she asked him to kill Billy. The only thing Bridget admitted was that she paid $1.75 for his dead carcass.

McGuire felt that Bridget was guilty, but he hesitated in his ruling. McGuire was a well-known popular public servant who was also a savvy politician. He had to be sure that it was in his best interests to throw a woman into jail. He scanned the angry faces in the room. He listened to their taunts. The crowd seemed unanimous, urging him to throw the book at Bridget.

First Billy, and then who next McGuire?

Yer a home boy Michael! Do what's right for yer citizens!

Shuro McGuire, but there must be justice for Billy!

McGuire straightened up in his chair and steadied himself so there was no hint of emotion on his face. McGuire knew it was political poison to ignore this much public opinion. Thus, with a look of great solemnity, he leveled his gavel for silence in the room and promptly sentenced Bridget the goat assassin to fifty-nine days at the Richmond County Jail.

McGuire gave the crowd what they wanted. They cheered and filed out of the court room, anxious to bring the news back to Rocky Hollow.

Did'ye hear? Did'ye hear? Billy's murder has been avenged!

That night, Bridget sat on a bunk getting acquainted with the other cell mates and sampling her first taste of prison food while the trial was the subject of small talk at supper tables all over the neighborhood.

In the Bascombe home, John confessed he had been there in case he was outed by someone else. Mary Ann frowned at him, and then leaned forward in her chair. She said,

Well, John, though I thoroughly disapprove of your actions you might as well spill the beans now and tell us every detail!

John shared his story while the girls dished out the beef stew and succotash. Over supper, each member of the family weighed in on the decision. Although the children felt she deserved what she got, the adults felt that McGuire had been a bit heavy hand-ed with his sentencing. All agreed on one point, however, that Billy's demise would give the city press yet one more opportunity to make fun of their hometown.

Sure enough, over the next few days a variety of tongue in cheek articles appeared in the New York newspapers. Reporters seemed to relish the perpetuation of negative impressions of Rocky Hollow and its inhabitants. One even wrote that Billy was a *shantytown sensation*, which irked Mary Ann to no end. Sitting at the kitchen table with her afternoon tea and biscuits, she frowned at the newspaper page and began to rant.

Bosh! Spooney! James, Rocky Hollow is no shantytown! Why if it was, I'd pack the children up this very minute and leave. And, you know this to be true because I have the means to do the very thing!

Mary Ann took newspaper articles like this personally. She was close to becoming the biggest property owner in Rocky Hollow and seriously committed to building homes of simple but solid construction. They were small, modest, and comfort-able living quarters, some of which housed her own family mem-bers. If there was an old dilapidated structure on a property she bought, Mary Ann razed it and built anew. She backed up the work of her laborers because she supervised them herself and did not tolerate substandard work!

She raged on as James sat at the table nibbling on his biscuit. It was certainly not the first time he had seen her worked up in such a state. A shantytown was a slum, a place where the im-poverished dwelled in dangerous substandard living conditions. His Rocky Hollow neighbors were workers who held steady jobs in the labor trades, the breweries, in town, or the docks. They lived in small but neat wood frame homes and cottages. Plus, Rocky Hollow was a part of the town of Stapleton in the Village of Edgewater, a municipality which was committed to the health, comfort and convenience of its citizens. Yes, Mary Ann was right to feel indignant, but now how to get her to stop yapping.

James munched away. He waited, confident of his ability to turn her rant off so he could finish his morning tea in peace. James had his faults, no doubt. He lacked serious ambition and liked beer way too much. Yet, he was in possession of something his wife needed desperately. His soothing and oft times comical nature were gifts he gave to her freely.

At the point where James sensed that Mary Ann had let off enough steam, he chimed in. Aye, he agreed with her, but James thought she was missing out on another way of looking at this.

Mary Ann lifted her eyes off the newspaper. She lowered her reading glasses down on the bridge of her nose and looked straight at him.

And what do you mean by that? she fired back at him sharply.

James took a deep breath and began to explain. He knew how hard it was for her to ignore any article that mocked their beloved neighborhood. Why no outsider would ever have the same feelings for the place as she, one who was born and lived close to her entire life on the same street corner. James likewise disapproved of use of the word shantytown in the article, but he also understood that reporters were given marching order to deliver only the most eye-popping articles to print. It was a cut throat business with many rival newspapers out there. Sometimes the editors had to embellish the truth to sell more copies than their competition.

Mary Ann gave him a curmudgeon look but did not say a word. It signaled to James that she was accepting what he had to say. He continued.

Billy was a most glorious beast, Mary Ann. Aye, and we will all fondly recall his regal stature high up on the hills. No finer animal could exist. So, the part they wrote about him was true. After all, wasn't he truly sensational?

James stood up. He swiped his cap off the back of the chair, placed it over his heart, and looked her dead straight in the eye. With serious face and a loud ceremonious voice, he then declared to her,

May God forever bless our Shanty's Billy!

Mary Ann could not help herself. She broke out laughing. With sweeping gesture, James then took his cap and threw it on top of his head. He winked back at her thinking,

Well James, you surely deserve a reward for this fine act. It'll be three pints this evening instead of the usual two!

Mary Ann's husband vowed to collect his prize on the way home from work. He kissed Mary Ann on the cheek, grabbed a second biscuit, and left the house whistling. James could not wait to visit his favorite saloon later in the day and down a few pints of Bechtel's Excelsior Ale. Surely someone there would pay for his drinks in exchange for an engaging story telling all how he controlled his wife's unruly behavior.

Reporters never used the word sensational in their descriptions of Mary Ann, but it would have fit her well. They enjoyed writing about her because there was no one like her in the town of Stapleton or beyond. With her eccentric ways and unusual accomplishments, Mary Ann was undeniably a newsworthy personality.

By now, Mary Ann had become very skilled at public speaking. She held her own in any debate whether it be at police court, a political gathering, the tax office, or a Village Trustees meeting. Reporters delighted in watching her talk, talk, talk until desperate opponents threw hands over their heads and cried for mercy. Reporters likewise took pleasure in recording her super woman feats like hauling bricks and lumber or using her stout stick to menace the deadbeats in her life. Her memory album bulged with newspaper clippings.

She was a bit of a local celebrity but tried not let it go to her head. Like her neighbors, she still had daily chores and responsibilities. On weekdays, she sent her children off to the Broad Street School and then cooked meals, cleaned house, and did laundry. She went to the butcher and the fish market and ran errands at Village Hall and the bank. She washed windows and swept the walkway in front of the small store she owned. Come Saturdays, Mary Ann went to confession and helped out at church socials and fire company fund raisers. On Sundays she attended Catholic mass, squeezed alongside her large and unruly brood in their rented pew.

As a small girl, the McDonough family belonged to St. Peter's Church, the first and only Catholic parish on Staten Island. Then, when St. Mary's was established, Mary Ann and her family joined the new parish because it was closer to home. There she met Father Lewis, a man she greatly respected. He was kind and humble and a tireless worker on behalf of his congregation. Because of his sincerity people listened when he spoke, such as the time he calmed the angry mob during the Stapleton riots. Lewis provided well for his congregants. He built a church and a school and purchased the Parkinson estate in nearby Southfield to establish a Catholic cemetery.

Father Lewis served as St. Mary's pastor for more than thirty years and during that time watched as the Catholic population soared. He was always pleased to welcome newcomers into his flock but was acutely aware that some congregants faced difficulties getting to mass. The church was indeed picturesque sitting high up off the road, but there were parishioners who were unable to climb the many stairs. Others faced challenges because of Staten Island's rutted, muddy, washed out roads. Father Lewis became concerned for the safety of the old and infirm in the parish. He felt their struggle personally, as he was getting on in years himself and having some difficulty walking.

The pastor consulted the New York archdiocese and was granted permission to open a mission chapel in Stapleton. He searched around and chose to locate the chapel in a Rocky Hollow storefront a few doors down the road from the Mary Ann's home on Broad Street. It was named Our Lady of Lourdes Chapel, though some nicknamed it the Chapel of Ease.

Father Lewis well understood the needs of his flock because the chapel was an immediate success. At first, the Bascombes obediently followed Father Lewis's request to limit chapel attendance to the old and infirm. They continued to make the trek to St. Mary's Church each week. Then, on one wickedly stormy Sunday morning things changed. Someone at the breakfast table suggested they forgo the trip to St. Mary's and attend mass down the street. All chimed in and it was unanimous. With mass no further than a few steps outside their front door, why travel in such nasty weather all the way down to Clifton?

After that, the family began attending Sunday mass at the Broad Street chapel on a more regular basis and they were not alone. Though the intent had been to meet the needs of those for whom travel was difficult, the locals had taken over the chapel. Rocky Hollow Catholics flooded the tiny space each week, causing perilous overcrowding.

Father Lewis tried his best to improve the situation. He spent $10,000 to erect a small wooden chapel on Broad Street to replace the storefront building, but this structure likewise quickly grew too small to serve the needs of the flock. He consulted Michael Corrigan, the Archbishop, who authorized the creation of a new parish in Stapleton.

Well, this was surely an exciting development! Although she would miss the sermons of Father Lewis, Mary Ann was overjoyed at the prospect of Rocky Hollow's own neighborhood parish. Reverend Father Gerald Huntman was announced as the pastor and celebrated his first mass in the Broad Street chapel on December 8th. The date was special because it was a Holy Day of Obligation for Roman Catholics. In tribute, the clergyman named the new parish the Church of the Immaculate Conception.

Mary Ann admired Father Huntman in his first days as pastor. Like Father Lewis, Gerald Huntman was an ambitious man. He bought up the storefront buildings adjoining the chapel for temporary use as priest quarters and a small school. He quickly raised $4000, enough money to purchase a number of small lots which when pieced together stretched from Targee to Gordon Streets. St. Mary's chapel was hoisted onto a flatbed wagon and moved from Broad Street to the land next to Mary Ann's house on Gordon Street.

Living so close to the church, Mary Ann became privy to the

comings and goings of the clergyman and his staff. There were some things she observed which she did not necessarily approve of but, *Pish! Posh!* that was none of her affairs so she put it out of her mind.

The parish finances, however, were quite a different story. This WAS her business, because the operating funds of the parish came out of her pockets and the pockets of her hard-working neighbors. Mary Ann had concerns about the parish finances but for a long time held her tongue. Mary Ann spent sleepless time in bed pondering the situation. She sensed there was something askew and it bothered her not to have all the facts. She prayed for divine guidance.

What would God think if I questioned the pastor?

What ultimately moved Mary Ann to take action was Father Huntman's announcement to build a church rectory. From the start, Mary Ann was skeptical that the parish could well afford a rectory. Then, after seeing how large and extravagant it was going to be, she was convinced. Only two priests were going to live there, but the rectory was bigger than her own home with ten people living inside! No, Mary Ann could not turn a blind eye to this blatant waste of money! She would finally speak.

The next day, Mary Ann cleared the breakfast dishes and dressed in her Sunday clothes. She donned her bonnet, grabbed her purse off the table, and walked over to pay a call to Father Huntman.

Mary Ann was still unsure if what she was doing was blasphemous, but that didn't stop her. Father Huntman saw her coming across the lawn and greeted her graciously. He asked if she wanted to have some tea and refreshments. Mary Ann accepted, and they walked back to his quarters.

After the tea was served, Mary Ann tried to be as amicable as possible. She stated all her concerns, including the belief that he was being frivolous in this new construction. Mary Ann pointed out that she wasn't asking this without any right to voice her opinion; she donated a good deal of personal time and money to support the parish.

Father Huntman smiled and remained cordial. When she

finished explaining, he thanked her but responded matter of factly that it was actually none of her business how he handled the parish finances. The smile never left his face as he then dismissed her from his quarters. Mary Ann said nothing. She excused herself and exited. Shaking her head, she wondered what to do next.

Mary Ann went home and consulted God, who advised her to keep going. She made an appointment with the trustees of the parish. They were a group of intelligent and well-to-do men of good standing in the Stapleton community. John Widdecombe, a prominent lawyer of English descent who lived up in the affluent hills above Rocky Hollow, served as the board president.

When Mary Ann met with the trustees, once again she was given the opportunity to make her case. She got a few heads to nod during her loquacious speech, but in the end, it was obvious that no one planned to join her in challenging Father Huntman. She left the meeting full of frustration.

Bosh Spooney! Doesn't anyone else have the gumption to stand up to this man?

Mary Ann was livid because she was acutely aware that this was one of those times when gender was holding her back. She was not being taken seriously because she was a woman! On the way home from the Trustees meeting, Mary Ann started up another conversation with the divine.

Help me dear God. What do I do next? How can I remedy this injustice?

Mary Ann did not get an immediate answer and in the meantime got angrier and angrier listening to the sounds of the ongoing construction. Then, one day, out of the blue, God enlightened her.

Pish! Posh! Of course!

There *WAS* more she could do about this.

Mary Ann wrote a letter asking for a private meeting with Archbishop. Her message was received, and a response sent back that an audience was granted. On the appointed day, Mary Ann woke up just a tad nervous. She boarded a ferry to New York and upon arriving in lower Manhattan hailed a cab. She gave the driver instructions to take her up Fifth Avenue. Mary Ann was not a frequent visitor to the city, so she relished the trip uptown. Like a small child she gaped out the window the whole way, intrigued by the unusual sights and sounds. By the time she spotted the marble façade and spires of the magnificent St. Patrick's Cathedral, Mary Ann's doubts were lessened. She knew that God was with her on this journey.

Mary Ann had left early to visit the cathedral before the meeting. After climbing the stone steps and entering through the massive wood doors, the woman with a reputation for incessant talking was instantaneously hushed.

Pish! Posh! What an amazing place to worship! Mary Ann knew she would never see another building match the magnificence of this fine structure. She genuflected at the rear of the cathedral and then walked up and around the perimeter aisles to view the stunning sculptures and window glass. She stopped at one of the many votive stands, opened her purse, and put a donation in the slot. Scrutinizing the rows of candles, she selected one on the very top row, and lit it. Then she lowered herself onto a kneeler.

Mary Ann made the sign of the cross and thanked God for her blessings. She prayed for her beloved deceased. Then, she asked for God's assistance. She had to deliver a speech that would make an impression on the Archbishop. She knew she was right but needed him to agree with her.

Mary Ann was well prepared. She carried with her a binder filled with notes that she had triple checked before leaving Stapleton. She would not be embarrassed in front of such a holy man! To stay focused, she reviewed the facts in her head as she sat outside the Archbishop's office waiting to be called into his chambers.

Any apprehension Mary Ann may have felt left her within the first few minutes of the meeting. Archbishop Corrigan was gracious and quite interested in hearing what she had to say. Mary Ann had many specifics to bring into the discussion. Before Father Huntman announced his intention to build the new rectory, the church debt was $7000. Its construction was budgeted at $7000, but in fact $24,000 had been spent on the ridiculously large building. Because of the extravagance, the parish now carried a mortgage in excess of $35,000.

There were other issues on her mind too. Mary Ann told the Archbishop that the parish finances were not transparent. Fundraisers which were held seemed very successful, but the proceeds were never reported. At the conclusion of their discussion, the Archbishop thanked Mary Ann for taking the time to see him in person. He told her he would look into the situation.

Shortly after Mary Ann's trip into Manhattan, Father Huntman received word that he was being transferred back to his former parish. When the *New York Herald* reporter got wind of what happened, they begged to interview both Mary Ann and John Widdecombe. Mary Ann did not hesitate to tell the reporters about her visit to the Archbishop. The board president avoided any mention of her name, but in his interview corroborated what Mary Ann said about the pastor's spending practices.

The incident resulted in sharp divisions among the parishioners. While some members of the congregation applauded Mary Ann, others were appalled and believed her actions were unjustified. A month after Mary Ann's meeting with the Archbishop, the small wooden church on Gordon Street was packed to the rafters for Huntman's farewell mass. His supporters were quick to point out that the transfer to a parish of equal standing was proof he was not culpable of any wrongdoing. Mary Ann paid her detractors no heed. God had stood by her side in what was right.

Father Huntman suffered no great loss but Immaculate Conception parish remained in turmoil for months. To many, the Archbishop's decision had been harsher than deserved because he ordered both the transfer of Huntman as well as Father Crowley, his assistant. Crowley was a popular priest, and parishioners petitioned the Archbishop to allow Father Crowley to stay. The request was denied. Thus, when the new pastor Reverend Father William J. McClure and his assistant Father Leahy arrived, they received a chilly welcome.

Mary Ann met with the new pastor as soon as possible and vowed to help in any way she could. She gave him an open invitation to come whenever he wanted to her house for supper. The priest was charged to find ways to build acceptance within the congregation and also take swift action to bring down the parish debt. Within a short span of time, parishioners came to appreciate the differences between their old and new religious leader. Parish policies radically changed. Income and expenditures were made transparent. Just a month after taking over, Father McClure published year end parish finances in the newspaper. The debt of the parish was calculated at approximately $36,000. John Widdecombe and the board worked diligently with the new pastor to manage the debt so that just two years later, the figure had already been reduced to $25,000.

Everyone in the Bascombe home wore their Sunday best on the days when Father McClure came to visit. On these special occasions, Mary Ann ordered a rare cut of beef from the butcher down the block. After supper, the youngest children made haste to excuse themselves from the table. They scattered to the far corners of the house while the older children and adults lingered over tea and cake.

They made small talk, but eventually the light banter turned into more serious discussion. Floods and major epidemics were things of the past, but new concerns threatened the neighborhood. Alcohol consumption was getting out of control. Lager ale free flowed at the many breweries, beer gardens, dance halls, saloons, and liquor stores throughout Rocky Hollow, and associated crimes were on the increase. All agreed that managing alcohol abuse would be the biggest social challenge for Rocky Hollow in the near future.

After the pastor left for the evening, Mary Ann told James how much she liked Father McClure. Finally, after all this time she felt at ease again as a member of Immaculate Conception parish. Father McClure was wise and clearly understood the importance of fiscal responsibility. And beyond that, he had also taken the time to get to know his community and appreciate the best and worst aspects of life in Rocky Hollow.

Father McClure surely did not see Rocky Hollow as a shantytown. To him, it was a tight knit community of Catholic brothers and sisters who had the potential to do good deeds for God and mankind by working together. That night, Mary Ann vowed to James. She would join Father McClure in his efforts to rid Rocky Hollow of the crime and delinquency that threatened the peace of their neighborhood.

Chapter Eight: The Terror Of Evil Doers

Mary Ann knew George Bechtel since the days when his family first moved to Stapleton. She admired George for his sound business acumen as well as his personal regard for the citizens of the community.

His father may have started the company, but it was George's talent in running the business which brought Bechtel's Brewery its great success. George was an innovator. He replaced his father's small wood building with a large brick structure on four acres of land at the intersection of Broad Street and Richmond Road. Its handsome square clock tower which soared above all the tiny homes in Rocky Hollow was attractive but also a useful design, for it stored the malt used to produce Bechtel's ale. Inside the brewery, George employed state of the art technology. He installed compression pumps and an ammonia process to create refrigeration and was the first business in town to use electricity.

The combination of pure artesian well water and modern factory practices helped Bechtel's beer win national and international acclaim. Bechtel's lager was recognized as one of the best beers in America at the Philadelphia Centennial Exposition. It won gold medals in Paris and Sydney and was a requested favorite of Japanese diplomats. It was no wonder then, that James and many other men in town preferred Bechtel's Excelsior brand above all others.

Mary Ann did not drink. She despised the stuff as she was intimately acquainted with the perils of excess drinking. Under the influence, a man took temporary leave of his senses. He could drink away his weekly wages. He could gamble away his life savings. He could get so drunk that he'd end up in the home of Mrs.

Baker down the block. And, sadly, he could even end up dead.

Although she had firsthand knowledge of the horrors of alcohol addiction, Mary Ann opened up a saloon area in the back of her general store. She sold liquor because it made sense. It kept James, her brothers, and older sons closer to home, and it was profitable.

Hers was a small operation so she did not bother to apply for a liquor license, which was typical. Lager ale free flowed at breweries and German beer gardens, hotels, dance halls, stores, and drinking holes all over town, but very few establishments sold alcohol legally. At one point, officials counted close to 200 drinking establishments in and around Stapleton, yet only 20 were licensed and paid taxes on the sale of alcohol. Officials turned their heads, because many of them were selling alcohol illegally themselves. The profits to be made were just irresistible.

Licensed or not, everyone ignored the Sunday laws. New York State ordinances prohibited target shooting, ball playing, and alcohol sales on the Sabbath, yet the bars were open for business all over Stapleton. They took their chances as saloon owners knew it was next to impossible for the police and courts to keep up with the high number of offenders.

When forced to take action by the press or angry citizens, officials liked to brag that they were in control of the situation. They called for the roundup of violators and sent the police out to drag the most egregious offenders off to jail. The problem with this though, was that many times when summoned to the scene of illegal activities, the police found Stapleton's local justices, constables, and elected officials were among those breaking the law. When this happened, the bust was called off and the officers turned their heads and walked away.

Bechtel Brewery and its rival competitors, the Rubsam and Horrmann Brewery and Bischoff Brewery, were vital to the local economy. They were a blessing to the town financially, but at the same time a plague. The expansion of the beer industry was a major contributor to growing crime problems.

One thing about alcohol: it did not discriminate. Beer was cheap enough for anyone to get their hands on, so it wrecked lives whether rich or poor. Though Mary Ann had a strong aversion, the memories of her late father reminded her to try to be kind to those cursed. If a person admitted their madness and asked for help, she could not refuse. Perhaps her assistance might enable a poor soul to get their life back on track.

Henry Fischer was an example of someone she helped. He was a fifty-year old painter who was one of her tenants. Henry immigrated to the United States from Germany around the start of the Civil War. He married a Scottish woman named Anna and together had five beautiful children. Mary Ann genuinely liked Henry. He was a family man. He paid his rent on time and never gave Mary Ann cause for trouble.

One bleak wintry morning, Henry walked into the Beach Street Police Station and asked to speak to the Police Chief, Captain Blake. The officer at the desk told him he would have to wait and that he did, sitting calmly and earnestly on a bench until the Captain came out to talk to him. Blake asked what he wanted, and Henry replied,

Captain, I need you to lock me up.

The officer was totally caught off guard by the politeness of the request. He pushed the glasses he was wearing down the bridge of his nose to get a better look at his face. Blake asked why. Henry told him he had been binging on alcohol for two days straight and had just run out of money. He knew that the tremors were coming.

I'm a threat Captain. I am going to get dangerous.

Blake saw no signs of the shakes or other impending disorders. Since drinking binges were all too commonplace in a town with three large breweries, it was impossible to lock up all those having alcohol withdrawal. The few cells he had in the police jail were reserved for true criminals. Blake told Henry to go home and sleep it off. Henry persisted.

I am very dangerous.

Henry refused to leave the stationhouse. Blake, short on time, dispatched him to talk to one of the police court justices. The justice told Henry that the police couldn't lock him up because no one had found fault with him. Henry replied in that case he'd write a complaint. That is not the way it works, answered the justice. A person cannot file a complaint against himself. He sent Henry on his way.

Henry exited the stationhouse with extreme dread. Deep down inside of him he felt the churning. Henry knew that something terrible was going to happen. Henry could not go home and risk endangering his family, so he began walking up to neighbors on the street asking if they would write out a complaint against him. Over and over they shooed him away. Either they could not be bothered, or, like the police chief, failed to take him seriously. Henry was about to give up and try to tie himself up somewhere, but then he thought about his landlady. Henry took off in search of Mrs. Bascombe. Why, certainly she'd help. Mary Ann always said if there was anything she could do to help the family to just ask.

By the time Henry caught up with Mary Ann he was beginning to feel a bit shaky. He told her his story and begged her to write out a complaint against him. Mary Ann sized Henry up from head to toe, similar to what the police chief had done. Then, she agreed to his request.

She said she was doing it just to humor him, but Mary Ann was truly concerned. What came into her mind were the terrifying moments of Thomas McDonough's last hours. Henry and her father were both decent men who craved alcohol in excess. She knew what delirium tremens was like and did not want his wife and children to go through what she had suffered. Henry needed prompt medical attention if he were to start to convulse. The only safe places for him would be in jail or the infirmary.

Mary Ann put aside what she was planning to do. She got into her wagon and drove down to the station house. Mary Ann walked up to the front desk and filled out the necessary complaint form. This obliged the Richmond County Police to find Henry Fischer and haul him off to jail.

In the end, Henry knew his body better than anyone. At first, he was a cooperative prisoner in his cell, but when the alcohol started to burn off in his system, Henry burst into a sudden rage. He howled, overturned his cot, and shook the bars wildly, demanding to be released. Then he became dangerously combative. Dr. G. Wilmot Townsend, a physician who worked at the Seamen's Retreat, was summoned to examine him. The doctor concluded it was a case of homicidal mania with little chance of recovery. He recommended committing Henry to an insane asylum.

The police kept him locked up preparing to do as Townsend said, but the diagnosis was premature. After all the alcohol had been purged from his body, Henry Fischer returned to his normal self. He was released from jail and took off for Broad Street to find his landlady. He had everything to thank her for. Mary Ann was happy to see Henry survived the detoxification without harm, but she was not about to let him get away scot-free. She launched into a very lengthy scolding.

You've beaten the devil this time but let there be no other occasions because I will not help you again. You have been given your one and only one chance Henry!

Henry agreed. No more alcohol binges. She wished him well, though she was not thoroughly convinced that her words had gotten through to him.

Alcohol was beginning to affect everyone in some way in the town of Stapleton. Even when there were no drinkers in the family, the peace-loving citizens of Rocky Hollow found it harder and harder to insulate themselves from the town's dark side. The beer gardens and saloons fueled the economy but at the same time produced a steady supply of drunks who tested the patience of the public. They also strained local law enforcement efforts. There were just not enough police officers on the streets or sufficient courts to handle all the cases of drunken misconduct.

One summery afternoon, Mary Ann's affable middle daughter Mary Ellen called out from the kitchen.

Mother, do you suppose that something is going on at the brewery?

The bold oompah-pah sounds emanating from George Bechtel's Beer Garden which provided live music that resonated throughout Rocky Hollow each weekend had abruptly stopped. Mary Ann was quite curious. She and Mary Ellen walked out the back door and strained their ears to listen. There was nothing. Then, they heard a lady's screams.

Mary Ann was repulsed as she read about the attack in the next day's papers. As usual, the beer garden was full of happy go lucky weekend day trippers. They were listening to the band and singing along with the music while cooling off with a few refreshing pints. These tourists had no idea their amusement would be interrupted by a bunch of local miscreants. *Red the Boss* and his gang of Rocky Hollow toughs entered the beer garden demanding to be served. As they were obviously already quite drunk, the staff refused and asked them politely to leave. The men did not exit. They swore loudly and then began to harass the patrons. One gang member overturned a beer barrel, starting a brawl between the gang and Bechtel's workers. Their fight escalated into a vicious one-hour melee. The tourists fled for safety as men battled with swords, stones, and clubs. Thankfully, by the time the police arrived only one of Bechtel's workers had been injured.

Bosh! Spooney! Those poor patrons and workers! I hope they dragged Red down to the stationhouse by his flaming crop of hair!

Mary Ann was concerned because it seemed that occasions like these were on the rise. Her son Thomas felt similarly and informed his mother of an intention to run for Village Constable in the November elections. Mary Ann was proud of her son but counseled him that there were many caveats in being an officer of the law. You can never underestimate a drunk, she warned. They were dangerous. She reminded Thomas of the day his brother Joseph was threatened in a simple but perilous child's play close to home.

Mr. Halloran was a smithy who owned a shop across the street from the Bascombe family on the adjacent corner of Broad and Gordon Streets. One hot afternoon, the smithy and his son were sweating away at their sweltering work over the iron forge when a stranger wandered into the shop. He called himself Cunningham. The man said he was just passing by and wanted to take a break.

Halloran took out his hanky, wiped his brow, and invited the man to sit with him. The men began chatting and after a few minutes, Cunningham said he'd like to send out for some cold lager. *No problem* said Halloran. *Bechtel's is just up the block!* Halloran sent his son out to buy beer, and when it arrived all three sat down to enjoy their beverages.

The ale was tasty and the banter congenial. They were having such a fine time that the boy was sent out for more spirits. They talked and drank and then suddenly without warning Cunningham pulled a revolver out of his coat pocket!

Halloran shot up quickly in his chair. Cunningham, who seemed quite composed, placed the gun in the palm of his hand. He asked Halloran's son if he wanted to fire the revolver. It was a peculiar request, so the blacksmith answered for the boy. Halloran asked if the chambers of the gun were loaded. Cunningham replied no. Then without further comment, Cunningham returned the revolver to his coat pocket.

The smithy wished to evict the man from his shop, but seeing this as potentially dangerous, sent his son away on an errand instead to ensure his safety. As the pair sat and continued to shoot the breeze, a group of young neighborhood boys which included Joseph Bascombe assembled outside the blacksmith's front entrance. One of them had a twig and drew a circle in the dirt. Then the boys started to play marbles. The game started out quietly but as it livened up the boys began to laugh and call out wildly.

The severely inebriated Cunningham looked over to the front door and remarked if it was his establishment, he wouldn't let those runts kick up a row outside. Halloran disagreed with him. They were good kids and he was used to them hanging around. He noted the man growing more agitated as the boys continued to play. Suddenly, Cunningham stood up and walked outside. Halloran sprung up from his seat and followed after him.

What happened next came about quite quickly. Joseph and his friends were sitting cross legged around the large circle on the ground. They sensed the presence of someone behind them, so they looked up and saw Cunningham hovering above their heads. Cunningham seemed to be looking right through them as he drew his revolver. The boys went silent. They were all frozen in fear.

Thankfully, Cunningham did not point his gun at a child. Instead, he put the revolver to his temple, pulled the trigger, and sent a bullet through his skull.

The loud BANG brought everyone on Broad Street to their feet. Mary Ann was among those who heard the sound. She jerked her head up from the saloon's work counter where she was pouring over bills. Mary Ann grabbed her stout stick leaning against the wall and bolted out the front door. She looked across the street and saw the young boys on the ground with adults running towards them. Mary Ann flew across the trolley tracks, pushed aside a few of the boys, and saw the body lying on the ground. She then spotted Joseph and grabbed him by the shirt collar. Kicking and screaming, she dragged him across the street back home.

People gathered at the site, gaping at the rivulet of blood oozing slowly from the dead man's head. A police officer showed up and asked a slew of questions.

Does anyone know this man? he asked. No, not a soul recognized him.

After Mary Ann warned Joseph to stay inside, she went back out across the street. Mary Ann plowed through the crowd in order to check on her neighbor. Halloran was in the back of the shop having a hard time holding onto a glass of whiskey. His hands could not stop shaking. He told her how relieved he was that their sons were safe.

Mary Ann did her best to calm him. Halloran asked himself over and over why he had not seen it coming. How could a man be so deranged and do something so horrifying in front of small children?

That evening, Mary lectured her entire family.

Be wary of strangers my dears. Watch your surroundings at all times. And most of all husband and children, stay far, far away from the drunks!

The incident across the street, frightening as it was, did not deter Mary Ann from continuing to run her small store saloon.

There she was in total control over who she served and how much alcohol was consumed. Gambling, however, was a totally different subject. Mary Ann had absolutely no tolerance for gambling. She who had struggled to save money her entire life could not comprehend how a person could ever chance throwing their money away. She could see how a cool refreshing draft on a hot sticky summer afternoon had some degree of value, but gambling? Pure insanity!

The men in the Bascombe house routinely received supper table talks on the evils of gambling. Mary Ann's position on this was as clear as the water that flowed from Gore's Brook: gambling in her saloon or anywhere else on her properties would not be tolerated. She drummed into their heads that once a man was smitten, little could halt the downward slide that would bring ruin to themselves and their family. Pitch and toss, card games, bets on boxing matches or cock fights – all were sinful activities in her eyes.

Mary Ann's saloon was a safe haven to keep her men away from such temptations. She knew full well that many saloon keepers were in cahoots with the bookies and encouraged gambling on their premises. There were illegal prize fights which took place in drinking establishments all around Stapleton. These prize fights were bad enough, but saloons also hosted cock fighting, something which Mary Ann found particularly ugly and inhumane. Cock fighting drew men from New York, New Jersey, and beyond. Birds were lugged into town in squirming sacks on the ferries or in row boats and let loose to go at each other in shoveled out pits in saloon basements. It was a big job to dig the pits, but the monetary rewards were great. After the fight got underway, saloon owners gladly filled and refilled the empty mugs of patrons while keeping an open eye out for the police.

The illegal assemblies were kept secret but at times wicked fights broke out among the drunk patrons, giving saloon keepers no choice but to call the Richmond County police. It was common for Mary Ann to hear that the night before a saloon owner down the road had the Richmond County police empty out his place. She became immune if she saw a bunch of men running willy-nilly coming from the direction of one of the more notorious saloons. She just naturally assumed there was a police raid.

Mary Ann was never one to hesitate backing up her words with actions. Neighbors gave her yet one more nickname after her efforts to reform a group of local boys. In addition to *Mrs. Mack* and *Counsellor Howe*, she was also dubbed, *The Terror of Evil Doers*.

One afternoon, an acquaintance dropped by her store to say hello. She called out to Mary Ann who was sweeping in the back.

Good day, Mrs. Mary Ann. Wonderin' did yer know what's goin' on down the street? A few lads are loitering on your property. Think they're tossin' coins.

Mary Ann stopped her work and walked up to the front of the store. After asking a few questions, she stated emphatically to her neighbor,

"I'll have no gambling in my neighborhood, not if I had to spend my last dollar in its suppression."[1]

Mary Ann grabbed her stout stick from behind the bar and took off down the road. About a block away, she spied a bunch of young boys playing pitch and toss in her vacant lot. Pitch and toss was a simple contest where players tossed coins up against a wall or upright surface and whoever threw the coin landing closest to the wall got to keep all the rest. It was a tame game by anyone's standards, but Mary Ann didn't care. She crept up on them surreptitiously. Then, just at the right time, she lunged at the group holding her threatening club high up in the air. They started to scatter, but Mary Ann called out loudly after them.

Stop right there. If anyone leaves, God be my witness for I shall whip him within an inch of his life when I catch up!

The boys, all who hailed from Rocky Hollow, knew *Mrs. Terror* quite well. Not willing to test her threat, they stopped short. Mary Ann demanded they march back into the lot. They warily returned, and she gave them a longwinded lecture on the evils of gambling. Then, she gave them a choice.

Come now with me to the police station house to admit to your gambling or off to church to confess to the reverend.

The boys panicked. Mary Ann was quite friendly with the

154

Richmond County police officers, Village Trustees, and justices. She was also in good stead with the parish priest, having been a longtime volunteer at various parish functions. Both choices were quite doable. Mary Ann could easily take them to either place and maybe both if she got any madder at them!

The young fellas thought it over as Mary Ann stood impatiently tapping her stout stick over and over on the ground. They decided it was better to be in God's good graces than on a justice's bad side. They told her to take them to the priest. So, in clear view of everyone, Mary Ann lined them up like ducks in a row. She marched the boys up Broad Street and into the church so their confessions could be heard and sins washed away.

Mary Ann was thoroughly convinced she was saving the lives of these boys by her vigilance. If she overlooked their deeds, however small they were, eventually they'd be tossing nickels instead of pennies and after that, dollar coins. Then, when the full-fledged gambling fever took hold, they'd squander their hard-earned wages and resort to crime to fuel their nasty vices.

Oh yes indeed, I am correct in my actions!

Later that week one of the boys' mothers came to the door to question her about the treatment of her son. Mary Ann was curt in her response.

Pish! Posh! But you shouldn't be making excuses for your son. You should be here instead to say thanks to me for undoing the ruination of your offspring!

Mary Ann shooed the woman away but thought to herself that taking the child's side in this matter was not helpful for the boy or the community at large.

CHAPTER NINE: I'LL REFORM YOU!

"*Yes. I have battled through life successfully and own a very handsome property now, and I have never had any friend in life except two—that club in my hand and the tongue in my jaw.*"[1]

When Mary Ann gave a reporter that quote, she meant every word. Other than her brother Michael's help she bought her first home, Mary Ann's major accomplishments were all through her own efforts. Her longwinded but efficacious speech was a great gift she could always rely on. And, if that wasn't helpful enough, there was also her stout stick.

Mary Ann's walking stick made excellent sense to protect her as a young girl and it was equally appropriate in the grown-up world in which she now lived. Every female needed to feel safe, especially on the first of the month when skirt pockets jingled with rent monies that had been collected. Though the stick was more of a prop, it reinforced the image that she was one woman not to be messed with. The combination of sharp sassy tongue and handy club left Mary Ann free to move about the neighborhood in ways that no other woman dared.

Mary Ann blamed errant youths for much of the misdeeds which took place locally and she was right. There were a number of Staten Island gangs circulating around Stapleton. The Duck Pond Gang was from New Brighton and loitered near the northern stretches of Stapleton. The Modoc Gang were boys from St. Mary's Avenue who met at the border of Stapleton and Clifton. The Sons of Rest Gang lurked in the dark recesses of the woods where Stapleton met Concord.

All these gangs were bad but the worst in Mary Ann's eyes was the Rocky Hollow Gang, probably because these punks prowled the streets closest to her home. The *New York Herald* nicknamed them the *Stale Beer Gang* because of their frequent patronage of the local breweries. Although the press mocked them, the boys' maliciousness was not to be taken lightly. The gang was heavily comprised of young Irish in their mid to late teens. They were hardened criminals and a worthy match for even the toughest New York City gangs who occasionally rode into town on the Stapleton Ferry.

Mary Ann knew several of the gang members since they were teeny tots in the neighborhood. She had nothing good to say about them because of the way they behaved but did hold some sympathy in her heart for their mothers.

Oh, how those poor souls must suffer over their sons' errant ways. Such a calamity that they are not able to control their unruly sons!

The Richmond County Police could not always be relied on to protect the community so citizens used what best suited them - guns, knives, fists - to protect themselves from assault, theft, robberies, or worse. The police department was a band of dedicated peacekeepers, but they worked at a severe disadvantage. The county force had once been attached to the larger New York City department, but in the late 19th century it became independent and as a result was grossly understaffed. In 1887, forty-three officers were employed by Richmond County. The Police Captain and his assistant, five sergeants and two detectives were included in that number, meaning that only thirty-four patrolmen were left to police the entire fifty-nine square miles of Staten Island day and night seven days a week. Technically speaking, one woeful police officer was responsible for an area about half the size of a New York City police precinct.

Richmond County Police Headquarters was located on Beach Street, near Washington Park. A mounted police force had been started a while back, but for some unknown reason it was disbanded. Officers made their rounds on foot, so when called to the scene of a crime, it was most often after the fact.

The police had a wee bit of help because constables were stationed in each region of Staten Island, but these men were of limited usefulness. They worked part time and were elected officials of the Democratic and Republican parties so more often turned out to be political hacks rather than actual crime fighters.

The limited police support was disturbing because crime was on the rise in Stapleton in the later part of the century. No one was immune. Not the wealthy folk. Not the businessmen. Not even Mrs. Edwards, an innocuous old woman who lived in the Old Ladies Home.

The Old Ladies Home was a nickname for The Mariner's Family Asylum. The Home had been created by the New York State Legislature in 1851 to provide living quarters for the wives, mothers, sisters, and daughters of sailors of the Port of New York. Sixty elderly women resided in a stately five story Italianate style building located on the grounds of the Seaman's Retreat. Their quarters were light and airy and complete with restful views of the white sails and steamers traveling up and down the Narrows. Mary Ann knew the place well. She passed the home regularly on her way back and forth to a property she owned on Vanderbilt Avenue.

Everyone thought the Old Ladies Home was a safe and secure building. Then, one dark November night, they were proven wrong. While the old women were curled up under the covers fast asleep, a thug seized a ladder he found on the grounds and placed it against the side of the building. Silently, he ascended the rungs. When the man reached Mrs. Edward's second floor bedroom window he stopped, took out a tool and carefully proceeded to cut out a pane of glass. Slowly and cautiously he reached in, unlatched the lock, lifted the window, and entered the apartment.

The criminal was too stupid perhaps to realize that not all old folk were senile for his movements stirred Mrs. Edwards from her light sleep. She sat up stiffly in her bed, pulled the blanket up to her neck and hollered out into the dark, *Who's there?* to which the burglar sheepishly replied, *Jim.* It was the name of the gardener, but the matron was not fooled. She began screaming at the top of her lungs. The criminal bolted and made it back to the window. He took off down the ladder and into the darkness of the night in possession of all the old lady's money, a whopping $4.50.

News of the crime spread quickly. The idea of a thief entering an old lady's bedroom in the middle of the night frightened a great many women in the community. As a precaution, the police went around town asking citizens to lock up any ladders inside their barns. It was good advice, although many were already doing this because it was not the first time that a criminal used a ladder to enter a local building. Gang members employed ladders, flagpoles, crates, barrels, or whatever else they thought was stable enough to bear weight and climb into the homes and offices of unsuspecting victims.

The Richmond County police were well regarded as local heroes. At great personal risk, they tracked down and captured criminals. One widely celebrated triumph was the day officers locked up two Rocky Hollow Gang members who went under the aliases of Red the Boss and Campbell. Red was the same thug who had started the big brawl at Bechtel's beer garden. After that fracas he teamed up with Campbell and the shameless pair went on a rampage in a string of brazen robberies all over Stapleton and Staten Island. Among the places they burglarized were the home of the famous abolitionist Francis George Shaw, the Rubsam and Horrmann brewery, the home of brewery owner Joseph Rubsam, and the offices of Stapleton real estate and insurance brokers.

Red and Campbell were apprehended one night at 2 a.m. when their break-in at the Empire Livery Stables on Canal Street was interrupted by a night watchman. It was yet one more brazen act because these stables were owned by the Deputy Sheriff of Richmond County. Shots were fired back and forth and Red and Campbell got away, but they were soon captured and brought to trial.

Rocky Hollow gang members took pleasure in preying upon the innocent, the weak, and the out of town visitor. The gang respected no one, not even God. One night, a bunch of inebriated punks entered the Union Methodist Episcopal Church on Riker Street during services. They disrupted the congregation with damn awful singing and dancing. When asked to stop, the boys refused and then a terrible fight broke out. The men in the church tangled with the gang members. Women cried, and little children shrieked. The pastor was physically thrown about the church. The brawl spilled out into the street around the same time that a contingent of police officers arrived. The offkey drunks spied the police and took flight down the road, leaving several male congregants seriously injured.

The police received no reprieve from the crime and mischief caused by the disrespectful Rocky Hollow youths, even in the holiest of seasons. Justice McCullough added to his collection of stories about the time spent as Justice of the Peace when four cocky Rocky Hollow teens were hauled into his court for Christmas Day shenanigans. On December 25th, the boys broke into a local saloon. They taunted and terrorized the owner and his holiday guests by pelting them with lumps of coal which had been stolen from a neighbor's supply. The owner and male guests rushed the boys and in the terrible melee which ensued, one man was stabbed and a woman hit over the head with a stone jar. A very Merry Christmas, indeed!

The gang was a topic of discussion at many Bascombe family repasts. Mary Ann was proud of her sons James, John, and Joseph because they had not been influenced by the gangs. The boys endured regular harassment by gang members but were smart enough to avoid any major confrontations. Living in the shadow of their mother's stout stick kept them on the right track.

Mary Ann was respected by many people living in Rocky Hollow but she was solidly despised by the gang members. They hated the fact that she was unafraid to speak out publicly against them, condemning their acts of violence and cruelty. To show their displeasure, up to twenty boys at a time congregated some nights on the opposite corner of Broad and Gordon Streets. There, out in the open they drank, smoked, and made a loud racket. Their goal was to be a public nuisance - bullying, cussing, and stealing from whoever passed - and they succeeded. In their gatherings, they indirectly taunted Mary Ann by shouting distasteful comments loud enough to be heard inside her open first floor apartment windows. Occasionally, they openly challenged Mary Ann by stepping off their side of the street onto her property. Mary Ann kept her stout stick leaning up against the wall at the front door entrance for just such a circumstance. She seized her weapon and ran outside to chase them. Holding the stick high up in the air she communicated her desire to let it loose upon them. Mary Ann took in a deep long breath and then held back nothing as she warned them.

Disperse or get a taste of my justice. Get off this property. NOW!

Her threat would force the boys to move, but not before they muttered a few well-chosen swear words under their breaths.

It was inevitable that sooner or later Mary Ann would become a victim of gang crime. She was their outspoken antagonist but more importantly, Mary Ann was the wealthiest person in the neighborhood. One afternoon, a few members of the gang were loitering opposite her corner, guzzling beer and bragging about their importance. Eying her home across the street, the boys swore that Mrs. Bascombe needed a comeuppance. As the boys continued to swig down bottles of dark smooth ale, they mulled over the possibilities. Mugging a woman who knew how to swing a stout club seemed a messy task, so they voted to break into her home instead. Two locals volunteered for the job. They were eager to prove their worth to their cronies as well as reward themselves with some valuable loot. The boys began inconspicuously tracking the movements of Mary Ann and her family, waiting for an opportune time to put their plan into action.

Watching the house, the boys could tell that in the early morning hours the Bascombe residence bustled with activity. Then, after James and the older children left for work and the younger ones trotted off to school, Mary Ann was home alone until she started her daily errands. If it was good weather, Mary Ann usually took off on foot. She walked near and far, making it difficult to predict the time of her return. When she travelled by wagon, however, they noted that Mary Ann was gone for hours.

The boys agreed they'd be less likely to be caught if they waited for one of these extended trips.

One day, Mary Ann had errands to run downtown. She walked out her back door to the barn behind the house. She went inside and brought out her horse. Mary Ann hitched the animal to her wagon and as she did so, the family dog emerged from his shady spot under a nearby tree and began barking. Mary Ann scolded him, and then helped him into the back of the wagon. She climbed up onto the buckboard, gave a sharp tug of the reins, and took off down Broad Street.

Mary Ann was preoccupied. She did not notice the two neighborhood teens who were watching her every move. When she was fully out of sight they crept into her yard. Then they pried open the back door of the house.

The boys knew they were on borrowed time, so they made straight for Mary Ann's bedroom. They rummaged through the contents of her dresser drawers before looking under the bed. There they found money stuffed into a nondescript tin box. It was a wad of small denominations and coins.

Mary Ann returned home later that day. She saw the jimmied door and guessed what happened. Mary Ann ran to her bedroom and gazed at the mess. She was fit to be tied. Her tin box with $400 in cash was missing.

Blasted miscreants! How dare anyone break into my home!

Mary Ann naturally suspected the gang across the road was to blame. She summoned the police and ranted to them to get out on the streets pronto and track down the thieves. She demanded that whoever was responsible be caught and prosecuted to the full extent of the law.

The police wasted no time in promptly apprehending the boys responsible for the burglary. They were two seventeen-year old Rocky Hollow neighbors who went by the aliases of *Steamboat* and *Hickory*. The boys made their capture very easy. Instead of playing it safe and lying low with the money, they went on a wild spending spree. It was a dead giveaway to the authorities.

By the time Richmond County Police caught up to them they had blown through about $100. When interrogated, they confessed and led authorities to their secret hiding place. The box with remaining cash was wrapped inside a copy of an old newspaper under a Gordon Street barn owned by John O'Rourke, a Bascombe family friend.

Steamboat and *Hickory* were charged with grand larceny which required their trial to be held in county court. Mary Ann drove down to Richmond to testify. It was hard to look at their mothers' faces at the sentencing because she understood the shame and sorrow they must have felt as their sons were whisked away to jail. However, Mary Ann sincerely believed that they needed to be locked up to teach them a lesson. If appropriately punished, maybe they would repent and when released from prison engage in honest pursuits.

Mary Ann liked to boast at times, saying *I fear neither man nor devil,* but she was most assuredly afraid of fire. And because she was not alone in her thinking, arson was one of the gang members' favorite crimes. It was a devastatingly effective way to show their defiance of the authorities and unleash revenge on anyone who got in their way. Local businesses were the usual targets. When the Staten Island Savings Bank threatened to arrest gang members squatting inside a foreclosed two story vacant house, they responded by torching the building. Eddy & Sons, the local lumber yard that supplied most of the materials used to rebuild after fires, was repeatedly torched.

The gang showed its hostility towards Mary Ann and others in one torturous week of serial fires. The week began when firebugs torched Mary Ann's stable on Patton Street. It burned to the ground. Mary Ann's political acquaintance, Michael Oates, was the next victim. Commonly known as the community's *Keeper of the Morgue,* Oates ran an undertaker business on Bay Street. Arsonists broke into Oates's carriage house and opened the back door of his brand-new horse drawn hearse. Then, they threw kerosene on its black curtains and set it afire. Flames consumed the interior, cracking the fancy French plate curved glass. The hearse was ruined but luckily the building was not destroyed. The air tight interior of the hearse smothered the blaze.

After the first two nights everyone in Rocky Hollow was on

guard, but the arson did not stop. On the third night, the fire-starters torched a second barn and a two-story carpenter shop close to the Bascombe home on Broad Street. Fires continued every night for seven days, ending after they victimized Mary Ann once more, this time in her own backyard. Ever so quietly, the criminals snuck into her barn on Gordon Street. They led Mary Ann's horse and cow outside and tied them to a tree. Then, they torched the barn and adjoining ice house.

This was the last straw for Mary Ann. The fire could have easily spread to the roof of her home while everyone was sleeping! Mary Ann and her neighbors gathered to discuss the attacks. They were fairly certain who was to blame. Two Rocky Hollow gang members had just been let out of the state penitentiary after serving 3-year sentences for similar crimes. Mary Ann and the fellow victims went to see Captain Blake of the Richmond County Police. They demanded he round up the boys and take them into custody.

Though gangs accounted for a good deal of the crimes committed in and around Stapleton, contemptible acts were not limited to the young. Once, on a pleasant spring afternoon Mary Ann and her daughter Emma were out taking a walk to view some properties she was thinking of buying. They had just passed the corner of Vanderbilt Avenue in Clifton and were chit-chatting away enjoying their time together, when in the distance they spied a small boy. He was moving ever so slowly, dragging a garbage cart up the side of the road.

As he approached, Mary Ann and Emma were struck by the pathetically sad appearance of the boy.

Egad! Mary Ann whispered over to her daughter. *Doesn't that little lad look dreadful?*

The child was grossly underweight and had oozing unbandaged cuts on his forehead and hands. He wore soiled ragged clothes. The boy grunted as he struggled to drag the heavy cart, which was filled to capacity and giving off a putrid smell. As they passed each other, the boy did not look up. His eyes were fixed to the ground, adding to his overall look of desperation and fright.

Mary Ann could not walk past him. She hailed the boy and

he stopped and turned around. Mary Ann walked up to him and spoke kindly, and he began to sob violently. Mary Ann let the sobbing run its course. When there was a pause she offered her hanky to blow his nose. Then she asked him a few simple questions. The boy trusted Mary Ann and answered. His name was Oscar Bradford. He was nine years old and lived in the town of Concord.

Mary Ann instructed the child to sit down next to her on a tree stump. Then she asked him to tell her his full story. With watery eyes, Oscar opened up and told Mary Ann that he was an orphan who had been adopted by a very cruel man and his son. They did not give him enough to eat. They beat him daily. At night, each took a turn whipping him with a leather strap.

Mary Ann stopped him. She had heard enough.

Oscar. Leave the cart here. Come home with me now.

Mary Ann was appalled and knew what needed to be done. When they got to her house, Mary Ann took out a scissor and cut off the boy's tattered clothing. She was sickened to see that Oscar's body was racked with bruises from shoulders to knees, and he had open cuts that were oozing blood all over his calves. Mary Ann cleaned and dressed the boys' wounds and gave him fresh clothes belonging to one of her sons. Then she prepared a feast for the starving boy. She served him chicken, pork, potatoes, green bean casserole, and cobbler. Mary Ann fed him until he declared that it was impossible to eat another morsel for fear he would explode. She put him in her own bed and tucked him in to take a nap. Then, she summoned the police.

Agent Corbett of the Society for the Prevention of Cruelty to Children was sent out to arrest Oscar's adoptive father. The man was arraigned before Justice Franklin C. Vitt on charges of cruelty to a minor. He responded by entering a plea of Not Guilty.

An investigation revealed that the adoptive father had been forcing the small boy to do the work of an animal ever since his goat died. Oscar was sent out daily with the cart and expected to go around town picking up garbage to feed to the man's pigs. The poor little lad had been hauling up to sixty pounds of garbage nearly two miles a day for the past ten months! And that was not the nastiest part. To make matters worse, the boy was whipped nearly every night and frequently given no supper. The father's response to the investigation was to deny everything. He said the child was a liar and accused him of stealing a watch and ring from him.

Justice Vitt ruled that it would be in the best interest of the boy to remove him from his adoptive father. He was placed in a temporary home with a farmer who lived on Richmond Road until one of the boy's relatives was located. Vitt fined the adoptive father $50. Mary Ann stood by Oscar throughout the hearing. She was pleased that the boy was now safe from harm, but less than satisfied with the degree of punishment that was doled out to his abuser.

Bosh! Spooney!

Oh, how Mary Ann wished that she had been allowed to add a taste of her own stout stick to his sentence that day!

Outwardly, Mary Ann carried herself with bullet proof self-confidence but inside she was really shaken the day she learned of the cruel murder of her neighbor Annie Deignan. She knew both the victim and murderer well. They were husband and wife and lived just a few houses up the block from her home. Mary Ann recoiled in disgust remembering the many times she had made small talk with Edward Reinhart on the street or even worse, how her own children knew him and visited his store regularly to buy penny candy. It was such an ugly tragedy and way too close for comfort just a few feet away from her front door.

Reinhart was a New Jersey native who had hidden from everyone the fact that he had served time in state prison. After Reinhart married Annie and landed a job at the Rubsam and Horrmann Brewery, the couple moved to Rocky Hollow. They rented a three-room apartment on the first floor of a two-family home on Broad Street.

The house was owned by Charles Herborn, the editor of a popular local German language newspaper. Annie, an ambitious young woman, set up one rented room as their living quarters, the second as a bedroom, and turned the third room that faced Broad Street into a small candy store. The Bascombe children loved having a candy source so close to home. They hunted for pennies in the streets and when they found one took it to the store to buy licorice. When they entered the store, they were always happy when Annie waited on them. She was warm and friendly, in sharp contrast to her husband who was sullen and quite distant.

Neighbors saw that the Reinhart marriage was a rocky union. Edward often said cruel things to his wife in front of others. He went missing for long periods of time and left poor Annie to manage their affairs on her own.

Annie became pregnant and as her belly grew, so did her worries. Annie and Mrs. Herborn had become close, so one day she confided in her friend. Her mother had not approved of her marriage to Reinhart. She would not be there to help when the baby was born. Mrs. Herborn saw the apprehension in her face. She reassured the young wife.

Don't worry Annie. I will be at your side when the time comes.

Mrs. Herborn took the young woman's hand and held it in hers. Annie heaved a sigh of relief. She began to look forward to the baby's birth and the happiness it would bring her as a new mother.

Annie was last seen alive by Mr. Herborn. He came into the candy store on the day the rent was due and asked for her husband. Annie went into the back room and sent Reinhart out to speak to him. Reinhart and Herborn exchanged words over the payment. The conversation went from civil exchange to a heated argument. Reinhart declared that the couple would be moving out the next day.

To the disappointment of the Bascombe children, the candy shop closed early that afternoon. The front door was bolted, and the windows shuttered. No voices were heard, but witnesses swore later on that they heard a sawing sound coming from the apartment.

The next day, Reinhart told the Herborns they were moving to New York City and he had sent Annie on ahead of him to set up their new home. Reinhart packed up the furniture. He took out a wheel barrow and placed in it a barrel with sawed off staves, covered with a piece of malt bag carpeting. Reinhart said that the barrel contained crockery and he was bringing it over to his sister's house on Richmond Road. Reinhart pushed the wheelbarrow up Broad Street. He turned right on Richmond Road, heading north. Reinhart passed his sister's house but did not stop. He kept going up to Silver Lake. On his way, he passed four people.

Two months later, a gory discovery was made. Three boys were herding cattle near Silver Lake when one of them noticed part of a barrel sticking out of the ground. It was a few feet from a wagon trail. Called Little Serpentine Road, the trail ran from Richmond Road near the intersection of Broad Street up the side of Grymes Hill. The boys began to dig out the barrel and saw that a piece of old carpet was nailed over the top.

They were boys and naturally curious, so they pulled away the carpet. What they found inside the barrel made them physically sick. It was the body of a partially nude woman in advanced stage of decomposition. The body was bent in half, with the arms folded over the chest, wrapped in burlap belonging to the Rubsam and Horrmann Brewery. County Coroner James Dempsey concluded that the cause of death was the result of a skull fracture. As no one had reported a missing person, the body was laid to rest in Potter's Field.

Richmond County officials appealed to the public to help solve the mystery of the dead woman. An old German called Water-cress Man came forward to talk to police. About eight weeks prior he had seen a young man digging a hole in a gully near Silver Lake. He had a barrel like the one found by the boys. The man said he was burying his dog.

The investigation continued and led authorities to Edward Reinhart. When the police arrived at his New York City apartment to question him, they found him living with another woman. Reinhart admitted to having once lived on Broad Street but denied all else. He stated he didn't know anything about the barrel or Annie's death, but changed his tune after being confronted with the testimony of the Water-cress Man. Under pressure, Reinhart admitted that yes, he had buried Annie near the lake, but insisted that her death was not at his hands. Annie's demise had been the result of a side effect of a medication she was taking.

Bosh! Spooney! Utter hogwash!

Mary Ann read the newspaper article and did not believe one iota of Reinhart's story. Neither did the police. Reinhart was going to trial for murder. If convicted, it would be only the second time in history that a man would go to the gallows for the crime of murder in Richmond County. Reinhart hired the famous New York City criminal lawyer, Counselor William T. Howe, to defend him.

Throughout the trial, Stapleton was a bee hive of activity. Carriages and wagons flew by the Bascombe home every day, bringing scores of people from the Stapleton ferries over to the county courthouse in Richmond. The trial was a great boom for Stapleton business. The beer gardens, saloons, and hotels made money hand over fist as they fed, housed, and entertained reporters and other out-of-towners who flocked to the proceedings.

William F. Howe was indeed larger than life in person. Mary Ann got a glimpse of Counselor Howe at his craft during the trial, but she was far too busy with business matters to make it a routine habit. Howe mustered up all the flamboyance he could to give a worthy performance in his defense of Reinhart, but in the end, there was too much solid evidence for the jury to be swept away by Howe's histrionics. Reinhart was convicted of first degree murder.

Edward Reinhart's day of reckoning was scheduled for the dead of winter. Mary Ann could have tried to get admitted to the hanging, but she was just as happy to pass on the affair. There was no need for her to go. She would find out all the gory details because of her friendship with Michael Oates. The court had appointed him Reinhart's undertaker.

Mary Ann predicted that the hanging would turn into a circus and it most certainly did. Faced with the once in a lifetime opportunity to make fast cash, local business owners advertised the gruesome event by printing up flyers and distributing them all over Staten Island and New York. By 9 a.m. that morning, the streets of Richmond and its neighboring community of New

Dorp were jammed with sleighs, wagons, and carriages. Vendors sold hot food while a large throng of people milled about in the streets.

The ghoulish curiosity seekers who showed up to attend the hanging were disappointed to find out there would only be a limited number of spectators. The execution was not to be held in an open field but inside the fenced courtyard behind the jail. To gain entrance, one had to have a card that read, *Admit the bearer,* signed by Sheriff Conner. The one hundred people who held these passes were allowed into the Courthouse and directed to stand outside under umbrellas and wait in the cold drizzle. When all the deputies, policemen, and reporters were added in, the actual number viewing the execution totaled close to one hundred fifty witnesses.

Mary Ann was less than pleased to hear of the considerations which were granted to her murdering neighbor during his last few hours of life. Reinhart smoked cigars and alternated between silent moments and casual chats with those who were on hand. He read and ripped up letters from his woman and the clergy. He thanked the county sheriff and deputy for treating him well even though he had joined others in a botched prison escape.

Around 4 a.m., Reinhart began to polish his boots and assemble his attire. He seemed to want to make sure he would leave this life well dressed. Then he laid in silence with his hands in his face for nearly an hour. Reinhart was served deboned quail on toast for breakfast. Having no appetite, he gave the food to an old sailor who was jailed close by. The last person he spoke to was his attorney, the portly red-faced Counselor Howe, who was overheard telling his client if only he had only dug three inches lower this unfortunate situation would not have occurred.

Oates told Mary Ann that after Howe left, the sheriff entered Reinhart's cell and read the death warrant. Then a hangman bound Reinhart's hands behind his body. Oates followed in line as the murderer was paraded through a crowded corridor into the courtyard. The noose was laid loose around his neck and a black cap placed over his face. A local clergyman read a long-winded Bible passage. Then it was time for the hangman to do his duty.

It took Reinhart six agonizing minutes to die. The ugly spectacle of watching him writhe and thrash about as he suffocated was so horrifying that Oates fainted at the scene. Those around him were surprised. They did not realize that Oates, who handled hundreds of lifeless bodies in his line of work, had never seen a man die. Oates was carried off by four brawny Richmond County police officers and given smelling salts while Reinhart's body was taken down from the scaffold. When he woke up, Oates was thoroughly embarrassed but resumed his duties as the undertaker. He supervised the burial of Edward Reinhart at Silver Mount Cemetery. As the casket was lowered into the ground, Oates thought about the irony of it all. Reinhart's place of eternal repose was eerily close to the spot where he had buried Annie.

Back in Rocky Hollow, the news of Reinhart's execution was greeted with a sigh of relief. Now all the hubbub would die down and they could all put this tragedy to rest. A bit of gloom had hung over the neighborhood for more than three years, but on this day, justice had been done. God was now his judge, and although the Almighty Father in Heaven might be so inclined as to grant Reinhart mercy on his soul, the inhabitants of Rocky Hollow held true to their beliefs. To them, his deed was unforgivable.

With the day ending, Mary Ann went into her bedroom and changed into her night clothes. She sat on a chair facing the room mirror and one by one undid the pins holding her hair up. Mary Ann watched absentmindedly as graying hair cascaded down over her shoulders. She reached for the brush on the dresser and ran it through her hair over and over until she felt it was properly smoothed out. Then she tied it back with ribbon. She got into her bed and gave sleepy James a peck on the cheek good night.

Mary Ann started her nightly prayers. Midway through she stopped, as Annie's cheery face came to mind. Poor sweet

Annie could now rest in peace. Amen to that. Mary Ann asked God to look after Annie and her unborn child up in heaven. She made the sign of the cross. Then she closed her eyes and let her thoughts drift.

Edward Reinhart is no longer of this earth. A terrible evil has been expelled from my hometown. All will sleep well this night.

CHAPTER TEN: MRS. MACK WILL BE THERE

" *S he was a politician as well as a landlord, and while sex prevented her from voting, she actually yielded such influence that she was for years and up to the time of her death, able to roll up an unfailing majority for the Democratic party.*"[1]

Mother! Oh, mother! Company at the door for you!

John Bascombe opened the front door and led a man wearing a stylishly vested suit to a chair inside the parlor. Then, he disappeared into an unseen corner of the house. Mary Ann had been busy in the kitchen preparing an array of light snacks. She was expecting the visitor. He was a reporter who asked to interview her about the newly founded Ladies Cleveland Club of Stapleton. With a broad smile Mary Ann bounced into the room, carrying with her a tray which held a pot of hot tea and assorted jellies and breads.

It was 1884, and Mary Ann was captivated by the national political scene. Everyone was. Male or female, few in America could overlook the excitement of the presidential campaign. Grover Cleveland, the Democratic Governor of New York State, was running against James G. Blaine, the former Republican U.S. Senator from Maine. It was a hotly contested campaign. On the line in the election was an unbroken chain of Republican presidents stretching back to 1860. Cleveland stood a good chance of winning, and his supporters were going all out for their candidate.

After tea and the requisite pleasantries were exchanged, the reporter asked if he could sit at her dining table. He took writing supplies out of his bag and arranged them before him. Then, he asked Mary Ann to tell him about the club.

Mary Ann spoke, and the reporter scribbled. She began by telling the reporter how pleased she was that he had come to speak to her. Mary Ann started the group because she was a staunch supporter of Grover's candidacy. She was the club president and had so far recruited thirty other dedicated women to the cause. She was eager to spread the word about Cleveland.

Mary Ann said that club members had a great deal of work ahead of them before Election Day to which the reporter agreed. As she began to explain her strategy, the man was somewhat disappointed to learn there would be no fancy parades, band concerts, or banner waving rallies like he was used to seeing from ladies' groups. Mary Ann was dead set against demonstrations of such sort as she thought they were self-serving and did nothing to guarantee the desired result. Besides, her club members would most likely balk at the notion, being too persnickety for such things. No, her club members remained duly focused on what was the heart of the matter - locking in votes for their man Grover!

Mary Ann told him that The Ladies Cleveland Club was not your typical women's group, a comment which intrigued the reporter.

So, if there are to be no public demonstrations, what will you do then? he innocently asked.

Mary Ann smiled, and then launched into a long and lengthy explanation. The reporter jotted down one specific quote and then stopped writing. He sat back in his chair to listen and take in the essence of what she was saying.

"The special object of this club is to advise such of our male relatives and friends as may be of doubt as of how to vote."[2]

The Cleveland gals were targeting men on the political fence and pulling them aside one by one to make persuasive arguments. Their goal was to secure a pledge from each man to vote for their candidate. Club members were not wasting their time with those who were the faithful, like staunch Democrats.

Instead, they were going after the self-declared Butlerites, luke-warm Democrats, and any undecided Republicans.

The reporter could not help but note the uncomplicated eloquence of her speech. Her words were straightforward, yet carefully crafted. She was not describing a social club here. Why, this woman and her lady friends were out there telling men what to do! Personally, he found the notion a bit appalling but realized if his true feelings slipped out she might stop talking. That would mean the end of the article and no paycheck for him. So, the reporter returned to his work and began writing feverishly. He let her ramble on, nodding his head here and there as if in agreement.

Mary Ann proudly proclaimed that she already had the promise of several Republican voters in her district. The reporter threw her a quizzical look and asked how she knew they would keep their pledge to vote for a Democrat. Mary Ann fired back.

Pish! Posh! I will be going to the polls on Election Day to greet the voters with a stack of Cleveland tickets in one hand and my stout stick in the other. Mrs. Mack will make sure they stay true to their word!

The reporter, who had been doing a stellar job hiding his feelings up to that point, finally lost his composure.

Pardon me Mrs. Bascombe, but did I hear you right? Are you planning to use your club on the men? he asked.

Well, it is not my wish to actually USE the stick, Mary Ann coyly replied.

The reporter now had more than enough information for his article. He packed up, thanked Mary Ann for her hospitality, and went downtown to finish his writing. Mary Ann was pleased to read the article about her club the next day in his newspaper. This publicity would surely help the cause!

By the time Election Day arrived, the campaigns of both presidential candidates had taken their fair share of lumps. Cleveland had his reputation as a hardworking man of integrity sullied by the revelation that he was contributing support to a child born out of wedlock. Blaine campaigned bearing the weight of having been accused of selling votes to big business during his tenure as a member of the House of Representatives.

Towards the end of the campaign, Blaine overlooked a slur made by one of his supporters against those of the Roman Catholic faith. He paid dearly for the mistake. Priests from all over New York State were incensed by the remarks. They began a campaign against the Republican, urging parishioners to come out in force and vote against him.

On Election Day, Mary Ann and her club members got to the polls early. At the end of the day, they went home and prayed. The press reported that Cleveland had locked up the South and Blaine the Midwest. In the end, it came down to the voters of New York State with its thirty-six electoral votes to decide the election.

New York was a divided state. Downstate New York was heavily Democratic. Upstate was of a Republican constituency. On Election Day, heavy rains flooded upstate New York and kept many Republicans away from the polls. When the polls closed, the winner could not be predicted. The count was extremely close.

When the results were announced, the count was disputed. A recount was ordered by the courts. Allegations were made that all the downstate ballot boxes had not been counted and some had been tossed into New York Bay. This was never confirmed.

By November 6th, the results were apparent. Governor Cleveland was awarded the electoral votes he needed to be declared the winner. *The New York Times* proclaimed a Democratic plurality in New York, New Jersey and Connecticut, and declared victory for Cleveland.

New Yorkers had backed their governor. Cleveland received nearly two thousand more votes than his Republican challenger. Mary Ann and her political ladies rejoiced! With their help a New York Democrat had been elected to the highest office in the nation!

As Stapleton was a solidly Democratic town, there was surely no better reason for a grand celebration. Mary Ann and the ladies of the Cleveland Club attended many local victory events held over the next few days. November chills filled the air but no one standing outside seemed to mind. Bands played, speeches were made, and the club members whooped it up in Washington Park with all the other Cleveland supporters. Included in the celebration was a walk over to St. Mary's Church to give special thanks to the Lord above for the fantabulous victory!

Mary Ann unabashedly accepted the credit she received for the local victory. The accolades helped manage the sting inside her that never went away. It was well known throughout the neighborhood that Mary Ann was sensitive about not being allowed to vote. The topic was so upsetting that locals made conscious efforts to avoid bringing the subject up in conversation. If it did get brought up, odds were that she'd launch into a long and drawn out tirade.

Good fer nothin' drunks in town have the vote. Old senile men have the vote. Yet here I am, a hardworking taxpaying member of the community and I am denied the right? I hold more property than most men in this town. I have more money than all the men I know. Doesn't that count for something? If I'm smart enough to tell the men folk who to vote for, why can't I just cast a ballot alongside with them!

Bosh! Spooney! Makes me so MAD!

James understood how she felt and knew the best way to handle Mary Ann after getting so riled up on the subject was to shift her thoughts to hopes for the future.

Yes Mary Ann. It's wrong but things will change. Just a matter of time. Those fools in Washington will sooner or later be brought to their senses. God willing, we both live to see the day!

In a few weeks, the presidential election excitement died down. Grover Cleveland began to pack his belongings in the Governor's mansion for the highly anticipated move to the White House. The holidays came and went, and Mary Ann settled back into her daily routines. Politics continued to take up a big part of her time.

There was no doubt. Mary Ann loved politics. In a way, politics mirrored the scrappy nature of her life. It was a rough and tumble mix of setting goals, fostering alliances, working interminably hard, and hopefully getting what one wanted in the end. She had been hooked on the thrill of politics as a small child listening to Thomas McDonough and his cronies in their spirited talks over a bottle of Irish whiskey. Now, as an adult, Mary Ann passionately followed in the footsteps of her father.

And, as luck would have it, Mary Ann lived in just the right place to stoke that passion. Stapleton was a place where political drama and highly charged partisanship was a way of life. As far back as Mary Ann could remember, political conventions were held here and candidates came to town stumping for votes. Throughout the season, Mary Ann and her neighbors were treated to grand entertainment sponsored by the competing political parties. There were delightful parades and demonstrations which featured flag displays, banners, fireworks, and gun salutes. There were concerts where musicians played gay patriotic music. And, places like Washington Park with its central bandstand which served as a focal point for major political debates.

Because of the superfluity of government positions, many offices were up for grabs each November on Staten Island – so many that it made the campaigning seem endless. County-wide there was an elected school commissioner, surrogate and county judge, district attorney, sheriff, county clerk, county treasurer, coroner, and justices of the peace. As part of the Middletown region of Staten Island, Stapleton voters elected an overall supervisor. And, as part of the incorporated Village of Edgewater which included the town of Clifton and a section of Tompkinsville, Stapleton citizens elected trustees, constables, tax assessors, tax collectors, town clerk, and a highway commissioner.

Edgewater's offices were located in Village Hall, a handsome red brick building situated at the edge of Washington Park in downtown Stapleton. It was of stylish Italian Renaissance construction with oversized windows, mosaic tile hallways, galvanized iron tower, and a slate roof. As an adult, Mary Ann's intrigue with politics intertwined with her business interests and civic causes. She saw the value of developing close working relationships with elected officials and thus, over time became a familiar face at Village Hall.

Stapleton was undeniably the political hub of the east shore of Staten Island and its citizens a worldly bunch. The daily arrival of visitors aboard the ferries, yachts, and commercial boats put Stapleton citizens in regular contact with a multitude of outsiders who lived near and far. For those who could read, there was a wealth of published newspapers which offered up news and information. *The Richmond County Gazette, The Staten Islander, Staten Island Leader,* and *Der deutsche Staten Islander* were all printed on a weekly or semi-weekly basis in Stapleton, while big city newspapers like the *New York Herald, The New York Evening Post, The New York Times,* and *The New York Evening Telegram* afforded daily coverage of newsworthy events on Staten Island.

If one was interested in understanding both sides of an issue, it was necessary to read a variety of newspapers because editors rarely disguised their biases in reporting the news. The articles written were often incendiary and spawned ferocious debates among the readership, no doubt aided by the town's seemingly limitless amount of free-flowing lager. In saloons, beer gardens and hotels around town it was quite common for political discussions to start up, heat up, and end up in a physical brawl.

Republicans and Democrats were the two main parties in town and with few exceptions, the political leanings of Stapleton residents fell predictably along nationalistic and socioeconomic lines. Around the time of the Civil War, abolitionists such as Francis George Shaw welcomed the burgeoning Republican Party to Staten Island by supporting John Fremont, the first Republican candidate for United States President. Years passed, and party membership grew to include many of the well-to-do businessmen and professionals who lived in and around the grand hills overlooking Stapleton.

After the War, the economy boomed and record numbers of immigrants came to New York. Stapleton's population soared because of its location and the ongoing success of the brewery industry. The Democratic Party, as the champions of unions and the working class, appealed more directly to Rocky Hollow citizens.

Mary Ann was a rock solid Democrat just like her father, although in her own unique way, she straddled both worlds. She lived among her Democratic brethren yet had a lot in common with the Republican bankers, businessmen, and lawyers with whom she was in frequent contact. She agreed with Republicans on subjects such as government efficiency and fiscal spending. However, she never strayed from her Democratic allegiances.

Besides family tradition, there was an obvious practicality for Mary Ann to remain a Democrat. In Stapleton, almost all key government positions were held by Democrats, so the sheer numbers of Democratic voters made it almost impossible for a Republican candidate to win.

Mary Ann's strong support for her father's party certainly pleased the Stapleton party organizers. They recognized her as a valuable asset. She attended most public hearings. She was well read and well versed on the issues. Mary Ann had no qualms speaking up and questioning officials at a political gathering or debate. And, she was quite willing to stump around town to lock in votes for her candidates.

Mary Ann was the only female in Stapleton who could lay claim to being a political powerhouse. So, even though the laws did not allow her to cast a ballot, she delivered real results time after time. Though her carried a stout stick, all that Mary Ann ever really needed to do to win over a voter was offer a few words of personal confidence in a candidate. Mary Ann's tenants trusted what she had to say. They voted for whoever she endorsed.

In Stapleton, political contests were battles to be won at all costs. Fairness took a back seat to winning and both political parties were guilty at times of questionable tactics. The unorthodox nature of elections combined with an overlapping bureaucracy and the appointments of many unqualified people to government positions contributed to an overall climate of collusion and corruption.

The season of election craziness started with political party conventions. Instead of meeting to have a healthy debate on the issues leading up to party consensus, the primaries were often winner take all events. There was so little compromise that often the events deteriorated into raucous, uncivil affairs. Sometimes the in-fighting went on and on for days until one of the factions stormed out of the proceedings. In that case, splinter groups such as the Independent Republicans or Independent Democrats were formed to challenge the regular party candidates.

Backroom wheeling and dealing for votes took place up to Election Day, which was also a wild and woolly affair. Secret ballots did not go into effect until 1890, so it was easy for voters to be openly intimidated. Since many citizens could not read or write, ballot tickets with the candidates' names written on them were handed out at the polling place. Everyone could see how a ballot was being cast. They were instructed to submit only one piece of paper, but some men surreptitiously stuffed the ballot box with additional tickets. Wielding a stout stick in the vicinity of voters wasn't shocking at all because all sorts of bullying tactics were being used. Party members and the candidates themselves turned out at the polls to bully voters.

Election inspectors stationed at the polls were supposed to prevent such events from happening, but they were often in cahoots with the political parties. They too contributed to the fraud and illegal activities by open electioneering.

Sailors were commonly at the center of election fraud schemes because of their transient living arrangements. Both Democrat and Republican officials went down to the docks and bought votes. In a close election, votes could cost up to $2 a piece.

The skullduggery that went on behind the scenes led to arrests and investigations resulting in criminal fines and jail time. Even the Village Trustees who should have known better than anyone else not to pull off such tomfoolery were occasionally found guilty of illegal acts. Mary Ann learned early on to steer away from such kinds of shenanigans. She campaigned vigorously for her candidates, but then let the will of the people run its course on Election Day.

Election craziness did make for good gossip, though.

Dang! Can you believe the gall of that Trustee? His brother is sheriff, and he goes and attacks a police officer in the middle of balloting! How did he think he'd get away with it? Did'ye hear he's out on $500 bail? Crazy enough, but what'ye think about that loser in the Trustee race? They say he's served papers on *the other Trustees! Twenty-nine votes cast by sailors livin' in a New York boarding house is pretty fishy, so he's right to git a full investigation!*

Mary Ann did not hesitate to endorse her friends and families for public office. And, in return for her efforts, she expected preferential treatment. When she headed into Village Hall to speak with an official, she was not there just to share her thoughts on problems in the community but instead dictate how to solve them! She fought for the installation of storm sewers to stem the flooding of Gore's Brook. She called for road improvements so people could get to and from work, school, and church more easily. She battled for fair taxation, and this is where she most likely became better acquainted with fellow Democrat Michael McGuire.

Mary Ann had known McGuire since he was a child. Like Mary Ann, he was born and raised in Stapleton. Handsome and well spoken, he was close in age to Mary Jane. McGuire started his career as an ambitious public servant in his early twenties. Career was the right word for it, as he was still young but had already been elected or appointed to many local and county positions. McGuire had been a Village Trustee and Highway Commissioner. He served as a Justice of the Peace, where he was well remembered by the locals for his infamous sentencing of the murderer of poor Billy the Goat.

Mary Ann and McGuire got to know each other well in the years he served as Middletown Tax and School Tax Collector. Some days she would drive down to Village Hall with a basket of fresh biscuits baked especially for McGuire. He'd sample her baking, they'd make small chit chat, and then she would turn to the business at hand. Mary Ann had a ton of questions about perceived unfair tax assessments, and she and McGuire would get into heated arguments. They battled, and then like most other officials, McGuire caved under the pressure. He gave in and made the desired tax bill adjustments.

When McGuire was elected to the New York State Assembly, Mary Ann had mixed feelings. She was happy that it was a political step up for him and a feather in the cap of the Democrats of her hometown, but she missed her pleasant adversary. She liked him so much that she remained a supporter even after a serious scandal erupted during McGuire's campaign for a second term. McGuire was pitted against Republican challenger Michael Conklin and when McGuire was named the winner, Conklin challenged the results.

The votes of sailors living at a northern Staten Island rest home called Snug Harbor were at the center of the controversy. The investigation revealed that Republican sailors' votes had not been counted and Democratic votes had been cast by men who did not vote, who no longer lived at Snug Harbor, by bedridden sailors, and even those dead for many years! Conklin got his satisfaction. McGuire was made to step down as Assemblyman.

The scandal generated headlines that sold a great many newspapers. County officials, recognizing that these practices needed to stop, tried to use the opportunity to educate voters on proper electioneering. The Richmond County District Attorney published abstracts of the New York State Penal Code in the newspapers. Among other things, the code clearly spelt out what was acceptable and unacceptable behavior for candidates and voters, what was considered unlawful behavior by election officials, and the penalties for violation of the election laws. They hoped that McGuire's disgrace had been a serious enough transgression to put an end to unscrupulous election practices, but this was not the case. Fraud, intimidation, ballot burning, and other improprieties continued.

Mary Ann had occasion to run into McGuire on the streets of Stapleton during the dark days of the inquiry. McGuire stuck to the story that he was an innocent who had been used by unsavory party members. Mary Ann thought about it. She knew the Democratic Party leaders well. Some were so shady she wouldn't trust them with a penny. Yes, it was possible that McGuire knew nothing of the Snug Harbor hanky-panky. McGuire had an appealing way about him, and it charmed the middle-aged lady. Mary Ann chose to believe him.

If McGuire believed he was off the hook after the Conklin affair, he was wrong. Soon after the State Assembly scandal, he was arrested again. A Richmond County Grand Jury indicted him, charging the politician with second degree grand larceny in eleven separate indictments. It was alleged that McGuire stole taxpayer money and then perjured himself by making false affidavits. McGuire's bail was set at $5000, an enormous sum of money.

McGuire was in a tight bind. He needed help from those who had deep pockets. He send word to Mary Ann and Robert Goggin, his friend and the village constable, to visit his jail cell. When they arrived, McGuire vehemently denied the charges against him and asked if they could please favor him by posting bail.

Neither Mary Ann or the constable responded at first. Mary Ann fired a series of questions at McGuire. Then, they excused themselves to go outside and discuss. When they returned, Mary Ann told him they would share the cost of McGuire's bail.

Mary Ann had been asked for handouts, bail money, and personal loans from people many times over and she had rarely complied with the requests. At the supper table that night she was peppered with inquiries. James and the children were quite curious to learn her reasoning.

Her husband asked: *What made you break your own rule Mary Ann? Why intercede on McGuire's behalf?*

Mary Ann told them that she was not sure she believed McGuire, but decided to post the bail as a business decision. When he was Highway Commissioner, McGuire gave the go ahead for some needed road work on Rocky Hollow streets and to get the project moving forward, Mary Ann paid some of the contractors from her personal funds. McGuire promised then that she would be reimbursed by the town, but this had not yet happened. By bailing McGuire out of jail, it gave him the opportunity to put together a solid defense with his lawyer. If he beat the charges McGuire might still have a measure of political influence. Maybe she'd get her money back.

Michael McGuire clearly had the luck of the Irish. In the end, there was no trial. All charges were dropped due to a legal technicality and the bail money was returned.

Mary Ann was relieved. She went to pay McGuire a call soon

after the charges were dropped. He thanked her profusely. Mary Ann was pleasant in return but by now was far less smitten by his charm. She followed his words of gratitude with a lengthy lecture. Thanks were not necessary. She wanted to be reimbursed for the money she fronted to make the road improvements. He promised he'd get on it right away.

Mary Ann looked warily into his obsequious eyes.

She had little choice but to wait.

Chapter Eleven: Greatest Woman Politician

Oh, how glorious it would have been to attend school!
A formal education was one of Mary Ann's nagging unfulfilled dreams. She vividly recollected when as a small girl she hid behind the trees surrounding the one room schoolhouse near her home. Mary Ann watched with envy as the boys filed inside one by one after the schoolmaster rang his bell. Sometimes she would brazenly stoop under an open window to listen to the lesson. What a true disappointment it was on the day she finally asked and was told by her father that she could not attend that little school. Mary Ann was glad that the times had changed. Formal schooling was the best way to equip a child with the reading, writing, and arithmetic skills necessary to be a success in life, so she encouraged all her children to take advantage of every opportunity to learn.

In 1855, the state legislature had authorized the construction of a new district school building in Stapleton which replaced tiny district schools like the one which existed near the McDonough's home. Land was purchased at the corner of Broad and Brook Streets in downtown Stapleton. Built at a cost of about $13,000, the school had six classrooms for the lower grades, and a separate upper boy and girl division. Oversight of the school district was delegated to three elected trustees and an elected school tax collector. Together, they managed the day to day operations of the main school as well as a small nearby school for children of color.

Pupil enrollment grew steadily, as did the overall Stapleton population. When Mary Jane and William were in school there

186

was ample classroom space, but by the time Thomas, James, and Mary Ellen attended, the school was overcrowded. Families with school age children continued moving into town, so that by the time Mary Ann's youngest children, Emma, John, and Joseph, were old enough to go to school, construction of an extension was necessary. Mary Ann kept watch on the construction and opined that the extension was too small to meet the needs of the ever-increasing student population. She was right, because soon after the overcrowding nearly caused a community catastrophe.

The maximum capacity of the Broad Street School was 300 students, but in 1885 over 700 pupils were enrolled. The main building was rather tall, standing at three stories high. There were only two ways to exit the building – through the main door porch and down a set of steps to the street or out a short corridor under the porch leading to the schoolyard. There were no fire escapes.

One day, a small child attending classes on the ground floor pulled on a big sliding door which separated two classrooms. The door was on a track, but it was loose with worn out rollers. It fell off the track and crashed down on its side, upsetting a large stove. Coals hit the ground.

FIRE! FIRE! the children shrieked.

Emma and the littlest ones on the first floor got out quickly and safely, but John and the older children upstairs panicked. They did not know how to properly evacuate because the school administrators had never conducted fire drills. They ran about helter-skelter. Some tried to jump out windows but were stopped by their teachers. Others, in a free for all, bolted to the stairs. On their way out, the children trampled the vice principal who was trying to keep the calm, knocking him clear to the bottom of the stairs.

A nearby Richmond County police officer heard the ruckus and ran down to the Washington Park fire tower. Men in the local fire brigades, hearing the toll of the bell, dropped what they were doing and bolted towards their respective companies to retrieve firefighting equipment. Black smoke rose in the skies, pinpointing the location of the blaze. News spread through the community as fast as a wildfire.

Oh, dear God! Our precious babies!

Parents took off in horror toward the school. Mary Ann jumped up into her wagon and drove her horse as fast as possible down Broad Street. She didn't bother to tether the animal. Mary Ann leaped from the wagon and joined the other parents who were searching the crowd, franticly calling out their children's names. Mary Ann spotted Emma and John standing together under a tree. She ran to them and gave them smothering hugs.

By the grace of God, there had been men at work inside the school at the time of fire. They extinguished the flames, saving the day for the children and the structure. When everyone in the building had been accounted for, the casualties amounted to a handful of adults and children with minor bruises. No one was seriously injured.

In the aftermath of the fire, Mary Ann joined an angry contingent of Stapleton parents who demanded a full investigation. Parents flooded the school at the next regularly scheduled public meeting of the district. One after the other spoke, insisting that the trustees mandate regular fire drills and devise a long-term solution for the overcrowding.

The trustees offered no excuses to the hostile crowd. They publicly admonished the school principal and ordered him to conduct fire drills from then on. They were not as forthright, however, in addressing the much bigger problem of the school building.

The fact that these men offered no concrete plan to address the overcrowded conditions was of no surprise to Mary Ann. The Stapleton School District was a disaster. Its politics were as bad or even worse than the nefarious wheeling and dealings that went on between the town's Democrats and Republicans. Unfair politicking for votes, misuse of power, and mishandling of monies were commonplace scandals. These matters, along with a host of other issues associated with the schooling of local blacks, ensured there was almost always some degree of turmoil.

Stapleton's one room schoolhouse for children of color had

been established around the same time as the school for whites. The school was not far from Mary Ann's house in Rocky Hollow at the point where Riker and Centre Street met. It was a small space but the center of big controversies. The parents of the Centre Street School were strong advocates for their children's education and stood up for their rights at every opportunity. One time when the regular black teacher took sick and a white substitute teacher was dispatched as her replacement, the parents went into a tizzy. A band of angry parents marched over to meet with the school trustees. They demanded a teacher of their own race. As far as they were concerned, only an inexperienced inferior white teacher would be willing to instruct their children, so they didn't want her. The parents gave the trustees an ultimatum: remove the white teacher immediately, or no one would send their children to school. The board trustees' hands were tied. They gave in to the parents' complaints and found a new black teacher.

It was uncharacteristic for the three trustees to come to quick agreement over what to do, but a boycott was something they could not ignore. The controversy generated some gossip around Rocky Hollow, but Mary Ann stood firmly on the side of the parents. Rocky Hollow was still a small enough community where she knew most of her black neighbors by name. These were God fearing citizens who had a gripe which most likely had some degree of truth. Yes, they did have the right to a say in who taught their children!

As the mother of eight, Mary Ann had years of experience watching the trustees in action and was quite unimpressed with the way they conducted business. Why, weren't they like children themselves at times with their self-centered, childish, and impractical behaviors! She let out an audible sound of disgust as she thought about incidents of the past that proved her point. A good example was the time two trustees ganged up on the third just because of personalities. Jealous that the one trustee had become too friendly with the principals of the schools, by a two to one vote they capriciously fired both educators without cause.

Mary Ann tried her best to overlook the minor shenanigans

of the trustees and concentrate on major issues such as school safety and the budget. Go ahead and feud, so long as it caused no harm to the town or its children. Monitoring the school budget was relatively easy for her since the district collected its taxes separate from the Village. Mary Ann kept an eye on purchases of books and supplies, staff salaries, and maintenance of the school property to ensure her tax money was being spent wisely. She was a regular at the public meetings of the school board. Though there were no assigned seats, just about everyone knew to leave one open front and center for her in the first row. It was a rare occasion if she showed up and wasn't itching to pepper the trustees with a series of questions.

She kept a particularly close eye on the monies being spent because of a history of problems within the district. School tax collectors varied greatly in their degrees of competency. Some men used the position as a springboard to other elected offices and were not skilled or very much invested in balancing the books.

One of the most perplexing episodes in the past involved a well-liked tax collector by the name of Scott. He was a career public servant who had served as clerk of the Village of Edgewater and a Board of Health clerk prior to his election as School Tax Collector. Scott was in office for two years when some irregularities in the school ledgers were uncovered. He was such a popular man in the community that not much was made of the error. He apologized and reconciled the books. All was forgiven, and he was easily reelected to a subsequent term of office.

Scott retained his job, but the troubles were far from over. When the next fiscal year ended, Scott did not turn over the district financial records. As a result, the trustees could not provide a required accounting report to the citizens at their annual public meeting. People were astonished at his behavior.

What's up here? What could that man be hiding? What gives with our tax money?

Mary Ann joined those up who were up in arms. An investigation was demanded, and the trustees met with the police chief and a lawyer to figure out what to do. The New York State

Superintendent of Schools was consulted, and everyone was shocked by the response. A law was brought forth that no one could demand that Scott turn over his books or any monies except his successor. And, since he had been re-elected to a second term, Scott was in fact his own successor.

Bosh! Spooney! Such fool laws!

Mary Ann was livid as she continued watching the situation worsen. The trustees decided that the only way they stood a chance of getting the records was to have Scott arrested and charged with embezzlement. In doing so, however, they were also forced to involve another well liked career public servant who held the dual positions of school district clerk and clerk of the Middletown region of Staten Island. The bond for Scott's funds should have been locked in an iron safe but the clerk claimed the document was missing and he did not know where it went. The police assumed that it may have been deliberately destroyed so they were forced to arrest the clerk too.

Gossip ran wild. Accusations were made that the trustees knew about their was something fishy the year before and turned a blind eye. Their lawyer, John Widdecombe, tried to sort matters out and recoup the money from Scott and his supporters. As the legal nonsense dragged on, innocent victims paid the price. The trustees were forced to freeze district's funds, and Stapleton's poor unfortunate teachers had to work without pay.

The bold and brazen high jinx that went on in local politics and the school district year after year got Mary Ann's blood boiling but at least in the school district she had some recourse. Though the laws of the nation prohibited her from casting a ballot in a government election, Mary Ann was the equal of any man in the Stapleton School District.

She had the vote.

New York State school laws were different from those which applied to government elections. Voter eligibility was based on independent home ownership not gender, so Mary Ann most certainly qualified! Mary Ann's properties were held in her name only. She hadn't known this years before, but if Mary Ann had placed her husband's name on the deeds of the properties she owned, by law she would have denied herself this most precious right.

Pish! Posh! How fortunate I was to keep my land purchases separate from James!

It did not quite match the thrill of casting a vote in a presidential election, but Mary Ann was proud of her active involvement in the crazy politics of the school district. In addition to the trustee antics and its various scandals, Stapleton was also widely known for its contentious school elections. The annual campaign to elect school trustees was a fight as ferocious as any partisan political match. Each year, the local newspapers admonished voters to leave politics out of the school elections, but in Stapleton this was almost impossible. As one reporter aptly noted:

"There are two factions in Stapleton that seem to be always opposing each other, and they have scarcely recovered from last year's fight...The vote is always close, and very exciting times are expected."[1]

Mary Ann held her right to cast a ballot in the highest regard, yet even with the vote Mary Ann was not fully satisfied. A single ballot was not enough to change the way the trustees operated. They placated the public by pretending to listen but then did so little to address their concerns. She was sick of their behavior as well as the scandals.

After the school fire she gave the trustees benefit of the doubt that they would act swiftly to relieve the overcrowding and protect the children of the district. However, as she monitored the situation Mary Ann saw that once again, the trustees promised but were doing nothing substantial to prevent another crisis. Their lack of action was the last straw for Mary Ann. She concluded that the time had come for a bold move. Over supper one night, she made an announcement.

James, children, I have news. I have decided to run for school trustee. Since I can't fix the schools' problems from the outside, I must tackle it from the inside!

The little ones stared at her blankly while the older children rolled their eyes. James ceremoniously put down his fork, stood up, and began to applaud.

Why children, let us wish your mother well! Here she sits, all set to make some Stapleton history!

Later that week, Mary Ann dressed in her finest Sunday clothes and drove her wagon down to the school commissioner's office. With great aplomb, she walked in and informed the clerk she was there to register as a candidate for school trustee in her district. The clerk looked her over for a second or two and then took out his fountain pen to write down the particulars of her registration. To the surprise of the clerk, she decided to use her longtime nickname, *Mary Ann Mack,* on the application. She had never quite given up use of the name, and on this important occasion it seemed appropriate to her. All should be reminded that she was the proud daughter of Thomas McDonough, born and raised in Rocky Hollow and fully committed to do right by the children for the good of the community.

Oh my, she thought as she signed the document. *Daddy, get a good gander at what your little Mary Anna is up to now!*

Mary Ann knew from the start that she was the undeniable underdog in the campaign. She had a vote because she was financially independent, but few women were in similar circumstances. In order to win, she needed the support of the men in town. Going after the male vote did not intimidate Mary Ann, but the incumbent placed her at a severe disadvantage. She had decided to run in a year when the extremely popular Felix O'Hanlon was up for reelection. O'Hanlon was likewise a native of Stapleton and thought by many to be a permanent fixture in the school district. He served as a trustee for more years than anyone cared to remember. Although he had been in the middle of many a controversy during his long tenure, O'Hanlon always seemed to walk away unscathed. His gregarious nature combined with a wide web of connections with other officials and the Stapleton business community made him impossible to beat year after year.

A few of her neighbors were cocky enough to ask Mary Ann straight out:

Why the dickens did you choose a year that O'Hanlon was up for re-election to run for office?

Mary Ann responded that O'Hanlon was part of what was wrong in the district and had to be replaced. She believed in what she was doing and felt that defeating O'Hanlon and his old boy network was daunting but not an impossible task. Mary Ann took her convictions and made it the central theme of her campaign.

District problems could not be solved by those who had had failed to fix them in the past! It was time for change!

The entire Bascombe family was involved in the campaign. Mary Emma cleaned up after breakfast, so Mary Ann could set out early on foot or by wagon to canvass for votes. Mary Ann knocked on her neighbors' doors every day but the Sabbath. The older children and brother Michael put in plugs for Mary Ann at their jobs while the younger boys pitched in doing extra chores around the house. James did his part by visiting his pals at the popular saloons in town. After buying the men a round of ale he'd let them know that it was Mary Ann who picked up the tab. Not surprisingly, James locked in a number of votes for her this way.

Mary Ann's children, who had not been so keen on the idea of her running for office initially, continued to have mixed feelings. It was both exciting and embarrassing at the same time. Their mother never seemed to know when to stop. She was always so involved in her work instead of staying home and taking care of them. Now that she was running for office, they felt more deprived of her time than ever before. What would happen to them if she won the election, they wondered? Secretly, a few of them began to pray that she would lose.

The newspapers ran a series of articles in the days leading up to the vote. Some openly stated their biases, emphasizing that voters should provide schools with the *best men* to run them. Others were less obvious. New York State law was reprinted on the front page of one newspaper to remind citizens who was entitled to vote. Section 12, Title VII of the Code of Public Instruction defined a qualified voter as:

"(1). Every person of full age, residing in any neighborhood or school district, and entitled to hold lands in this State, who owns or hires real property in such neighborhood or school

district liable to taxation for school purposes. (2). And every resident of such neighborhood or district who is a citizen of the United States above the age of twenty one years, and who has permanently residing with him or has a child or children of school age, someone or more of whom shall have attended the district school for a period of at least eight weeks within one year preceding. (3). And every such resident and citizen as aforesaid who owns any personal property assessed on the last preceding assessment roll of the town, exceeding fifty dollars in value, exclusive of such as is exempt from execution, and no other shall be entitled to vote at any school meeting held in such neighborhood or district."[2]

After weeks of hot and sticky door to door summertime campaigning, the day of the school elections arrived. Mary Ann stretched, got out of bed, and said a short self-serving prayer.

Dear God, if it pleases you may this day be one of the few times in my life I will count on the men to come through for me!

When the polls opened that afternoon, Mary Ann was one of the first on hand to cast her vote. Then she went home to greet the neighbors who came to call throughout the day. Their chit chat took her mind off the balloting. When the polls closed at 9 p.m., Mary Ann and her family piled into their wagon and drove downtown. The ballots were to be counted, and the results announced to the throng of citizens who gathered in Washington Park.

In the battle of incumbent vs. dark horse, the incumbent once again won. Two hundred seventy-nine votes were cast for Felix O'Hanlon to top Mary Ann's one hundred thirteen votes. Her children who had been secretly wishing she would lose suddenly felt very guilty. Mary Ann was disappointed but did her best to hide her feelings. She walked over and offered an open hand to O'Hanlon. In return, O'Hanlon offered up his very best political smile, took her hand in his, and congratulated her on running a laudable campaign.

Mary Ann brooded for a bit, but after a few days her spirits began to lift. Thinking it over, she made peace with the results. Over one hundred voters had shown enough confidence in her abilities to entrust her with the safe keeping of the children. This was a grand accomplishment. So what that she lost! She could run again someday if she chose.

Mary Ann was not the winner, but defeat did not silence her agenda. Not at all! She still had the tongue in her jaw and the ballot in her hand to fight for her beliefs. When she stood up to speak at the first school trustee meeting after the election she was humbled by the applause of her supporters. Others believed as she did, encouraging Mary Ann to keep questioning the way things were being done in the district. They viewed her as a true school reformer.

A few months after her defeat, the district experienced yet another major controversy regarding the Centre Street School. Mrs. Johannes was a black woman with children in the district. She had taken classes at the Normal College founded by Thomas Hunter in New York City, and thus was better educated than the majority of white residents in the community. One day, she went to the trustees to voice complaints. Mrs. Johannes was concerned with the quality of education her children were receiving. She was also fearful of health risks in the vicinity of the school. A recent widening of Centre Street had caused a chronic stagnant water pool to accumulate close to the building. Mrs. Johannes believed it would become a major breeding ground for mosquitoes. On the basis of her complaints, she demanded the right to send her children to the Broad Street School.

The trustees, who were so rarely unanimous in their opinions, adamantly refused her request. Reporters got wind of the story, and went out to talk to people around town. Those they interviewed freely voiced their doubts in the abilities of the trustees to manage the situation. Some brought up Mary Ann's name and said it had been a mistake not to elect her.

Too bad that Mrs. Mack isn't on hand. No doubt she could fix the situation to the satisfaction of all.

Mary Ann proved she was a legitimate problem solver a year or two later, when the school election was held on a day of very stormy weather. With dirt roads and no storm sewers, the torrential rain led to flooding and impassable muddy roads throughout Rocky Hollow and other parts of the district. Voting hours were late in the day, and the combination of darkness and muck and mire on the streets kept almost all the women who could vote at home. In her district, Mary Ann was the only female who dared to come out. After reading about this in the newspaper, she questioned the trustees. Why not change the voting hours and make it easier for all citizens to get to the polls? They agreed and next year, the polls opened at 2 p.m. to better accommodate women, the elderly, and infirm.

Mary Ann watched closely when the Trustees proposed changing from a Public School to a Union Free School District. She joined the jam-packed meeting held in the Broad Street School to discuss the possibility. As a Union Free school, the board of trustees would hold power separate from the county. They would be able to levy and collect independent taxes to build and maintain school buildings, run the district library, maintain the school for black children, and pay the salaries of teachers, principals and a librarian. The trustees would serve 3-year terms which would be staggered annually so that each year one trustee spot would be up for reelection. Mary Ann worried about the idea of giving more power to the trustees, but concluded that the overall proposal seemed advantageous to the district.

That same year the state legislature passed new laws governing school elections. The changes were significant, and the local newspapers published a series of articles so that citizens understood the new rules. The New Consolidated School Law required citizen status to vote and specified that a woman who had school age children and was the head of the household (such as a widow) could vote. The change meant that Mary Ann would now have more female company at the polls. She was thrilled.

Though she lost the election, Mary Ann did not stop arguing over the need for a new school. Problems at the Broad Street School persisted. Parents began complaining that the school was causing their children to become sick with lung ailments. The trustees had no choice but to appoint a committee to investigate the complaints. What they found was that the structure was very damp. Mold was growing on the seats in some classrooms. Walls were cracked and in some areas at risk of falling down. They also noted that the overcrowding was inexcusable. In one primary classroom a total of 70 children were packed into a space of only 12 feet square.

The Trustees could put off the inevitable no longer. A special meeting of the taxpayers of the Stapleton Union Free School District was called to discuss the construction of a new school. It had been the talk of the community for days, and Mary Ann was part of the lively crowd of over 150 citizens who gathered. William M. Mullen, then chairman of the School Board, presided over the meeting.

There was no great debate as almost everyone in the room agreed. The public vote was cast overwhelmingly in favor of erecting a new building. The trustees authorized the spending of $90,000 for the construction of a new school and demolition of the old one. To provide adequate space for the larger structure, the purchase of additional land in the rear of the present school was also approved, along with money set aside for architect fees and furnishings.

Mary Ann was in one of the seats up front, sitting on her hands and eagerly waiting for the time of public comment. When the moment came, her hand shot up high in the air and she was recognized by the chair. Mary Ann said she was totally in favor of a new school but she did have a question about the construction bonds. Mary Ann asked if they could extend the term of the twenty-year bonds to stretch out the burdens of repayment over a longer period of time. The question touched off a fierce debate. The trustees went back and forth and modifications to the original proposal were drafted. Then they put it to the voters and it was rejected. Mary Ann spoke again. Further deliberation ensued. In the end the original motion passed and though it was not what she proposed, Mary Ann was satisfied. The debate made her feel certain that everyone in attendance at the meeting thoroughly understood the fiscal implications of the decision.

The children attending the Broad Street School were temporarily relocated and construction began on a new brick school building. And amid its construction, quite peculiarly, the school for black children burned down. Mary Ann and her neighbors speculated that someone intentionally set the fire but it was never proven. A replacement school was not proposed. Integration of black and white children took place at the brand new Broad Street School.

The last Stapleton district school board election was held in the summer of 1897. Everything was due to change in January because Staten Island was becoming a part of New York City, but as usual there was still intense community interest in the election. A year before, the frenzy of the voters nearly caused a riot, and the sentiments which spurred the uncivilized behavior were for the most part unchanged. Everyone expected the campaigning to be fierce.

Instead of staggered terms, all three trustee positions were up for grabs this time in a one-year fixed term. Incumbents Felix O'Hanlon (a.k.a., the perpetual trustee) and Captain William Cole were running one last time. It was expected they would be shoe-ins. Michael Brennan, Thomas Barry, and Edward C. Meurer were in the running for the third available slot.

Mary Ann watched the politicking with her usual degree of intense curiosity. A few years had passed since Mary Ann made her own run for office, and despite the occasional rant here and there her family was sure she had given up the notion of running again.

They were wrong. One night at supper Mary Ann announced as a matter of fact that she was going to run again for school trustee.

Holy cow! But WHY, Mother? Joseph blurted out.

Mary Ann glanced sharply at him and then replied.

Well, the better question is why NOT, son! This morning a grand notion dawned on me. I got out of bed and thought how fine it would be to get a peek at those district accounting books before they get all tangled up in the new city budget!

Time was not on her side. It was a last-minute decision, so late that her name did not even make it into the newspapers until the eve of the election. Mary Ann had only a precious few hours to campaign, and soon realized she had only the slimmest of chances to win.

On Election Day, it seemed that every able body in town wanted to get out and vote. Multitudes of horses, wagons, and carriages clogged the roads driving back and forth to the polls. The Richmond County police were dispatched to prevent citizens from being crushed by the huge crowd that gathered in Washington Park to hear the ballot results. All who were there felt the significance of their presence as witnesses to history. The night dragged on. It was 12:50 A.M. before the final ballots were tallied and winners announced.

There were no surprises. The old boys conquered one last time. William Cole came in first with 443 votes. Felix O'Hanlon came in second, garnering 415 votes. Charles Bruns secured the third seat on the board while Mary Ann, who had entered the contest on a whim and without sufficient time to politick, garnered a mere handful of family and friend votes.

A parade through the downtown commercial district led by a local drum-corps started up after the announcements. It was a delightful, relatively bug-free summer night. Mary Ann chose to hang out in the park and make small talk with friends and neighbors before going home. She did not fret over the results.

The female candidate walked away from the last school board election with head held high.

Chapter Twelve: Stapleton Romance

"*E*mma and her mate will be welcomed home whenever they seek the safe harbor off Stapleton again."

As unsavory a neighborhood as it could be, Rocky Hollow also held its share of delightful romantic charm. In Rocky Hollow, the soft green carpet of the surrounding hills beckoned couples to come and pay humble reverence to the grandeur of the harbor. Hand in hand, lovers could scale the hills and find a shady spot to lay out a blanket and sample a picnic basket filled with gastronomical delights. With the splendor of New York Bay laid out at their feet, they lost track of time and place. The waterways below churned in slow graceful movement as vessels big and small glided almost imperceptibly up and down the Narrows. The hoot of a train, the low moan of a boat signal, and sounds that people or livestock make might in town could occasionally drift upward but to those smitten, a private walk along the primitive trails was as good as it could get.

Mary Emma Bascombe – Emma for short – was a dark eyed beauty who adored the graceful hills that overlooked her home on Broad and Gordon Streets. As the 19th century was winding down to a close, Emma was in firm possession of the title of grandest dreamer in the family. Her lofty future aspirations rivaled those of her mother and the grandfather she never met.

Her mother's house was cramped and noisy but up in the hills Emma could always find serenity and solitude. As a child, Emma delighted in spending free time up above Rocky Hollow sitting on a rock, gazing out at the harbor, and imagining the possibilities of life. Emma was an accomplished young lady. She played piano, sang in a choir, and was a member of a ladies bowling team. She acted in local theater productions and hoped one day to become a professional actress. Like her mother, she loved her neighborhood, and actively volunteered for the church and fire companies.

Emma was also a hopeless romantic. She firmly believed someday she would meet a charming young man who would sail into town, sweep her off her feet, and then take her off on a series of most magnificent life adventures. Mary Ann knew of her youngest daughter's dreams and ambitions, and while she didn't actively *Pish! Posh!* them, she also didn't greatly encourage her. She was not going to admit it publicly, but Emma was her favorite child. She never wanted her to leave Stapleton.

Mary Ann was blessed that all her grown children had chosen to remain close to home. She owned close to 70 properties now, so Mary Ann was able to provide housing for her sons, daughters, spouses, and the ever-growing number of grandchildren. The entire clan lived no more than a few blocks away from her home, a brand new multifamily three-story brick apartment building she built on the corner of Broad and Gordon Streets.

Mary Ann was relieved that her highly headstrong first born, the intractable Mary Jane, had found stability in her life. She and her husband Harry were rearing a large brood in one of her homes on lower Broad Street. Mary Ellen was married and lived just a little further down the block from her sister. Her husband, Michael McGuigan, was Irish and from a nice family that was very active in the Immaculate Conception parish. Thomas was married to a local girl named Rose McGinley. He and his family lived a few doors away on Gordon Street.

Her eldest son, William Richards, was likewise married and lived a few blocks away. William's courtship had concerned Mary Ann at first, but in the end, all turned out well. William won his wife's hand in marriage on the rebound, but Mary Ann knew it was a good match.

Mary Emma Wall was well known to the Bascombe family, having grown up just down the block on Gordon Street. William, who was a few years older than Mary Emma, always thought well of her. She was the pretty lead soprano in the Immaculate Conception choir. She came from a good family. Her father, Robert Wall, was an industrious Irish immigrant who supervised on the ferries.

Mary Emma was betrothed to an Englishman named Thomas K. Green. He was a steward at the United States Marine Hospital, which was the name they gave to the Seamen's Retreat after the hospital was purchased by the federal government. Green was deeply enamored with Mary Emma. He converted from the Protestant to Roman Catholic faith just to prove his affection.

A few days before the wedding, Green picked up his wages at the hospital and told friends he was going to the bank. Green saw Robert Wall in passing and told him he would head over to his house later to pick up Mary Emma and take her into New York for furniture shopping.

Mary Emma eagerly awaited Green's arrival. Hours passed, but he did not show. Robert called the Richmond County police. He suspected foul play but hoped the police might find Green lying somewhere sick or injured. The police discovered that Green never arrived at the bank and all his belongings were still intact at the hospital. He had disappeared without a trace.

Mary Emma was distraught. Three hundred guests had been invited to the church wedding and reception at her home. What should she do? Her father tried to spread the word, but some of the invited did not receive the news in time and showed up at the scheduled date and time. The doleful group gathered at the church entrance, giving more of the appearance of being there for a funeral than a wedding. It was a sad sight.

William was at his mother's house that night, eyeing the lingering crowd. He could not believe Mary Emma's bad luck. She was such a pretty girl and sang like an angel. How torn up inside the poor girl must be feeling.

William was a carpenter by trade and nearly thirty years old at the time. He was still a bachelor, not having met a girl he wanted to marry until the next Sunday morning when he spotted Mary Emma in church. There was something about Mary Emma as she struggled with her grief that struck a chord within him.

She seemed so amazingly engaging in the courage she showed. William went up after mass to offer his condolences. He reassured her that everything would turn out alright in the end.

Thomas K. Green was never found. William and Mary Emma became close friends, and then started keeping company. He was good for Mary Emma's spirits. It took nearly two years for William to fully win over her heart, but in the end Mary Ann's eldest son healed the girl's lovesick wounds. When William finally gathered up enough nerve to ask Mary Emma to marry him, she gladly responded yes. They were married in Immaculate Conception Church, surrounded by a close circle of Rocky Hollow family and friends.

A big reason why Emma Bascombe loved her hometown was that it was still a small and intimate place where almost everyone knew each other by name, yet the presence of local breweries and beer gardens in town ensured that there were always new faces around too. Boats and ferries brought newcomers to Stapleton daily, thanks in part to a man that had long since passed but who left a great legacy.

Cornelius 'Commodore' Vanderbilt was born on Staten Island in 1794, a descendent of one of the first Dutch farmers who settled the land. At a young age, Vanderbilt realized he had little interest in the family business. He was given the responsibility of ferrying his father's crops to market across the bay. Weaving his small piragua across the harbor, Vanderbilt uncovered his life's passion as he fell in love with the New York waterways.

At the age of sixteen, legend held that Vanderbilt borrowed money from his mother and started a ferry service from Stapleton to lower Manhattan. His business flourished, and Vanderbilt expanded from ferries to steamboats and then later to railroads, creating a multimillion dollar transportation dynasty. Vanderbilt's ferry brought outsiders from Manhattan to Staten Island daily. It was likely that Thomas McDonough rode one of Vanderbilt's ferries on the day he first scouted out Stapleton as a place to live.

The Stapleton docks were a busy place. Longshoremen put in long hours hauling cargo. Shipyard workers labored hard, building, repairing, and readying vessels for sailing. Ferries arrived here daily, filled with businessmen and day trippers. Though ferries were the most commonly seen type of boat, there were also large steam powered cargo ships, passenger steamers, tugs, yachts, and fishing boats in the New York waterways. For some travelers, Stapleton was their final stop and for others just a transfer point to catch a stagecoach or train to another part of the island or New Jersey.

There was no doubt about it: Emma was partial to seafaring men. To Emma, they seemed far more exotic than the homegrown variety of boys who always wanted to court her. Sailors were well traveled and had grand stories to tell. These men lived life with gusto, taking advantage of all that Stapleton had to offer, which included free-flowing beer and many social events.

One of the best things about sailors Emma thought, was that an emotional attachment to a sailor was not at odds with her personal goals. Emma was not really certain how she would feel being a fulltime wife having to cook, clean, and be home every night. She figured if she married a sailor, life would be perfect. When he went off to sea she would still be free to pursue her singing and acting career without any distractions. Such a practical idea for the girl who liked to dream!

A job at sea was not always safe so sailors had to be strong and courageous and unafraid to battle the elements. Storms sunk vessels of all sizes and varieties plus there were unexpected tragedies, like the boiler explosion which tore apart Staten Island's Westfield Ferry as it sat in its slip in lower Manhattan. On that day, over one hundred men, women and children were killed, with many more hurt and disfigured.

There was big money to be made recovering flooded, disabled, burnt out, and sunken ships. One of the biggest specialists in maritime salvage was the I.J. Merritt Wrecking Company. Headquartered on Wall Street but with a large shipyard at the Stapleton docks, they used trained divers, specialized steamships and state of the art machinery to get the dangerous job done. Originally called the Coast Wrecking Company, the business had been started during the Civil War, establishing a stellar reputation during the time that vessels transitioned from sails to steam power. Merritt Chapman investigative teams were worldwide experts in the forensics of ship wrecks and explosions. When the U.S.S. Maine exploded in Havana harbor, the Merritt Chapman Company was one of only two private salvage companies authorized by the U.S. War Department to attempt to recover parts of the hull.

Many of the men who worked for the Merritt Chapman Company were likely to fit Emma's image of a dream man. Thus, it came as no one's surprise when Emma announced at the Bascombe supper table one day that she had met a handsome young mate who worked aboard an I.J. Merritt steamer ship. His name was John Lyons, and they had taken an immediate fancy to each other. Knowing full well the rules of the house, Emma dutifully brought John home soon after to introduce him to her parents. James took an immediate liking to John. He thought he was an excellent chap. Mary Ann also thought well of John after their first meeting. He was friendly, polite, and humorous. John held a steady job at Merritt Chapman and hoped to rise through the ranks to become a supervisor someday. His overall ambition sealed the deal. Mary Ann gave her approval of their courtship.

Emma and John kept exclusive company over the next nine months. She packed picnic baskets full of cured meats, breads, and cheeses and introduced him to her glorious green retreat high above Rocky Hollow. The hills afforded them a degree of privacy, while Emma's hometown below provided tons of public fun and entertainment. They passed by the Bechtel and Rubsam and Horrmann beer gardens and stopped to dance to the music in the streets. They waved patriotic flags at parades and holiday celebrations. The one-thousand-foot-long Staples Dock was theirs for a cozy mid-afternoon perambulation or rendezvous on milder nights. And, Washington Park was but a few minutes stroll in the summer months to catch a live act or band concert.

It was a course of smooth sailing for Emma and her sailor and then out of the blue, a second man of the sea got into the act. A handsome sailing yacht breezed into the Narrows one day, captained by a young man named Robert Conklin. He was charming, self-assured, and oh so easy on the eyes in his nattily attired nautical dress blues. After he made land, the captain spied Emma from a distance and was immediately smitten. Robert was told she had a steady beau, but it did not faze him. He was a confident man. Robert vowed to do whatever it took to make Emma change her mind and favor his company.

At first, Emma disregarded the advances of the yacht captain, but he persisted and eventually wore down her resolve. Emma admitted to herself that he was quite handsome, and she was attracted to him. How very exciting being pursued by two sailors at the same time!

Emma confused everyone in the Bascombe household one night by bringing Robert home for supper. She introduced Robert to her wise mother to get her opinion on which man should be her beau but was surprised by her mother's response.

Pish! Posh! My dear Emma! The Captain is a fine catch, but I like John too! Both would make fine husbands. I think it is up to you to figure out whose company to keep.

For once in her life, Mary Ann did not offer up a strong opinion. She counseled Emma to be fair and give each of them a clear chance to win her heart but other than that left the decision strictly up to her daughter.

Choosing between John and Robert seemed an almost impossible task for the young woman. She had strong feelings for both. They were different, each with their individual draws. Robert was tall and handsome and a gentleman who clearly was well situated financially. John was considerate and good natured and a pleasure to be around. Should she go with Robert who would be the better provider or John with whom she had the stronger natural ties?

John found out about Robert and grew increasingly impatient as Emma vacillated between the two men. He began to pressure his girl, and the previously calm and steady waters between them began to get choppy. The captain, realizing he now held the upper hand, countered John's steadily growing anger with his example of gentlemanly patience.

The pressure took a toll on Emma's relationship with John. Just before his boat was ordered out to Halifax, Nova Scotia, they had a huge fight. There they were, standing and sniping at each other on the pier when in a fit of rage, Emma pushed her mate overboard. John was mortified to have such a thing happen in front of all the other sailors. He told Emma to get out of his life forever. John boarded his ship and sailed away, leaving Emma free to do as she pleased.

With John out of the picture, Robert finally had the edge he needed to win the favor of his sweetheart. For the next three months, the couple kept steady company. Then, the captain received orders to ship out to sea. Robert did not want to leave without a promise, so just before he left, he donned his fine blue captain's uniform asked for Emma's hand in marriage. She accepted, and Robert jumped for joy. He could leave town now feeling happy and secure. He had won the competition for the heart of his fair lady!

The Captain caught a ferry to take him back to his yacht which was berthed in Brooklyn. There was much work to do in supervising the crew and making the necessary preparations to equip the yacht for a long sea voyage. When all was ready, Robert took a brief trip back to Staten Island to bid Emma goodbye. Then he returned and ordered the crew to pull up anchor and take his vessel out past Sandy Hook, New Jersey. Robert stood out on the deck and called out a loving tribute to his Emma as they sailed past the town of Stapleton. Then he turned his full attention to his job. Robert ordered the navigator to set course for a protracted voyage to foreign ports.

Emma wandered high up into the hills above Rocky Hollow to watch her fiancé's yacht pass through the Narrows on its way out to sea. She sat there waving and imagining her future with Robert as her husband, but this mindset did not last long. As if by magic, no sooner than Robert's vessel was fully out of sight, John Lyons appeared with a bouquet of fresh picked daisies in hand!

Johnny! You always knew daisies were my favorite!

The young woman could not believe her eyes. She was glad to see John but now it was even more complicated. Emma began to tear up. She confessed to John that she was engaged and watched as the buoyant look drained from his face. After a moment or two of silence he asked,

I understand what you say Emma, but may we linger here awhile to put aside our differences?

John told her how he had been torn up by the way their romance ended. He wanted to remain amicable. Emma agreed, and they began a strange new chapter in their relationship.

Emma brought John back to the house with her and shocked everyone by saying she had invited him to stay for supper. Mary Ann watched with growing suspicion over the next few weeks as John started to show up at the Bascombe house with increasing frequency. It seemed that whenever he was within hailing distance of the Stapleton piers, John hopped off the boat and paid a call to Emma. Mary Ann asked her daughter flat out what was going on and got a response that it was nothing serious. They were just friends.

Yes, they were friends, but in her heart, Emma knew it was more than that. After their fight, Emma realized she loved John best but did not know if she would ever see him again, so she turned to Robert. Now with Robert gone, she understood she did not have strong feelings for him. Absence did not make Emma's heart grow fonder for the handsome young captain. It had all been a good test of her emotions and she knew now what must be done.

John came back to Rocky Hollow determined to win Emma back. He knew that with the yacht captain out of the picture, it was his chance to gain the upper hand. John was worried, but knew he needed to be bold. He asked Emma to reconsider her engagement. Emma did not waste time keeping John in suspense. Johnny Lyons, the cheerfully persistent kind of chap that he was, had swept Emma off her feet once more. Yes. She said she would.

She was head over *keels*.

Emma was sure they would be the gossip of the neighborhood when the news broke. Declaring her love for John while she was promised to Robert meant that the seas were going to get extra rough for the pretty woman living on Broad and Gordon Streets, but Emma took heart in the fact that she was not alone.

Others had successfully maneuvered through the rocky seas of love without running aground. Her oldest sister was a prime example. When she was younger, Mary Jane had the dickens of a time managing her perplexing affairs of the heart. She was just a small girl at the time, but Emma still remembered how mad her mother was and how messy it all was at first. Yet, it did eventually work out. Mary Jane was now a very happily married lady.

True love works out.

Emma was thinking something like that on one particularly hot summer afternoon in August when John Lyons showed up at her front door. He asked Emma if she would like to take a leisurely stroll with him. She agreed and went to grab her bonnet and parasol from the front hallway coat tree. *Goodbye all!* she called out to her mother and father. Then she scurried out the front door on the arm of her man.

The couple was out an unusually long time, but it was a busy day and with the usual comings and goings in the Bascombe house so no one thought to question her about it upon their return. John bade Emma's family a very good night and left to return to the bunk on his boat. Emma kissed her mother and father on the cheek, wished them good rest, and then went promptly to bed.

Emma proved just how talented an actress she was in the days which followed. Her behavior gave no hint of anything out of the ordinary. Towards the end of the week, the doorbell chimed. Emma, who was home at the time, went to the front door. It was a postman who had a special delivery letter addressed to Mary Ann. On the envelope was the postmark stamped *Clifton, Staten Island.*

Emma greeted the postman nonchalantly. She called out upstairs.

"Mother, there is a registered letter for you. Shall I sign for it?"

The young woman asked although she knew quite well the answer that would come back to her.

"No, dear, I'll sign for it myself."

Emma directed the postman to wait for her mother at the

foot the stairs. Then she went to the coat tree near the front door, donned her favorite sun bonnet, and scooted out the door. Emma bolted down Broad Street as fast as she could in her heels and long skirt, and she didn't look back.

Mary Ann came downstairs and chit chatted with the postman for a moment or two. Then, she escorted him to the door. Mary Ann went to her little roll top desk in the corner of the parlor and took out her letter opener. She pried open the envelope and started to read. It was an unsigned message, written on St. Mary's parish stationery.

Mary Ann was immediately suspicious.

Why would I be receiving a letter from my former parish? It's been almost twenty years since I last attended mass there.

The dame from Broad and Gordon Streets continued reading and then suddenly she stopped. Mary Ann could not believe her eyes! She started again from the beginning, reading slower this time to digest the full meaning of each word.

Mary Ann put the letter down on the desk and let out a piercing shriek. Last Sunday when Emma and John had gone out, they had walked all the way over to St. Mary's Church in Clifton and gotten married.

Egad! Another elopement! What the dickens is wrong with my girls? How could my sweet Emma do this to me? And how on earth did she keep this a secret all week long?

Mary Ann was honestly caught off guard, for as far as she knew Emma was still betrothed to Robert the yacht captain. She scrutinized the wording and guessed that it was Emma who had dictated the letter. Emma did not have the courage to tell her mother face to face so it was her daughter's way of breaking the news.

Emma. Emma! MARY EMMA!

Mary Ann called out loudly and repeatedly for her daughter until she realized that Emma was not home. She ranted on and on, likely scaring the pants off the tenants on the floors above her, but it helped to purge all the rage out of her. Mary Ann began to calm down and think rationally. Emma was a smart young woman. She knew full well that her mother was a hot head. She had heard one too many stories about how her oldest sister made Mary Ann crazed when she ran off with O'Leary and then later with Harry Marshall. Emma chose not to risk her mother's wrath, so she went into hiding until she could come up with a good enough explanation for marrying John Lyons without her knowledge. It was a defiant but sensible move on Emma's part.

Mary Ann took in a deep long breath and relaxed. Mary Ann was certain that her daughter was safe. She was probably staying at the home of one of her girlfriends.

In her haste to flee, Emma failed to see that her situation was somewhat different than the days of her older sister's turmoil. Her mother clearly disapproved of Mary Jane's first husband and knew very little about Harry Marshall at the time that Mary Jane eloped with him. Mary Ann liked John Lyons. She knew he and Emma got along well. John was not a yacht captain, but he was a hard worker. He would be able to provide adequately for Emma in the future. It was a very different set of circumstances.

The only real problem was that Emma was betrothed.

Age and experience had mellowed Mary Ann from her younger days of broomstick and soapsuds torments. After the immediate shock wore off, Mary Ann discovered she was not angry at all. Her feelings were a bit damaged, yes, but she was relatively amused at the way her daughter schemed to break the news. Mary Ann was thankful that Emma had enough common sense to make it a church wedding. Her only wish was that she had been there herself to see the union take place.

The reporters who had by now become a familiar part of Mary Ann's life lined up at her front door when word got out about Emma's elopement. The men knew her well and were startled to see that instead of confronting an enraged woman, they were greeted by a well composed mother of the bride. Always eager to report the worst, they seemed visibly disappointed by her calm demeanor.

Privately, Mary Ann would have a few choice words to say to John when next she saw him, but she did not tell that to these men. Mary Ann realized she could use the newspapers to her advantage so she instructed the reporters to print that she was happily waiting to greet the couple and confirm upon them a proper maternal blessing. Mary Ann, who could be a bit of an actress herself on occasion, kept smiling and offering them food. She hoped Emma and John would read her words and decide to come home.

The new Mrs. Lyons prepared herself for the inevitable gossip as the news leaked out. Her mixed up love story was plastered all over the newspapers. Reporters used the word *heiress* to describe her, which Emma interpreted as a mocking comment. They were alluding to the fact that her mother had considerable assets as one of the biggest property owners on Staten Island, but Emma knew that it did not merit the use of such a hoity-toity title. The Bascombes lived a sensible, almost frugal existence. Emma had grown up in a cramped clapboard house on the busy corner of Broad and Gordon Streets. She attended public school as did all her brothers and sisters. She had no finishing school education, had not been introduced to society circles, nor had she ever attended a fancy soiree. Emma was a Rocky Hollow girl. The only true heiresses were found up in the fancy estates in the hills above Stapleton.

Emma eventually returned home, and she and her mother had a long talk. Then John came over and all three talked some more. The reporters, more interested in scandal than happy endings, stopped stalking the Bascombe residence and life began to return to order.

Robert came back to port and was sadly informed that he was no longer engaged. He reluctantly stepped aside. Emma and John moved into another one of Mary Ann's apartments down the road.

One day, a few months after everything settled down, Mary Jane dropped by her mother's house with some of the grandchildren for an afternoon visit. The little ones ran around out back while the women sat at the dining table and enjoyed some tea with jam and jelly. After a while, Mary Jane broached a question that had been on her mind for some time.

Mother, even at this age I still don't understand you. Why didn't you raise the same kind of fuss over Emma and John that you made over me and my men some twenty odd years ago?

Mary Ann looked at her daughter, then threw back her head and laughed long and hard. Mary Jane, who was quite serious in asking, saw her mother's face and couldn't help it. She began to chuckle too.

When the laughter stopped, her mother answered the question. Mary Ann told her eldest daughter that she had actually given some serious thought to this. Perhaps she was just getting more sedate as she grew older. Or maybe she realized that Emma's choice of a husband could have been a heck of a lot worse.

Mary Jane attempted to probe further but her mother hushed her.

Pish! Posh! Mary Jane, and don't you of all people know by now that true love sails in defiance of all logic! You can offer up common sense to young lovers 'til your face is blue as the ocean but it's a futile affair.

You have children. You'll see for yourself soon enough.

Chapter Thirteen: Consolidation
(*To Be or Not to Be One Big City*)

"*T here is dissatisfaction in this borough, no doubt, but so there is everywhere. Some of it has been engendered by disappointed politicians and some of it doubtless is based on real grievances, but if anybody entertains the idea of getting out of Greater New York now that we are in, he might as well give it up. Consolidation has come to stay and we must make the best of it.*"[1]

A steady rain fell on January 1, 1898. It was stinging cold, but the precipitation did not hamper the celebrations. This New Year's was special. It was the first day of the year but also the beginning of the consolidated City of Greater New York. New York City, the city of Brooklyn, and a number of small towns and villages in Queens, the Bronx and Staten Island merged on January 1st into one five borough metropolis.

Throughout the new city there were a series of planned commemorative events. In Manhattan, the crowds were joyous. They took to the streets with parades, fireworks, and one hundred gun salutes. In Brooklyn, it was a more subdued occasion. Some chose to ignore the whole matter, while other displeased shopkeepers showed their sentiments by hanging funeral drapes on store windows.

On Staten Island, the inhabitants were generally cheerful. Mary Ann, however, was an exception. The woman could not stem her irritation. It was cold outside but inside her blood was boiling.

A few days earlier, Mary Ann attended the last official board meeting of the Edgewater Trustees before the local government was disbanded. It was a bitter wintry day, but Mary Ann paid no mind. She bundled up in her warm wooly coat, went outside hitched up her horse cart, and drove down to Village Hall. Seizing upon this one last chance to settle her personal business, Mary Ann carried with her copies of bills for local street repairs from the years 1893, 1894, and 1895.

When Michael McGuire served as an Edgewater trustee, he instructed her to make street repairs in conjunction with scheduled road improvements. Mary Ann agreed and paid for the work, expecting to be reimbursed afterwards. Then all the trouble started for McGuire, and no one now wanted to pay her.

Bosh! Spooney!

She would have never spent the money if she thought she wasn't going to get it back!

Mary Ann stood in front of the Trustees as she had many times before and argued her case. It was not the first time Mary Ann had asked them to pay these bills. She had been unsuccessful up to this point but knew it was her final shot, so she argued ferociously. It ended up as one of her finer oratories, imbued with a strong measure of common sense righteousness, but the speech did nothing to change the status quo. Politely, they told her they could not help. The work had not been authorized by trustee vote. Mary Ann thanked them for their time and walked out of the room.

The denial of her request coupled with the unpleasant cold weather made it a gloomy day indeed. It was days later, but she could not help but continue to dwell on the outcome of the meeting.

Mary Ann was personally disappointed. She knew her speech had been spectacular and yet it got her nowhere. Why? Why hadn't she walked away with what she was after? In the past, Mary Ann would have been able to wear the Trustees down and walk away with check in hand. What was the real reason behind their decision? Did they just want to distance themselves from McGuire and his past? Yes, she thought. It was quite possible they thought of it as their last chance to show disapproval of the man as well as a distain for Mary Ann's decision to put up bail for him a few years earlier.

She thought some more and came up with one more possibility. Maybe there was just too much financial uncertainty at this time to grant her request. Staten Island was joining the grandest city in America, but there were lots of unanswered questions on what would happen next. Matters such as taxes and public services were not yet finalized. Perhaps the Trustees foresaw budgetary difficulties in the coming months?

Why, of course! That must be it, she rationalized. *Otherwise, they would have surely given me what I asked for.*

Staten Island was entering unchartered territory. The trustees were being fiscally prudent. This was an explanation she could accept.

Like everyone else, Mary Ann could only speculate on how joining the City of Greater New York was going to affect her personally, but she had to tip her hat to Andrew Haswell Green for finally making good on his idea. Green was a city planner who dreamed of New York as the biggest city in America. After the Civil War this did not seem possible, as Chicago's population was fast exploding and New York was slowing down in growth, but Green postulated that if New York united the waterfront and acquired more land it would beat out its western competition.

At times it looked as if Green would have to abandon his dream. There were fierce opponents along the way. New York businessmen feared that their tax burdens would increase. Tammany Hall worried about the ramifications of uniting the Republican voters of Brooklyn, Queens, and Staten Island. Brooklyn was already the third largest city in America, and residents there were concerned that consolidation would affect their quality of life. In upstate New York, Republicans were leery of creating political domination downstate.

Despite the opposition, in 1894 a bill in the New York State Legislature was enacted calling for a popular vote on the consolidation of Greater New York. Public meetings were set up throughout the five proposed boroughs to debate the pros and cons of the merger.

Mary Ann was confounded to see so many of her neighbors so eager to jump on the consolidation bandwagon without carefully examining the pros and cons. Why, they didn't seem to be giving due credit to Richmond County as a thriving community in and of itself! She'd read the statistics in the papers and was very proud. There were 60,000 people living on Staten Island who traveled on 54 miles of macadam and Telford roads. Staten Island had 53 churches of 8 denominations, 29 public and 11 private schools, 9 banks and building and loan associations, 20 post offices, and 12 newspapers. Twenty-eight industries employed Staten Island workers. There were 35 volunteer fire brigades, and 66 policemen who protected the citizens. There were over 41 social and scientific clubs and societies and 15 benevolent organizations. Staten Island boasted ferries, trolleys, a railroad, gas, water, electric, and telephone companies. It was a stable and well-established community, and yet Staten Islanders could not see there were possible disadvantages in giving up independent rule? Her neighbors were way too intoxicated with the allure of becoming part of a big new city.

Mary Ann played devil's advocate for a while but eventually gave up trying to get others see both sides. She was a realist and would deal with whatever the vote came down to. There wasn't much of a point offering logic up to those who lacked good old fashioned common sense.

Though she would not be able to cast a vote either for or against, Mary Ann had a vested interest in the decision. As a major taxpayer she had many questions and concerns. When rallies were announced to be held in Washington Park in support of the Greater New York campaign, Mary Ann told James he would have to fend for himself for his midday meal. She drove her wagon downtown extra early to ensure a place at the head of the crowd. Mary Ann had with her a pencil and a paper with a long list of questions folded neatly inside her coat pocket.

A large number of citizens turned out for the event. The atmosphere was festive, with banners, band anthems, and speeches. When it came time for questions, Mary Ann's hand shot up front and center and was quickly recognized. The matron made sure to step up to a place where she would be well heard by those around her.

Mary Ann took the paper out of her pocket and rattled off questions in rapid succession. What would happen to taxes under the new government? Would water, gas, and electric utility rates remain unchanged? What services would Staten Islanders receive that we didn't already have? How about new roads and sewers? How about new schools?

The meeting organizers were not from Stapleton. They had never seen or heard of Mary Ann Bascombe. The men were caught totally off guard by this seemingly innocuous grey-haired lady which the crowd clearly supported by clapping, whistling, and egging her on. Mary Ann kept firing questions at the organizers who struggled to respond. Clearly, there were no definitive answers for many of her concerns.

After three decades of intense debate, politicking, and maneuvering, Andrew Haswell Green and his supporters won out. On Election Day 1894, approximately 40,000 more Manhattanites voted in favor of consolidation than against. In Brooklyn, however, the story was different. There the proposal passed only by a couple hundred votes. Mount Vernon voted nay by a large majority. In Westchester, consolidation passed by only one vote. The inhabitants of Queens, Eastchester and Pelham voted solidly in favor.

On Staten Island, it was a victory for the proponents of a new city. The final count was approximately 5500 votes for vs. 1500 against consolidation. The majority of Staten Islanders went to the polls believing that the consolidation would result in a better life for themselves and their families. They gambled on giving up home rule in exchange for the promises made during the campaign. Citizens wanted better public services and capital improvements the local government could not afford. They now looked forward to more and better schools, roads, docks, transit systems, water, and sewer lines.

Mary Ann fought back a bit of grumpiness that set in over the election. It had been so darn frustrating to be denied the vote in such a history making event! Seeking solace, Mary Ann got on the consolidation bandwagon. She began to let her mind roam freely, envisioning some of the grand civic improvements which would now be possible as part of a consolidated New York.

Her musings stirred up the memory of a recent fire at her home.

Well, that was one day where I surely could have benefitted from better public services!

Mary Ann was very proud of the brick multifamily house she built to replace her tiny wood frame house. Mary Ann's family and four other tenant families occupied the building. One day, Mary Ann had been out running errands when neighbors caught up to her and told her that the house was ablaze. She gave out a loud gasp, then hiked up her skirts and took off up the street as fast as her laced boots could take her. By the time Mary Ann arrived at the scene, the fire was under control. She saw her tenants sitting on the curb and went over to check in on their health. Then she conferred with her firefighter friends who informed Mary Ann of the events that had taken place.

BaBOOM!

The sound caught the attention of everyone in the vicinity of Broad and Gordon Streets. Mr. Fricker, Mary Ann's second floor tenant who worked at the Bechtel Brewery, was startled out of his seat by the loud explosion of a kerosene lamp in his room. He tried to smother the flames, but smoke quickly swept from inside his apartment to the hallway. Women and children present in the third-floor apartments heard the explosion and fled to the stairway. They wanted to get out, but smoke and flames blocked their egress. The mothers ushered their children back into the apartments, closed doors, threw open the windows, and began screaming loudly out into the street.

HELP US! HELP! HELP!

Luckily, members of the Enterprise Hook and Ladder Company were close by and quickly responded. They ran ladders up the side of the building to rescue Fricker and the stranded mothers and children. Then the Benjamin Brown Hose and Robinson Hose Fire Companies arrived. As the rescue of the inhabitants was already underway, it was their job to put out the fire. They hooked a hose into the fire hydrant on Gordon Street to put down the blaze.

After the fire was extinguished, the Village Engineer came by to investigate. He examined the scene and interviewed the residents and firemen. He told Mary Ann that the solid brick construction had been the saving grace of her home. There had been no structural damage from the fire but there was other destruction. Unfortunately, $700 of home furnishings were lost, but only $100 of the damage could be attributed to the fire. Most of the ruin came from hose water which flooded the interior of the house.

Mary Ann was perturbed to learn that there had been a problem with the hydrant. Members of the Robinson Hose Company tried to shut the hydrant after the fire was out but couldn't turn the valve. The pipes installed by the Crystal Water Company were defective, clogging the valve with stones and mud. Mary Ann was thankful that no one had been hurt, but angry over such inferior construction. She had made it a point to register her complaint at a Village Trustee meeting. As she pondered the changes coming as part of Greater New York, Mary Ann hoped that the new city would provide better oversight of the public utility companies and include regular inspections of the hydrants.

After the bill became law, the governor appointed a commission to draft a new city charter. The commission, which included one representative from Staten Island, worked until February 1897 when their work was submitted to the New York Legislature for review. A charter was approved in which there would be one mayor of the city and a number of other elected city officials. Staten Island would stay intact as one of five distinct boroughs of the expanded city. Each borough would elect its own president having the authority to oversee certain local functions.

Elections held the following November were highly politicized. There were many offices to fill in the new government. On Staten Island, the campaign to elect the first Borough President of Richmond proved to be quite contentious. Voters had a difficult choice to make as two very popular local men were vying for the position.

Mary Ann solidly backed Dr. John L. Feeney as the Democratic candidate. He was a lifelong resident of Stapleton, and Mary Ann knew him well. She was pleased to go out and stump door to door for him. Feeney was a graduate of the Medical Department of New York University and had been a physician at the Seaman's Retreat, a doctor to the Richmond County police, and the Health Officer of Edgewater and Middletown. He was a man of medicine but was also well entrenched in Staten Island politics. Feeney had been Chairman of the Richmond County Democrats for ten years and an elected Town Supervisor.

George Cromwell, a Brooklyn native and relative newcomer to Staten Island, ran on the Republican side. Cromwell was the son of a wealthy steamship company president and also a well-respected politician, He was a Yale graduate and an attorney by profession who served Staten Island as a New York State Assemblyman.

As usual, Election Day in Stapleton and all over Staten Island was a wild affair and the vote so close that both sides claimed victory. The staunch Democrats of Stapleton were surprised at the results. Staten Island was generally considered a Democratic stronghold and yet Cromwell was able to hold his own. It took six tense months of appeals before the winner was officially declared. In the end, Cromwell won, but by only a handful of votes.

Cromwell learned quite quickly that the first few years of the consolidation were not going to be easy. Under the charter, the five borough presidents held very little real power. This put Cromwell at even more disadvantage as he was the only Republican dealing with four Democratic Borough Presidents and a Tammany Hall connected mayor. The sparse population of the borough also ran counter to his aim of grabbing a substantial piece of the city budget pie. In 1894, the total number of registered voters on Staten Island was around 7000. This was miniscule as compared to New York County which had approximately 166,000 voters and Kings County which had close to 130,000. Citizens in the least densely populated areas of the new city like Staten Island and Queens clearly underestimated their political influence under a new regime. The politics of the new city was obviously going to be driven by the needs of New York and Kings County.

Cromwell had immediate concerns about the condition of Staten Island roads. He requested funds for a topographical survey of the island as there had never been one done in the entire history of Richmond County. Mayor Van Wyck, who controlled the sewer, highway and street cleaning departments through his political appointees, gave him an emphatic no. Despite the protests of Cromwell and others, during the first years of consolidation only a half mile of new pavement was authorized for Staten Island.

Defeat in the battle over road construction did not deter Cromwell from following through on other ideas. Government offices existed all over Staten Island, so he proposed moving all city services to one central location. The move, he projected, would provide convenience for citizens and officials alike. George W. Vanderbilt offered up land he owned in Stapleton but was turned down as it was decided to consolidate as close as possible to the isle of Manhattan. The decision was made to move the county seat from Richmond to St. George. Plans were drawn up to build a new central office building.

The prestigious architectural firm of Carrere and Hastings was selected to design the new structure. Staten Island resident John Carrere and his partner Thomas Hastings had designed many magnificent structures, including the New York Public Library on 42nd Street in Manhattan and the Senate Office Building in Washington, D.C. They presented plans for a three-story high French Renaissance style brick building situated on top of a hill overlooking the harbor. Adorned with lavish limestone trim, stone entryways and window columns, the new Borough Hall would have a massive two story mansard roof and distinctive clock tower. A stately new courthouse separated from Borough Hall by rows of formal side gardens and a new police station were also proposed.

These buildings were a sharp contrast to their smaller and more humble predecessors and symbolic of the power and influence of the new great city. As each building was completed, the consolidation of government offices in St. George started to shift business and political power away from Stapleton and the other parts of the island.

The creation of the City of Greater New York also resulted in the creation of a whole new bureaucratic structure. Staten Island remained a separate county of New York so a representative seat was retained in the state legislature but all other town and village officials were legislated out of office as of January 1, 1898. County taxes would now be collected and paid by the city, doing away with the need for a county tax collector. Staten Island communities were turned into New York City political wards. Mary Ann and her neighbors were notified they now lived in Richmond Borough, Ward 2.

Mary Ann watched the changes in government, trying to figure out new business strategies. A few of her allies in government were still in place, but without home rule Mary Ann saw that her voice would not carry as far when it came to challenging officials.

Bosh! Spooney!

This ate at her mood at times, but did not halt her business activities. The dame of Broad and Gordon Streets was not going to let anyone, not even the great big City of New York, hold her back. She hitched her wagon and drove down to St. George to introduce herself to the crew of newly hired municipal workers. Mary Ann asked a multitude of questions and slowly learned the ins and outs of the new bureaucracy. And, she continued buying local properties.

Mary Ann made sure not to let up on the issues which were near and dear to her heart just because of the new regime. When President Cromwell organized a public forum on mosquito extermination at Village Hall, Mary Ann, like always, claimed her seat up front and center. She listened to the Commissioner of Health from the City of New York and an expert employed by the city make promises to rid Staten Island of mosquitos. She patiently heard the other officials' commentary, then got up as the last speaker of the night. Mary Ann offered her point of view, breaking the crowd up in laughter as she made her point that the Health Department was more interested in issuing fines than actually doing the work to rid the pests.

The creation of Richmond Borough meant more than just the elimination of old and the establishment of new public government offices. It mandated the reorganization of all public services. The Crystal Water Company which had been contracted to supply water to Stapleton and Rocky Hollow since the 1880's continued to bring water to town but the New York City Department of Water Supply began the process of taking over the service. Eventually the city would own and operate the water supply of the entire borough. The City Charter placed control of ferries under the New York City Department of Docks and Ferries and public parks, playgrounds, and public squares under the New York City Department of Parks.

There were all kinds of newfangled licenses required if you wanted to do business, which were not welcomed by the locals. The Police Department now controlled the licensing of public exhibitions, theatres, shows, dance halls, dances, and boarding houses. The Fire Department licensed the sale of explosives. The Department of Docks and Ferries issued permits for the erection of sheds on piers and bulkheads. The city legislators had the power to enact ordinances regarding push carts, car drivers, salesmen, hawkers, peddlers, venders, pawn brokers, junk dealers, circuses, and the keeping of dogs among other things.

Mary Ann was speechless over the extent of the bureaucracy.

Egad! What in blazes have we gotten ourselves into with all these fees?

A local newspaper pointed out the insanity in all the new rules by describing one farmer's plight. This poor man now needed a permit to walk his cow from the barn to the pasture because by doing so he crossed a small road considered a city street!

The public schools were the only place where Mary Ann saw a clear benefit from the consolidation. First of all, that old relic Felix O'Hanlon was finally out of a job! Secondly, the District trustees and county administrator were now replaced by a single Richmond Borough Superintendent.

Before joining Greater New York, Staten Island public high school education had been limited to a two-year curriculum held inside the crowded district schools. Just a few years after consolidation, the cornerstone was laid for Staten Island's first public four-year high school. Mary Ann, who always regretted not being able to attend school, was ecstatic. The plan had been held up by a controversy over its location, but this had been finally resolved. The first site was directly across from the freight train tracks in St. George, but citizens protested that the location was far too noisy and dangerous a place to locate a school. The city backed down and an alternative tract of land was found at the corner of St. Marks Place and Hamilton Avenue. Mary Ann wholeheartedly approved of the new location. She too had been quite leery of the thought of her precious grandchildren jumping train tracks on a daily basis!

The site of the new school was truly inspiring, perched high on a hill overlooking the magnificent New York harbor. It would resemble a castle when completed, with an exterior of three stories of Indiana limestone and four-story tower in the center. The school was named in memory of George William Curtis, the Staten Islander who was a prolific author and lecturer, a friend of Thoreau, Hawthorne, and Emerson, and related by marriage to the famous Shaw abolitionist family. Although Mary Ann would have preferred the first high school on Staten Island being named after a Democrat, even she could not help but admire the man who was so honored. There was no doubt in Mary Ann's mind that her grandchildren would receive a top notch education attending classes in such a fine facility.

As the transition to city borough continued, town residents felt it important to honor those who served the community so well under independent rule. While the local fire companies remained active during the switch over in municipal governments, the New York City Fire Department was mandated to absorb the voluntary firefighter system. Mary Ann, always a fervent supporter of firemen, was personally thrilled when they asked her to participate in one of tributes given to these very brave men. When the day arrived, she proudly took to the streets of Stapleton. Linking arms and marching side by side with former Court Crier John Rooney, she paraded downtown in tribute to the valorous men of Protection Engine Company No. 7.

Acknowledging the best of the past helped Mary Ann and other citizens cope with problems of the present. There were some big glitches in the transition from home rule to city governance. The city charter commission addressed the major operations of government, but had apparently overlooked what would happen in the immediate as a result of the merger.

Perhaps, the most glaring oversight was the failure of the city to provide localities with adequate funds to operate during the transition period. In its last year of operation, the Village of Edgewater faced a most serious financial dilemma. Edgewater provided public services to 16,000 citizens and had annual expenses of about $60,000 a year. City officials failed to listen to the Village Trustees and thus did not plan for emergency funds to bridge the calendar gap between the last tax collection in Edgewater in May and January 1st when city taxation kicked in. As a result, village ex-officials were forced to go to Albany and petition the state to fund essential public services through the end of the calendar year.

Another concern was that the tax structure was a big unknown at the time of city consolidation. No one was sure what the tax rate would be. After the city charter went into effect, the first step was to complete audits of all local government ledgers. Then a real estate assessment throughout the five boroughs was conducted. The process was time consuming and of serious concern to Mary Ann as a major property owner. Although they were estimating the tax rate to be lower than what she currently paid, the value of her properties was likely be assessed higher. It appeared to Mary Ann that she and her Rocky Hollow neighbors might end up paying more taxes than ever before.

And, to make matters worse, the tax payment schedule was also changing. Under independent rule, state, county, town, and school taxes were staggered so Mary Ann and others were billed at separate intervals during the year. This was a big help to those who were just struggling to make ends meet, but it was not to be under the new government. Greater New York required all taxes to be collected at the same time. Mary Ann adjusted her financial practices to comply with the new city regulations but wondered how this change would affect the poorer members of the neighborhood.

Pish! Posh! Rocky Hollow better get nice new roads and more sewers for all this tax trouble. Because if not, by gumption, I'll go down to City Hall and talk to the mayor myself!

Public utilities became one huge headache for all after the consolidation. Well aware of the city's plan to take over the entire private water supply, Staten Island water companies sought to rake in as much profit from their customers as possible before that day arrived. A running feud developed between the city and private companies which featured a most vigorous fight over the price of water being supplied to fire hydrants. The city wanted to decrease the price per unit while the water companies refused to negotiate. Their inability to come to mutual agreement resulted in the companies' refusal to furnish water for street cleaning and the city's refusal to permit the companies to extend water mains.

Citizens were caught in the middle and would not be quiet about it. Mary Ann, never a fan of shenanigans when it came to her pocket book, got invited to a public meeting held at the German Club Rooms. She and other local landlords came together at the gathering to bitterly criticize the Crystal Water Company. She was one of those who spoke at the meeting.

Tell us now, what nature of skullduggery is going on here? We here on the east shore are paying four times the cost of city water being provided to those living on the north shore! Why in Stapleton it's cheaper to down pints of lager ale than the water supplied by the Crystal Water Company!

Mary Ann and her fellow landlords threatened to sink their own wells if things did not change. The meeting ended with resolutions to formally condemn the officers of the water company and send a sub group to the mayor to demand construction of an additional public water plant to meet their needs.

The electric company was likewise guilty of locking horns with the city. In the dispute, the city failed to pay its electric bill and streetlights were turned off all around town, but this action paled in comparison to the travesty which occurred around Christmastime, 1898. The New York and Staten Island Electric Company sent out notices to its customers stating that all existing contracts were null and void and new contracts had to be signed. Under the new contracts, all electricity was to be metered. Although the quote rate was 25 cents per unit cheaper than in the past, customers were now required to buy all their lamps from the company and pay for the installation of fixtures. In the end, instead of saving money the new contracts would end up raising the costs for customers.

Those who had existing contracts with one to two years left before expiration were quite upset. They consulted lawyers who advised that the existing contracts were valid and urged them not to yield to the intimidation.

Come January, the electric company retaliated against the customers who held their ground. Like ancient barbarians who tore into villages to pillage the poor and unsuspecting, bullying work crews suddenly began invading private homes and businesses of Staten Islanders to savagely rip out meters and fixtures.

Mary Ann was probably angrier than she had ever been in her life. She had way too many homes to personally defend against the vandalism of these workmen who were deliberately and carelessly defacing walls and ceilings. She anxiously waited for them to dare to show up at her home.

Dear God, please keep these evil men from trespassing into my home at Broad and Gordon. For if they do, I will be forced to deliver a smack to the side of their heads that will send them crying home to their mothers!

These were her thoughts but she had to admit that if the electric company henchmen arrived at her door, she'd probably give them nothing but a scolding. If Mary Ann used her club in this crazy new world she was now a part of, she would likely be the one who'd get hauled off to jail. Still, she kept vigil with her stout stick leaning up against her front door.

Lawyers for the wealthy sought restraining orders to bar the removal of service. Meanwhile, the power thugs were pulling the plug on everyone. They even showed up at the county sheriff's office. Since the sheriff was there when the goons arrived he was able to stop them, insisting that the office was used for official government business. Then, as soon as they left he ran home, worried that they'd go and rip out the wires there next.

Not everyone suffered. The Richmond County Gas Company did a bang-up business during this dark period. They were inundated with requests for conversions back to gas fixtures and had to hire extra plumbers to do the work.

Staten Islanders watched these and other discouraging developments and began to question what other negative consequences they would suffer because of their decision to join with Greater New York. A debate began over whether or not the deed could be undone.

Democratic Former State Assemblyman Daniel T. Cornell took a practical approach. He believed there was no way out of the merger and if there were increases in taxes they would be justified by the new and better services to be put into place. It would take time, but in the end all issues would be resolved and result in positive change for Staten Island.

The opposite viewpoint was expressed by John De Morgan, a Democrat who had run in the past for the State Assembly. De Morgan strongly believed that Staten Island was being short sheeted in its merger with New York. In addition to higher taxes and the utility struggles, he brought up a host of other concerns. City officials were collecting salaries that were much higher than their predecessors who did the same job under the old regime. Yet, there were negligible improvements in services rendered. Residents elsewhere in the city could travel for free back and forth to other boroughs while Staten Islanders were forced to pay to ride the ferries. And, although they were now living in the greatest city in America, citizens living in rural Staten Island still had no United States postal service.

De Morgan disagreed with Cornell's view so strongly that he formed a local citizens' coalition to look into secession. De Morgan obtained a petition which he took to the state legislature requesting a break from the Greater City of New York and the creation of a separate City of Richmond. The petition went nowhere, but De Morgan had peace of mind because he followed through on his beliefs.

Back in Rocky Hollow day to day life went on, despite the blowing winds of change. One thing Mary Ann and her neighbors looked forward to under the new regime was the fulfillment of a promise to make valuable Stapleton waterfront improvements. A new municipal ferry was being pitched, and the construction of new docks to help support the economy. As municipal offices began to relocate to St. George, the locals were a bit melancholic, sensing that their beloved Stapleton might no longer hold the same sphere of influence as it did in pre-New York City years. The comfortable small town feeling was giving way to unfamiliar insecurities in a new city bureaucracy. It was an exciting yet painful time.

The economy which had long supported Stapleton was changing too. By the turn of the century, three familiar faces in town disappeared. George Bechtel was gone first, dying of heart failure. Then his closest competitors, Joseph Rubsam and August Horrmann of the Rubsam and Horrmann Brewery on Canal Street, passed away. Joseph Rubsam died of apparent apoplexy at home. Poor suffering August Horrmann took a razor blade to the neck to end a deep melancholia over the death of his child. Members of the Bechtel and Horrmann families stepped up to take over the breweries, but the big men were missed. The glory days of Stapleton breweries seemed to be ebbing.

Everything was different and yet the same. Mary Ann continued to scour the public auctions for good deals to add to her real estate holdings. Between 1898 and 1904, she added nine more properties to her already substantial real estate holdings.

She tried her best not to let the bugaboos of the new government slow her down.

Chapter Fourteen: Never Ruled By Man

"*Few persons in the borough before or after its absorption by the city were prouder of the place than she. She was of the type of Staten Islander fast being supplanted by more metropolitan dwellers in Richmond.*"[1]

Hip. Hip. Hoo-RAH!

At the stroke of midnight, Mary Ann and her family and friends threw open their front doors and went out into the street to usher in the first day of the new millennium. Neighbors greeted each other with warm and friendly hugs. Wooden spoons in hand, they proudly marched up and down Broad Street banging away on their pots. Church bells rang, and ship horns tooted. Young men set off firecrackers somewhere in the hills. Groups of Immaculate Conception parishioners came together on Gordon Street. They went inside the church to light candles and offer up prayers.

The Bascombe family bundled up and traveled downtown to join the large crowd that collected in Washington Park. There was music and speeches and great frivolity. The future was in God's hands, but for the residents of Rocky Hollow, Stapleton in Richmond Borough of the City of Greater New York, spirits soared with the prediction that the coming year would be their best yet.

John De Morgan and others were still fighting to undo the vote to join the City of Greater New York, but Mary Ann, practical as ever, had come to terms with the situation. She was well aware that Staten Islanders had lost something special when they gave up independence but that was over now. Rather than fight for something destined to go nowhere in the state legislature, she focused her efforts on making the new system work for her.

Mary Ann was getting on in years and old school in her beliefs. She could not fathom the way people treated each other nowadays! Being neighborly seemed to be on the decline. In all her years owning properties she never faced any serious problems with her tenants. They had always felt like an extension of her family. Now it seemed to be different. Her tenants were less friendly and more resentful.

Actually, it was more serious than that. Some of Mary Ann's tenants were downright angry and belligerent people. One wintry day she prepared to make her rounds to collect the rent. Mary Ann bundled up with scarf and gloves and set out on foot down Broad Street. In one of her homes there lived a tenant by the last name of Smith. She knocked on the front door and he let her in. Mary Ann followed the routine she had used in dozens upon dozens of homes each month for many years. Mary Ann made a little chit chat and polite inquiries as to Mr. Smith's general well-being, and then asked for the rent that was due.

No, Mrs. Bascombe, Mr. Smith said matter of factly. *I'm not paying your rent today. Get out of my house.*

Mary Ann was stunned. Did she hear him correctly? She snapped back.

Well, I'm quite sorry Mr. Smith, but no one can order me off my own property!

Mary Ann refused to leave, and they got into a heated argument. Suddenly, Mr. Smith knocked her to the ground and began to kick her about wickedly. She screamed loudly and help soon arrived, but not before Smith severely injured his landlady. The police came and arrested the tenant. They sent for James, who arrived a few moments later with the family wagon to take his battered wife home. Mary Ann insisted she was fine, but James was not sure. He called for the doctor.

The physician who examined her sent James off to the druggist for a tonic to ease the pain. Over the next few days he returned periodically to manage the pleurisy which set in. Every time Mary Ann coughed she was in agony. Mary Ann hated to sit still, but found she was unable to walk freely because of the horrific pain across her ribs.

Mary Ann was weakened both physically and mentally by the attack. She sat in a chair by the window in her front room staring mindlessly at the comings and goings out in the street. Mary Ann relived the attack over and over again in her mind.

How could I ever have rented to a man like that? Why did I not see the evil in him? What in blazes was wrong with me? I should have never let this happen.

Her tenant was evicted and sent to jail. Mary Ann slowly recovered. A month later when she next went out to collect rent money, Mary Ann made sure her stout stick came along with her. Mary Ann continued to trust her long-term tenants but found herself holding back a bit on the degree of benevolence she extended toward her newest renters. Over time her attitude mellowed, but Mary Ann maintained that she never wanted to be caught off guard again.

It was a fine mindset, but a few years later she was attacked again. Mary Ann had a female tenant the locals liked to call Crazy Annie and unfortunately, the nickname fit her well. Annie had fallen behind in her rent over many months, way too long a time for Mary Ann to ignore. Whenever Mary Ann asked her about payment, Annie made an excuse. One day, Mary Ann was mulling over her financials and decided enough was enough. She took out her stout stick and walked over to have a serious talk with Annie.

Annie let her in when she rapped on the door, but after a few minutes of listening to Mary Ann, told her she was not interested in discussing how to pay back the rent she owed. Mary Ann tried to be reasonable but the brick wall she faced left her with no recourse but to tell Annie to pay part of what she owed or risk being evicted. Annie said nothing, so Mary Ann turned away and started to leave.

What came next shocked the landlady. Crazy Annie rushed her from behind, throwing herself upon Mary Ann like some kind of ferocious animal! Somehow, Mary Ann was able to stay on her feet but she dropped her stout stick, rendering it useless.

Mary Ann attempted to push Annie off her and out of the way so she could leave.

You're a barbarian Annie!

The matron, still strong at 60 years, held her own as they wrestled. Then, Crazy Annie seized Mary Ann by the left arm and bit it savagely. Mary Ann shrieked in both pain and horror, which summoned her neighboring tenants to the scene. Annie and her landlady were still going at it when the police arrived, and only after a strenuous struggle did they succeed in subduing the feral woman. Three brawny police officers were required to drag Crazy Annie into the police wagon.

The neighbors who came to her assistance looked over Mary Ann's injuries and offered to stay with her to make sure she was alright. She brushed them off, preferring to follow the police wagon down to the station house and file a formal complaint against her tenant. On the way back home, Mary Ann stopped at the drug store on Broad Street and had her wound cauterized.

That evening, she was smarting from the procedure as well as having a hard time digesting what had happened. She wondered if Annie would try to reenter the apartment when released but thankfully, Mary Ann did not have to deal with Annie again. Annie was arraigned before Richmond County Magistrate Marsh, who committed her to the almshouse in Richmond for reasons of insanity.

In the days that followed, Mary Ann found it difficult to put Annie's attack out of her mind. Once again, she had been taken by surprise which was the worst part of the experience. Her arm, wrapped from elbow to wrist in linen bandages, served as a visual reminder of the vicious assault. Mary Ann sat in her rocker while recovering and could not help but wax nostalgic over the old days. In her childhood, the greatest dangers to Rocky Hollow were infectious disease and the flooding of Gore's Brook. Now, at the turn of the century, it seemed that the biggest threats came from the men and women of Rocky Hollow itself! Crime and violence were taking over and testing the will of all God-fearing people in the neighborhood.

Criminal activity in Rocky Hollow was not ameliorated after

the Greater New York consolidation. Although there were more police officers on the streets, their ranks remained inadequate to curb the numbers of drunk and disorderly. Plus, race and culture conflicts were on the rise. Italians were among the newest residents of Stapleton, moving to Staten Island as part of a great new wave of immigration from southern Europe, and the Irish and Italian population did not mix very well. Italians spoke an unfamiliar language. They had different cultural and culinary traditions. Plus, they were vying for the same laborer jobs alongside the Irish.

One June evening, a huge fight took place between Italians and Irish youths in Rocky Hollow. It was warm dry night, so Mary Ann had the bedroom windows open in order to catch any chance of a breeze. Everyone in the house was in deep sleep in the wee morning hours when roused by the sudden commotion outside. Mary Ann lifted her head off the pillow to better hear the screaming of expletives down the road.

James! What the dickens is going on!

Mary Ann got out of bed and stuck her head out the window, but did not see anything in the darkness. All she could tell was that the voices seemed to be escalating.

Though no one still knew what happened at breakfast, all were certain that alcohol must have played a part. Mary Ann went out to talk to the neighbors and filled in the details of the night before by reading the dailies.

A number of Italians (who the Irish liked to mockingly call a bunch of oily rag pickers) were dallying at the corner of McKeon and Varian Streets. On the opposite corner, Irish and other English-speaking youths showed up and likewise began to congregate. The numbers grew until there were close to two hundred young men hanging out on the street. An insult was hurled across the road which was answered by an angry retort and soon both sides were viciously taunting the other. Then, someone picked up some rocks and chucked them across the road.

Both factions moved into the middle of the road and a physical brawl ensued. What started with a few shoves and punches quickly escalated into a savage fight with knives and clubs. The police were called, and drew their pistols and fired shots off into the air to disperse the crowd.

Close to a dozen young men were injured. John Fritz of Varian Street was stabbed with a knife in his left side so severely that he collapsed on the ground. A police ambulance was called and he was taken to the R. S. Smith Infirmary and hospitalized.

Two Italian brothers who lived on Varian Street were arrested in the melee. One of them attempted to dispose of his knife, revolver, and stiletto along the way to the police station but the weapons were recovered by police and held as evidence.

As Mary Ann was reading the newspaper article, she thought how easy it could be for one of her male progeny to find themselves in the wrong place at the wrong time by accident or to get inadvertently mixed up with these unscrupulous kinds of people. Mary Ann called for her grandsons to come over to visit and when they arrived, she fed them and then engaged the boys in a long lengthy discourse.

My dear grandchildren. Be mindful of your surroundings at all times and stick to your own business. And for heaven's sake, steer clear of the saloons! That's where the gangs and bad seeds in town hang their hats. People like that Harry Keeley!

Though she had no proof, Mary Ann theorized that Harry Keeley, a local Irish mobster, had somehow been involved in the fight. Keeley was a thirty-year old ex-convict from Clifton with a reputation so bad that even the fearless Mary Ann would not dare to confront him.

Keeley had a dark history. He murdered a man during a fight and was sentenced to five-years in Sing-Sing prison. Keeley did his time, but incarceration did not change him one bit. One night shortly after his release from prison he went to a community social and terrorized the attendees. The police were summoned and when Officer Jose arrived an ugly fight erupted. Four men in addition to Jose were needed to bring Keeley to the ground. He was taken away by the police in a crazed condition. Keeley went to court, where his attorney argued insanity. He was committed to Manhattan Hospital Mental Asylum.

Three months later, Keeley was released from the asylum.

Like prison, Keeley did not benefit from the time spent in confinement. He returned to the streets with a heart full of poison. Keeley was consumed with an intense hatred of Officer Jose and all who helped subdue him at the social.

One Saturday evening, Keeley left home and started making the rounds of the saloons in and around Stapleton. At many of the establishments he flashed a six-chamber revolver and boasted that he was going to make trouble before the night ended. He wanted to kill a policeman and go to the electric chair. The men who heard his threats believed he was serious and they were right. It was not known at the time, but Keeley was carrying 134 bullet cartridges on him. A few of them ran over to the Beach Street police station and reported that Keeley was drunk and out of control. A score of brave NYPD police officers were then sent out into the streets to find him.

It was now the middle of the night, and the highly intoxicated Keeley stood dawdling near the lamppost at Broad and Centre Streets when suddenly John Fritz and Henry Wintermeyer turned the corner and ran smack into him.

Fritz was a most unfortunate young man. He was an example Mary Ann liked to use when she spoke to her grandsons because Fritz had the worst of luck. Fritz had just recently recovered from being stabbed by the Italians in the street fight just a few blocks from where he was standing. Now again, he was in deep trouble for it had been him and Wintermeyer who helped hold Keeley down the night of his last arrest.

When they spotted Keeley the pair froze where they stood out of panic. Keeley flashed his pistol. He began to taunt the men, asking why they chose to help a policeman over him. Seeing that Keeley was mentally unhinged, Fritz chose his words carefully while looking for the best opportunity to run. When sounds in the distance got Keeley distracted, he nudged Wintermeyer and the two fled the scene. While running, they met up with Officer James McGrath and told him what had happened.

Officer McGrath ran to the scene and found Keeley was still in the same spot on the Rocky Hollow street corner. Now he was talking to a black man by the name of Scudder. McGrath approached him cautiously. He asked Keeley to go home, but he refused. Then, he ordered him to leave. Something caught McGrath's attention and turned his head to the side. In the brief instant that he looked away, Keeley whipped out his pistol. He fired five shots, three of which hit his target. One bullet entered McGrath on the left side above his heart; the second pierced his right shoulder, and the third went through his right hand.

Fritz and Wintermeyer heard the shots and returned to the scene. Keeley saw them and started firing upon them too. Fritz was shot in the foot and fell to the ground. Somehow Wintermeyer was able to drag him away to safety.

A crowd was quick to gather as the gunshots woke many in the neighborhood. The alcohol must have dulled Keeley's common sense as he chose to hang out in the crowd rather than run away. Patrolman Durkin was the first officer to arrive at the scene and went straight to his fallen comrade's side. Durkin asked what McGrath happened, and despite the obviously great distress he was in, the officer was able to lift his finger to point out the perpetrator.

Durkin rushed at him while Keeley attempted to pull out his revolver. Durkin got to him before the gun was fired and dealt him a heavy blow with his billy club. He hit him straight across the mouth, bloodying Keeley's lips and expelling some teeth. Then he slapped him smartly over the head.

Durkin asked someone in the crowd to stay with the wounded men and another to call for an ambulance. If the sound of gunshots, screams, cursing, and other loud crowd chatter hadn't yet woken up every Bascombe family member from their sound sleep, the sound of the ambulance wagon in the middle of the night surely did. Both McGrath and Fritz were loaded into the wagon and taken to the S. R. Smith Infirmary to be treated for gunshot wounds.

Durkin did not call for a police wagon. Instead he dragged Keeley off by foot. Those who watched wondered how much sense that made in that the gunman fought Durkin tooth and nail the entire way. When Keeley arrived at the police station it took four officers to hold him down and search him.

Over 128 bullet shells were taken from his pockets and piled up on a desk. He had no gun but on the basis of McGrath's positive identification, he was arrested for assault in the first degree. Scudder was also brought to the station house. The intent was to take Scudder's testimony as a witness to the crime, but as he was acting strangely he was likewise searched. He had Keeley's revolver in his pocket.

Keeley was held without bail, which everyone in Rocky Hollow applauded. Mary Ann and her neighbors counted the days, waiting for the day of Keeley's trial to arrive. Of all the criminals around town, he was the one who kept them up worrying at night. Everyone wanted him put away permanently!

At the trial, the judge declared Harry Keeley legally insane. He was committed to the Dannemora Criminal Asylum, a prison mental hospital in upstate New York. Mary Ann and everyone she knew rejoiced at the decision. She cooked a special celebration supper and invited all the tenants living in her Broad and Gordon Street apartments to join her.

There was no doubt among her family and friends: Mary Ann was uniquely qualified to offer an opinion on crime, politics, and other affairs in the Stapleton community. She had been born during Stapleton's infancy and lived almost her entire life on the same corner at Broad and Gordon Streets. She watched history unfold with the start of the brewery industry, the Civil War years, the introduction of modern inventions such as electricity and indoor plumbing, and the transition of Staten Island from independently governed county to a borough within the City of Greater New York. She had lived long enough to see changes in the status of women in American society and had high hopes that the future would usher in even more positive developments for her daughters and granddaughters.

In June 1900, the U.S. Census workers were out in force knocking on doors up and down the streets of Stapleton. A man by the name of George Koffer showed up one day at the front door of Mary Ann's Broad Street home. She was there and invited him in, offering him a seat at her dining table.

Koffer opened his business bag and took out paper, pens, an

inkwell, and a large census roster. He had been up and down the streets for a few weeks now and knew his job by rote. It was boring work if not for a bit of cordial chit chat here and there, so Koffer engaged Mary Ann in some conversation prior to rattling off the same series of questions he was asking all over the neighborhood. Mary Ann was pleased, as she enjoyed telling anyone and everyone about her life and business enterprises.

Gee! Gosh!

Koffer was both surprised and impressed at Mary Ann's accomplishments! Based on their conversation, Koffer noted something unique about the Bascombe family. In the column where he had to identify the relationship of each person in the family Koffer inked the word *Head* next to Mary Ann's name. And, on James' line, he scribbled *Husband*.

Koffer returned to the census office and submitted his records. In the office, a supervisor reviewed the ledger. Scrutinizing each line for completed data, the man stopped at the Bascombe listing.

Look at this, he said to himself.

Obviously, Koffer made an error.

The supervisor did not bother to ask Koffer about the entry. Whether deliberately altering a federal census form was legal or not did not matter, for the supervisor knew full well no one was going to make a fuss. With a heavy hand and distinctly different penmanship, he boldly wrote over Koffer's script. *Wife* was inserted over the word *Head* and James was given back the traditional family title.

The New York census officer was probably unaware that around the same time, the U.S. Circuit Court of Appeals in Virginia was examining this very issue. Their court ruled that a woman could indeed be the head of the house. In the decision, the presiding Justice opined that:

"When an intelligent, active, industrious, frugal woman finds she has married a man who, instead of coming up to a standard of a husband, is a mere dependent, who acknowledges that he is only a helpmate to his wife, obeys her instructions, pours his little earnings into her lap, acknowledges her to be and always

*to have been the head of the family, and leaves her its support,
it would be contradictory of fact and an absurd construction of
law to say he, and not she, is the head of the family..."²*

Koffer had recorded the truth, whether or not the census
supervisor cared to investigate or acknowledge. And in the
end, what did it matter? Census workers were head counters
and pencil pushers. Their characterizations of individuals were
limited to name, age, gender, and a few basic facts. Mary Ann's
amazingly atypical life could never be accurately reflected in
census records because the sensibilities of the day did not allow
her to stand out. There was no doubt, however, to anyone who
knew her that Mary Ann was the head of the Bascombe family.

And, she had never been ruled by man.

As the new century unfolded, Mary Ann Bascombe was still
going strong. The grand dame of Broad and Gordon Streets
celebrated her sixtieth birthday in December 1900, surrounded
by a large circle of family and friends. It was a happy day
for Mary Ann. She and James were healthy. She had many
grandchildren to smother with hugs and kisses. Her career as a
lady lawyer had come to an end with the new government, but
she still had a lot to say about what the city should be doing
for its citizens. Neighbors continued to seek her advice and
pay attention when she spoke out at public forums. Her real
estate business was still going strong with more new properties
coming on the market every day to catch her eye. Money was
never a concern.

When the birthday festivities ended Mary Ann and her
daughters washed, dried, and put away the good china and
silverware. Mary Ann said good night to her family, and then
she began to prepare for bed. She went to the bathroom, washed
her face at the sink, and made good use of the indoor plumbing.
Then she went to the bedroom where she took off her clothes
and placed them neatly on a chair. Mary Ann put on her sleep
gown and then went over to the dresser to turn off the electric
lamp. She climbed into bed. James was already snoring after
having one too many beers. She smirked and gave him a light
peck on the cheek. Then, Mary Ann closed her eyes to relive all

the wonderful moments of the party. It was relaxing, and after a bit her mind drifted from the here and now to the distant past and her parents.

Dear father and mother up in heaven, how much you would have enjoyed today's party. Rest assured your big brood of grandchildren and great grandchildren make you proud. Life is good here in Rocky Hollow but my, how surprised you would both be to see how much the neighborhood has changed since we all lived here as one!

Aside from the magnificent view of the harbor that could be seen from the soft green hills, the Rocky Hollow that Thomas McDonough fell in love with in 1840 was no more. What replaced the pastoral landscape of farms, fields, woods, and brooks was a modest working-class suburb of homes and businesses. Naturally, she missed some aspects of what Rocky Hollow was like in years past but realistically she was a sensible woman. Time and progress was inevitable. There was much for Mary Ann to cherish looking back, but perhaps even more to look forward to in the years to come.

Mary Ann and her family and friends embraced their new city, the 20th century, and the early years of Richmond Borough. They always found things in life to celebrate. Before her conscious mind gave way to sleep, Mary Ann made certain to thank God for the many blessings which had been bestowed on her.

She smiled as she drifted in the dark. Through a combination of faith and hard work, Mary Ann had been the survivor of many hardships in her life. She was a woman of great accomplishment, both personally and for others.

Mary Ann had one last conscious thought before falling into a deep sleep.

Pish! Posh! Life is good.

What Happened Next

No one was prouder of her community than Mary Ann Bascombe. Though at times she liked to project an intimidating image, in reality she loved the citizens of Rocky Hollow and the feeling was reciprocated. In November 1905, when it was learned that she had come down with the same deadly strain of pneumonia to which her husband James had succumbed, neighbors set up a vigil outside her front door. People came to offer help and provide comfort to family members. Each hoped to speak to her one last time, but they were turned away. Mary Ann was far too ill to receive visitors.

Mary Ann's last will and testament was handwritten on her deathbed. The struggle to summon enough strength to sign her name is noted by the shaky lettering on the page. Apparently, departing for God's Kingdom anytime soon had not been on her mind prior to getting sick. She had not yet run out of things to accomplish here on Earth.

There were many newspapers that reported her death. Some papers showed their distaste for her even at her end. The *Richmond County Advance* reported James's death as frontpage news, but a week later relegated Mary Ann's passing to page four. Other friendlier newspapers such as the Stapleton based *The Staten Island Leader* turned her obituary, "Never Ruled by Man", into their lead story.

Up to seventy properties were assessed to settle Mary Ann's estate. Her assets – brick and wood frame homes, vacant land, bank accounts, horse and wagon – were divided equally between her six surviving children. The only exception was her piano, which was left to daughter Emma. The execution of the will was fraught with controversy. Some of her children challenged the actions of the will's executors. Lawyers got involved and the decision went all the way up to the New York State Appeals court. Mary Ann's estate was not settled until years after her death.

The majority of Mary Ann's homes were built on Broad, McKeon, and Gordon Streets. In the 1920's, her modest structures became close neighbors of one of Staten Island's most popular sports attractions. A wealthy lumber yard owner built a ball field on land which had once been part of the Seamen's Retreat. Inside its stockade fence, Thompson's Stadium had 8000 uncovered bleacher seats. The stadium became home to local amateur school and sports clubs, the professional Staten Island Staples team of the National Football League, and semiprofessional baseball teams. Those living in some of the houses she built were able to hear the wild cheers and jeers of the crowds on game day. Her homes on Warren Street were close enough perhaps to provide inhabitants with a glimpse of the action.

Stapleton residents were made promises in the consolidation of Greater New York, and not all were delivered. Thanks to Andrew Carnegie, a New York Public Library building was erected in 1907. A municipal ferry complex was built but the service quickly abandoned after government offices opened in St. George. In the 1920's a mayor envisioned a monstrous waterfront complex which was ultimately abandoned but not before earning the nickname, Hylan's Folly. The landscape changed, sometimes by deliberate intent and other times by freakish accident. In the 1930's, fires burnt down landmarks like the German Club Rooms and the Bechtel Brewery. Time went on. The Rubsam and Horrmann Brewery was purchased by Piels Brothers. Eventually it closed and was demolished.

Midway through the twentieth century, the New York City Housing Authority announced plans for a large state financed housing project in Rocky Hollow. Thompson Stadium was to be demolished to make way for over 690 apartments, a recreational playground and ball fields. Many of the small homes built by Mary Ann would be torn down. At the groundbreaking ceremony, Harry Reid, Chairman of the New York City Housing Authority, was one of the main speakers. He emphasized how hard it was to find decent housing in urban areas. The Stapleton Houses would help fill the continuing need for modern homes and apartments in New York.

The locals who attended the ceremony were likely caught off guard by Reid's words. In 1959, Staten Island was still mostly a place of modest one and two-family homes, family farms, marshes, and undeveloped woods. They were part of the greatest city in America but in no way did Staten Islanders consider their borough *urban*. Urban communities were large and impersonal places. They lived in a small *town* called Stapleton where everyone knew each other. Few wanted that to change.

Construction of the Verrazano-Narrows Bridge a few miles away began just a few weeks prior to the ground breaking. Some wondered how a bridge to Brooklyn in addition to these massive apartment buildings would impact their community. In a few years both projects were completed, bringing an influx of new families to Stapleton. A new and modern Public School 14 was built. The school on Broad and Brook Streets was torn down.

Crime did not go away. In fact, sometimes it was more violent than ever.

Stories of the breweries, Thompson's Stadium, and other parts of town survived, but tales of Rocky Hollow and the people who first settled the community seemed to fade away. Mary Ann was a larger than life personality, but was forgotten over time. Even her own family lost track of the fact that they had an ancestor who was special.

Mary Ann's name is written on a yellowed index card in the office of St. Peter's Cemetery on Staten Island. It confirms that she is buried there with James on the property. The problem is no plot map exists at the cemetery to identify the exact location where they were laid to rest.

Though the exact location of her final resting place is not certain, who Mary Ann Bascombe was is no mystery. She was a daughter, sister, wife, mother, friend, factory girl, housemaid, washerwoman, landlord, business entrepreneur, lady lawyer, public advocate, school board candidate, community volunteer, and local Democratic powerhouse. She was a woman who did not let men dictate to her who and what she could be. Mary Ann was a woman ahead of her time.

Mary Ann's spirit must soar high in light of the changes in American society which resulted in equal rights for women. Mary Ann's daughters and granddaughters got the vote and broke through major social and economic barriers. It is now much easier for women to achieve their dreams, but there are still challenges. In today's world, Mary Ann would be a strong supporter of initiatives such as the Me Too Movement. She would want all women to appreciate their own power to create the life of their choosing.

This book was a journey which took a few unexpected detours, but it was my dream to publish her story. Mary Ann Bascombe is my great-great-grandmother and she was all about not giving in to the naysayers and obstacles in one's way. It was not an easy feat, but I was not going to let her or myself down.

Mary Ann and I grew close over time. I felt I got to know her well. After completing my final edit, I realized the need for some sort of approval from her to go forward. So, I asked out loud what she thought of the finished product. To my delight, I received an immediate response. Her words shot forth in my mind, crisp and clear as I could only imagine the waters of Gore's Brook.

Pish! Posh! she answered.

You've done the job. Thank you my dear girl for not forgetting me.

Phyllis Barone Ameduri
July 17, 2018

Notes

A variety of source materials were consulted to write this book. The stories about Mary Ann and people living in Stapleton came from historic newspaper articles. Bascombe family facts were found in census forms, wills, deeds, tax records, maps, church records, death certificates, and family documents. Gaps in surviving public records led to conjecture on some events such as the deaths of John McLoughlan and William Richards. No claims have been made that this is a scholarly work. The source materials should thus not be judged critically but are included for anyone interested in doing additional reading.

Quotes

Chapter One
All quotes are from "Bride and Maiden. A Controversy in a Staten Island Court in Which Mrs. 'Counsellor Howe' Appears – A Tintype and the Trouble Which it Caused," *New York Herald*, February 10, 1882, fultonhistory.com.

Chapter Two
[1]"The Lounger. The Lounger on a Hill-top," *Harper's Weekly,* November 28, 1857, fultonhistory.com. [2]"The Health of the City. Cholera in Staten Island," *New-York Daily Tribune*, August 11, 1866, fultonhistory.com.

Chapter Three
[1]Ira K. Morris, *Morris's Memorial History of Staten Island,* (New York: Memorial Publishing Company, 1898), Volume 2, 367.

Chapter Four
[1]"Woman Politician Dead," *The New York Press*, November 24, 1905, fultonhistory.com.

Chapter Five
[1]"Enforcing the Cattle Ordinance," *The Staten Islander*, June 26, 1878; [2]"A Woman Who Takes Her Rights," *Saratoga Sentinel,* January 12, 1882 fultonhistory.com; [3]"This Factory Girl a Moneymaker," *The Washington Morning Times,* March 7, 1897, chroniclingamerica.loc.gov.

Chapter Six
[1]"Hiding the Girl He Wanted to Marry," *The New York Sun*, February 23, 1881, chroniclingamerica.gov; [2]"A Staten Island Romance," *The New York World,* June 29, 1884, fultonhistory.com.

Chapter Seven
[1]"Personal and Political," *The Philadelphia Inquirer,* December 31, 1881, 4, newspaperarchives.com.

Chapter Eight
[1]"I'll Reform You!" *The New York Evening Telegram,* January 3, 1884, fultonhistory.com.

Chapter Nine
[1]"A Strong Minded Woman. How She Punished Her Husband for His Beer Drinking," *New York Evening Telegram,* December 30, 1881, fultonhistory.com.

Chapter Ten
[1]"New York News and Gossip. A Staten Island Woman's Original Way of Dealing with Tenants," *Rochester New York Democratic Chronicle November 30, 1905,* fultonhistory.com; [2]"Mrs. Mack Will Be There," *Wheeling, West Virginia Register*, October 29, 1884, fultonhistory.com.

Chapter Eleven
[1] Last School Elections," *The Staten Islander,* July 31, 1897; [2]"School Elections," *The Staten Islander,* August 1, 1891.

Chapter Twelve
All quotes "Jilted the Captain; Wedded the Mate," *The Syracuse Journal,* August 20, 1904, fultonhistory.com.

Chapter Thirteen
[1]"Now Richmond Complains; Some Taxpayers Dissatisfied with Consolidation Results," *The New York Times,* August 8, 1899, nytimes.com.

Chapter Fourteen
[1]"Woman Politician Dead," *The New York Press,* November 24, 1905, fultonhistory.com; [2]"A Wife's Separate Rights," *The New York Times,* November 9, 1900, nytimes.com.

Source Material

Newspaper articles which mention Mary Ann Bascombe and/or her family: "A Dishonest Servant," *New York Tribune*, September 7, 1858, fultonhistory.com; "A Female Lawyer's Peril," *The New York Evening Telegram*, October 6, 1884,fultonhistory.com; "A Portia in Court," *The Glen Falls Daily Times*, February 3, 1882, fultonhistory.com; "A *Weekly Globe, February 14,1882, NewspaperArchives.com;* "A Woman's Moving Plea. The Controversy Between Bride and Maiden and How Mrs. Bascombe Talked to the Justice," *Detroit Free Press*, February 14, 1882, ProQuest Historical Newspapers; "Abduction Ending in Marriage," *The New York Times*, February 23, 1881, nytimes.com; "Annual Entertainment," *Richmond County Advance*, March 16, 1901, chroniclingamerica.gov; "Arrest for Robbing a Safe," *Brooklyn Eagle*, September 6, 1858, eagle.brooklynpubliclibrary.org; "Black vs. White," *The Staten Islander,* May 23, 1891; "Bitten by a Negress," *The New York Sun*, September 20, 1903, fultonhistory.com; "Bitten by an Angry Woman," *The New York Times*, September 20, 1903, nytimes.com; "Bowling Notes," *Richmond County Advance*, March 7, 1903, chroniclingamerica.gov; Brutal Treatment of an Adopted Child," *The New York Herald Tribune*, April 20, 1886, fultonhistory.com; "Captain Sails, Marries Mate," *The New York Times,* August 19, 1904, nytimes.com; "Charged with Child Beating," *The New York Herald,* April 7, 1886, fultonhistory.com; "Crazy Annie Bites Wealthy Woman, "*The New York Herald,* September 20, 1903, fultonhistory.com; "Disastrous Fires," *The Staten Islander,* April 6, 1892; "Engaged to Captain, But Fled with Mate," *The New York Press,* November 19, 1904, fultonhistory.com; "Engaged to One; Weds Another. Staten Island Girl Disappears While Mother Reads Notice of Marriage," *New York Tribune*, April 19, 1904, chroniclingamerica.gov; "Fires Set on Staten Island," *The New York Sun,* October 7, 1884, fultonhistory.com; "Foresaw Himself a Murder," The New York Press, January 10, 1898, fultonhistory.com; "Going Mad, He Sought Jail, *New York World,* January 10, 1898, fultonhistory.com; "He Knew it Was Coming," New York Tribune, January 10, 1898, chroniclingamerica.gov; "His Prediction Fulfilled," *The New York Times,* January 10, 1898, nytimes.com; "In the Public Eye," *The Los Angeles Herald,* April 25, 1897; "Incendiaries on Staten Island," *The New York Times,* October 7, 1884, nytimes.com; "Jilted Captain; Eloped with Mate," *The New York Evening Telegram,* August 18, 1904, fultonhistory.com; "Mary Ann Bascombe," *Richmond County Advance*, November 25, 1905; "Mary Ann Bascombe Kicked by a Tenant," *The New York World,* December 23, 1898, fultonhistory.com; "Mrs. Bascombe's Daughter Wed," *The Staten Islander,* August 20, 1904; "Mrs. Mary Ann Mack and Her Pretty Daughter, " *Boston Herald ,* June 29, 1884, genealogybank.com; "Mosquitoes and Drainage," *Richmond County Advance*, July 25, 1903; "Negress Bites Rich Woman," *The New York Daily Tribune*, September 20, 1903, fultonhistory.com; "O'Hanlon Defeated Mrs. Bascombe," *The New York Press*, August 7, 1890, fultonhistory.com; "Othello in a Police Court," *New York Herald Tribune*, February 23, 1881, New York Public Library; "Plain Truths. Something About the Board of Health at Edgewater, Staten Island," *The New York Evening Telegram,* August 2, 1887, fultonhistory.com; "Personals," *The Newport News,* May 12, 1897. chroniclingamerica.gov.; Protest Against Water Rate," *The New York Press,* July 1, 1902, fultonhistory.com; "Remarkable Woman," *Wheeling Daily Intelligencer,* March 10, 1897, fultonhistory.com; "Removed a Priest," *New York Herald,* December 8, 1895, fultonhistory.com; "Said to be Thieves," *The Staten Islander,* June 3, 1893; "She was Lawyer and Bricklayer," *New York Herald,* November 24, 1905, fultonhistory. com; "Staten Island," *The New York Daily Tribune,* June 1, 1893, chroniclingameri-ca.gov; Staten Island," *The New York Evening Post,* February 5, 1895, fultonhistory. com; "Sudden Death," *Richmond County Advance,* November 18, 1905; "Suitor Not Discouraged," *Syracuse New York Herald,* August 19, 1904, fultonhistory.com; "The Drama of Real Life," *The New York Evening Express,"* February 25, 1881, fultonhis-tory.com; "The Public Eye," *Los Angeles Herald,* April 25, 1897, chroniclingamerica. gov; "Workwoman Becomes Rich," *The Anderson (S.C.) Intelligencer,* March 17, 1897; chroniclingamerica.gov.

Bascombe family records: Certificate of Baptism of Mary Anna McDonough, dated December 17, 1840, St. Peter's R.C. Church, Staten Island, New York; Certificate of Baptism of William Richards, dated August 17, 1862, St. Mary's R.C. Church, Staten Island, New York; Certificate of Marriage of John McLoughlan and Mary Ann McDonough, dated August 22, 1857, St. Peter's R.C. Church, Staten Island, New York; Certificate of Marriage of William Richards and Mary Emma Wall, dated May 6, 1893, Immaculate Conception R.C. Church, Staten Island, New York; Death certificate of Mary Ann Bascombe (State of New York Certificate and Record of Death Number 1277, The City of New York Municipal Archives); Deed of Sale from George Coyne to Thomas McDonough, dated August 27, 1840, (recorded November 6, 1840) in the office of the Clerk of the County of Richmond in Liber 7, page 312, Richmond County Clerk, Staten Island, New York; Deed of Sale from James and Harriet M. Coyne to Mary Ann Bascombe, dated August 8, 1864, Office of the Clerk of the County of Richmond, Liber 58, page 28, Staten Island, New York; Deed of Sale from Michael and Bridget McDonough, John McDonough, James McDonough and Julia D. McDonough to Mary Ann Bascom, dated April 24, 1873 in the office of the Clerk of the County of Richmond in Liber 103, page 514, Richmond County Clerk, Staten Island, New York; 1851 Census of England and Wales; ancestry.com; 1892Webb's Consolidated Directory of Richmond County, New York;1895 -1896 Standard Directory of Richmond County, New York, 24, Staten Island Historical Society, Richmondtown; Index to Death Certificates, Richmond County, New York, 1847 – 1886, microfilm, New York Public Library; Index to Deeds, Richmond County, N.Y., (Microfilm), 1630 – 1972, New York Public Library; Index to Petitions for Naturalization filed in New York City, 1792-1989; ancestry.com; Last Will and Testament of Mary Ann Bascombe dated November 18, 1905, Surrogates Court, Richmond County, Index P36645; Letters of Administration for the Estate of Thomas McDonough dated January 6, 1853, Surrogates Court, Richmond County, Index A/635/1853; Marriage Record of Mary Anna McDonough and James Bascombe, June 15,1864, St. Mary's R.C. Church; "New York Deaths and Burials, 1795-1952, Index," *FamilySearch*, accessed 2012, familysearch.org; New York State Census 1835, 1855, 1865, 1875 of Richmond County, New York, microfilm, Staten Island Institute of the Arts and Sciences; Passenger Lists of Vessels Arriving at New York, New York, 1820 – 1897; National Archives Microfilm Publication M237, 675 rolls; Records of the U.S. Customs Service, Record Group 36; National Archives, Washington, D.C. accessed at Ancestry.com; Staten Island," *The New York Evening Post,* February 5, 1895, fultonhistory.com; U.S. Censuses, 1840 – 1920, ancestry.com.

Descriptions of Rocky Hollow and Stapleton, Staten Island are found in "A Model Brewery on Staten Island," *The New York Times,* August 18, 1885, nytimes.com; Richard Mather Bayles, *History of Richmond County (Staten Island), New York from its Discovery to the Present Time* (New York: L.E. Preston and Co., 1887); "George Bechtel; One of Staten Island's Prominent Citizens Passes Away," *Richmond County Gazette,* July 24, 1889; F.W. Beers, *Atlas of Staten Island, Richmond County, New York* (New York: J.W. Beers & Co., 1874); "Brewer Ends His Life," *The New York Times,* February 10, 1900, nytimes.com; Reau Campbell, *Rides and Rambles on Staten Island* (New York: C. G. Crawford: 1889); J. J. Clute, *Annals of Staten Island: from its discovery to the present time* (New York: Press of C. Vogt, 1877); "Death of George Bechtel," *The New York Times,* July18, 1889, nytimes. com; "Delightful Village" *New York Spectator,* April 18, 1837, genealogybank.com; Richard B. Dickenson, ed., *Holden's Staten Island: The History of Richmond County* (New York: Center for Migration Studies, 2003); "Edgewater Up in Arms," *The New York Times,* July 7, 1884, nytimes.com; "Father Huntman Transferred," *The New York Sun,* December 9, 1895, fultonhistory.com; "Father Huntman's Farewell," *The Staten Islander,* December 4, 1885; James G. Ferrari and David Goldfarb, *Images of America. Stapleton* (Charleston, S.C.: Arcadia Publishing, 2010); "Facts About The History Of St. Peter's R.C. Church On Staten Island," *St. George Civic Association,* Accessed May 12, 2018, http://www.preserve.org/stgeorge/stpeter.html; "Fourth of July Excursion for the Million," *New York Tribune,* July 4, 1860, fultonhistory. com; "Gas on Staten Island," *The New York Times,* November 28, 1856, nytimes.com; "Good Church Work," *The Staten Islander,* January 15, 1898; Great Conflagration at Staten Island; The Health Officer's House Burnt Down, Destruction of the Quarantine Establishment," *The New York Times,* Sept 2, 1858, nytimes.com; Leslie M. Harris, *In the Shadow of Slavery: African Americans in New York City, 1626 – 1863* (Chicago: University of Chicago Press, 2003) excerpt found at http://www.press.uchicago.edu/ Misc/Chicago/317749.html; C. G. Hine, *History and Legend of Howard Avenue and the Serpentine Road, Grymes Hill,* (Staten Island: Hines Bros.Printery,1914); "History of Merritt-Chapman & Scott Corporation," *Mystic Seaport The Museum of America and the Sea,* accessed June 29, 2018, http://library.mysticseaport.org/manuscripts/ coll/coll002.cfm; Historical Records Survey, Division of Professional and Service Projects, Work Projects Administration, *Inventory of the County and Borough Archives of New York City* No. 5. Richmond County and Borough (Staten Island) (New York: The Survey, August 1939); John Hogrogian, "The Staten Island Stapletons," *The Coffin Corner,* Vol. 7, No. 6 (1985); "Housing Started on Staten Island," *The New York Times,* September 29, 1959, nytimes.com; *Illustrated Sketchbook of Staten Island, New York, its Industry and Commerce* (New York: S.C. Judson, 1886); "In Brooklyn and the Suburbs," *New York Tribune,* July 6, 1874, fultonhistory.com; *Insurance Maps of Staten Island, New York* (New York: Sanborn Map & Publishing Co., July 1878); Charles W. Leng and William T. Davis, *Staten Island and its People* (New York: Lewis Historical Publishing Company, 1930); Alyssa Loorya and Christopher Ricciardi, *Phase IA Cultural Resource Documentary Study of the 210 Broad Street (Stapleton Housing) Project – Staten Island (Richmond County), New York (Block 545, Lot 100 (portion only) Final Report,* prepared for BFC Partners and City of New York - Landmarks Preservation Commission, November 2007, http://www.nyc.gov/ html/lpc/html/publications/archaeology_reports.shtml; "Maine Wreck Abandoned," *The New York Times,* April 3, 1898, nytimes.com; "Mass Meeting of the Democratic Republican Electors of Richmond County," *New York Herald,* July 6, 1844, fulton-history.com; Carmelo Melluso, *St. Peter's Roman Catholic Parish, New Brighton, Staten Island,* accessed on May 12, 2018, http://www.fordham.edu/halsall/medny/ melluso.html; Harlow McMillen, "Staten Island's Lager Beer Breweries, 1851 – 1962," *The Staten Island Historian,* Vol. XXX, 3; Anthony Medditto, Jr., Kevin Cummings, et al., "The Police Departments of Staten Island," *The Staten Island Historian,* XXXI: 14, April – June 1973; Ira K. Morris, *Morris's Memorial History of Staten Island, New York* (New York: Memorial Publishing Company, 1898); Mud Lane Society, Staten Island, New York, Mudlanesociety.org.; "Obituary," *The New York Times,* October 23, 1890, nytimes.com; "Parish History," *Church of St. Mary Rosebank Staten Island,* accessed October 2012, stmaryschurchrosebank.org; "Property on Staten Island," *New York Spectator,* June 30, 1836, fultonhistory.com; Patricia M. Salmon, *Stapleton: A Walking Tour,* brochure prepared for the Staten Island Institute of Arts & Sciences exhibition "Stapleton: a Community of Contrast and Change," February 20 -August 25, 2002; Seaman's Retreat: Main Building, *Landmarks Preservation Commission,* April 9, 1985, http://www.neighborhoodpreservationcenter.org; "Stapesville," *New York Spectator,* July 7, 1836, genealogybank.com; *Stapleton, Tompkinsville, New Brighton, West New Brighton, Clifton and Port Richmond, Staten Island: Their Representative Businessmen and Points of Interest,* (New York: Mercantile Publishing Company, 1893); "Staten Island," *New York Evening Post,* January 9, 1896, fultonhis-tory.com; "The Death of John Bechtel," *New York Sun,* May 28, 1882, fultonhistory. com; "The Draft," *Richmond County Gazette,* July 15, 1863; "The Meeting in New York Avenue, Clifton, on Wednesday," *Richmond County Gazette,* July 22, 1863;

"The Quarantine War: The Burning of New York Marine Hospital in 1858," *Public Health Reports,* Vol. CXIX119; "The Riot," *New York Tribune,* July 18, 1863, chroniclingamerica.loc.gov; "The Riot on Staten Island." *Richmond County Gazette,* July 22, 1863; "The Staten Island Jubilee," *The New York Times,* May 4, 1859; nytimes.com; Joseph Thiesen, *History of the Parish of Immaculate Conception on the Occasion of the 75th Anniversary, 1887-1962* (Stapleton, New York: 1962); W. S. Webb, *Webb's Consolidated Directory of the North and South Shores Staten Island,* 1886, VI – VII.

Description of health and safety conditions in and around Stapleton are found in "A Deluge," *Albany NY Evening Journal,* Aug 23, 1843, fultonhistory.com; "Cholera," *Centers for Disease Control and Prevention, Atlanta, Georgia,* Accessed on October 27, 2012, cdc.gov/cholera; "Excelsior Hose Company's Fair," *The Staten Islander,* April 6, 1892; "Facts in Relation to the Fever at Staten Island," *The Albany Evening Journal,* September 6, 1848, fultonhistory.com; Jacques Noel Jacobsen, Jr., *They Answered the Alarm: The Fire Department of Staten Island 1805-2005* (Daytona Beach Shores, FL: Jacques Noel Jacobsen, Jr., 2010); Charles W. Leng and William T. Davis, *Staten Island and its People* (New York: Lewis Historical Publishing Company, 1930); *Morris's Memorial History of Staten Island,* (New York: Memorial Publishing Company, 1898); "On Staten Island," *The New York Daily Graphic,* August 2, 1889, fultonhistory.com; "On Staten Island," *The New York Times,* August 5, 1854, fultonhistory.com; Patricia M. Salmon, "Volunteer Firefighting: The Early Years," *SIIAS History Archives and Library* brochure, Staten Island, SIIAS, 2003; "Staten Island," *The New York Times,* July 15, 1871, nytimes.com; "Staten Island, *The New York Herald,* August 27, 1875, fultonhistory.com; "Staten Island Deluged," *New York Herald,* August 14, 1875, fultonhistory.com; "The Fireman's Fair," *The Staten Islander,* March 26, 1890; The Yellow Fever at Staten Island," *New York Herald,* September 7, 1848, New York Public Library; "The Yellow Fever at Staten Island," *The Albany Evening Journal,* August 31, 1848, fultonhistory.com.

Information about women and the times come from Otto Bettman, *The Good Old Days – They Were Terrible!* (New York: Random House, 1974); Gail Collins, *America's Women: Four Hundred Years of Dolls, Drudges, Helpmates, and Heroines* (New York: Harpers Collins, 2003); Hasia R. Diner, *Erin's Daughters in America: Irish Immigrant Women in the Nineteenth Century* (Baltimore: The John Hopkins University Press, 1983); "Henrietta "Hetty" Howland Robinson Green (1834 – 1916), National Women's History Museum, accessed September 2012, http://www.nwhm.org/education-resources/biography/biographies/henrietta-howland-robinson-green; "Married Women Property Laws," *American Women. A Gateway to Library of Congress Resources for the Study of Women's History and Culture in the United States,* Accessed May 12, 2018, http://memory.loc.gov/ammem/awhhtml/awlaw3/property_law.html; Celia Morris, *Fanny Wright. Rebel in America* (Cambridge Mass:

Harvard University Press, 1984); "New York's First Female Lawyer," *The New York Times,* May 21, 1886, nytimes.com; Tammy A. Sarver, Erin B. Kaheny, and John J. Szmer, "The Attorney Gender Gap in U.S. Supreme Court Litigation," *Judicature,* 91: 5 (2008); "Suffrage History", *The Susan B. Anthony Center for Women's Leadership at the University of Rochester,* Accessed on May 12, 2018, http://www.rochester.edu/ sba/suffrage-history/; "Women Learning to Vote," *The Staten Islander,* July 21, 1880.

Stories about Stapleton people come from "An Aged Justice Resigns," *The New York Times,* February 3, 1884, nytimes.com; "A Shantytown Sensation," *St. Louis Republic,* January 1, 1893, genealogybank.com; Aiding Charity," *Richmond County Sentinel,* February 26, 1881; "Bridget and the Goat, *The New York Herald,* December 30, 1892, genealogybank.com; "Bridget's Explanation Was Weak," *The New York Herald-Tribune,* December 30, 1892, genealogybank.com; "Commodore Vanderbilt's Life," *The New York Times,* January 5, 1877, nytimes.com; Conspired Against the Goat," *The Evening World,* December 30, 1892, chronclingamerica.gov; "Dr. John L. Feeny Dead," *The New York Times,* June 1, 1901, nytimes.com; "Events in Society, *The New York Times,* February 19, 1881, nytimes.com; "William F. Howe, Dean of Criminal Bar, Dead," *The New York Times,* September 3, 1902, nytimes.com; "Legalized Lottery," *New York Evening Telegram,* February 21, 1884, fultonhistory.com; "McKow's Billy Goat," *The Washington D.C. Evening Star,* January 13, 1893, chronclingamerica. gov; "Mickey the Duck's Defiance," *The National Police Gazette,* September 24, 1881, fultonhistory.com; "Mr. Brock's Dog," *New York Herald,* July 9, 1880, fultonhistory.com; "Rival Justices," *New York Herald,* December 31, 1879, fultonhistory.com; "Staten Island's Charity Ball," *The New York Times,* February 22, 1881, nytimes.com; "Suing the Board of Trustees," *The New York Times,* January 5, 1885, nytimes.com; "Thomas Green Disappears," *The New York Times,* November 11, 1891, nytimes.com; "Too Old to Be a Justice," *The New York Times,* October 15, 1883, nytimes.com.

Information on crime comes from "A Life Taken for a Life," *The New York Times,* January 15, 1881, nytimes.com; "Another Clue," *Richmond County Gazette,* October 9, 1879, 1; "Battles of the Gamins," *The New York Sun,* December 19, 1875, fultonhistory. com; "Bloody Fight with Knives," *The Washington D.C. Evening Times,* June 26, 1899, chroniclingamerica.gov; "Busy Firebugs," *The Syracuse Standard,* October 7, 1884, fultonhistory.com; "City and Suburban News. Staten Island," *The New York Times,* November 25, 1879, nytimes.com; "City and Suburban News. Staten Island," *The New York Times,* July 11, 1881, nytimes.com; "Connecticut Cocks Victorious," *New Haven Register,* November 28, 1883, genealogy.com; "Harry Keeley, ex-Convict, Insane," *The New York Times,* October 17, 1903, nytimes.com; "History of the Crime," *The New York Times,* January 15, 1881, nytimes.com; "Home News. Staten Island," *The New York Daily Tribune,* December 2, 1879, chroniclingamerica.gov; "Home News. Staten Island," *The New York Herald Tribune,* December 30, 1879, genealogybank.

com; "Home News. Stapleton," *The New York Herald Tribune,* November 27, 1897, genealogybank.com; "Incendiarism," *Richmond County Gazette,* October 8, 1884; "Mr. Brock's Dog."; "Staten Island," *New York Daily Tribune,* April 7, 1880, fultonhistory.com; "Policeman Shot by Former Convict," *The New York Herald,* June 29, 1903, fultonhistory.com; "Reinhart to be Arraigned in Court," *The New York Times,* October 14, 1878, nytimes.com; "Reinhardt's Doom," *Richmond County Gazette,* January 12, 1881; "Riot in a Staten Island Church," *The New York Times,* August 2, 1887, nytimes. com; "Ruffian Shot Officer," *The New York Daily Tribune,* June 29, 1903, chronicling-america.gov; "Staten Island," *The New York Times,* July 1, 1871, nytimes.com; "Staten Island," *Commercial Advertiser,* August 17, 1875, genealogybank.com; "Silver Lake Horror," *The New York Herald,* May 22, 1879, fultonhistory.com; "Staten Island," *Commercial Advertiser,* November 2, 1875, genealogybank.com; "Staten Island," *New York Daily Tribune,* April 7, 1880, fultonhistory.com; "Staten Island," *New York Daily Tribune,* May 23, 1880, fultonhistory.com; "Staten Island," *The New York Daily Tribune,* November 9, 1880, chroncilingamerica.gov; "Staten Island," *The New York Times,* June 13, 1881, nytimes.com; "Staten Island Justice," *The New York Evening Telegram,* December 28, 1883, fultonhistory.com; "Staten Island's Gangs," *The New York Herald,* October 20, 1887, fultonhistory.com; "Strange Suicide at Stapleton," *The Staten Islander,* December 4, 1889; "Suburban Notes," *New York Herald,* September 17, 1880, fultonhistory.com; "The Body in a Barrel," *The New York Times,* October 8, 1878, nytimes.com; "The Silver Lake Murder," *The New York Times,* October 9,1878, nytimes.com; "Various Paragraphs," *New York Evening Post,* March 1, 1880, fulton-history.com.

Background information on elections comes from "A Great Party Rebuked," *The New York Times,* November 6, 1884, nytimes.com; "Accused of Taking Middletown Money, *The New York Times,* October 1, 1895, nytimes.com; "Asserted Fraud in an Election," *The New York Times,* June 8, 1888, nytimes.com; "Charged with Embezzlement," *The Staten Islander,* August 31, 1895; "Detailed Election Results; The County Goes Democratic," *Staten Island Gazette and Sentinel,* November 5, 1884; "Frauds on Staten Island," *The New York Times,* February 1, 1879, nytimes.com; "Kernan on Staten Island, *The New York Sun,* September 21, 1872, fultonhistory.com; "Important to Voters and Election Officers," *The Staten Islander,* October 26, 1895; "Mass Meeting of the Democratic Republican Electors of Richmond County – Erection of a Young Hickory Tree," *The New York Herald,* July 6,1844, fultonhistory.com; "Michael McGuire Arrested," *The New York Times,* August 31, 1895, nytimes.com; "Ordered to Appear in Court," *The New York Times,* October 27, 1893, nytimes.com; "Political," *The New York Evening Post,* October 29, 1879, fultonhistory.com; *Prominent Men of Staten Island. 1893* (New York: A. Y. Hubbell, 1893); "Reform Won Against Odds," *The New York Times,* May 3,1890, nytimes.com; "Richmond County Town Elections," *The New York Times,* February 13, 1879, nytimes.com; "Suburban Notes," *The New*

York Herald, February 22, 1885, fultonhistory.com; "Staten Island," *The New York Evening Post,* February 5, 1895, fultonhistory.com; "The Results on Staten Island," *The New York Times,* November 6, 1884, nytimes.com; "The Village Hall," *The Staten Islander,* March 27, 1889; "Voted on Dead Men's Names," *The New York Times,* December 29, 1893, nytimes.com.

Background information on the schools comes from "A Disgraceful Condition," *The Staten Islander,* May 27, 1891; "A Free School Opened," *The New York Times,* July 18, 1856, nytimes.com; "Blacks and Whites," *The New York Sun,* April 27, 1883, chroniclingamerica.gov; "City and Suburban News. Staten Island," *The New York Times,* July 11, 1881, nytimes.com; James D. Folts, *History of the University of the State of New York and the State Education Department 1784 – 1996,* accessed on June 5, 2018 at http://www.nysl.nysed.gov/edocs/education/sedhist.htm#free; "Frightened School Children," *Staten Island Gazette and Sentinel,* January 28, 1885; "Had Made Away with the Bond," *The New York Times,* October 25, 1892, nytimes.com; "High School and Freight Yard," *The New York Daily Tribune,* April 20, 1902, fultonhistory.com; Carlton Mabee, *Black Education in New York State from Colonial to Modern Times* (Syracuse: Syracuse University Press, 1979); "Panic in a Crowded School," *The New York Times,* January 28, 1885, nytimes.com; "Panic in a School," *The New York Herald,* January 28, 1885, fultonhistory.com; "Paying off the Jokers," *The New York Times,* April 2, 1884, nytimes.com; "Richmond Borough's New Public School," *The New York Times,* December 21, 1902, nytimes.com; "School Elections," *The Staten Islander,* August 1, 1891; "School Elections," *The Staten Islander,* August 3, 1892; "School Trustees," *The Staten Islander,* August 6, 1890; "Stapleton Poker Players Arrested," *The New York Times,* March 27, 1893, nytimes.com; "Stapleton's School in Bad Condition," *The New York Times,* Sept 28, 1893, nytimes.com; "Staten Island, *The New York Evening Post,* January 20, 1894, fultonhistory.com; "Staten Island," *The New York Evening Post,* August 6, 1894, fultonhistory.com; "Staten Island," *The New York Evening Post,* May 4, 1895, fultonhistory.com; "Staten Island," *The New York Evening Post,* August 3, 1897, fultonhistory.com; "Staten Island," *The New York Evening Post,* August 4, 1897, fultonhistory.com; "Study the Points," *The Staten Islander,* August 1, 1894; The Richmond Borough Association of Women Teachers, *Staten Island and Staten Islanders* (New York: The Grafton Press, 1905);"The School Funds are Short," *The New York Times,* September 14, 1892, nytimes.com.

Background information on the beginnings of the City of Greater New York comes from Edwin G. Burrows and Mike Wallace, *Gotham: A History of New York City to 1898* (New York: Oxford University Press, 1999); "Charter Revision Report is Made," *The New York Times,* December 2, 1900, nytimes.com; "Cromwell's Great Trump Cards," *The Staten Island Gazette,* May 25,1903; "Dr. Feeny Gets the Office," *The New York Times,* December 17, 1897, nytimes.com; "First Hearing on Charter Revision," *The*

New York Times, May 18, 1900, nytimes.com; "$421,512,876 Rise in Tax Valuation," *The New York Times*, January 10, 1899, nytimes.com; "George Cromwell Dead at 74," *The New York Times*, September 18, 1934, nytimes.com; Historical Records Survey Division of Professional and Service Projects, *Inventory of the County and Borough Archives of New York City, No. 5, Richmond County and Borough (Staten Island),* (New York: Work Projects Administration, August 1939); "Ignored by New Charter," *The New York Herald,* December 17, 1897, fultonhistory.com; Charles W. Leng and William T. Davis, *Staten Island and Its People. A History 1609 – 1929* (New York: Lewis Historical Publishing Co., 1930); Michael Miscione, "A Man, a Span, a Plan, *The New York Times,* May 20, 2001, nytimes.com; "Mixed Borough Accounts," *The New York Times,* December 30, 1897, nytimes.com; "Municipal Register", *Brooklyn Daily Eagle,* July 26, 1902, brooklynpubliclibrary.org; NYC Citywide Administrative Services. *Staten Island Borough Hall,* http://home.nyc.gov/html/dcas/html/resources/si_boroughhall.shtml; "Richmond Borough Dark," *The New York Times,* October 2, 1899, nytimes.com; "Richmond for Secession," *The New York Evening Post,* August 18, 1899, fultonhistory.com; "Staten Island Light War," *The New York Times,* January 12, 1899, nytimes.com; Henry Steinmeyer, *Staten Island 1524 – 1898* (Staten Island, New York: The Staten Island Historical Society, 1950); "Suburban News," *The New York Evening Post,* December 29, 1897, fultonhistory.com; "The New City Ushered In," *The New York Times,* January 1, 1898, nytimes.com; "The State Vote Canvassed," *The New York Times,* December 15, 1894, nytimes.com; "Tore out Electric Lights," *The New York Times*, January 11, 1899, nytimes.com.

CPSIA information can be obtained
at www.ICGtesting.com
Printed in the USA
FFHW020341040619
52796200-58338FF